Dear ✗✗

I hope that you enjoy reading your copy of Trupio!

Thanku,

[signature]

In creating this novel I had invaluable assistance from so many
people and places including the School of Metaphysics, editor Dan,
artist Gary, Breeden Photography, Kevin Knox, Howard Behar,
my family of origin, my young adult children, everyone at the Power Collective
and Indiana Writers Center, the folks at Fedex, both Marion County Libraries
and my neighbors and friends who were there to ask about Tripio along the way.

Tripio is dedicated to the fantastic four and their mom

Tripio

by

Jerry VanSchaik

Prologue

If You Love Coffee, Sell The Best!

Maybe it would be good to live and write in Chicago. It is Monday, and I have the Chicago Tribune in front of me. I'm drinking some coffee, putting thoughts into my journal and listening to The Replacements. It is almost noon, and I am only just now up and moving.

I step out to the front door of my mother's house to get a feel for the weather of the coming day, and I see someone familiar walking past. I let the screen door shut behind me, and the noise attracts his attention. He looks at me from the sidewalk. We make eye contact, and recognition hits me.

We called him John John, and I hadn't seen him for years. My gang of friends had started calling John John "Gravel Throat" around the fifth grade because his voice was so harsh and raspy for a kid his age. I hadn't seen John John for years, but it didn't surprise me that he hadn't left the neighborhood. I had once seen John John square off at midcourt during a pick-up basketball game at the gym of our local park. A hard foul had pissed him off moments earlier, and he and the perpetrator of the foul were throwing real punches at midcourt. I stood nearby, held the basketball, and watched. It was not a big deal for a fight of some kind to break out during these pick-up games. It was that kind of court in that kind of neighborhood. John John won that fight. I was not on John John's team the day of that fight. After my teammate had surrendered, John John headed for me. In that instant I knew, he was not done taking revenge. He wanted to kick my ass too. But no. John John simply reached out, took the ball from me, and

indicated it was his team's possession. A replacement was chosen for our bleeding

teammate from other guys watching the game courtside, and the game went on. Yet,

that instant of terror, when I thought John John was coming to kick my ass too, came

back to me on the front porch right then. I took a short quick breath and reached behind

me for the door handle, ready to retreat inside if John John headed for me.

John John looks at me from the sidewalk, just a stone's throw beyond where I

stood. He simply nods. He remembers me, but most likely because we played a good

deal of playground hoops together. He probably didn't remember the fight I am

recalling now. John John got into too many fights to remember them all.

Seeing John John alive and well brings on a feeling of relief that he had not

kicked my ass that day on the court. The second emotion that hits me is one of

motivation. I have the Sunday Chicago Tribune waiting downstairs. Now more than

ever, I am determined to find a job in Chicago. Once I do that, I could live and write

there. Plus, I would most likely never run into John John again.

***

I bought the Tribune after yesterday's shift at the Oregon Street Coffeehouse

had ended. The bookstore I frequented had out of town papers and was within walking

distance of the coffee house, so I had headed over there arriving just before it closed.

They had several Tribunes left. Rather than opening the one I bought right away, I took

it with me to the Trolley Stop Bar for the Sunday night dollar Heinekens. My new life

could wait until I spent my tip money on beer.

After warming up my coffee in the microwave, I head back downstairs to the table where I dropped the Tribune late last night. I retrieve the classifieds and before long find what I am looking for:

Chicago Tribune, Sunday, July 1, 1990

Retail Managers
★★★★★★★★★★★★★★★★★★★★
IF YOU LOVE COFFEE
SELL THE BEST!
Starbucks: We are a quality oriented specialty coffee roaster/retailer with ambitious plans and a 20 year history. Our 15 Chicago stores will grow this Autumn as we develop in the N.W. suburbs. We are looking for friendly, enthusiastic, energetic coffee lovers with 1 to 3 years of management experience in retail, specialty food store or restaurant to join us. Experience must include responsibility for P & L performance, hiring and staff development. We offer: the challenges and opportunities of growth, competitive salaries, and bonuses, good benefits and great coffee. Send resume:
Tony A., Starbucks, 948 N. Rush, Chicago, 60611
Equal Opportunity Employer
★★★★★★★★★★★★★★★★★★★

About the only real qualification I have is that I'm a coffee lover. Well, here goes. Even if this company goes under in a few years, by then, I'll be published, and it won't matter.

Chapter One

I was sitting at my writing desk, shirtless on a muggy day in Chicago. It was too early in the summer for the soggy heat. It was sticky in my apartment, and I knew it was going to be like that when I ventured out to take the trash out to the alley dumpster early that morning. That was the only time I left my apartment. I spent some of the morning scrubbing the tub, toilet, and kitchen floor. My face was greasy with one dried layer of sweat and grit worked up while scrubbing. A new light sweat appeared on my face while I sat drinking hot black coffee and reading.

I read to keep my mind off work. I was reading *Quiet Days in Clichy* and was miles, years, bodies, and minds away. I thought that I should be working on my own book. But, I looked to the back of this book to see how many pages I had left. I wanted to finish this short book and work on my own novel. That would arm me against the world outside my apartment and provide energy for my steps later at work, on the bus, shopping at Osco, or doing all I do over the days. Yes, to finish a short book would fortify me and help me through the coming weekend at work. Too busy to think there most times. Plus, I switched my days off to help out. I was regretting it. I usually had Thursday to get ready for the weekend shifts. *I won't be so fast to do that again.*

I had but fifty pages left and was glad. I noticed the list of other books by this publisher and was relieved. Kerouac, Burroughs, Robbe-Grillet. So far removed. I looked at that list of names, and it felt good to have read them. Read a good deal of some of them, a little of the others but knowing all the names. The list mattered to me. Sitting in front of my typewriter, I was surrounded by my notes, filled notebooks, and nearly finished novel. But I was worrying about day-to-day life. When I wrote a good

9

passage for my own book or short story or even one line in my notebook, I was more connected to myself. Sitting shirtless and smelling a bit ripe and having only had coffee as noon approached, I looked over the list of names to feel good again.

As hot morning became hot afternoon, it seemed foolish to participate in the outside world. I thought of showering, eating, doing errands but could not do those things just yet. I was hungry but hated taking orders from my stomach. I thought of making more coffee and staying there deep into the afternoon to continue reading and do some writing. *But it can't last, can it?* The mixture of sweat, hunger, and caffeine buzz somehow gave me the permission to stay out of the outside world and do what I want. *Damn, I know I have to close tonight. No day is even remotely like the one before or after it. Nothing ever adds up the same way. So, stay in and read or write of some the novel or even just keep pecking away at it. Soon enough, I'll be on the eight, thirty-six, or twenty-two bus, heading for work.*

And there I was on the number eight bus heading for the intersection of Diversey, Clark, and Broadway and the Cosmodemonic Coffee Company store #204. I took the word Cosmodemonic from Henry Miller. He called Western Union "The Cosmodemonic Telephone and Telegraph Company" when he worked there well before being published. I use the word to try to keep work out of my mind as I take notes and go about my off hours. Not sure how well it works though. As lead clerk, it would be my store when I punch in at three until the two other closers, and I leave after midnight sometime. I'll have the keys and the code and will count the money for the next day's deposit, so that put me in charge of #204. I liked it for the most part. *The free coffee is nice.* Having to throw out angry and crazy people and getting spat on while doing it wasn't a thrill. Neither was counting down the tills. Every so often one of them came up

short, and I wasn't able to find out why.

A week before, I was in the back counting the money when I noticed my right

knee pressed hard against the bottom of the table due to the anxiety I felt while doing

the tills. I didn't realize it got to me so much. It was then I decided it was okay to take

from the accumulated weekly tips in the safe to balance the drawer.

Mark, the manager of #204, always divided the cash tips by actual hours

worked. I vowed to myself to replace the ten dollars by payday. Which was the next

Friday. *A long way off. I don't have it now, of course.*

But it would be Denis the actor and Chuck the gay male stripper that night. Both

were good closers so I could make it on autopilot. Of course, Mark would open the next

morning. He could be bleary from tonight's pints at Boru's, but he'd notice a bad close

no matter the state he is in. And he scheduled both Sarah and Kati to open with him. *Not*

fair. But Mark had the power to make the schedule. Controlling the scheduling would

be a benefit of moving up the ladder at the Cosmodemonic. They seemed to want me to.

But it was hard enough to write as it was.

***

Friday morning and my knees were sore. The close with Denis and Chuck went

well, as expected. Chuck was just starting his workday, and Denis talked about

rehearsals for *Lysistrata*. Denis was funny and had the looks to make people want to see

him. Chuck did too, for that matter. Then again he was making more than Denis did, as

far as applying that asset went. I had good looks and had my admirers among the #204 regulars too. That morning I had sore knees, and no one sees an author while he is

working, which was in contrast to Denis and Chuck. Though you'd get to see most, if

not all, of Chuck. Sitting at my typewriter, I was relieved that the previous night was

done. My shift was spent standing, lifting, tilting, and stooping. The coffee order came

in, and Mark's shift didn't have time to put it away, so I had to. I didn't mind too

terribly since I got to hide in the back and do it. Not unusual, but it took its toll

physically. The Christmas time shipments left me with a sore back and sore knees. But

both were easily felt and identified. Not quite the same with writing. *Why am I doing*

this? Was not really stopped by easing up or resting. I could be working and saving for

five years, and then I'd be able to afford a new car. Measurable. Insane. *Are the*

thoughts and events of my life worth recounting? That went back and forth in my mind.

Arms folded and unfolded, nose wiped, brushed arm hairs: all took their time to be

done. Tangible actions offering a prize of completion. At work, with my knees sore, I

was cheerful. We got busy an hour before close. I jumped up on the bar, and we got the

line out. Nothing much to be remembered about that day but my sore knees.

I sat with my back rigidly upright. No usual pillow. Five years and then a car

would be paid for. I could put last night toward that. Then again, I didn't need a car

living in Chicago.

I took a walk to the Belmont Rocks and found a good spot. Two good things

happened on the twenty or so minute walk there and confirmed it was worth it to pack

my journal and water and a little food for the time there. *One day, I will bring a cooler*

and beers. I would work later and knew it would be a long and busy night. The first

good thing was that I walked into the lake effect, like through an invisible curtain into a cooling mist. I felt it get cooler yet I was still blocks away from the lake itself. I was

confirmed by the cool and soothing difference in temperature. It welcomed me after the

walk there. Next came the man-made effect. The tunnels under the highway were cooler

still. The concrete was wet at times and usually, but not always, smelling of urine. I

found the man-made tunnel telling me that I live here now. I wouldn't find this in

Dayton, my hometown, or something comparable in many cities anywhere else in the

world. Because I knew that after I passed through this cool, damp, urine-scented tunnel,

I would step out to the see Lake Michigan and look south to the skyline of Chicago, the

second good thing. And for me then, the city was part of my day-to-day life. I would

find it hard to believe it was really me and my life if not for the damp feel to my skin

and the urine scent in my nose telling me it was quite real and very much my life.

***

I crossed through the beat-up vestibule to the aroma of coffee being ground,

coffee brewing, and coffee grounds spent and still steaming in the trashcans. That last

one was the defining aroma that hit me hardest when I stepped into #204 midafternoon

Friday. That of the grounds, still hot, dumped in the trashcans behind the counter and

heating up what was already in there. No time to let the grounds cool down. I didn't go

to Mark or the back to check on how things were for the morning shift. Instead, I took

the two steps up to the espresso bar itself, in order to talk with Mikey G on the bar, to

get a feel for the day. The bar was elevated, and you could see the entire store from

there. Mikey G was good and had everything stocked but had no time to clean. Mark

had been on the phone a lot. Some big shot is visiting next week, and all the other

managers were checking with each other to see who knew what and who was coming

13

and why. It wouldn't be that weekend, so I didn't care all that much. My concern was to get through the next three shifts and just make it to Monday. I would close the next two nights and open Sunday, and it was supposed to be a beautiful weekend in Chicago. It would take its toll.

With the close done efficiently, I stepped out of #204 revived. My fellow closers already off for their nights, and I only waited a couple minutes until my bus pulled up. A small victory. At times, I've had to walk almost halfway back to the apartment before catching the bus. It was becoming a common occurrence for a passenger sitting near me to look around to identify the source of the coffee smell. It was most pronounced on me the day I used my free pound of coffee benefit and would carry that onto the bus with me. I sometimes offered up, "It's me," but mostly sat in silence, choosing not to explain where the coffee aroma was from. Lately though, if I did explain, more and more people had heard of Cosmodemonic coffee. I didn't wear my Cosmodemonic hat or shirt home. I changed those parts of the uniform for the trip, putting them in my backpack and retrieving either a book to read or my current journal.

***

It was cooler that morning, and as soon as I woke, I thought of my mark-out, my Kenya-AA, steeping in my French press. I had to get up to make that happen, but I loved the ritual of grinding the beans, boiling the water, and waiting the four minutes to press the coarsely ground beans to the bottom of the glass carafe. I remembered that I had told Irene at Liberation Book Distributors on Sheffield that I'd stop by that morning to discuss me working there as a book reviewer. Not working for money but as a volunteer. In exchange for book reviews, I hoped to acquire a name of someone who knew someone from a small publishing house who would consider publishing my novel when complete. Irene didn't know about the publishing connection plan and didn't need to. But, I felt that I need a haircut. I wanted to look a little more presentable, even for a non-paying position with the Maoists at Liberation.

***

I was back in my desk chair facing my bulletin board filled with postcards, notes, and quotes. The bulletin board leaned against the wall I faced when I worked on the novel or when taking notes in my journal, which I had just decided to call a Sketchbook of the Mind. I thought it fit me better. I had my first assignment for Liberation Distributors. It was to read, and then write a blurb for their latest catalog on a book called *Beyond the Border: A New Age in Latin American Women's Fiction.* Fair enough. I probably didn't need to worry about the haircut. Nevertheless, I had just enough time to run into a barber a few doors down from Liberation. I was the only one there who spoke English. I used my Spanish to ask for *corto*, which must have meant very short because it was really short. Looked to me like I just got out of boot camp.

I wondered—and maybe now will feel even more like this considering my haircut—wondered if people think I'm odd. Did the people at the Cosmodemonic think I'm strange? Was writing inevitable for me? Did I start writing to run from life and reality and responsibility? Or did it just awaken in me? Was I kidding myself writing? *If I keep it up and am happier for it, then it's worth it.* Others played weekend softball games in their spare time or worked on cars. I wrote in that allotted time. I'd be going to work later, and it's not going to matter to Cosmodemonic if I worked on my book or

not. Or if I'm a writer or not.

***

I got in a good stretch on the novel before heading off for Saturday's close.

Nothing makes the time go by faster than thought with concentrated effort. A couple

times, I had to stop and bargain with myself for another five minutes. I had no choice

but to make for the Halsted bus. On weekday closes if I had the time to walk a little, I'd

catch the Clark or Broadway buses heading south to #204. Today I had to jog to the

Halsted stop and hope for the best. I didn't have to worry as two buses were waiting.

***

Once I made it in to work, I had to navigate my way through the line of

customers to get to the backroom of #204. Both Denis and Sarah were on the bar. Two

on the bar meant the morning rush had become the afternoon rush and there was a

chance we had hit a thousand transactions already. I would run a tape to see the counts

when I got a chance. I knew the close would be long and busy. I'd have to pull money

from the drawers several times, putting the bills first in a pastry bag then stuffing that

deep into my front pants pocket until I could dash to the safe in the back. It was too

busy to enjoy the sensation of a fistful of bills on my person. I only felt the urgency to

get them to the floor safe, to get that quick task off my list, and move on.

The first thing Mark said when I made it to the backroom was that he had #206

send a case of large iced cups over in a cab. They'd be here soon, so I needed to be on

the lookout. He was on the phone, apron crooked at the waist and smeared with coffee grounds of various vintages. I nodded. He finished his phone call and tossed his dirty

apron toward the hamper, missing badly. I pretended not to notice as I grabbed a clean

one. I took my hat off to tie my clean apron around my neck. I could see from his

glance at me that Mark noticed the hair, but he didn't say anything. His own hair was

always short and dyed with a little more intended style since his wife worked at a salon.

He had faith in my ability to get the rest of the masses out and the store in shape

for the morning when it would start all over. I had been a key holder since before

Christmas, and it was early summer. I had heard #204 was unique before I transferred

over here from the lower key, steadier, and predictable #206. I took the position for the

small pay increase and because it was closer to my apartment, but I was unnerved at

first. Store #204 was way busier but also had a reputation for being offbeat in both

customer and partners (which is how Cosmodemonic refers to the store employees). I

found myself fitting in quickly though. No one batted an eye if I said I was a writer.

There was opera singer here already and all types of actors, actresses, comedians, and

performers on staff at #204. Mark's assistant, Rebecca, was a graduate of the Manager

in Education system (which was how the Cosmodemonic referred to its training

program for store management candidates) and had arrived at #204 just a month or two

before me. She was the most conventional of us, and between the three of us, the store

was in good hands. So, for the close, Mark's only other piece of information for me was

that Tony was running late. There was one more bit that I already knew: Mark was

heading across the street to Brian Boru's for some post-shift pints.

***

It was Sunday after work. I had a shower and some sleep in front of my TV. Rebecca opened this morning, and I got in at seven to deal with the first wave of customers. Rebecca and I didn't work together much, and she made me a little uneasy watching me in a way Mark never did. Maybe Rebecca felt I was invading her territory. It wasn't my fault that that staff at #204 came to me for help on any given shift. Rebecca had asked Allison from #206 to close for her tonight. Rebecca had to be somewhere so couldn't do the closing shift. In any case, it was unusual for two key holders to work the same shift.

***

The Saturday and Sunday shifts ran together: iced latte after iced latte, cup after cup, and customer after customer so that it felt, sitting at my desk in my apartment, that I hadn't even made it back here last night. I knew I did because the beer in my hand was not in my fridge last night. Four left. I had one last night before crashing. After this one, I decided to head to the Duke of Perth or Bento's to wash the shifts away. To wash away the waves that brought the people in. The customers who bought the drinks, the scones, and the whole bean coffee. I called them waves because I always knew there was another one on the way in. Just as the wave of a dozen was out the door, there came a group of three women, two guys in Blackhawks hats after them, a couple on a walk next, an older man who needed an explanation of *doppio con panna* appeared behind them. Then came the *café misto* regular, the well-dressed men taking their time with their decision, Kenny-the-street-guy looking for a sample of coffee cake, the women getting four *grande* drips to go. They all came through the doors as one wave. The milk steamed, the cups were pulled from under the counter and refilled, the cash register rang open and shut, the brew button was pressed again, espresso beans were poured to fill the

hopper, and steam wands were wiped clean. That group receded to make room for

another group who crashed onto the shore of #204. A breath. They are out the door and

make way for the rush, crush, and pounding of the next wave.

I felt like I'd been washed ashore and washed up and washed out by it all. My

reward would be Monday off. Mark and Rebecca go to the Pow Wow on Tuesday, so

I'll open with Kati and Sarah, the usual weekday openers. Both Cosmodemonic

veterans. I worked more with Sarah, who was full-time and also closes. But, Kati reeled

in my thoughts. We had worked together during the holiday madness, but her name is

never on the schedule for one of my shifts. I have hoped to see her name appear on one

of my shifts every time the schedule had been posted but to no avail. I hardly ever

opened weekdays.

The beer was gone, and I headed to the fridge for the next. I needed to grocery

shop tomorrow and stop by the Maoists for the working copy of my book. I wanted to

take the El downtown to the art museum and take in the actual Picassos and Hoppers

there. Before sitting down with the next full beer, I relieved myself. I glanced in the

bathroom mirror. In the madness of the weekend, I had forgotten about the *corto* cut.

***

I awoke to Monday, my reward, my day off. I sat up slowly and recognized the

full beer next to me on the nightstand. I had been too tired to go out and too tired to

finish my last beer. I remembered planning to finish all my beers and then go out for

one or two more. It was a much cheaper buzz that way. Payday wasn't until Friday, and

I didn't have the money to go out anyway. All for the best. I was relieved. I needed the money for my trip to Jewel.

I decided to skip the art museum. I told myself I might go on Thursday, my day off. I remembered that I had my book and assignment from the Maoists and felt good. I could tell people that I work in publishing or that I review books. It is as far as you normally get in any conversation, a sentence or two before the person starts talking about themselves anyway. With that book in my smaller backpack, not the work one, I took off to the basement bookstore on Broadway. It was a favorite day off destination for me. It was easy to kill a free hour or two there. I could walk and therefore was spared waiting on the platform for the El or dodging workday loop-pedestrians downtown. Also, I would not be tempted to duck into a downtown Cosmodemonic. They had it made. A five-day workweek. Busy as hell and cramped but closed weekends. A few downtown stores were open weekends though, including the one I heard was the busiest Cosmodemonic in the country. I wouldn't be caught dead working there; my store was busy enough.

As I stepped out of the bookstore and up on the sidewalk, I was stopped by an older man, nicely dressed but in a disheveled, professorial way. He spoke with a heavy central European accent, and I wasn't sure what the hell he wanted until he showed me a scribbled map he had in one hand, drawn on a piece of light blue paper. I thought at first he was looking for cassette tapes but then understood that he was looking for sheet music. The bookstore had some, so I smiled and pointed down the steps. He thanked me, and called me mister, and looked happy. I walked on, feeling good that I had helped him and knowing he played music for a living and maybe even had been heard by Paul Bowles or someone else from my list.

I continued walking to keep my spirits high. From Broadway, I cut into the neighborhood streets away from the noise. The city was so deep, so layered. The courtyards of the apartment buildings certified that to me. My building didn't have one. It was smaller and not grand enough. These buildings I passed had a look-but-don't-touch appeal for me as I walked past at a slower pace in order to take them in. I lived here now. I walked on these sidewalks, under these trees, and stood on these corners or, even better, crossed halfway down the block, timing the passing cars like an old-time resident.

I had moved here just under two years ago. My former lover had moved here, to the South Side. She urged me to move, to get out of Dayton. It seemed destined to be when I saw a want ad in the paper soon after that conversation. The ad said a lot of stuff about qualifications but included, "...enthusiastic, energetic coffee lovers." That was me, and the company was opening stores in Chicago. It wasn't too difficult to leave. I wasn't making much of a life for myself in Dayton. Yet, there I was, walking these streets. I decided to call Natali when I got home. *Yeah, I will call her.* Any romance was over between us, but I needed to see someone who was not from work. It would do me some good.

I turned south and found myself only a few blocks from #204, my workplace. I could use a tripio. Technically that is three shots of espresso, hot and served in a small demitasse cup. The cup should be warm and the crema on top thick and light brown.

That is all well and good. But the drink should be consumed almost immediately because its flavor elements begin to break down almost immediately. No matter how perfectly it is made, it is only really sweet and strong, not bitter, for a short time. And that combination is what I wanted. When I taste it, I know. Quickly the crema dissipates, the aroma weakens, and the tripio is just a few ounces of black, inert liquid. In order to stave off that inevitability, I pour mine over ice. That helps. That allows me more options. I can then— *Hell no. Not on my off day.*

I needed to call Natali. The Cosmodemonic was in my head way too much. *I should be thinking of my novel.* I changed direction and headed north on Clark. I was forced to cross the street at Bento's. The sidewalk was blocked off. I stopped and joined the small crowd of people formed across Clark. I didn't want to come off as a tourist type but asked the guy next to me what was happening.

He said, "They are shooting a movie. It stars John Candy and is called *Only the Lonely*."

I wondered to myself as I strolled past the crowd, affecting my big-city nonchalance, if anyone from #204 had auditioned for a part. Again, I realized that the Cosmodemonic Coffee Company was winning the battle for my thoughts.

The walking and thinking had made me hungry. I was forced to pass up too many restaurants with tempting aromas pouring out of them. With some effort, I resisted stepping into one for a non-budgeted lunch and turned for my apartment. *There must be a game at Wrigley tonight.* It was Monday, and there were more people around than usual. Looked like they planned on having some fun. I loved living there, walking the streets, and making them mine. I began to realize that my job at Cosmodemonic gave me something of an edge on everyone else. It was becoming a place to be. A new place. One that gave me a bit of notoriety over all the people on these sidewalks who have lived here way longer than I had. They were not a part of the growing thing that was the Cosmodemonic. I passed the Man Cave Bar and passed through the beat-up gate leading to my second-floor apartment. I adored being part of this day, this city, and these streets. I simply needed more money and time to take it all in. I had to get in and make my own lunch. My book needed to get done. It felt like an escape as I passed into the small vestibule and up to my second-floor place, relieved to be there but also pissed that I had to be.

I was back at my desk and smelling my pot of chili. I was hungry when I got home and had to eat as soon as I could. The chili is for today and the rest of the week. The walk did clear my head after all, and I felt ready to write. I had to. *Today is the day for it.* I left Natali a message about possibly seeing her on Thursday. At least with my windows open, I would hear the cheering from the ballgame when the seventh inning stretch arrived. That was my goal. I should have written a good deal by then.

***

I shut off the alarm and sat up quickly, looking around my small bedroom for an answer. First, I was disoriented. A moment of confusion occupied my head, then it hit me. *What I am doing? Work.* I switched with Mark so he could go to the Pow Wow. I hardly ever opened during the week. I didn't leave any time to spare. I quickly showered, dressed, and inhaled a half cup of yesterday's Kenya, which I liked almost

23

better at room temp. With keys in hand, I stopped to look over my desk. I took in the

typed pages from yesterday and felt good. As I hustled down the steps, I realized I

didn't even give myself a glance in the mirror but hoped the walk yesterday gave my

face color. I needed to look good for my fellow openers, Kati and Sarah. I also hoped

the big shots wouldn't bother with stopping in at #204 that morning.

The music from the store audio system was classical in the mornings. It was not

a rule but just the norm at #204. We always played jazz at night. That morning the piece

was the "United Airlines Theme" as I jokingly referred to it. My fellow openers Sarah

and Kati had the morning routine down. Kati took the bar and Sarah the register for the

rush. I expedited and pulled pastries, grabbed the occasional whole bean order, and

darted to the floor to clean the counter and refill the creamers and sugar packets when I

could.

The Monday close was spotty, and I had to make a run to the back and drag

down a five-pound bag of decaf espresso from one of the shelves. That should not have

happened if the store was restocked correctly the previous night. I quickly returned from

the backroom and stepped up to the elevated bar to find the scissors to cut the bag open.

Kati handed them to me, stepping quite close to me to do so. A bit distracted by the

proximity of her body, I filled the hopper too full and too fast and a good couple

handfuls of beans cascaded to the counter and then to the floor. *Fuck*. The #204

morning regulars looked over at the guy who wasn't Mark who just made the mess. It

didn't concern them too much as at they were used to being taken care of. I smiled an

apology at Kati as she steamed a large pitcher of milk. Surprised at the big, somehow

inviting smile she returned, the spilled beans made my morning. I promised her I'd be back to help her clean her bar after the rush. From the many times I came in after her

morning shift, I knew she would leave the bar spotless. But it didn't matter; I wanted an

excuse to stand close to her again.

But of course, the deposit came first. Mikey G had been made lead clerk

recently and had done one of his first deposits last night. It seemed all in order, and I

stuck it deep in my backpack and headed for the door. Dennis-the-Juice-Guy was

coming in as I was leaving. He was short, always hustling, and too young be balding.

But he seemed to be Chicago personified to me: sharp eyes always looking things over

and ready to work hard for his Old Styles. He had the end of the morning rushes of each

store timed as he arrived just when #206's ended also. And he always made time to chat

with Tracy and Allison at #206. And he did the same here with Sarah and Kati. I got the

sense he knew he had happened into something really good with the Cosmodemonic

juice account. His OJ was great, but I hated that it separated after a while in the case. I

felt it made the whole pastry display look old. I would make it a point to swirl the

display cups around a few times to reinvigorate the case. We had formed a mutual

respect based on a regard for each other's work ethic. We stopped on our respective

paths and talked for a moment on the floor.

"Got you opening I see?" Dennis-the Juice-Guy greeted me as a hello. He had

no option, but a verbal greeting as each hand held a gallon of OJ.

"Yeah. Everyone's downtown." I responded blandly.

I liked Dennis-the-Juice-Guy. I remembered him from my very first days at

#206. That, in turn, created a feeling in me of duration and longevity in the world of the

Cosmodemonic. I needed that today. The Pow Wows always meant change. There was more of that these days at the Cosmodemonic. And that morning, post rush, the stools and small tables filled with #204's regulars, I felt at home. I didn't want all the coming stuff to affect me and my world. Dennis-the-Juice-Guy knew about the Pow Wow downtown and in fact was heading to the Embassy Suites store next, where it was taking place. But, I also knew Dennis would take his time during his delivery to flirt with Sarah and Kati, especially with me heading to the bank. Maybe that was the true source of my anxiety. I had been looking forward to finally working with Kati. I had even stood close to her and carved out a plan to follow up. I had the deposit on my back, so there was no going back. I had to get the deposit done by a certain time, or the phones would ring, and I would have to explain why it wasn't done.

"You know Doug still misses you. He and Allison don't see eye to eye." Dennis-the-Juice-Guy gave me a quick update on my old store. Allison had replaced me as lead when I departed #206.

"Doesn't surprise me," I responded truthfully and as calmly as possible. I suddenly liked Dennis-the-Juice-Guy again. His news had inflated my ego. I shifted the backpack and stood a little taller. Dennis-the-Juice-Guy rolled his shoulder back as a signal he was ready to take the two gallons of juice out of his hands.

"You know the drill. Sarah or Kati can sign." I nodded in the direction of the bar and counter, where both were doing their post-rush cleaning. Dennis-the-Juice-Guy and I headed to our respective destinations.

As Dennis-the-Juice-Guy headed for the back past the bar, I added over my shoulder, "Look out for Kati's mess!"

As I hoped, she heard me and looked up to send me to the bank with a smile that said, to me, that she was waiting for me to come back and help her. Just as I had hoped.

I got the bank and deposit done. Relieved to have the money off me, my thoughts went back to what Dennis-the-Juice-Guy said. Doug had hired me and then promoted me to lead without much fanfare. I had immediately taken a liking to the job and soon was #206's resident coffee expert. It felt good to be recognized with a promotion, but I hadn't really thought of moving up the Cosmodemonic ladder much at all. I moved here to write, to get out of Dayton, and see what I was made of, but not to find a career. But, there had been twenty or more applicants for my old job at #206. I left the bank thinking that I must be better at this job than I thought.

It was odd to live my day in reverse. On the morning bus to work, I couldn't wait to get back to work on the book. But with work done, body cleaned from coffee grit and scent, and stomach fed by chili, the thought of the book irritated me. It was pointless to write anyway. *Who am I kidding?* My more practical thoughts saved me as I remembered to check my messages. *Yes!* There was one. I smiled at the message as I listened. It was left for 'The Lover' and was from Natali. She got my message and is going to see *The Mahabharata* at a small theater with friends. If I got this in time, she said, we could meet there, and she could take me home. *Perfect. No writing.* It was a chance to see an old friend. A chance for maybe some fellowship and nostalgia sex.

27

She started calling me 'The Lover' after I came to Chicago several times to visit her. Natali was living with her theatre colleague from college. She and Craig had one side of a double, and the Serbian landlady lived alone in the other half. It was the landlady who gave me the nickname, 'The Lover.' The colleague and now playwright, Craig, was clearly gay, so it was only obvious to the landlady that I was Natali's lover there on carnal visits. The Serbian landlady pronounced 'The Lover' with a southern European lilt that Natali and Craig loved to repeat to me, embellishing the words as it were a key phrase from a play they were running lines for.

I could make it on time if I took the Howard El. I repeated 'The Lover' in that accent several times over to myself, smiling as I made off for the station.

***

When I woke up, Natali was gone. I hadn't heard her leave. I must have been too tired from the open yesterday and also from sitting through the endless movie. The only part I really remembered clearly was the gambling scene and one actor saying, "I have won" about fifty times. I was edgy and distracted by Natali sitting right next to me. It was good to see Craig and Anita again. They were at school with me and good friends with Natali. There were more acquaintances from our school up here, a sort of an émigré troupe from Wright State. Craig was the leader since he had moved to Chicago first. He had helped Anita write her one-person show, which I had promised to see when it was all set. I was sure Natali had not planned to sleep with me. She had her life, and so did I. We both knew our time together was over and last night was not meaningless, but wouldn't awaken complications. The actual sex was slow and familiar.

We remembered what to do and when to do it. *Damn, rethinking it, it doesn't seem real already*. I wondered if Kati was single. Not sure. Probably not. She must have been asked out five times every morning at the Cosmodemonic. *Got to close tonight but Thursday is not too far off.* Couldn't stay with Natali's side of bed reminding me she was here. It happened. I put my Sketchbook of the Mind in my bag and headed out somewhere to try to clear my head.

I ended up walking to my favorite coffee house. It sat on an alley under the El tracks. The atmosphere was great because there was no conscious effort in creating it. I was getting through *Beyond the Border* for the Maoists and still had a week before I saw them again to turn in my paragraph for the catalog. But I was mentally returning to Natali and our time together. I told myself I was taking charge of my life when I moved here. But I was sure a lot of me was hoping to get back together with her. After all, I gave her a lot of credit for getting me to start writing seriously. And, as I became friends with her theatre friends, I saw they were just like me. They were not touched by angels or muses or what the hell else. If they could do it, then I could. And if Craig could call himself a playwright and director, then I could call myself a writer. But I was there, and Natali was at work somewhere near Wicker Park. We made no concrete plans to see each other again, just that I would see Anita's play. Natali would be there of course. I'm sure I would need a ride home.

***

Still too restless and edgy over the unmade bed in my apartment, I wanted to leave my place almost as soon as I got back. I found a reason to leave in skipping the bus and walking in for my close. It would take a lot longer to walk than the usual bus ride. And, it was not a bad walk down Clark as it had cooled a little outside. There was always a lot to see and the lovemaking last night had given me a bit more lift to my back and length to my stride. By the time I made the doors of #204, my blood was flowing, and I had just started to break a small sweat on my forehead. I was ready for a great close to send me to my day off.

Sarah was the only one on the floor. A beauty herself with a square chin and raspy voice she fit #204 because she was hard to categorize. She was athletic and played lacrosse or field hockey or both at Loyola. But it seemed she came from money, and I couldn't figure why she worked here. Not that I cared as I smiled at her. She smiled back and turned back to her conversation with a regular. I didn't care if she had money, nor did I care if she was talking now. I knew Sarah would not be talking if there was work to be done for the shift change. I passed the whole bean counter, and it was in fact wiped clean. It was free-pound day for me. A benefit I always took advantage of. I usually took the Kenya or the Ethiopian Yergacheffe since I felt the African Varietals had the most complex flavors. I stepped into the back feeling even better, knowing I'd have my free pound to take home at close. No Mark. Rebecca was counting the money. She was focused, so I didn't ask any questions while I put on my apron and hat. As I did, I noticed the handwritten sign above the time cards: "Store Meeting Sunday at 7pm. Everyone must be here. You'll be paid. Mark."

***

"The struggle with oneself, the trying to better oneself, the renewal of one's energy, all this is complicated by material difficulties." That was a great quote. I wished I knew who had said that. I wrote it early on in my Sketchbook of the Mind but did not attribute it to anyone. As I reclined doing my laundry and leafing through the nearly full Sketchbook of the Mind, I came across that near the front. I thought it applied to me because I hoped to find a dryer with time on it when my load finished in the washer. Trying to conserve quarters counted as a material difficulty. Either that or I could possibly luck out with a new dryer. But since those actually dried clothes, they were staked out and almost always taken. *Tomorrow is payday, and I remember that I owe the tips ten dollars.* The tips added up for me since I always got my forty hours, but ten dollars taken from that was still ten dollars. I didn't care so much about the Cosmodemonic, but everyone deserved their tip money for putting up with the craziness at #204.

Why did I volunteer for the Maoists? No money in it. Yet I put in the time. I would finish *Beyond the Border* later if that day went as planned. How much chili was left? It didn't matter; I'd eat what's left. I needed inspiration for next week's menu. It could be turkey meatloaf. At least the coffee was free. And damn was it good from the thermos I brought with me. I usually brought a thermos of coffee with me when I did the laundry.

About thirty minutes before, when I first opened it, I heard a fellow laundry doer comment out loud to a friend that she could smell coffee. I didn't volunteer it was me. The aroma was so strong that it carried to the female whose voice came from the other end of the laundromat. Later, when I saw the two friends leaving with their baskets of

31

clean clothes, I regretted that decision since they were both quite pretty. I didn't want to

be bothered. I was brooding over how to finish my novel. Not smart. I consoled myself

by the fact that the thermos was also free, a mark-out from #206. It had been dented so

we couldn't sell it, so I figured that it was perfect for me to take home.

I was glad to have returned to my relatively cooler apartment. It felt good to be

at my desk, even if I was alone. The clothes were clean and dry. A success. I felt at

times like I didn't want to be too big a part of this world. It hit me again after the night

with Natali that I was alone a lot. I had family in St. Louis and Dayton and could have

used a visit to either. It was hard for me to leave the city without a car. I daydreamed

about bluffing my way into Pops for Champagne like Henry Miller would have done.

Or I could have ingeniously panhandled money from a pedestrian and then spent it on

wine at La Commercial across Halsted. I decided to not go to the art museum. Instead,

I'd go lie on my floor shirtless, pillow under my head, and turn on the ceiling fan above

me. That felt better. Thoughts. Thinking. Maybe the days of the week didn't mean

anything anymore. *Today is today, that's all.* I wondered if I wrote crap. I didn't think

so. Maybe it was a thing I never should have worried about in the first place. Only it

might have taken years for anyone to notice. Years for any kind of confirmation. My

eyes were heavy. I thought I'd sleep. At least for a little while.

***

I woke up slowly and realized I had been out for a while. The ceiling fan was

still turning above me. It had done its job and cooled me, allowing the sleep. I was

hungry, so it must have been close to five or so. I couldn't see the clock, so I sat up. It was odd to be eye level with my desk and notes. That was the night I had hoped to see Natali. I couldn't say I regretted it happened Tuesday but wished that it would be that night. Still sitting on the floor, I saw *Beyond the Border* on my desk. The bookmark showed how little I had left. If I finished reading it and then wrote the paragraph, I would have been able to call today worthwhile.

The writing was a success. But, it was on my novel. The novel was almost complete, and I am not sure I knew what it was even about. I just sat for a long while after reading the last bit of *Borders*. As I scribbled ideas for the paragraph, my novel came out instead. That was fine by me. I had some stamina from the floor siesta, and it just took off. Yet it was not entirely fair to say I was not sure what it was about. It covered the trip I took across the country with friends in my VW van. It seemed to me that it was partly a head-trip minus any drugs. I mean, no drug trips, just beer as far as that goes. My mind went backward as the van and my friends headed forward. Eventually, they must meet. I do know I made better progress when I was not trying to define it too much. I did have to finish it soon. I was coming to the last pages of the journal I kept for the whole trip. When the journal ends so did the trip and so will the novel.

I will close tomorrow. So I could finish the Maoist paragraph in the morning and drop it by Saturday if I have too. I needed some TV as a reward. I hoped for a rerun of *WKRP* or *MASH*.

***

I woke up and felt the energy back in my body. The first task was to open the kitchen door to welcome in this sunny day. I heard the El several blocks north as it passed Wrigley. The sound it produced was big-city to me. Never heard anything like it growing up in Dayton. I brought the Kenya home and was glad I did. Its distinct winey taste was more defined and refined as it cooled. Over the second cup of the morning, I finished the work on *Beyond the Border*. My favorite line was: "The stories focus on women, yet this wide-ranging collection is interesting enough to be useful in several fields." Just the right mix of restraint and praise to help it sell, I thought.

I needed to do a few odd things before closing shift tonight. The first close of all three weekend nights. The meeting Sunday struck me as early for the quarter. Maybe it was a week or so early, but I didn't track them all that closely since they were usually during my Sunday close, so I was going to be there by default anyway. Doug's meetings at #206 were quiet affairs. I remember the meeting when Doug introduced me as the new lead clerk, and everyone smiled and gave me a round of applause. Mark was more animated and let the actors and performers at #204 have more input on any changes he announces. I needed to buy stamps. Writing letters now and again helped me warm up for the novel. And, I thought my refrigerator was going south. I left my landlord several messages. I thought he got the first call, but he didn't confirm. It was summer, and my beers the other night were not that cold. I needed to call him again.

***

After buying stamps at the post office, I couldn't come straight back to my place. It was warm but somehow not a humid day out, and I heard music from down the block. I followed it from the post office steps to a small street fair off Halsted. There

was an Ecuadorean band featuring a pan flute, and its enchanting, almost hypnotic feel

was what drew me to the fair. I didn't know what the occasion was, but I took in the

booths and people and activity. There was enough activity by enough people but with

enough room to easily maneuver. I was alone but became part of the street fair. I was

the guy with the backpack on. I was that ingredient in this mix. Some others were the

people who came for the food and walked with it in their hands, stopping to take a bite.

Others forming the mix were the ones pushing a stroller, the parents in hats and

sunglasses pushing the baby in the stroller who was pacified by something plastic in

their mouth. Trying to get around them were the de rigor guys without shirts on. But my

eyes found the skin of the legs, arms, and shoulders of the women. I soaked as much in

as I could, knowing my day was coming to an end later that afternoon. I wanted so

badly to stay and to buy food and beer and really listen to the band. It was these small

fairs and festivals I liked best. Who needed the Pier and Grant Park? I wanted to extend

my time there by buying just one beer. I would still be good for work of course. It

would help keep the fair and festival feel in my mind and bones for the walk back to my

apartment and help dilute the usually moral crushing preparation for work. *No, I can't. I*

don't have the money. Yeah, I could afford to spend around ten bucks. But the tip

money I owed the till came to mind. Wait. That's right. It would be tip and paycheck

day on the same day. That only happened because Mark and Rebecca each thought the

other had done the tips last week. I knew this week was a little leaner than most. The

Cosmodemonic worked it out so the staff got tips one week and paychecks the next.

Hell yeah. I would delay this beer and get six for the same price later. I heard through

35

the grapevine, Dennis-the-Juice-Guy, that Mark and Rebecca got into it over the tip

thing. Someone at #204 had called the district manager, Katherine, to complain that the

tips were not done. I was so glad I didn't get those calls. I felt better when I

remembered that. I had a new plan in my head, and I was able to bid farewell the fair

and pan flute. That made it easier on my legs to make their way back to my place.

Before I knew it, I was unlocking my door.

***

The vibe in the store felt off as soon as I stepped in #204 for my Friday close.

Mike G, Denis, Sarah, and Patty were on. There was no Mark in sight. He must have

switched with Mike G. I could immediately tell that it was, and had been, busier than

usual. Both condiment stations were trashed. No one had been able to clean them.

Those were my barometers when I arrived for a shift. I could gauge the day buy what

condition they were in.

I dropped my backpack on the floor in the back, not even taking a second to put

my leftovers in the fridge, and was out on the floor. I passed Patty helping a whole bean

customer and saw five or six open five-pound coffee bags torn open tossed on the

counter. *Damn*. Bad sign number two. I tried to catch a quick glimpse of her as I tied

my apron on and I headed for the espresso bar. She was engaging with the customer, but

I could see fatigue on her face. Patty was Mark's first hire at #204 and a bit older than

most of the staff. Bad sign number three: the pastry case had not been rotated. What was

left of the morning's muffins and scones were broken if there at all. Mikey G was on the

register and Sarah was expediting and brewing, so I jumped up on the bar to help Denis.

"Okay. What do you want me to do, steam milk or pour shots?"

That is how I asked. Denis and I had been in the trenches together before. We knew that a customary greeting was a waste of time now. Besides, I knew how Denis was. Behind. That was why I asked that question with only two possible answers. If I had asked Denis about his dying grandmother, he would have responded only with one of those two options.

The line of customers almost out the door wanted drinks, and they expected them fast and exactly how they had yesterday's, the day before's, and even last month's.

"Shots."

I got the response from Denis, took a deep breath, and reached for a five-pound bag of espresso beans, found on a knee level shelf, and refilled the nearly empty hopper. We needed ammunition. I had a second before I actually started pulling shots because Denis had half a dozen pre-pulled shots already sitting on the bar, crema thinning, temperature declining, taste waning. I had no choice but to ignore this breach of drink prep rules. I had seen him do it on slower weekday mornings too. I would dump them out when he stepped off the bar so he'd have to pour a good shot for the next customer. I believe the drinks should be made right. I loved my triple shot over ice, my tripio. I only used perfectly pulled twenty-second shots that were sweet at the finish and full of the coffee's heart. I lived on them. At the same time, I liked Denis and hated to play boss, so we had an unspoken agreement. He knew I dumped the shots and I knew that he knew. With a line out the door, his old shots were going into the drinks until I got into my groove. We had to catch up.

Below us and to our right, Mikey G and Sarah called out drink orders to Denis and me. In response, Denis fired up the steam wands and sets the milk on its way to foam. I quickly pulled the grinder's release lever, tamped down the ground coffee, and set the filter baskets in place. After several pulls, the automatic grinder clicked on and noisily ground beans for the next dozen or so drinks. The din of the grinding and shriek of the steaming milk made it mandatory for Mikey and Sarah to shout out the orders.

"Tall latte! Double tall mocha! Grande skim latte! Iced Grande Americano!"

Denis and I were veterans of the trenches. Now that I'd joined him, we would win this battle eventually. After all, the espresso bar was elevated, and we looked down on the line of customers. Their lines would form and reform to no avail. We would win this. We held the high ground. We quickly found the cadence we needed. He pulled the cups for the drinks as they were called out. They could be written down, and some who toiled on a busy bar rush preferred that. But neither Denis nor I did. That took too much valuable time.

"Grande skim mocha No whip! Short hazelnut latte! Grande skim latte!"

Denis quickly set the cups on the counter utilizing survival techniques familiar to us bar veterans. We used the Cosmodemonic logo on the cups themselves to guide us. The label facing us was for latte, label facing away was for cappuccino. Mochas got chocolate shots in the bottom. Same with flavored drinks. Decafs were upside down. A lid on the skim drinks. Iced drinks and sizes were self-identifying.

Three grande iced mochas! One skim, no whip! Tall decaf misto! Double tall skim latte!

Sarah and Mikey kept the orders coming at us. Neither Denis nor I spoke. We didn't need to. We didn't have the time to waste. The milk, skim and whole, squealed and shrieked as the steam was repeatedly put to it. I pulled double shots from three of the four filter groups. On the fourth group, I produced triple shot after triple shot. I tamped the espresso into the group's filter basket with my right hand, swiping any overflow off with my left hand and in turn wiping that off on my apron at the hip. In no time, that part of my apron was covered in a brown smear.

"Three tall skim lattes! Short decaf mocha! Iced vanilla latte!"

The hail of orders continued. "What size on the iced vanilla latte?"

I had a steaming wand at my side of the bar and took over steaming milk for the skim drinks. Denis called out drinks and handed them to the customers. He was able to do that with more clarity and precision. How was that possible? Hadn't we just blasted through about fifty orders? Damn, now we need milk for the fridge under the bar. We caught a break as I saw Patty ringing up a whole bean customer on the second register. There was no one in line behind them.

"Patty!" I called in her direction.

No response. The grinder had just clicked on and drowned out my yell.

"Patty!" I yelled louder, giving up the courteous and more civilized tone in my attempt to get her attention. It was no time for civility.

Success. She looked up to me, and I nod to fridge at my feet. She knows what I mean and heads for the back to reappear shortly with a case of four beautiful red-capped gallons of milk. Survival on the bar was assured. She didn't even wait for me to ask and headed out to the condiment stations.

"Short latte double cupped! Double tall decaf hazelnut latte! Two grande lattes!"

Over at Mike and Sarah's station, the trash was overflowing, and they needed drip. Patty had to refill the creamer and sugar at the stations. Money needed to be dropped. No cakes for the upcoming evening shift in the case. Onward, the customers came. None of this mattered to them. Why should it? I glance glanced at the line and saw two guys in roller blades were in line without shirts. Two rules broken at once. *Damn, if that isn't Gene Siskel in front of them.* No time to care about either. I knew Gene's drink and some others, so that brought a second of relief. I knew Denis had to leave soon. He would stay for another thirty minutes if I asked. It had been two hours since I stepped on the bar. The only one of us working this rush to have moved more than a step or two off their station is Patty. But this was it, this was the bar at rush time, and if you were up here, you had earned your stripes. I remembered my first morning rush at #206. I had butterflies in my stomach but knew I had to get on that espresso bar and get through the line. To me, it was the heart of the store, the beating heart of the growing Cosmodemonic Empire, and where you earned the respect of everyone you worked with. As the rush wore on, Denis and I reached that point when we know it just couldn't get any busier, but we had established control. We had held higher ground. We had won.

"Two short cappuccinos! Tall skim latte! Grande decaf latte! Grande iced
hazelnut latte!"

They came and went now. The shouted orders came and went but to little effect.
We took them, processed them, and didn't waver. Denis and I had weathered this rush.
We had done it well enough to make sure the customers would be back in #204 for
more tomorrow. And the next day. And the next.

Then, for the first time in those two hours, someone I wanted to see walked
through the doors. It was Mark. In the immediacy of the rush, I had forgotten he'd be in.
We almost never closed together. He looked up right at me on the bar and grinned from
ear to ear. He knew.

Denis stayed long enough for Mark to do his stuff in the back. Denis would still
make it on time for his *Lysistrata* rehearsal. Tony came in just as Denis left. Since Mark
was there, I eased off mentally. But, I still told Denis he did a great job. The lines began
to slow, and the transition to close began. Half an hour after Denis left, Mikey G took
off. And Sarah left an hour after him. We would get busy again later, but for now,
Mark, Tony, and I went into recovery mode. Anything empty was filled. Anything
spilled was cleaned up. Anything empty was stocked. Anything opened was closed and
shelved. Counters and surfaces got wiped off. Sanity, hope, and humor came back to
me. Tony was quiet and efficient on pre-close, but long-winded with customers,
especially when explaining drinks. I have tried to tell him to say, when it is busy, that a
certain drink or type of whole bean is 'my favorite' so the customer will bite and the

line will move. He didn't do that much, but I was sure glad he was there. He was in grad

school somewhere was always good to call if a shift needed filling.

Finally, I made a second tripio over ice and leaned by the door to the backroom

to catch my breath. It was almost nine. Mark came from the back carrying a sleeve of

pastry bags, one of the less dire items that needed filling. But he was already thinking of

the Saturday morning rush. It would be another thousand-customer morning. As he

passed me, he stopped and put his free hand on my shoulder and said that he and I are

going to Boru's after close. He's buying the pints. He added one last thing, and that

was, "We need to talk."

***

My body felt the couch in my apartment as my eyes eased open. I knew I wasn't

in my bed. I saw my unpacked workbag on the floor right by my front door. I thought

that I stumbled, leaned, and staggered my way from where my bag is to where I am

now. And I passed out. Sitting up to look at the sun through my window in order to

guess the time, my head felt like a wet sandbag and my stomach like a fishbowl filled

with eels. Draft does that to my stomach.

Mark bought pitcher after pitcher of draft beer at Boru's. Tracing the night in

reverse, the end was the haziest and the beginning clearest, although that isn't saying all

that much. It did stand out that big things were coming at the Cosmodemonic. Not just

in Chicago and the Pacific Northwest but more big cities like Washington, Denver, and

even New York. Rebecca was leaving #204. Mark ordered shots over that news. That

explained the sandbag head. I can handle beer after beer, but add shots, and the head pays the price. And, yes, Mark wanted me to be the assistant manager at #204. I think I said, "I'll think about it." But then, I remembered another round of shots. Did that mean that I said yes or that we just wanted more shots? Did I say no because I'm writing a novel? I hoped I didn't say that.

At that point, on my couch, it was too much for my brain to attempt to recall. Too much effort. The sun wasn't all that strong through my windows. I took a deep breath over my fuzzy tongue and stood. I took my clothes off and let them form a pile on the floor. I made it to my room and under the sheet. A half-filled glass of water stood on my nightstand. It was a sign of absolution to me. My better-behaved-self had water a couple nights ago when reading in bed. I inhaled it in one gulp. I was hopeful of being human upon waking again. If I rested my brain, the details would come back to me.

***

It was nearly one when I braved food. There wasn't much offered by the indifferent refrigerator. What was in there had no appeal. Gold Coast Dogs had saved my life a couple times when I was in this state. That was what I wanted. There was one just across from #206 and one Sunday about a year ago, I remember making it through a Sunday open with a hangover only because I could see Gold Coast across the street. Despite the hangover, I worked the bar the entire rush so I could see their storefront. Made it over there at lunch. The hope of a couple seven-ways got me through that brutal morning. But it occurred to me I had to drop off the paragraph at Liberation, and I wanted to talk to someone when I did. Sadly, that didn't leave time for the Gold Coast.

I headed north several blocks to Liberation. It was in the opposite direction of #204, and I was cutting it close anyway, but I had no choice. I'd just get the bus from Liberation to #204 for the close. I liked their bookstore and the people there. I had hoped to feel better when I brought in my work. But it was too late for that. All I could do was pace the floor. I wanted to make a good impression, get a second assignment, and then who knows? As I glanced at book titles and posters of Mao and Bob Avakian, I felt guilty, useless, and talentless. I was still a bit hungover. I was handing in my assignment at the last minute. And worst of all, I just found out that the company I work for plans to take over America. Maybe the Maoists already knew. I think that maybe they did somehow. To my hangover-ravaged mind, that made sense. Based on that certainty, the Maoists would surely reject my paragraph and send me packing. My hope of making a connection to a publisher, already tenuous, now lied in the dumpster behind Boru's next to one of the plastic cups I used last night. And to top it all off, the guy behind the counter asked me to wait for Irene, who was in back. She was in charge and who I needed to talk to. I was already cutting it close. I hoped to slink in, hand in my paragraph, and be on my way. I barely recalled last night, and that is suffocating any confidence I had planned on having when I got a quick face to face with Irene. I had flushed my bravado and self-esteem down the toilet at Brian Boru's. *Fuck*. I just want to go to work. I don't need Liberation to get me published. It wasn't even much of a plan. Since it's fucked now, it doesn't even matter. I'd get the novel finished soon enough and it would take care of itself. *When I finish it.* I should have been working on that instead. Instead of their book. Instead of drinking last night…

"Hey, Irene can see you now!"

***

I was back at my apartment and took a long, hot shower to wash off Friday night

at Boru's in addition to tonight's close. I had Phil and Chuck tonight. Sarah left at eight,

and it stayed busy but under control the rest of the way. As she left, I reminded her of

the meeting Sunday. Mark had asked me to remind everyone since it was an important

meeting. I then had a thought to call Kati and remind her too. It was a perfect excuse to

call Kati and let the conversation lead somewhere. It wasn't much of a plan, but it was

something. But just as Sarah passed through the doors on her way out, a group of tourist

types came in. Always the worst because they didn't know the drill. Chuck was his

usual self. Not the greatest and not the worst closer. But he could charm the customers.

I let him do the talking and jumped on the bar to await their decisions. Phil was already

doing the pre-close cleaning. I let him go at it. It was really too early, but my hangover

had been replaced by simple, uncomplicated fatigue. I wanted out as soon as possible.

Phil was the quietest person of all the #204 staff and only closed every other Saturday.

That was a bit of a favor from Mark since Phil had been here since before Mark. There

was an unwritten rule at the Cosmodemonic that any staff had to work at least ten hours

a week. But since Saturday nights were the hardest shift of the week to staff, Phil stayed

at #204. Phil was tall, blond, and fair with blue, deep-set eyes. We all joked that he was

the perfect Arian specimen. He always joins in with the kidding, and as we joked about

his fake genealogy, he vowed to create the 'Master Roast' to help the Cosmodemonic

Coffee Company rule the country. The humor got us through the close, but I never

found the time for the phony reminder call to Kati.

***

I woke up early on Sunday morning in Chicago. I put my kettle on the burner to heat the water for my French press pot of Ethiopian Yergacheffe. My senses were back, and I wanted to taste the floral Yergacheffe, not the winey Kenya. I didn't need any reminders of alcohol. I always had some backup coffee kept in my cabinet, away from light and heat. I didn't have to freeze it since even my back up stash didn't last very long. I was aware and pleased with my clear head and calm stomach. It was the perfect time to sit down to work on the novel. I looked forward to an easy close tonight. We would lock the doors an hour early, have pizza for the meeting, and I could get out and have my Monday off. I was free of booze binge guilt. But also, I had a clear conscience because I added the ten dollars back to the tips last night.

I couldn't do it Friday as planned since Mark was there. It all worked out. Though it was funny how often the money came into my head. There were more times than I care to admit that I thought of keeping it, or just telling myself that I forgot to return it.

I had no idea how much more an assistant manager made than a lead. I heard it wasn't much more since managers and assistants were not allowed to take the tips. Tips could add up when it was busy, and if you got forty hours like I always did. Lord knows I loved the feel of the cash in my wallet. With the newfound clarity in my head, I recalled some of Friday night. I remembered Mark saying I had what it takes to qualify for the Management Training Program, a college degree and a love of coffee. I remembered back farther to Carlos at #206, who would call me 'Mr. Cosmodemonic' because I got so into the coffee as soon as I got hired there. I heard the water. It needed to be just off boil for the perfect temp to extract maximum flavor from the grounds. In a press pot, you let the coarsely ground coffee steep for four minutes, break the crust with

a spoon then press the screen down. Couldn't wait for that first cup and then what? Oh

yeah, the novel.

I swear I was physically lighter after a good session at the typewriter. As I

wrote, my clear head became clearer. I'd felt this before when I wrote and have

promised myself that I was going to weigh myself before I sat down at the typewriter.

Then after a good hour or two, I'd step on the scale to find out whether I was really

lighter or not. But, I didn't have a scale. Yet, the end of the novel was in sight. I had a

good three hours on it. Three hours that seemed like half an hour. I needed to get a

ribbon, or there would be no finishing it anytime soon. Plus, I needed to pay bills. That

would work since I had to stay here in the morning. The landlord, Karl, was finally

sending the maintenance guy over to check out my fridge.

***

I arrived for the shift at #204, and it seemed an entirely different place than

yesterday. It wasn't of course, but I was entirely different today. Mark opened and left

as soon as he could after I got in. He would be back for the meeting. Mikey G was

leaving in an hour would be back too. It was Patty and Tony with me for the duration.

We could use another hand. Mikey G said Mark had called around for someone to fill

in, but all the city stores have been doing similar meetings, and there weren't that many

bodies willing to fill another shift and then go to their own store for a meeting in the

same weekend. Fair enough. I was energetic and felt ready to conquer the world.

Sunday afternoons were never slow but never the crush that Fridays and Saturdays could be. I could stay on the floor, do mark-outs for the week and even get in a little

restock of the retail shelves if all went well.

It did. I knew it may have been the residual buzz from the progress on the novel,

but I felt like I was at home here. Like I had always been at this store just off the corner

of Clark, Diversey, and Broadway in Chicago. I even allowed a little self-esteem to

come back to me. The time eased by, and I was in fact, able to slide from beans to bar to

retail and soon #204 looked great. It was still a little beat up of course from all the

customers coming and going. But, I liked that. I liked the character it gave the place. I

liked the story told by use, by decline, by the passing of time. But the Cosmodemonic

was also right. This store could have used a facelift. I got a moment and stood with the

bar towel tossed over my right shoulder and took it in. Again, I was struck by the

possibility that I was a better Cosmodemonic partner than I perceived myself to be.

Mark had seen the wars at Cosmodemonic longer than most. And #204 was designated

as a training store, hence Rebecca. That meant it was considered to be well run enough

to be an example to new hire management types. That was a designation of distinction

for Mark. And Mark wanted me to move up as assistant here. Tony called me over to

the bar to get help with a short line. I'd been able to set the grinder to produce beautiful

espresso shots. They looked like honey dripping off a spoon. The drinks I made were

perfect. I loved the product, and it showed. Mark and Rebecca were not exactly peas in

a pod. They never got hammered at Boru's together. But it wasn't just that. It couldn't

be.

***

The doors were closed, and the chairs pulled around in a circle on the retail floor. Again, I was proud of the way the store looked and how that reflected on me. The #204 staff arrived a few at a time. I was finally feeling fatigue coming on and was already in my chair, hat off, apron off my neck. Glad to be sitting, I tuned out for a moment and then she sat down right next to me. Only a few chairs were taken and none of them all that close to me. In fact, Mark and Mikey G were not even back with the pizzas yet. But Kati took the seat right next to me. My fatigue left me. She looked at me with a wide smile as she took her seat. "How was boot camp?"

I didn't say anything for a second. What did that mean? I forced a quick half-smile on my face and leaned over pretending to tie my shoe. Kati was in shorts. She had long, smooth legs with a line of muscle definition running up her left thigh highlighting the separation of her thighs and hamstrings. Her skin was a light caramel color from the sun. Her legs seemed to not sit still but flow smoothly from her ankles up to her khaki shorts. In the two seconds it took for me to pretend to tie my shoe, it suddenly hit me that she was referring to my haircut. I raised myself back up to respond, "Got out yesterday."

Kati responded with a second smile, and we fell into easy conversation about what to expect at the meeting. I wished again that I could recall more of Friday night at Boru's so that I could use that information to impress Kati. I could have elevated myself by telling Kati all I knew about the Cosmodemonic's expansion plans. I knew that the march of the Master Roast is underway. I decided then to join the march as a management trainee. That is if I hadn't told Mark that already. If I said yes on that bleary Friday at Boru's, then I would confirm it again. Confirming because a change in positions would mean more opening shifts with Kati.

***

I had passed L'escorgot countless times on my walks up and down Clark. It was tucked in between bigger more noticeable establishments on both sides. The aroma of garlic made fragrant by the heat of olive oil was always oozing from the interior. As much as that aroma enticed me, the restaurant itself seemed to say to not enter unless you were with someone. Since I was usually just with my Sketchbook of the Mind, I felt I should pass by. And I always did until that night.

Mark had run the meeting as quickly as he could. There were lots of questions from the staff. He covered Cosmodemonic's expansion plans, Rebecca's leaving for a suburban store of her own, and something called an IPO, and lots and lots of policy changes. He, of course, mentioned the assistant manager job being open and that it was being posted citywide. When he did, he avoided looking at me. He added that the actual official posting would not be in his hands until Tuesday. That, coincidence or not, was my next workday at #204.

I don't recall who suggested it. Maybe Kati, maybe me, maybe neither, but we found ourselves stepping together into L'escorgot just a few minutes after the meeting ended. We were asking each other questions about what we had just heard from Mark. A lot of it was discussion worthy, so we talked and walked in step out the vestibule of #204, across the street, up a half block, and into the doors of L'escorgot. It struck us simultaneously that we weren't hungry when the waiter greeted us with the menus. We

50

had just had pizza. To quickly save face, I drew on a cursory knowledge of wine and ordered a bottle of a sweeter after dinner wine. Our server seemed impressed and gave Kati a quick smile, which I imaged to mean, "You are in good hands."

Kati was from Charleston, Illinois, and found herself in Chicago partly because of that. I want to say that I was relaxed around her after a glass of the wine. But there was no time that I didn't feel relaxed around her, no stage where I even noticed feeling otherwise. It could have been that she was from a big family like mine and from the Midwest. That description fit a lot of people in Chicago. She carried herself with confidence and aura that conveyed a sense of purposed movement. On the bar at #204, she did the half spin from the espresso grinder to filter basket with a directness and a swift grace that I had noticed the first time I worked with her. She worked at the Cosmodemonic mainly for the schedule and the benefits for part-timers. And the free coffee. She almost exclusively opened six to twelve on weekdays. She also made some decent money posing in the nude for art students at Chicago Art Institute. She said that she was always a little uncomfortable doing it. Not because she was squeamish or shy about nudity as I first concluded. No, she corrected me; it was just a little too cold just be sitting there posed and still with nothing on.

Our conversation took in movies, politics, food, and songs liked and disliked. Neither of us had a car. She hoped there would not be a war in the Middle East, and I agreed. I felt a touch of relief when I ventured an opinion, and she shared a similar view. There wasn't much talk of store #204 after the second glass wine was poured. Those cares were overtaken by more closely held hopes of forming a connection between two people. These hopes were carried somehow by the almost visible, life-giving aroma of dinners eaten and being eaten. We still didn't order anything though, as I was easily content by the occasional moments of lingering eye contact across the table.

Writing this in my Sketchbook of the Mind and glancing up to where Kati sat until about fifteen minutes before, I knew I would see her again. She had to open tomorrow and needed to leave. She had a train ride back to her place with no transfer and a good walk to her apartment from the station. I had the last glass of *vino relaxo* before I mounted up and headed north on Clark for home myself. Only I couldn't sip the wine slowly enough to save my life. I wanted to keep Kati with me via the glass of wine. If I finish it, the evening would be over officially. I bought myself some time by pulling out my sketchbook and taking notes. I wanted to drink the wine, the glass of Kati, and have it refilled again. I wanted to swirl her around, hold her on my tongue for a moment before swallowing, and let her aftertaste linger in me. It would fortify me, warm me, and leave me appreciating her even more than when we arrived here together. I did the best I could but noticed a couple guys from the kitchen in food stained chef gear take seats at a table across from me. That was their way of saying that it was time to leave. I complied and finished the wine less poetically in one gulp. Sketchbook jammed into my backpack, I made a right out of the door of L'escorgot. It was Sunday night, so it was nearly empty on the sidewalk, and even the traffic on Clark was scarce. A cab or two, lights on, slowed in my peripheral vision. It had been a great day and an even better evening, and I considered treating myself to a cab as a reward. *But no.* Tonight I'd be walking home alone.

Chapter Two

It was almost two on Monday afternoon, and I had my seat at La Bamba, the

shoebox-sized Mexican restaurant just up my street. It was to be avoided on Cubs'

game days and late nights on weekends. But, to the unhurried trickle of the small

fountain by the front door, I waited for my post-three-close-weekend reward to be

brought to the table. I had a seat by the window at one of the eight tables that made up

the small dining room. I faced the big window looking down Cornelia toward Halsted. I

could see almost as far as the Manhole Bar at the end of my street. If I were to turn and

look behind me, I would see Wrigley Ville and its stadium, bars, restaurants, and bars.

But what I took in as I waited was just a residential street. With just a little bit of effort,

I could have convinced myself that this could be any street in the Midwest that time of

year. I couldn't help but wonder why sometimes these streets were filled with the

movement of so many people and cars. *Not now, thank God. I've seen enough people*

over the past three days. Mark said at the meeting, we had the most customers ever for

a Friday and Saturday since #204 opened. It struck me again that Cosmodemonic was

considering a remodel. They wanted to move the bar back away from the door and

lower it. No more espresso bar as theatre stage. Of course, that brought the most protest

from the staff of all the new changes coming down the pike. *That might be it.* That

might be what I didn't understand and what was on my mind. It wasn't the fact that the

maintenance guy never made it over, not that the only reason Irene wanted to see me at

Liberation was to double check my phone number to call me if something came up.

Those relevant facts and day-to-day challenges were not uppermost in my thoughts. Not

even the great time with Kati held my mental attention. I looked down the now quiet tree-lined street and wonder why it wasn't enough? Why wasn't a record-breaking

weekend at #204 enough?

In my situation, I felt just about there, like just a bit more would be enough. I

took the time waiting on the maintenance guy's visit to get in a work a little more on my

novel and even settle on the title: *Back Outta the World*. I had just over two pages from

the trip notebook left which likely meant four or five typed pages remained. That's all.

With the novel done, I could focus on finding a publisher or editor or both. And that

couldn't be as hard as the writing. So, that left me with the time I would need. The time

I would need to give to Cosmodemonic. I had decided to go in tomorrow and tell Mark

that I wanted to be the assistant manager at #204. Sober and official. But I wouldn't let

it consume my life. Mark didn't seem to let it consume his life, though it may be why he

boozed so much. Rebecca seemed to want it to be her life, hence the suburban store.

Me, if I could just make a little more money, then I would be all set. Might even have

enough to have food next time Kati and I went out. *Speaking of food, here it comes.*

Time to eat. Time to put the Sketchbook of the Mind away.

***

Okay. I turned my typewriter on, and it was humming again. It was late Monday

afternoon in my apartment, and I was back at the desk. The hard-shell tacos, beans, and

rice at La Bamba did not disappoint. After an errand and beer run, I hit my couch for a

siesta. The weekend had taken its toll as they always do.

I had been sitting for twenty minutes or so to the silence of the typewriter in

front of me. I had turned it off twenty minutes ago. That didn't help either. Since no day was the same and we were always changing, always becoming someone new, I had

hoped that twenty minutes of time passing might bring something. It did not. Before

that, I randomly punched keys to warm up. The sound the keys made me think of bugs.

The kind with long legs, like crickets or even roaches. Then I remembered a battle I had

with a two-inch roach in my kitchen. The kitchen door of my place faced the alley and

all that it brought. My neighborhood was quite densely populated, and there were

restaurants and bars and clubs not too far away from my front and back doors. I had

always kept a clean kitchen. So when the two-inch brown roach scurried out from under

my stove one day while I was cleaning, I had to kill it. I took it personally even though I

knew no matter what I did, no matter how clean I kept my apartment, I could still get

bugs or even mice. After the first moment of surprise at seeing the brown two-inch

roach racing across the kitchen floor away from me toward the main room and lots of

potential hiding places, I acted. I swept a copy of the *Reader* off the sink counter and

smashed it down upon the offending roach with authority and malice. I confidently

looked under the paper. I had to clean the spot where I smashed it. But no, all two

inches of it took off again. *Damn.* I couldn't let it find safety in my living room. I stood

up to the surprise of its life force continuing and saw the phone book on top of my

fridge. Certainly, the roach would meet its end. In the hallway where the bathroom,

kitchen, and living room met, I crushed the phone book down upon the roach, and I

meant business doing it. The apartment shook with the impact. Again, I lifted the

weapon to see the result, and again the roach lived! It had been wounded though. I

could see that it could get to the safety of a corner or under my couch if I allowed it. But

I had been able to buy some time. This time I grabbed the *Reader* again and smashed it down on the roach as it reached the actual floor of the living room. Then to assure

victory, I put my right foot on the *Reader* and stood on the spot directly above my two-

inch adversary. I listened until I heard the unmistakable sound of roach exoskeleton

being crushed. I had won.

The roach story took up time I could have used to write *Back Outta the World*. I

didn't know how many times I had turned my typewriter on and off to hear the

humming stop and start so far today.

In the back of my mind, I thought of how it would go with Mark tomorrow. I

knew he just couldn't give me the position of assistant manager. I had to go through the

training. Cosmodemonic calls it Manager in Education or MIE, and it took a while. I

only knew what I overheard Rebecca say to Mark and what they said in the backroom

when they talked about her progress. I didn't think too much about her since she arrived

at #204. But now I was trying to get a picture of what her days were like. She was good

enough on the floor, and her shifts ran well. She was not as good as me on the bar.

Neither was Mark. I remembered an incident with Andrea who just left #204. She once

told Mark the pour was off on the espresso machine. Mark walked up to the bar and

dismissively brewed a shot that ended up being eighteen seconds—in the acceptable

range. It was December and so busy that I didn't think he wanted to take the time to

really check more than one pour. Andrea was a bit put off, and life and the rush went on

but I watched from time to time and the rest of Andrea's shift the shots ran fast. She had

been right. I should have said something to make her feel better, but I was still too new

at the time.

I felt like only Sarah and Denis were my match on the bar. But, being good on the bar didn't make you management material by itself. My days at the coffee house in Dayton likely didn't amount to much in Katherine's eyes. I know she'd had to sign off on any type of MIE training for me. As a district manager, her vote counted more than Mark's. *God damn, where was I? Back Outta the World. Not happening at all. Okay. I give up.* It was still before five in the afternoon. That meant that it was time for a retreat to my spot. It was safe to go up there now before anyone else came back. I knew I wouldn't be bothered.

I had my sketchbook and my copy of *Tropic of Cancer* with me. I was shirtless, barefoot, and on the roof of my apartment building. It was four stories high but seemed higher from the roof. The sun was out, and the heat it produced on the roof was more all-encompassing. I got there by climbing the wooden ladder from the uppermost landing. I first went out my back door and up two flights of the back staircase. I would go down the other two flights when I need to take my trash out as the back staircase faces the alley. That day, I put my things in my backpack and climbed through the porthole up to the roof. I needed two hands to get through, so I always put anything I brought in a backpack so I could be hands-free for the climb. There were a couple chairs and about half dozen empty beer bottles, which were not mine. I had mine still full and coldish from my fridge. I figured this was my spot on Monday afternoons in the summer, and everyone else could have it for evening beers if they wanted. A good decision to stop forcing the novel. Yes. I looked all over, all directions. I could see the top of Wrigley and dozens of roofs close to the height of mine. The roof oozed heat, but the breeze up there matched and equalized it. The sound of the train passing was different up here. Life seemed different up here. My perspective was different up here. My life was different up here. It was a good place to come to cleanse, alter, or shake up my mind. I loved it here because I sensed the city, I heard the city, and I felt the city. But at the same time, I saw no one.

I took my preferred chair. I opened a beer but not *Tropic* and felt the heat find my body. It soothed me and settled me. The city below going about all the business it goes about also soothed me. It would go on, and I would sit here, neither getting in the other's way. The fact that I could hear it going on, while I was spying undetected heightened my anonymity. I heard the train and knew that no passenger could see me from ten blocks away. I heard buses pulling off from what was most likely my stop five blocks away. Cars' honking reached me as did the occasional shout or door slam from a nearby building. The heat on my skin felt even better, more pronounced because I was spying. The sun and its warmth were for me only. No building near me had roof access, or at least I'd never seen anyone else on them. This was my spot and my heat. I stood up to slide my shorts off. I put them on the seat of the old chair and placed my naked backside on it. It struck me as odd that the sun felt the same on the whiter flesh of my pelvis and penis. I reflected that my nudity had no effect on the scene below.

***

Tuesday morning and I was up and going about my business. My laundry was finished, and I had clean clothes for the workweek. My fridge had food and provisions for eating all week at home and on break at #204. The fridge was still not cold enough for me but hadn't gotten worse. I left another message for my landlord Karl. I didn't have to be here for the guy to check out my fridge. Maybe Karl didn't trust his

maintenance guy. Whatever the case, I crossed that call off my list. It felt good to have

control over my environment. The rest of the bills had been paid. I had a bit of time

before heading in for the close. I wanted to write but felt a little off. Were the coming

changes at Cosmodemonic putting me on edge for work? Or was it just that I knew the

writing wasn't flowing right? I did know I wanted to get out of the city. I had an older

sister in St. Louis. She had a nice condo with a pool. I loved my rooftop and the sun up

there. But I wanted to sit by a pool with a beer and have the option of jumping into the

water.

Just as I begin the letter to my sister, the phone rang. I didn't get a lot of calls. I

noticed the time. It was close to eleven a.m., so I was not too surprised when it was

Mark's voice on the other end. That was the time of morning when the rush would be

over, and breaks would have been started, and Mark would be at the desk in back

ordering supplies for the weekend. Mark called because he was hoping I could come in

a bit early so we could talk. He had to leave right at three, and it would really help him

out. I had no good reason to say no, so I agreed, and he sounded pleased. Before I hung

up, I heard Kati's voice from the background "Tell him I say hi!" My pulse quickened

for just second without any conscious effort. She must have been on her break in back

by Mark's desk. If I got there really early, I could see her. But, no way. She would be

long gone. I realized that I didn't have her number. Mark hung up. I stood holding the

receiver and pissed at myself that I didn't have Kati's number. We did get along

famously Sunday night, but I failed to follow up. I stood in my spot and decided on a

compromise. I would finish the letter to my sister, inviting myself to her pool and maybe receiving an offer of financial assistance to do so. Then I would leave early for

work, thus meeting my desire to see Kati today about halfway. I would mail the letter

when I came to a mailbox. Crossing that off my list would take some of the edge off my

lack of follow up with Kati.

***

I got in at two-thirty, and Mark stood up from his desk as soon as he saw me

enter the backroom. With a smile on his face, he greeted me by declaring, "In life,

timing is everything."

Mark nodded to me to drop my bag on the table. There was more to tell.

"There's new round of Managers in Education training set to start next week.

Katherine is coming Friday on her regular rounds, and she called me to ask if I had an

answer from you."

Friday at Boru's came back into my head. Or at least some fragments did.

"What about our interview?" Looking Mark in the eyes for some hint. It was

only then that I realized he might not have the best memory of the Boru's night either.

"That was at Boru's." He replied shrugging his shoulders as to say it was time to

move on.

"Then, yeah, I'm in," I said.

***

I had an interview with our district manager on Friday and needed a white shirt

and a tie. I had decent khakis but could really use new ones for my confidence if

nothing else. My favorite resale shop, the Brown Elephant, would not fail me. It was the

size of a warehouse yet immaculately kept up. I could trust the Brown Elephant but

didn't know if I could trust myself Friday. What did I know about actual management?

A little late for that. The Cosmodemonic Coffee Company was growing fast and needed

people. I was one. Plus, I had a real passion for the coffee. Cosmodemonic would have

to teach me the rest.

The Tuesday close was the Tuesday close. We were busy enough to keep my

body moving. My mind moved to Friday often enough to speed the passing of the

evening. I didn't have to worry about Denis and Sarah doing their jobs. Before I knew

it, my keys turned the lock for the front door, and I was in back filling out the deposit

and nightly recap sheet. I noticed myself making an effort to make my numbers more

crisp and legible than usual. After all, I thought, Katherine looks these over at the end of

the week.

***

I was at the doors of the Brown Elephant before they opened at noon on

Wednesday. They opened, and I headed over to the dress shirts. At the very first rack of

white shirts, there were two my size. They didn't even look like they'd been worn. Now

I had momentum. Fortune was smiling on me. The instant good luck in finding shirts

steered my mind in positive directions regarding Friday. I had a supporter in Doug from

#206. He hired me and must have said good things about me to Mark. And there was

61

Candace, the district trainer. She knew everyone and must have trained everyone at Cosmodemonic on how to pour shots and a million other things. I knew I had made a good impression on her during my new hire training classes. I had taken the classes seriously and did the workbooks and read McCoy and Walker's *Coffee and Tea* from cover to cover—except for the tea parts. It showed in my class participation and answers. And Mark told me Candace was a bigger wheel for Cosmodemonic than it would appear.

Content with two shirts, I headed for the pants section with a resolve, hoping to sustain the momentum. I did train with at least one other new hire who was a manager. Back when I started, they lumped everyone together. One I recalled for sure was Sue who now runs the store on Webster, further south of #206. She would surely remember me. Plus, Sue and Doug talk a lot. I think Katherine was her district manager too. But now there were more districts to manage, and I am not sure. I know for sure more districts were on the way because more stores were on the way. And more after that. Latte by latte and cup by cup Cosmodemonic had created the need for bodies. And I had well over two years of actual Cosmodemonic experience. I understood that the coffee wasn't bitter or burned. It was just brought to its peak of flavor. And the oily sheen on top of the bean was the evidence. I knew that the crema on a shot of espresso was due to the water being forced through the grounds. I knew that the company was not named after that female skater.

On cue, I had a good pair of khakis. I knew they would fit. My waist hadn't grown since my last trip there. I saved the ties for last, counting on them being the easiest. But, with my confidence increased and spirits lifted, I had a hard time deciding.

They all appealed to me, especially the brighter colored ones. Then I remembered that

Mark hired a new guy to start that night. Training people was not easy. They slowed

everything down. His name was Dennis too. But he was from Boston, and Mark was

already calling him Boston Dennis. Mark said it would look good to be training

someone when I was interviewing with Katherine on Friday. He told me to look for

examples of progress in Boston Dennis that I could point out to Katherine as evidence

of my ability to train people. Because that was going to be incredibly important to the

Cosmodemonic: a demonstrated ability to train people. I already did that at #206 as

lead, especially training closers but couldn't remember an example for the life of me. I

reserved that mental space for the novel. I found a good tie. It was colorful but not too

much. I decided to get one more just in case. During the rushes at work, the coffee in all

its forms seemed to find clean clothes way too easily.

***

I was back on the thirty-six bus for the Wednesday close. I took the thirty-six

again since it felt right. Yesterday had been a good day, and I wanted to keep the

momentum going. It was usually a little less crowded than the twenty-two or the eight,

and I could find a seat alone most times. It felt good to settle in, let the bus's AC cool

me, and keep my backpack next to me instead of at my feet. I had the *Reader* in my

hand. I grabbed it from the seat in front of me, which was also empty. I knew it would

be a good close tonight no matter how busy. My dad had said over the years that pretty

much all you could do was "give 'em a good day's work." I would do that tonight, even

with training Boston Dennis on my plate. It struck me that with all the coming changes

in my head, I didn't know who my fellow closers were going to be. Now that Mikey G was a lead, he could open and close and would be the best option to have around. He could do all the things I usually did and leave me to focus as much as possible on Boston Dennis. If I did make it into MIE training, I'd have to get to the district office. It used to be in the back of the Rush Street downtown store. Now it was a real building somewhere else downtown. I didn't yet know where. My thoughts traveled ahead to Friday and back over my time with Cosmodemonic until I reached the corner stop and store #204. It seemed like it was my first day at #206 all over again. I had a small case of butterflies as I stepped in through both sets of doors. But that was just in my head, not in the real world of #204. I realized that as soon as I saw the elevated espresso bar. No one looked up from their stations. They knew it was me, and I was always on time. Sarah didn't even acknowledge me as I stepped next to her and prepped my tripio over ice. Again, she knew it was me doing the normal. I checked the schedule in back, and Boston Dennis was due in at five. Tony for Sarah at four. Then Chuck. We'll be fine. I was glad for the two hours to clean what I could. I always felt like I had to have the store looking great to create the impression that it should always look like this whenever possible. I put my food in the fridge and tied my apron on. Better get to it.

***

Almost one in the morning. I knew the close would be slower with a new person to train. And since that was the case, we were unexpectedly busier than usual for a weeknight. Tony ended up with all the new customers who didn't know an Americano from a hole in the ground. Luckily, Chuck took orders from the espresso bar, stepped down to the register to ring that order up, and then jumping back up to make and hand off the drink. It wasn't ideal, but it worked when it needed to. I was at the whole bean counter for Boston Dennis's first couple hours, so I let Chuck and Tony handle the rush.

To his credit, Chuck did not complain about the bar hopping as he jokingly called it

later. Boston Dennis had bartending experience, which should have helped, but I didn't

let him near the bar for now. He would close with me Friday, so maybe I could get him

started then. He seemed to take in the whole bean set up well and was very deliberate in

measuring out the ground batches for the next day's brewing. At close, it could be hard

to picture why we did what we did unless you also experienced the morning rush. As

the batches piled up on the counter for tomorrow, he remarked that it was a lot of

coffee. We weren't halfway through prepping at that point. We were not even prepping

for a busy weekend morning.

When I made it home, I used my residual tripio over ice energy to reset my

writing space. It might help me finish *Back Outta the World*. It couldn't hurt. My desk

was cleaned up, aligned for a better view out of my window, and visually more

appealing to the user, who was me. A big pile of writing instruments, collected from all

over my apartment, and stuck in one of my old coffee mugs, provided the finishing

touch. I called it a night.

***

I was awakened up by knocking on the door. *Who the hell?* My first thought was

of Natali. *Hell yea!* With that hope, blood began to flow to my pelvis, and I felt the

emerging of an erection. She still has a key to both doors from when she helped me

move in, right? A second knock and the muffled voice of a man came through my door.

Not Natali. It was Karl the landlord, of course. I had made it to my room and bed last night. Pulling some pants on, I checked the clock. It was past nine and late for me to be still asleep. My thoughts before opening the door for Karl was of calling Natali to see if there was a date for Anita's play.

Despite Karl not being Natali, it was a good visit from Karl. He had been out of town, and the maintenance guy was, by Karl's orders, converting a small space in the basement to a laundry room. With that explained, he excused himself and checked out the fridge while I got dressed. As I washed my face, I wondered what he thought of my desk and the notebooks and papers accumulated on it. He most likely didn't care. But he cared enough to pull out the fridge and use a little vacuum he brought to clean off all the dust and grit off the cooling coils. I heard the fridge click and hum to life. I thanked Karl and thought of cold beers later. Before he left, he mentioned that the year would be up in a couple months and that the rent would go up due to the addition of the laundry room. It was going to go up anyway, he assured me as he left.

My first reaction was to cancel my planned trip to Modi Mahal for some great Indian food. It was a decent walk, but the place was worth it. *No.* Now I didn't have the money. *No! I do have the money for it now.* But I couldn't go, the rent was going up in a couple months. It would be great to do laundry downstairs, and the machines would be newer and more efficient, and I wouldn't have to plan so carefully on laundry days. And, I really needed to impress Katherine with my sharp attire and get the promotion to assistant. Clean clothes demonstrated attention to detail, and that would help me get the promotion. If that happened, I wouldn't have to look for a cheaper place. Natali did help me find this apartment, and it turned out to be perfect to get to both of my

Cosmodemonics. But, if I had to move due to increased rent. *Okay, stop.* Walk to Modi

Mahal. The walk would help. The reveries as Henry Miller called them, always help.

***

The walk helped calm the mind and clear the head. I was at the table I wanted,

and it was midafternoon. I was the only one in the dining room at Modi Mahal. I was

practiced at eating when there was no one else around. If I brought my Sketchbook of

the Mind and had it open, it appeared I was deliberately by myself. I actually was alone

because I wanted to be. My legs moved my mind, and I felt better after my walk here.

The city was at its best in the summer, I thought. It did occur to me as I sat alone that

Kati was off work at #204 a couple hours before. *Damn.* I had all week to get her

number from the list at work. And I didn't do it. So maybe I really wanted to be alone.

No, on second thought, not that badly. I needed to write it down in my sketchbook to

get her number on Friday. *There.* I did it and left a blank space for her number next to

her name.

That done, I looked up from my table out the window. I liked this view because

I could only see a part of one other building. It had a white stucco-like façade and

wasn't tall and modern looking. The dining room and entire feel of Modi Mahal are

authentic India to me. So, I could pretend to be Ginsberg or Kerouac as I wrote and

waited for my food. That was one of the reasons I was here. I did get a plate of filling

food for a great price to be sure. But, I came two thousand miles from my apartment.

Any voices I heard were not speaking English unless they addressed me. The aroma

was all spice and depth and warmth. It brought something faraway with it. I breathed deeply to take it in. It helped. But, I remained afraid of everyday life. I couldn't think

straight after I heard the news of my rent going up. But Jack and Allen just took off all

over the world. And wrote about it. Come to think of it, here in this dining room it could

have been forty years before in India. Ginsberg and Orlofsky could have walked in and

sat down on the other side of the dining room. Easily. I didn't want to leave until they

did. I didn't want to interview with Katherine tomorrow. *I'm in India, lost to my*

apartment, lost to my bills, lost to my plans for more a bigger paycheck. I'm here now

in India with the Beatniks. So there is no need to finish the book or prep for the

interview now.

***

I'd been getting ready for the workweek on Fridays for as long as had I lived

here. I was so used to it that it barely occurred to me that most people's workweeks

were winding down on Friday afternoons. Why did so many of them spend their

weekends going in and out of #204? I bet I knew over half the customers' drinks by

now. I couldn't tell you their names. I knew Gene Siskel drank double tall skim lattes,

but that's about it. I knew the customers who wanted flat lids or double cups. I knew the

ones who wanted their sugar put in the bottom of the cup before the drip goes in. I knew

the customers who wanted no room, a lot of room, or a couple ice cubes in their drip. I

knew the customers who always got the grande-of-the-day, the ones who got half caff-

half decaf. I knew the ones who got a tall-of-the-day with a touch of steamed milk on

top. I knew the ones who get depth charges or red eyes. I knew the ones who ordered

beans ground for flat bottom, cone shape, or French press. I'd get to the espresso drinks, but I didn't have time or space in my sketchbook. I didn't want to be late. I wanted to

feel as upbeat as possible for the interview.

***

The last twenty-four hours had zoomed by. It seemed like I had been just at my

desk, writing in my Sketchbook of the Mind. No matter, yesterday could not have gone

any better. As soon as the interview with Katherine was over, Kati came in with a

friend. She had forgotten to get her free pound for the week during her morning shift.

Kati and her friend were out and about on a Friday evening and wanted a break before

heading off down Clark or Halsted to a play or movie. I forget Kati's friend's name, but

they seemed close, so I tried to remember. My head was spinning a little since they

came in just as Katherine left. I had my Brown Elephant outfit on and felt like I looked

good since I had not yet been on the floor for the rush. Katherine had Mark call in Tony

early so she and I wouldn't be disturbed in back. We weren't. I can't recall much of the

interview, but I do remember telling myself I came off sounding like I knew about

coffee. Before I could begin to evaluate myself too harshly, I saw Kati and her friend

walk in. I had just stepped out from the back for the first time all afternoon. That may

be why I felt so good about it all this morning. I went from the interview to talking to

Kati and thus didn't have time to properly destroy myself, as I would have normally

done. Was it Gayle? Sounds right.

But the really important part was that Kati and I picked up where we left off

Sunday. Again, we talked easily, bouncing from one topic to the next. She was

seemingly without an agenda. She read a lot. She wasn't trying to be something she

69

wasn't. Just a Midwesterner in the big city, and like me, looking for something. She had

a confidence in her stance and speech. But it came with a sharp sense of humor, often at

her own expense. I was proud to say I possessed that trait as well. Gayle suggested we

join the march against the Gulf War the next weekend. She seemed more excited about

it than either Kati or me. I was not all that politically minded, but before I knew it, I had

said I would be glad to join them downtown at the march. That came only after Kati had

said she would be going. Since it was the three of us planning to go, the rest was easy. I

had Kati's number now. Yes, right in the blank space a few pages back. She would call

me with the details in a day or so. I hope her call would come before Katherine's. That

way, I would be in a good frame of mind with whatever Cosmodemonic decided about

the promotion. I thought a walk to the rocks was in order. I had plenty of time before I

headed to work.

For the second day in a row, I found my favorite spot. That time it was on the

shore of the great Lake Michigan. The water was blue on that Saturday. I brought some

old Sketchbooks of the Mind with me. The earlier entry got me wondering about them,

and about me. I had a good sense of humor, based mostly on timing and situations. Not

a joke teller. But my Mind Sketchbooks seldom revealed that side of me. For that

matter, neither did my fiction. At least I always kept these sketchbooks. I wondered

what other people would think if they read them? Sometimes they were more journals,

despite the name change. Sometimes just quick thoughts, observations, or small

occurrences noticed on the bus or on foot. Other times there were drunken entries too

hard to read. And at other times they were hopeful, but mostly they were growing in

value to me. I wanted to stay and journey through them. For the shift that night, I told

Boston Dennis he could get on the bar at the rush. I would be with him as much as I could, but it would be a challenge. My near future created the wish to jump from page to page of my past. I thought the lake agreed. It was quiet overall. But the water was wavy enough for its splash to be heard as it crashed onto the rocks. If ever a sound were created to make you want to travel in your own thoughts and memories, this was it. So, I did. I flipped my sketchbook pages to the slap of the water on the rocks. Every minute or so I turned back a page. The more recent sketchbooks had become smaller to accommodate bus trips and walks. This one folded open away from me with a coil at the top with nineteen holes, which a section of coil slid through on its way to the next hole. At the top of this page was Butch Hancock's address in Austin, Texas. Complete with a phone number. Maybe I wrote some lyrics to send him? Funny, no idea why that was there. It would give me something to think of on the walk back, besides tonight's close, that is.

***

I made a stop at the Duke of Perth last night. The close took its toll. The rush was out the door as I arrived. That was no surprise. My thoughts were on Cosmodemonic during the bus ride in. I made no sketchbook entries. No *Reader* to read. There were only thoughts in my head of my next few days, or months, or years working there. Having committed to the MIE program, I wondered where it would lead me? Would it be worth the extra money? What about the book? I couldn't follow those thoughts much farther as my bus pulled to my stop.

My first thought then, as I crossed through the vestibule, was that I did hope they hurried up and opened more stores so these people could go somewhere else. Denis, Sarah, Mikey G, and Patty were holding down the fort. Mark expediting, cleaning, and patrolling the floor with a bar towel in hand. Grinder grinding, steam wands steaming, brewer brewing, customers waiting. It was all familiar. I knew what I had to do to get ready for Boston Dennis.

First, of course, was to make my tripio over ice. It was my chance to check the grind and shots as was the procedure for the start of each shift. But the drink was more than an example or test pour. I packed my cup with ice and no water at all. I used the triple group from the four-group La Marzocco espresso machine that served #204. It once had two double groups and a filter group for a single shot. That single group filter basket was long lost in a drawer somewhere. We needed shots and shots and more shots. So, in theory, and often in practice, we could pour nine shots at a time. The machine seemed to never fail. The ice machine, brewers, and in-store music system had all crashed since I arrived at #204. I liked the triple group even though there was debate among the coffee purists that it was not a true pour. A true pour was from a single or double group. I could see that reasoning because it was a bit more difficult to create a twenty second shot from the triple group. You had to tamp a little harder, work a little more. But once the three in one shot brewed correctly, it was worth it. I could also see the beautiful tan crema on top of the coffee after the brewing was complete. I knew there would be a unique sweetness to the coffee as I drank it, even hours later. That was why I chose that drink to propel and sustain me for my shifts. It was efficient and low maintenance. I could simply sip it when I got the chance during a lull in the rush. If it was too strong, which was rare, I could add ice. For the opposite case, I could grab one

shot from the bar and strengthen it. No milk to steam, nothing to warm up. It was my

crutch, my momentum, and my solace when the rush, and then the close assaulted me.

My tripio stirred my mind, enhanced my present condition, and created momentum for

what was next. After my first sip, I stepped next to Denis on the bar. As we exchanged

hellos, I noticed he had used the dry erase black marker that we keep on the bar for the

baristas who wrote on the cups. He had drawn a new button on the top panel of the La

Marzocco, where only the baristas could see it. He labeled it, "Death Ray." I smiled at

him and said, "That kind of day, huh?"

***

And there I was at the Duke splurging on a single malt Scotch. I reasoned that

what I saved on bus fare, I could spend on the single malt. So it was not that expensive

by my formula. Of course, it was still the second least costly item on the whole list. But

I deserved it. I also considered my cold beers waiting in my newly cold fridge. All in

all, it would be a cheap night's recovery and entertainment. I took the table closest to

the back wall and away from the small stage. As a way of deflecting attention, I took

out my Sketchbook of the Mind. That way, it appeared I was alone by choice. Over sips

on my single malt, I recalled the evening.

At shift change, all Mark said was that Katherine and he always talked on

Mondays and he would let me know when he heard anything. He seemed like he wanted

to get the hell out of there, and I couldn't blame him. I spent the rest of the close

wondering if his nonchalance was a good or bad thing. Was he so sure I'd get the promotion that he didn't even have to convey anything reassuring to me? Or was he resigned to the fact that he was getting another MIE trainee? Why didn't I ask, clarify? It was too busy. Plus, The Broker was in his spot, and Mark said I had to get him to move. His reasoning, which he had told me a few times during the last week, was that the Cosmodemonic likes to see its applicants do the job they were applying for before they get it. But The Broker was as much a part of #204 as the La Marzocco. He'd been coming in since before Mark was the manager. Always on weekday mornings after the rush. He was always dressed in a powder blue pants and a matching V-neck sweater. He would then take his coffee to the customer seating counter that faced Diversey. A great spot to people watch. But he chose otherwise. He proceeded to spread out newspapers, Barron's, several hard-backed books on finance and sit there for hours taking up two or even three seats. Since he was a fixture on weekdays, no one seemed to mind. The Broker was one of the things that kept #204 a unique location in the Cosmodemonic collection. But now he was showing up on weekends, and we were getting complaints. Mark had talked to him last week, so it was my turn.

My first thought was that I could use Denis's Death Ray on him. Not practical. I had the very real thought of doing nothing. The Broker wasn't doing anything, except once in a while talking to himself. And he was a customer. He did purchase his usual coffee-of-the-day for here. Although it was usually several hours between refills. But, if I did nothing, I felt sure Mark would hear from a customer. We had weekday and weekend customers. But we had plenty who were both. Could that be enough to sabotage the promotion? After considering that possibility, I hated The Broker. Before today, he was a nuisance fairly easily tolerated. But now I couldn't stand him. I hated the ugly matching blue pants and sweater. I hated confrontation. Who likes it? But The Broker stood in between me and all I wanted to achieve at #204. He stood in the way of my ability to keep my apartment, to have more money, to get more opening shifts and have a real social life with dinners, females, and sex. And all of that sat in front of me taking up three seats with piles of the Investors' Daily and old Wall Street Journals.

I was halfway through my single malt and now good with my decision on The Broker. I told him that Cosmodemonic had instituted a new policy and that there were no more refills after the second cup. It was halfway true. We charged half price after the first refill. Then, I told him about my off-day coffee house under the tracks not too far from #204. There, I said, refills were always on the house. He bought it. Of course, it took him twenty minutes to pack up all his stuff, and I felt sure he'd be back on Monday. In the meantime, several customers stared over at me in my Brown Elephant white shirt and colorful, attention-drawing tie waiting for me to do more. I was sure The Broker wouldn't recall our conversation. That didn't matter to me then and there. In those twenty or so minutes I knew I was more noticeable in my tie and white shirt. I was visible. I was clearly in charge.

The Broker finally left, and I remembered that Boston Dennis was due any minute. The incident had drained me though. As I took a sip from my tripio, I wondered if there were any more lessons for me somewhere in that whole situation.

One Denis left for the other Dennis. The shift change was done, and Phil and Tony were on for the duration. I had money to count and figures to record in the back, so I had to send Phil to the bar and bought some time having Boston Dennis do the drip for Sunday morning. I had trained enough new people on the bar at #206 and #204 but found myself almost nervous for Boston Dennis. It felt like I was being watched, judged by his performance. At #206, there was the spillover to Doug. What I didn't get across he would have to. It was his store. Mark had told me more than once that training was the skill that the Cosmodemonic needed from its managers. At #206, Linda from Ireland turned out great. I had trained her, and she was great on the bar and with the customers after that. So, I had done it, but that was a while ago. There was no record of that success carved in stone anywhere. Maybe Doug could confirm my achievements back at #206. But it was starting to feel that I had the MIE position already. I was good enough. I had proved it over the years. But, I had to continue to prove I deserved it. That early evening, as the line stayed steady, was the time that counted. I put down my tripio and headed to the La Marzocco.

Phil went to help Tony at the register, and Boston Dennis and I took the bar. It was time to make Boston Dennis a great barista. He was deliberate and to my mind slow, but he would get faster. He knew he had to be able to make multiple drinks at once. That was the key on the bar. But that concept was grasped right away on the bar or, it seems, never.

"Again, you have to be able to make several drinks at once," I said again, looking Boston Dennis in the eyes for recognition.

"Yeah, you've said that before." He assured me

"If the called drinks are tall latte, tall cappuccino, tall mocha, you don't make the drinks one at a time. You don't steam three small pitchers of milk. Don't pour three separate shots. You don't reach over for one cup, three times."

I caught a break just then as the line ceased for a moment. We had a short run of drip only customers.

I took a deep breath and continued. I had his attention and had to get a lot into him in a short time. I knew the line would be back.

"For those three drinks, you first grab the whole milk pour it into the pitcher and begin steaming. For the cappuccino, you need foam. So even if it is the second or third drink in line, you must get the foam first. You do that because you cannot generate foam from already warmed milk. Pour more milk that you need for the drinks on hand during a rush. You will need it. After the milk has reached the proper temp as shown on the required thermometer stuck here on the side of the pitcher, put it down under the nozzle to work on the shots. For these drinks, you'll need three shots. A tall size gets one shot of espresso. Pull the lever under the grinder. Use a full range of motion. Don't flip the lever. Good. Now tamp the coffee down into the filter basket. Don't put it down on the counter to smash it down. You tamp it, you don't smash it. Hold the filter basket firmly with one hand and tamp the coffee down forcefully with the other. Now, wipe off any excess from the rim. You want a tight as fit as possible when you place it in the group fitting. See the notches? Now, up and in. Perfect. See how it the handle point straight at you? That's perfect. Put the shot glasses, if rinsed out, under the spouts and start right away. The coffee can start to burn if you keep it there too long. When you start the pour, press the timer to make sure the shot is between 18-23 seconds. Like

honey dripping off a spoon. Are your cups ready? What are the drinks again? Put your

chocolate in the bottom of that one. Quickly. Good. Nineteen seconds. Perfect. Okay.

Shots in the bottom. One each. Swirl the chocolate around with the coffee to help it

melt. Good. Always brew the shots after your milk is ready. The coffee starts to lose its

peak flavor right away. Okay. Which one has more foam Latte or Cappuccino? Okay,

then pour it first. About half foam, half milk. Good. Now, do the mocha about a third

and swirl it all together. Okay, now finish it off. Leave room for the whip. Okay now

finish the latte. Lids. Call them out. The latte will be heavier than the cappuccino. And

you can tell the mocha by the whip. Okay, there you go. You got them."

Boston Dennis did fine with me walking him through it. I kept the three drinks

on the shelf under the counter and out of sight just in case a customer ordered in the

next minute or so. Who needed to know? I would let Boston Dennis find his own

shortcuts. I truly cared about making the drinks right, every time. But also know it

wasn't always done because it was not possible. It just wasn't. It was too time-

consuming. We had to get the lines out the door. The money in the tills. That wasn't

going to happen as often as the Cosmodemonic wanted if we timed every fucking shot. I

think I had more trouble reconciling that than most. Oh well, I'd let Boston Dennis deal

with it in his own way. Since today was what mattered to me and hopefully to

Katherine, I preached the gospel of the Master Roast by the book.

"That was the easy part. Now, here are the exceptions…" I took a deep breath

and continued.

"If just one of those three drinks is decaf, a different domino falls. If one is skim milk another, different domino falls. If one is a double tall. If one is double cupped. If two are iced. If the cappuccino is hazelnut. If the mocha is no whip. If the cappuccino is dry or the latte extra hot. If you need milk or espresso beans filled. If you need lids. Set the timer and keep checking the shots all the time. The decaf gets timed too. So, when…"

"Tall skim mocha, no whip! Grande iced hazelnut latte!" Class was over for Boston Dennis. Sarah's voice had brought us back to reality. I am not sure how long I was on the bar with Boston Dennis, trying to maintain the drink standards and my own sanity.

I didn't even cover the troubleshooting, like when if the grind was off or the filter baskets slid to too far over, and you needed to change the gasket inside the fitting. That needed to wait. More drinks were being called out. "And if you drop the tamper to the ground. Open the drawer. Find another. A customer asks to buy some beans. Now? You scald the pitcher of milk you desperately needed. Once you smell it, you know. Start again. The line is getting longer and drinks are piling up. People are staring at you and milling around at the pickup point. Wait. He just grabbed the wrong drink! Sir! Wait!"

"Wait! Sorry. Yea, I'll have another." I said to the server at the Duke of Perth as I emerged from my sketchbook. I couldn't remember how long I was on the bar with Boston Dennis. Not sure I wanted to remember much of it now. That was why I wrote in this sketchbook. And that was why I just ordered my second single malt.

***

That may have been a mistake. I couldn't read my last few entries, which I wrote once I got home. I couldn't resist a few beers since my fridge was keeping them crispy cold. I do remember I watched an old episode of Colombo and fell asleep

***

Despite the long day and the single malts, I woke up feeling good. I had taken home some earthy and full-bodied Sulawesi for this week. I had to get through a Sunday alone in a big city. Not always easy. In the middle of Sulawesi number three, I reached for *Back Outta the World* for the first time in a while. Maybe it was the caffeine, but my disposition had slowly eased from cheerful to uneasy. It seemed the whole neighborhood was listening in on me. The windows were open, and a good breeze was blowing. It was strong enough to slam the bathroom door shut and make me jump. That made me want to leave my apartment but I felt like that would lead to spending money. Like I did last night. I might do that again at La Bamba tomorrow. I decided to pick up some recent pages of *Back Outta the World*. "It don't cost nothin," as Bluto said.

It was no coincidence that the section I read ended with the parting of two friends after the long trip together. The pages felt to me like they were typed a long time ago. Maybe I couldn't move on from there because I needed the book with me. Part of me didn't want to move on. I was already lonely enough on days like that windy Sunday morning. When I finished the book, then I would be truly alone. The book had been my companion since I moved here. For better or worse, it outlasted Natali. And it was always here waiting for me when I came back from trips to Dayton, St. Louis, or elsewhere. But I had to write that last part. The part where I left the van on the side of

the road wasn't straight out of my journal. But the end had been forming in my mind.

But it had not yet made it to the paper. The van did die, but it was earlier in the trip. But

the rental van we actually used was without character. My old VW van was almost a

character in the book. So, it stayed and was in the final scene of my book. That I knew

for sure. The breeze again kicked up, and my papers and journal notes responded with

movement. I smiled in my mind and said to myself that it was not really that easy to get

the pages moving.

***

After all the disruptions of Friday and Saturday, it was good to be at

Cosmodemonic #204 on a Sunday and be steadily, but not overly busy. That was

familiar. It felt like I belonged here in my hat and apron as my workweek ended. Sarah

and Chuck had closed, so everything ran smoothly. No sign of The Broker, and the rush

was just busy enough to move the clock but not overwhelm us. I counted down the tills

and everything balanced out. Work had a way of purifying. And I was soothed by my

job and the beat-up store on the familiar corner. It felt more like home to me than the

city, my neighborhood, or even my apartment.

***

Up and busy on Monday. Most people were starting their workweek. I had the

day off. But, I realized I couldn't make the phone ring. After two cups of the Sulawesi, I

was out the door, down the steps, and off to Treasure Island. It was a bit pricey grocery

store for me on most occasions. But I had recently discovered that if I go early enough

81

on Monday mornings, I could find some usually too expensive items already marked down from the weekend.

On the walk back with a small bag of finds bought for sale prices, I passed and was hissed at by a toothless old hag of a woman. She half yelled, half snarled at me, "Beef and gravy!" I did not change my stride during the entire episode. Nothing about the encounter was particularly memorable. I had taken enough walks and rides to enough places at enough different times the over years that I had lived in Chicago that I was accustomed to such episodes. Though, I was not immune from a quick angry flush in my cheeks caused by her hissing. I had scored at Treasure Island and was full of high expectations for the coming day. I had no desire to think of this woman who chose to hiss and snarl at me. Me, out of all the people going to and fro past her on this Monday morning. I wanted my thoughts on me. I got back to my apartment. No light on the phone. Too early for Mark. As I put my stash away and planned my weekly food, I reran the hissing incident in my mind. It hit me as I did that the hissing and the "Beef and Gravy" comment had nothing, in fact, to do with me.

***

"One must not wait till it reveals itself. By painting one becomes a painter." That must be from Letters to Theo. I had read that since living here. I am making a sauce for pasta that would be the main meal of the week. I would have it three or four times. I am using the marked down sun-dried tomatoes. I have the sauce on and simmering. When I need the noodles, I would boil enough for me, for one dinner. Boiled pasta noodles did not hold up well in the fridge. Once the kitchen was cleaned, I checked the phone for messages again even though it hadn't rung since I had made it

home past the hissing lady. A quick glance at on older sketchbook brought me the

above quote. I read it over several times. The content did not settle in. Each time I read

it I listened for the phone. Each time, nothing.

I had not checked the mail in my box at the downstairs landing all weekend.

That was where I was when the phone rang in my apartment two floors up. I had just

turned the key to the small, worn metal door and grabbed the several waiting envelopes

when I heard the ring bouncing downward toward me off the wooden staircase. The

ringing zigged and zagged on its way to me, taking its time, and knowing that only one

ring was needed to get me moving. Two other rings came along unneeded. At the

completion of the third, I passed through my open door and reached the phone. It was

Mark. It was official. I was in Cosmodemonic's Manager in Education Program.

Mark sounded about as happy as I was. He was so anxious to tell me that he left

the floor early to call me. I would start Thursday at the new regional office. I would still

work every day this week, but next week I would have to start opening at least one

weekend morning. The best part of it for the two of us was that I would stay at #204 for

the duration of the training. He had to hang up and get back to the line but would have

more information for me when he saw me Tuesday. I hung up. I thought to myself that

it felt good, really good, to have made it in.

With a deep breath of relief and accomplishment, I slowly placed the receiver on

the cradle. I took my time in order to prolong the call, to prolong the moment. I

considered going in to work for a tripio and just tell Mark I was on the way somewhere.

The cleaners. I had decided to drop my white shirts off a place next to work to save time. That would be believable because I was going to get my shirts laundered now. An investment, not an expense. That way I wouldn't have to wait for the details until Tuesday. No. Slow down. That's stupid. I have laundry going in the newly rehabbed laundry room in the basement. Yea, bad idea. But the laundry room. That was a wonderful addition. Everything was coming up roses. I calculated that the laundry room would be at my disposal every Monday with only the odd chance that one of the five other occupants in my building would be home to use the facility on Monday mornings. Energy came into my limbs. I paced a couple times around my place. At my desk, I shut the sketchbook with the old quote. I put that one under the three other ones in chronological order. I grabbed the current one, placed it on top of the others, and realized it contained Kati's number, the acceptance into the MIE program, and the laundry room for my nearly exclusive use. It all added up to create the courage to call her. I had vaguely promised myself that if I did get the call from Mark that'd I celebrate. The Green Mill for the Ellington Dynasty show. Six-dollar cover and they played for a couple hours. She'd love it. I thought I knew her well enough to know that. Here goes the call. *Fuck.* The recording started. Oh, yea, she's at work at #204 for a couple more hours.

The sauce had been simmering for a couple hours. I took it off the heat and rummaged around my plastic container drawer for the right size container with a matching lid. If I had just put the lid on the container when I put it away, then this would not be such a pain in the ass. I had left the rambling message on Kati's phone around an hour and a half ago. Since then I'd taken my nervous energy to take the trash down to the alley, cleaned my bathroom, and put my cleaned sheets on my bed. I was

ready for the week. Those physical actions disposed of enough energy to allow me to

read the letter from my sister which had come over the weekend. I was certainly invited

for a visit. In fact, they had rehabbed the pool in their condo, and now they had an

outside area with a grill and space to sit and dine al fresco. The thought of food then led

to a recollection of my sauce on the stove and from there back to my desk and my

sketchbook. I was sure Kati had things to do before she got to her place. I had to get my

white shirts to the cleaner next to La Commercial. Then I will feel even more ready for

the upcoming long week. I had time. And I would get a six pack at La Commercial in

case the Green Mill plan falls through.

***

The Green Mill night was almost too good. I'm reading that last line in my

sketchbook from yesterday. "In case the Green Mill plan falls through." It seemed at

first to be a long time ago and second to have not seemed like even a possibility from

yesterday morning's vantage point. Kati called back midafternoon. Vanity had driven

me to my rooftop chair and about an hour of sun and some of *Tropic*. That of course,

was when she called. I felt relieved that her message rambled on as mine did. We had

that in common. We shared a fear of sounding stupid on answering machines, so we

both tended to ramble in an attempt to cover all bases. I would have started with that as

an icebreaker, something we had in common already. But, as it turned out, there was no

need.

I met Kati at the corner of Lawrence and Broadway out front, after waiting just a couple minutes. She looked great. Confident in her features, she had no makeup on. The smile when she saw me outside the Green Mill seemed not made up either. A quick hug. I imagined or maybe didn't that it was just a bit longer than a first date hug would have normally lasted. She had told me at L'escargot that she felt compelled to stay in shape for the other job as she called it. Her body enforced that as we pulled together for that first hug plus a microsecond. She felt strong to me. Kati was only a few inches shorter than my 5'11" and not runway model thin by any means. But her firm lower back in my hands and her body as it leaned into mine held a strength I liked right away.

We found a table for two on the left as we faced the stage. It was higher than all the other tables and back in the corner. Yet we could see all eight musicians. I did not even get to my icebreaker as Kati was anxious to tell me that our fellow would-be-protester, Gayle, was transferring to a Cosmodemonic in Portland, Oregon. It was one of only three other cities that had a Cosmodemonic presence. I responded quickly that there were many more cities on the way and that Chicago was chosen as a test city for expansion because the weather was like the Pacific Northwest. I used my access to information to build my confidence. It turned out Mark had already told her about my promotion and that I would be staying at #204. Kati was genuinely pleased to hear it. She went on to say that one of the reasons Gayle was transferring to Portland was that she did not get along with her manager at the five-day downtown store she worked, on Van Buren. The five-day stores had no assistant and just a manager and lead clerk. As the lead, Gayle felt she was made to do way too much for the money. As I listened to Kati, I tried not to stare too deep at her untouched features, defined jawline and cheekbones, slightly sharp nose, and dark brown eyes. I was successful in part because I was evolving a plan in my head to become a manager at one of those five-day stores. I hadn't even started officially as a Manager in Education, but know I didn't want the responsibility of a busy, seven-day store. I had to finish my novel and work on getting published from there. A five-day store became my goal.

We talked so easily that we had only time to have a couple glasses of house white wine before the music came to an end. As we were reminded to tip our waitress by Greg Sergio himself, Kati remembered the protest march downtown. She still wanted to go. I did also, for both political and now increasingly more important personal reasons. We discussed the details as we headed out of the Green Mill to the corner of Lawrence and Broadway. I was going back by bus, but Kati hailed a cab. The corner was busy for a Monday night. But Kati got a cab way too quickly for me. Before she stepped away to the waiting cab, she leaned over and gave a quick goodnight kiss. Again, it seemed just a microsecond too long. As we separated, a passing car of teenagers spotted us at that moment and honked at us, accompanied by various cheers from the backseat. That, in turn, generated a laugh, smile, and goodbye wave from Kati. I don't have much memory of how I made it back home that night. I relived the evening over in my head. I do remember waking up around three in the morning on the couch to an old *Mayberry RFD* on the television. I must have decided to have a couple of my beers and watch some TV in order to come down from the great evening. It worked.

Chapter Three

I was in the middle of the four-minute wait before I plunged my pot of Sulawesi. My back door, my kitchen door, was open for the morning air. The alley was calm, but it was morning yet. I was up early for the day but had to get moving. The second I woke up I began to look ahead to seeing Kati again. I could not stay in bed. After the usual morning ablutions and quick cleanup of the kitchen, I looked forward to the first cup of the day. While I waited, I noticed a pigeon sitting on one of the many wires that ran up and down my alley. Nothing unusual about that but I watched as a squirrel on the same wire approached the pigeon. The bird flew off. After a couple seconds, the pigeon landed again in pretty much the spot. The squirrel again headed toward it. This time the pigeon didn't notice or didn't care too much. I watched the squirrel get even closer, within a couple feet of the bird. Suddenly the pigeon took off again. The squirrel and I waited in our respective spots for a few seconds. The pigeon did not return. The squirrel continued toward Halsted. I returned to the wait until my plunger pot was ready.

It was Tuesday, and so it would be the usual close. But already I felt like it had to be great. I thought I would clean the condiment stands really well if I got the chance. I would shut one down early and run all the shakers for the cinnamon and chocolate through the dishwasher. And then I would clean the chrome napkins holders. And I would also wipe up underneath, behind the doors, getting the built-up sugar grit that no can see. Those stations got a lot of use and abuse. I could then wait to put it all back together after we close and no one can use it. I would do the other one Wednesday when I close again. It was the little details that made the difference. No one might notice it, but they could feel it. The details matter in writing too. Maybe even more. That being said, I felt the need to finish *Back Outta the World* even more now. Thursday had been taken away from me. Mark told me the new regional office was easy enough to get to. That was not the problem. I wouldn't have that day on any given week to work on the novel.

Some sort of '70s music was coming in through the window. I should have known who it was and found it familiar and soothing. My desk looked out to another building over the small courtyard. There were more units and windows in that building than there were in mine. A lot of the people living around there worked different hours. I was not the only one. That fact and the familiar music helped calm me. I was thinking too much about work and the last night at the Green Mill. And thinking too much about the book, but not doing anything about it. I took the coffee in my right hand. It might have been too hot for other hands to hold but the heat felt good in my hand. After two-plus years at Cosmodemonic, my hands had grown desensitized to heat, at least to some degree. The freshly brewed coffee was close to two hundred degrees. Since we were always busy, we were always brewing. No time to wait for it to cool so we pulled one hot cup after another time after time after time.

I turned on the typewriter but couldn't hear it hum. The '70s music was covering it up. I am the seventh of eight children in my family. All my older siblings loved music, and there were lots of albums playing in the house I when grew up. The music coming through the window was from one of them. I knew it. It must have been from the summer I got my nose busted open in a game of dodgeball. That game, that incident was at the core of *Back Outta the World*. I got my nose busted open by a dodgeball thrown point blank, and I relived it several times mentally on different parts of the trip. I could see the blood on my T-shirt in my mind. I caught the ball, and we won the game.

Maybe this same album was playing when I ran into my house to hide my tears from

my friends. It was possible. I ran in and sat on the washing machine and held the ball

and bled. I must have bled on this album. Anyone of my siblings could have been home

on that summer day. Yeah. I must have bled on this album. Okay. I have just concluded

that it is fine if I don't know what the book is about as I write it. It will reveal itself

when it is ready. What was that quote I found the other day? Something like that. I was

meant to hear this album all these years later. Maybe I would just have to wait until the

time is right to figure out my own book. The held mug has lost some heat. I liked the

coffee a little cooler than most people. I think you get more discernible flavors that way.

It was time to put the mug down, however. If ever there were a time to finish *Back

Outta the World*, this was it.

***

The past two closes were routine. Yet, I think I took more interest in them. I was

at my desk, attempting to wind down as it neared midnight. I'm clean, fed, and have

opened my current sketchbook. And since I was attempting to come up with and record

a grand paragraph or learned wisdom on the momentous occasion of becoming a

Manager in Education tomorrow, nothing was coming out. I did deep clean each

condiment station. One each night as planned. Sarah, Chuck, Denis, and Boston Dennis

all went about the closes as usual. They knew I would be in training and thus replacing

Rebecca as their official boss as soon as the weekend. But, I was pleased to see that

none of them acted much differently toward me. They had seen me work hard enough,

long enough not to hold anything against me, even if they cared enough to. It was funny though when Chuck asked me if I had been in the military. At first, I didn't make the connection. It was around seven and the time between post-work small rush and start of pre-close. Since #204 was old, we were always battling the lines. The customers seemed to want to order at the wrong register. So, sometime before I arrived, maybe even just after #204 opened, someone had hung a small "Order Here" sign above the register where the customer should in fact order. But, it was too small and didn't quite hang far enough down to be seen by the masses storming the gates for their double tall skim lattes. Tonight I noticed how dusty it was and decided to clean it. That is when Chuck asked me if I had ever been in the military. I said no and smiled. It was a little excessive to clean a sign that nobody saw. But, I was just doing my job. In fact, cleaning a sign that no one sees was a lot like writing a book that nobody will ever read. That was the wisdom I got out of it. Nothing grand.

I was just back to my desk from checking my clothes for tomorrow. They were ready and just where and how I left them before I left for tonight's close. I chose the yellow tie from the recent Brown Elephant score. The alarm was set. And best of all: the train stopped within a block of the new regional office. *It's hot in here, or it was all day.* Trying to cool it off was working some. I got the back door open to the air and alley. The ceiling fan was on above me and likewise in my room. The windows in my living room and my bedroom were all opened as far as they will go. Only two of the three along the wall in front of me actually opened. And only went about a quarter of the way up. My bedroom window went all the way. That was enough to convince me to try to get some sleep in my own bed. Thursday would have been my usual day off. But, things were changing, and I needed to try to get some sleep so I would be ready for

tomorrow.

***

I felt like an official commuter with a tie and regular work hours. I also had a

small black attaché case with me. That was what I called it at least. I brought it on the

first interview I had with Cosmodemonic a couple years before with Doug at Dickens. I

must have bought it in Dayton. I felt confident and calm waiting on the platform for the

train. I had taken the train a lot and knew the transfers between trains and train and bus

and all that. But, this was the first time I felt like a true Chicago commuter. On that

interview with Doug at #206, I knew I had the job before the interview was even over.

About ten minutes in, Doug asked me to describe a coffee and then said, "Bridget might

ask you this type of question when she sees you behind the counter."

I didn't miss a beat and answered the question, but realized Doug had

mentioned his boss's name. He already saw me behind the counter and had decided to

hire me as we talked. He and I finished the interview, and the rest is history.

***

The MIE day went so fast I couldn't seem to slow my thoughts down enough to

write them down. I should have tried typing it. That might help slow them down. No

point. I was so hungry and suddenly tired too. I was drained and washed out in a

different way than after a regular shift at #204. Drained by the listening and taking it all

in. Drained mentally but my body wanted to move. There were new faces sitting around

the big table in the conference room. I didn't remember many of their names. I knew

92

one guy had a bow tie on. But I was glad to see a familiar face in Kerry. He was from

the Cosmodemonic on Webster, not far from #206. He had been around for a while like

me. We got to know each other the times he came into #206 to borrow or return cups or

bags of espresso. And, of course, when I returned the favor. And, there was Candace,

the regional trainer. She did remember me of course and smiled at me when she saw me

arrive that first morning. Once we were all seated around the main table in the

conference room, we introduced ourselves. I had the most actual coffee experience but

the least actual management experience. Be that as it may, Candace gave her opening

presentation on behalf of the Cosmodemonic, welcoming us to the MIE training

program. She could not get across in words how big an opportunity was before us. She

took both hands and tugged at her curly hair in frustration at not being able to get it

across to us in words. But, I think it worked on me.

***

Just back from La Commercial with a six pack to celebrate, I wanted to call

someone to tell them how it went. Someone I went back some time with. If I called any

family, it would most likely make me feel the distance. I decide on Natali, who was

pretty much my only other choice. I called under the pretense of asking about Anita's

show. I didn't want to come off like I was bragging. And we hadn't spoken since the

nostalgia sex. Got the answering machine. At least I asked about Anita's show. And I

did say I had good news about work but tried not to sound too excited. She was

probably rehearsing, but I felt sure that she would call back. That done and a beer

quickly gone, the hunger returned. I thought of La Bamba, but the five beers were the

93

investment that kept me home to finish the weekly food. I was a bit off my routine due

to the MIE class and commute. It had been my normal day off.

***

I ate in front of the TV to a baseball game. Two more beers and I faded. I

looked at my attaché case, filled with workbooks and training materials. It sat next to

my desk and seemed out of place. I wanted to do something with it. I stood up, stepped

over to pick it up and carry it to my room. There was no room for a desk in there, my

place was too small. My desk for the novel and notes was in the main room for a reason.

My work stuff needed to be separate from my writing stuff. It just had to be. That made

sense to my fatigued, slightly buzzed head. There. In my kitchen with the coffee maker

and coffee. Perfect. I hardly ever ate at the actual kitchen table. While I was there, I

finished off a beer and grabbed one more, still relishing the fact that it was cold. The

events of the day slowed. I still couldn't remember much of the class itself. But I pulled

out my chair and had one more try.

I remembered the train home due partly to the eye contact with the women who

reminded me of Uma Thurman. She held my eyes for a second before looking away. I

was good enough looking with my green eyes and olive skin. Sure. But also, I was

wearing my tie and white shirt and not my beat-up, dirty, coffee stained work clothes.

In that tie and white shirt and attaché case filled with training materials, I

looked over the city as it passed. I found a seat facing forward next to the window. I

didn't really like sitting with my back to the window so felt fortunate to have such a

great seat at that time of day. MIE class ended around 3:30 and I got on before the main rush. Some of the passengers were likely stopping at Addison or close to my

neighborhood and maybe even going to #204 or #206 after the ride. I looked on them all

just a little differently. They could all have been my customers from the morning rush.

Not just in my car, but the entire train. And not just this train heading north, but the one

after it and the next and the next. Maybe that was getting carried away. But that was

how it felt in the middle of the rush. But in my commuter apparel and Brown Elephant

tie, loosened enough to affect the proper after-work look, I saw them less as adversaries.

Yes, they would fill my store, and Doug's and Gayle's and all the Cosmodemonics and

make me tired of them. Tired of every glare if their drink took too long. The glare that

said, "I'm still waiting for my iced latte." The glare that was oblivious to the fact that its

owner was twenty-third in line. Scanning the commuters, I realized they were a part of

the opportunity Candace was pulling her hair out trying to get across. That opportunity

was commuter after commuter, car after car, train after train, again and again and again.

As long as there were mornings, coffee breaks, and long days when you needed a cup of

coffee, then my opportunity was there. My hair had grown since the *corto* cut but not

enough to pull at. Or else I would have.

I thought of titling that last entry "Visions of my Future" or something corny

like that. I almost never assigned titles to anything in my sketchbooks, even the longer

passages. And I was too tired to start then.

***

All those trips to La Commercial for beer and other necessary items and I had

never paid any attention to the dry cleaners that was the next door to the right. I knew that the door to the left of La Commercial was Little Jim's bar. Since I lived on the edge

of Boystown, I wondered more often about who Little Jim was than what was going on

at the dry cleaners. Now that I had to use the dry cleaners for my white shirts, Karl's

brilliant new basement laundry was just that—brilliant. But I knew it couldn't get the

coffee stains out from a white shirt. Hence the dry cleaners. I had just stepped back into

my apartment from dropping off my shirts for Tuesday pick up when the phone rang. It

was Mark. We talked easily as usual. Nothing had changed between us. I was

disappointed for a moment. I wanted our talks now to be more formal and business-like.

But I didn't have time to dwell on that. Katherine had called, and I was to be the

opening manager on Sunday. Mikey G would close. I would close on Saturday and

Mark apologized for the coming short night, but he couldn't help it. Plus, it would only

help since once Mikey G got up to speed I could even get more opens. And since it was

what Katherine wanted, it was what Mark wanted. I got that and agreed verbally and to

emphasize my agreement, I nodded my head for no one to see. Even better news: Kati

told Mark to tell me to call her tonight sometime.

***

The call to Kati. The close, the close, the open. It became Sunday 4 p.m. I guess

I should have seen it coming. No entries in the sketchbook since the awkwardly titled

"Visions of the Future" passage. Wait. Here is a little from Friday morning. "Getting

too busy for notes." The bright side was that I would be meeting Kati at #206 to head to

Sterch's for a beer or two. Then maybe to see *Killing of a Chinese Bookie* at the Music

Box. Never did make it the protest march downtown. Oh well.

***

I planned a train trip with Kati to Illinois. The night was that good. Last night. It went so well that I woke up in her apartment. It's not far, and it is a lot like mine but with higher ceilings. I remember her reading my palm on her futon. We were sitting next to each other halfway discussing the movie. She just suddenly asked if I would like a palm reading. I don't remember responding. Just putting out my hand. Wrong one. She pulled me closer to get "a better look," she said. She held my hand in her left and ran her right forefinger slowly over the lines in my palm. I didn't know if she knew what she was doing. But, it didn't matter at all. It was just the prelude, the breaking down of the outer body required before lovemaking. And we did. We had sex on the futon. She was in the lead so to speak. It wasn't until later in her bedroom that I could clearly appreciate her. Was it really me? I had to look down to make sure. In her bed, and on top for a time, I saw myself, my erection sliding into her. And slowly pulling partially back. She responded, pushing slightly and adjusting her pelvis when it was needed. It was me, erect as I could be and just barely, discernibly covered in a shiny coating. Yeah, it was me, entering Kati, just below her smooth and firm torso. Yes, it was me, and I was making love to the owner of this aligned, beautiful body. I had to look up to slow myself down. But not at her even better face and eyes. That excited me more and made it worse. If a word like worse could ever be used to describe the occasion. I had to look at her bedroom wall. A giant street map of Paris was taking up most of the wall to my left. I put my focus there.

***

97

Monday afternoon around one. I just made it home. Kati had switched a shift with Tracy at #206. I remembered Tracy as a good morning person, if not quite as fast as Kati on the bar. Tracy usually worked later in the morning. The #206-morning rush was not nearly as bad as #204's so there was a longer mid-morning to pre-close shift there, as the dollars taken in would require. I had to start paying more attention to this. Which reminded me of my attaché bag on the kitchen table. It hadn't moved, and I had to study some of it for Thursday. The Tuesday and Wednesday closes loomed. I had my Monday stuff to do. I had to shore up the visit date with my sister. Kati and I would go to Charleston to her family's house for a night. Then I would continue to my sister's. Kati didn't know if she wanted to go with me to St. Louis. Depended on if her mom was driving her crazy or not. I had the vacation time. I could still use it without interfering with the training. I needed to get to Osco, plan food for the week, and clean the place. I was hungry again. Kati and I had a quick cup of coffee and some easy conversation before she headed off for #206 and me to my place. She drinks her coffee black, as I do. She had the La Minita—my favorite Central American. Very important, I think, *Okay. Put this Sketchbook of the Mind away.* I needed to get to my coffee house under the tracks to study coffee.

***

I made it to my coffee house under the tracks. It was just far enough of a walk to clear the head. I had to use this as a carrot to get me to get other chores done. I made it to Osco and decided on fish for the week. It was on sale. I would thaw a couple at a time before I headed to work. Then a quick fry and it's done. I got back from Osco and started cleaning but made myself stop short moving furniture. I only did the essentials;

toilet bowl and both sinks. But the place was cleaner. There was no grey area in cleaning. It was either clean or not. I took comfort in that. Maybe Chuck was right. I had been in the military but in a past life.

Our assignment was to read, or reread for me, the history of the Cosmodemonic Coffee Company. But I kept thinking of the auto parts place I passed on the walk. It looked like an old auto parts place should look. Sort of dingy and unkempt. But it didn't matter because all the guys who worked there knew where everything was. They had all worked there forever. Through the dingy front window, I could see the calendars on the walls. Girls in bikinis, not nudies. Those, in turn, reminded me of the time Mark was joking around and said that #204 needed to do a calendar of the guys there. He was the exception, but he had said that Denis, Chuck, Mikey G, and I would be on the calendar. He said he was going to send the plan on to Katherine for approval.

That, in turn, reminded me that we were getting a new regional director. He had been in charge at some high-end clothing chain in New York. So, by title, he was taking a step down to join Cosmodemonic. At some point, he was scheduled to show up at one of our Thursday MIE training sessions. I had only met the first and only regional director once at a work party for an occasion I don't remember. I wondered if the new guy would green-light Mark's calendar plan.

The ambiance is why I was at the coffee house under the tracks. Not the coffee. The Cosmodemonic does the coffee right.

I wondered if the guy behind the counter could make out the Cosmodemonic logo on my workbooks. He seemed disinterested in just about everything except his female friend at one of the stools along the counter. That was fine. She was not as

beautiful as Kati. I hoped Kati goes to St. Louis so I can show her off. I was sure the

guy manning the counter knew about Cosmodemonic. It was getting hard not to know

it. I had just seen an ad for apartment vacancies in #206's building. It must have been in

a discarded Sun Times on the bus or train or left on the counter at #204. Store #206 was

on the ground floor corner space of a large apartment building near the Lincoln Park

Zoo. A great spot for a lunch break on nice days. But the ad did not contain a photo of

an apartment but one of the outside of #206, showing the Cosmodemonic there. The

hook was that it was great to have a Cosmodemonic downstairs of your future

residence.

At least all this material was review. I knew the differences between the five

coffee families. I knew the various definitions of espresso. It is a roast, a grind, and a

drink. I knew what ours was blended with. I knew the story of the logo, what book it

was from. But it was good to refresh the memory and be sharp for Candace on

Thursday. There were a lot of MIEs who didn't know coffee but were way ahead of me

on actual management skills and experience. Especially the guy with the bow tie. He

knew all the management terms, like "controllable costs" and "walking meeting." Plus,

there was the woman with the English accent, who had already been made the acting

manager of #214 on Armitage. I didn't know why I felt intimidated by them. They were

peers, not rivals. And I was getting the feeling that there would be enough train cars for

all of us.

***

It had been rainy and cloudy for the last several days. The weather in Chicago was one of the reasons Cosmodemonic chose Chicago to expand outside the Pacific Northwest. Apparently, the Chicago weather was the most like the Pacific Northwest. Work was busy all weekend, to say the least. All I did was work, come home, and veg to TV and movies. I was avoiding *Back Outta the World*. I was going to have to get better at keeping Cosmodemonic out of my head when I was not physically there. But, as I had taken more responsibility, it got more difficult. There were hardly any entries in my sketchbook either. Kati was also on my mind in a different way. She had things to do that weekend, and I took her word for it. What choice did I have?

I opened my back door to let in the damp, cooling air. It was Monday. When the temperature goes up, this would be a humid mess. But, the open door let the air in. It came in to circulate the stagnant air of my small place. But it also stirred and moved my thoughts.

Every once in while a grey cat showed up on my stoop. It wasn't a kitten but wasn't fully grown either. It must have lived around here. So, I gave it milk and sometimes sat out on the stoop and talked to it. The cat didn't show up every time I opened my back door. That's good. I didn't want it to go hungry, but I had no desire to take care of it either.

I got two fillets of the Osco fish out. I had them olive oiled, salted, and peppered. My kitchen chair was out on my stoop overlooking the alley, and I had a cold beer to drink. To relish. To reflect on last few days with. It tasted crisp and had just enough bite for me to take notice. Just before I took my second sip, I remembered that I had to check my messages. Another thing I didn't do all weekend. I should have waited

until I think the fillets are at room temp and ready to coat in bread crumbs, and fry. But

I didn't, dammit. There could have been something from Mark. Work crept into my

head more. I stood up.

Good thing I did get up. It meant more time to take in and enjoy the good news.

It was Natali. She got my message but didn't call because she was working a lot on

Anita's play. She sounded curious about the jobs news. But best of all she said Dayton's

own Tooba Blooze was in town to play a couple shows. And they were going to open

for Maestro Subgum at Lower Links starting Thursday night. My first thought was of

how I would get home. Maestro was the Bobby McFerrin style group made up of

mostly our ex-WSU friends. Sure, they were mostly Natali's friends, but I was not

really going to see them anyway. I was too much of a hermit the last forty-eight hours.

With little to show for it. I put down my glorious cold beer and dialed Natali's number.

I'm not sure why I said what I said when Natali picked up. Maybe it was the two

beers. The two-beer buzz is a great state to be in. You are aware, but just off the dock.

You are in your boat, untied, and pushed away from the dock and floating on the water,

not having started the motor or taken up oars. A great place to be, floating easily and if

a destination has been decided on, no action has been taken, and the shore is still visible

and easily reclaimed. Out on the water, there may be rocks, sharks, and rapids. But here

and now drifting in the two-beer buzz boat, all was well.

So, in those waters, when Natali picked up, I decided to say it was 'The Lover.'

There was the combined moment of hesitation and recognition in her voice. I had thrown her off and knew it right away. I was only 'The Lover' in the past and not the

present. I knew that of course. She did too. We both did, as did our relationship. In that

hesitation, I knew there was someone else who had taken my place. I recovered, I think,

quickly enough thanks to my sense of humor and the history of our times together. We

quickly moved past the awkwardness and returned to the matters at hand. Since MIE

class would hopefully be over by four, I would have time to get back and change, eat,

and then get to the show. I would get to see the WSU gang and tell them all that I was

climbing the Cosmodemonic ladder. I would certainly count on taking a cab home if I

felt rich enough.

Back to my beers, which were hitting me just right on that early evening. Mr.

Chet on my tape player. I found that putting my tape player in my bathroom and leaving

the door open amplifies the music. That surprised and pleased me.

I knew it was over with Natali. Yet it was never made official. At least not until

I heard the hesitation in her voice. It surprised me somehow. I didn't know why I was

dwelling on it. Maybe I was insecure enough to have wanted to be the one to formally

end it. No. Not me. Kati was here now. Kati was the one I thought about most. She was

working. That called for her to be naked now in front of the artists. It would have been

fine with me if she quit that second job, as she called it. But the second job showed her

confidence. The same confidence showed in her movements on the bar at #204. Kati

possessed the confidence to do that second job. I didn't make myself sit down over the

weekend and try to finish my book. Why? It must have been a lack of faith, of

confidence in myself. I did work a lot. But that was just an excuse. I bet I'd open

Sunday again. I would get see to Kati then. If not sooner. I wanted to try the Kingston

Kitchen. I wasn't sure she'd be up for it. I thought a run to La Commercial was in order. I'd call when I got back.

I had a change of mind halfway down the loud steps. I wanted some wine with dinner. I could always find the money for a good, not expensive, bottle to have with my fillets. I had green beans and some day old crusty bread. Not beer food. It was a longer walk to get wine than to La Commercial. I head farther north on Halsted. On the way back, I passed the pizza place. The scent of garlic and herbs ignited my hunger. I had mostly beer in my stomach. A couple blue-collar guys passed the window the same time as I did, headed the opposite way. One said to the other, "Hey, the guy making the pizza looks like Pete." Sharing a laugh, they walked on. The man who looked like Pete was, in fact, pouring tomato sauce on the dough and applying it in concentric circles with his ladle.

My walk for the wine was worth it. The wine helped make my dinner more appealing. The beans with garlic and tomatoes turned out best, the fish almost as good. I wisely opened the bottle as soon as I got home. I knew with time, it would become better. The lemon I drizzled on the fish seemed to dominate the scene via its scent. Not a bad thing. The earlier the better on opening wine, especially if it is the kind in my price range. I thought of the L'escorgot and Kati. She would be home, and I was just about to call her, I stopped. I remembered the mistake with Natali and didn't call. I couldn't afford a mistake with Kati. Instead, I cleaned up the kitchen. My faucet had started to drip if I didn't shut it off by twisting as hard as I could. Time for another call to Karl.

***

My kitchen was clean, so I sat back with the wine at my desk. I had forgotten to clean my dinner plate. The lemon was there among the olive oil and remaining bits of beans and bread. The scent was still hovering. I poured a glass. It was in small beer glass that looked like it came from a bowling alley. It wasn't ideal, but it suited my buzz. My stomach was quiet and my sink clean. I put on King Curtis from on my bathroom-enhanced sound system, leaving the plate where it was. I was congratulating myself on the dinner I made. There was a bouquet of flowers in a half-gallon milk jug in front of me. It was from #204 and free since it was the week-old one. I was not frustrated about the plate I left sitting there. The wine, the King Curtis, the flowers, and the plate of remains form a scene of comfort, a collection of parts to make a whole. An evening at home alone, but one of effort. The scene created comforting thoughts as I looked at it. The full stomach helped as the wine maintained the buzz in my head. I had three beers left. I was less worried about the last weekend when I created nothing. My thoughts came from all places. They mixed with my recent and distant faces: the walker, the reader, the worker, the bus-rider, the lonely TV watcher, the ex-tennis player, the dinner eater, the appreciator, the sibling, the Chicagoan, the Ohioan. Maybe I could open my Sketchbook of the Mind and allow them all to come out and play.

***

Up Tuesday morning with my coffee. I forgot my mark-out last week but always have some whole bean Kenya in the freezer. It was plunging. The grinding of the whole beans did not do my head any good. Two closes awaited me. I looked over my entries from last night, and I notice I left out 'The Lover' and 'the writer.' Not a big deal. The

rest was not worth deciphering that morning. A few pages of scribbling and exclamation

points. I did like that I wrote very clearly, "I Want a Red Silk Tie." But I wasn't sure

why.

I was glad I had a good dinner last night and because of that was back to form

soon. It was time for a walk to complete clearing my head and cleansing my system.

What better destination than Belmont Rocks? I wanted to square myself with myself for

last night's overindulgence. It wasn't bad but lingered. I decided to do that by stopping

in at Liberation. I missed the smiling face of Bob Avakian.

***

I was heading back to work on the bus. I looked over my homework for the MIE

class. We had to set up a demonstration area around the whole bean counter in each of

our stores. It was more of a challenge for the trainees working downtown, but that was a

small price to pay for having weekends off. We had to use the French press pot and

engage the customers at #204. The goal was to generate whole bean sales and then share

what worked with the class on Thursday. Whole bean sales are a focus. But I liked

doing it. I got to talk coffee and explain all I knew. Looking over my Cosmodemonic

workbook on the bus to #204, I felt confident that I could do this assignment.

Cosmodemonic is a coffee company after all. My reliable #8 bus rolled past my usual

old sights and sounds and street corners. I found myself looking out on the familiar path

and judging whether I thought that this or that building would be a good one for one of

the next Cosmodemonic locations. They liked corners with foot traffic. I had a great spot in mind just across from Wrigley for my own store. I imagined the rush there

around game time on Sunday. Or even day games during the week. I heard that brokers

or floor traders at Van Buren inhale mochas with extra shots all the time. Made sense. I

liked the stories from the other MIEs about the devotion of their customers. I forgot

who told the story about a woman in labor insisting her husband stop and get her a latte.

Seemed made up, but you never know. I saw a good spot not too far from the Duke of

Perth. It occurred to me that there would never be enough foot traffic on any corner in

Dayton for the Cosmodemonic to ever put one there though.

***

My first day back for the week Sarah and Boston Dennis close. Mike G is still

on for an hour in when I stepped to the bar to make my tripio. He needed to run the

deposit to the bank still, but it wasn't very busy for a change. Sarah was glad to see me,

and we talked for a minute on the bar. Everything seemed to be in order. But when I

checked the fridge thermometer, I had to put the old milk in front of the newer gallons.

Sarah noticed and joked that she hoped I didn't write her up. I didn't know why I

bothered since we went through so much milk that it was never in danger of going bad.

Still, I was in charge and just displaying that I didn't miss anything. Sarah said Mark

had been paranoid the last couple mornings. The new regional director was apparently

going around unannounced to the stores. He carried a tape recorder and talked into it

while he was doing his thing. She said she'd never seen Mark on the phone so much.

Sarah then surprised me when she said that yesterday morning, Dennis-the-Juice-Guy

asked how Kati and I were doing. She smiled when she saw the surprised look on my

face. Dennis-the-juice-guy knew about us? Then I remembered that Kati went to work at #206 the morning after our night together. He must have overheard Kati talking about our night at the Music Box that next morning. Fine by me. It felt quite good to me that people knew about us. Kati worked hard, didn't put up with crap, and was a great partner here at #204. It made me feel proud, as a matter of fact.

The exchange was finished perfectly as Sarah took off her apron and looked at me as she stepped down off the elevated bar and said, "I always thought you two would make a good couple."

***

I loved making lists and then crossing things off. I had always done that as a student, at home, at #204, and #206. I wanted to find the books-read list in an old sketchbook for evidence. Wednesday night post close and with a bottle of sparkling water, I pictured all that I had crossed off the last two days. I sold a lot of whole bean, both nights. I called Kati from work and set a trip to the Kingston Kitchen on Sunday. We also set the date for our train trip downstate. And I sent a confirmation postcard to my sister. In addition, I left Karl a message about the sink. I picked up clean shirts and dropped off dirty ones. I was ready for tomorrow. I had my best Brown Elephant clothes selected and hanging on the nail on my bathroom door. And in my actual closet, was my outfit for Lower Links, just in case I had a long commute or class goes long. Also, I finished the MIE workbook. Nothing left to chance if I could help it. Nothing like a little post-binge guilt to motivate me. I still wanted to look good for Natali, for the hesitation in her voice, and oddly, for the new "lover."

But I couldn't find it. The list of books I've read since I moved to Chicago. It was in one of my sketchbooks. I liked to refer it when I felt down or like my life was going nowhere. At least I had read these books! I was pissed all of a sudden. It triggered my stomach growling, and my patience was suddenly vanishing. I'd find that list later. The faucet was dripping also. *Fuck!*

Okay. Better. Ate the last of Monday's bread and some butter. I wrapped the dripping sink faucet in aluminum foil. I made a spout for the drip to silently crawl down to the drain. Better. One more thing from the list popped into my head now that I am sane. They thought enough of me at Liberation to give me a second book. Not sure why they didn't call. Irene wasn't the most organized Maoist I've ever known. This one is about Haiti. Title: *In the Parish of the Poor*. They wanted a review in a couple weeks. I was relieved that it was only a little over a hundred pages.

***

Friday morning. I was awake and physically fine. Only drank a couple Lienes at the Blooze & Subgum show. MIE class rocked. Sat next to Kelly. He had a great sense of humor. Tall with curly hair and a bit goofy looking when he tried to be. He was at Webster with Sue. We all had a good conversation comparing famous regulars. Kerry's store was near Steppenwolf so he could drop names like Ally Sheedy and John Malkovich. I had Gene Siskel of course. And Bill Kurtis from #206. But Chris from #209 downtown was the winner with Oprah. Kerry and I hit it off. Good to have a buddy in class. *Can't write now.* Up and overwhelmed I resorted to once again cleaning the apartment.

***

I couldn't focus earlier. For some reason, I turned on the TV. I never turned on the TV during the week. But I did earlier. Found a Family Feud Special: Playmates of the '80s versus Playmates of the '90s. Fortune favors the restless. I didn't need my mind for that wonderful thirty minutes. And that was just what I needed.

Natali didn't think I fit in at Cosmodemonic. Plus, it was Ned. I always hated that guy. I thought his vocals were the weakest of the group, beating on his chest to keep time. Everyone did that those days. She even said he wasn't quite as good looking as me. No kidding. Not sure if she said it to give me something to feel good about. Didn't know if she even meant it. He irritated me from day one, back in WSU days. She didn't see me climbing the corporate ladder. But I told her it would be at my pace, and I would go as far and as fast as I want to. A five-day store and later maybe the one across from Wrigley. If they got it, then I could walk to work. She reminded me that I hated corporate America. *True.* I remember countering loudly in order to be heard over the music. But I added, this time not nearly as audibly, that I wasn't sure exactly why.

I became part of it and was seeing some benefits, and feeling more comfortable. But I had to research the IPO I kept hearing about. I couldn't ask anyone because it would show just how little business jargon I knew. Bowtie at MIE knew all about it apparently and seemed quite happy to hear it mentioned.

Back to Ned. No way was he good enough for Natali. I had Kati, but Natali was a beauty too. Was. Still is. Then why was I upset? I couldn't wait for Sunday. Needed to start on *Parish of the Poor*. Got a new MIE workbook. *Tonight, I close. Saturday I close and then Sunday I open.* Not easy but doable. I was too scattered in my mind. *Damn, no more Family Feuds on.* I was wasting time on the sketchbook. Had things to clean.

***

I couldn't write. Not much anyway. I'd had a long, busy night. It was rush after rush for longer into the evening than usual. Never slowed. Boston Dennis had not yet found second gear on the bar. He made the drinks correctly but slowly. I jumped up to help him on the bar. Burned my left hand on the steam wand somehow. Hurt worse than any time before. Work kept my mind off it. It was my left hand at least, but that was about all I could do. I was trying to write holding a cold beer with the burned hand. I grabbed the wand to move it. That'd be okay at slow times when you are using only one but not when you are in the second hour of a rush. The wand was on fire. Not very MIE. I could hide it Thursday if I needed to. Boston Dennis needed to speed it up. Would I be measured by his bar performance? Really? He made the drinks right but almost one at a time. But they were by the book. It was what Cosmodemonic wanted, right? But they wanted the lines to move, the money to come in. The grey area drove me nuts. *Can't get into it now. I need another Family Feud.* Got the beers on the way home. I wanted a movie. Just too wiped to do both. I was dirty, tired, and burned. It was almost one-thirty.

Tonight would have been a good night to come home to someone. Kati came to mind.

***

111

Forgot I wrote that last line, all by itself at the bottom of the page. I do that sometimes. If I fall asleep on my love seat couch to the TV. I'll wake up and scribble a dream fragment or a quick thought. Usually after taking a whiz. Then to bed for the duration.

Kati was from a big Midwestern family, not quite as big as mine. Like mine, it's one of those big families where you have to take care of each other. However, unlike me, Kati had younger siblings, and it showed in her. I knew she would have known what to do for my hand. I just knew it. Without running to the store for something. She had a talent for caring for people in small, simple ways. Kenny, the sample stealer, knew. He was officially banned from #204 as of two weeks ago. He was banned from #206 before that. Kenny was his name, but that is just about all anyone really knew about him. He was "off" to put it politely. I have had to toss him out of both #204 and #206 my share of times. He pushed through the lines by the register and grabs the samples of scone or muffin put out for paying customers. The samples act as part pacifier, part sales tool for the masses of customers. Kenny seemed to know to always leave some as if that would have made it okay. But his home was on the streets, though no one was absolutely sure which ones. Maybe a halfway house. So, the customers complained in both Cosmodemonics. Mark and Doug banned Kenny, and so we all looked out to keep him away. Of course, that was impossible. We would have had to post a guard at the door. Kenny always swooped when it was busy, grabbed his samples, and beat it. I hated it when it happened, mainly due to the looks some customers gave me. Not sure what they expect me to do about Kenny. I couldn't do anything but dump the samples and take the plate back to back like I was throwing it away. I just put it in the sanitizer. Once Kenny took his share, he didn't come back that same day. And once the look of disgust went of the faces of the people in line, things went back to the normal chaos. The people must have their double tall skim lattes after all. Damn if Kathrine didn't somehow hear about Kenny from a customer or somebody. It was big a deal now. No more samples are to be left out. Customers would have to request one. And we would have to provide a slice of Cinnamon Scone or Lemon Knot upon request even at the height of the rush. But Kati couldn't stand the idea. She told me last week she has worked it out with Kenny to come to her when she working the bar in the mornings. Which she always was because she was good up there and knew all the regular's drinks. I knew Kenny understood me when I tossed him out but never really tried to have a conservation with him. But Kati told me she saw him on Clark and told him the plan: If she were on the bar in the morning, she would have a scone in a takeout pastry bag and would slide it to him as secretively as possible. Kati said Mark was good with it, but only if no customers saw her doing it. And only if it was a day old or broken scone or one of the awful Oat Bran Muffins. Kenny didn't care which one it was

***

I was off to read some of *Parish of the Poor*. Saturday closes could be better than Friday's. The open got killed each and every Saturday but the evening could occasionally find a mellow vibe. I hoped it would tonight. My hand was better already. Kati was up for the Kingston Kitchen. She even left me a message confirming that she was looking forward to it.

113

I couldn't believe I hadn't written this yet, but I did finish *Back Outta the World* to the '70s music. It has been a while by now. Of course, I realized that I didn't note it because it didn't feel finished to me.

***

Sarah was on the bar as I came in and made my tripio over ice. Phil on tonight for his every other Saturday night close. Tony would be in later. Sarah and I chatted for a second. She knew Kati and I were going out again Sunday. I felt a tinge of pain return in my burned hand as I made my drink. But as I looked around from the bar, the remote pain triggered memories of all the hours worked on this bar, and of those at #206. But not just of the drinks made. I looked around from this elevated bar to the rest of my store. I had swept the vestibule and entryway dozens of times. I had stocked and dusted the retail shelves, cleaned the bathrooms, swept, and mopped this floor. Did the same for the backroom floor. I had even pulled up these thick and heavy mats under our feet, which saved my knees to some degree, and cleaned them in the slop sink in back. I have changed the light bulbs when they needed it. I have shined the bean counter scale and cleaned the oily scoop that sat on it, waiting to hold a pound of shiny, dark Italian or French roast. I have restocked the stickers that went on the bags many, many times. And many, many times I have taken this four-group espresso bar apart as much as I could to clean the trays and filter groups. I had spent too much time here not to treat #204 as a home away from home. And once I was established, I treated #206 the same before coming here. And now I was an owner. Or would officially soon be. The second biggest Cosmodemonic wheel, HB, was coming to town in a few weeks. The Cosmodemonic Coffee Company was going public, and I had shares of stock, having been full time for over two years. Or it would be stock options. They were almost the same thing. Instead

of reading *Parish of the Poor* earlier, I had made it to the library on Belmont and got a

book or two on the stock market. Good bus reading on today's commute. I had a lot

more reading to do to understand it all. For now, the shots were perfect. Mark came out

from the back. I hadn't seen him in a while and couldn't help but smile when I saw him.

He smiled back. I knew it had been the usual madhouse all day. He said to punch in

because he had a project for me. I did.

The first thing Mark said was that we needed to hit Boru's again. I agreed. But

the real reason he wanted to see me was that Cosmodemonic was pushing a summer

blend of coffee. And #204 had to sell it. That is, he and I had to sell it. Sell it by

plunging and sampling the hell out of it. It was my job tonight and Sunday too.

"We are competing with everyone in Katherine's district," Mark added for more

incentive for me to get the ball rolling.

"Since Phil created the Mater Roast, we should win," I replied dryly. I actually

liked the contests we had. But I knew I had to put up the signage, stage the display,

grind the coffee, keep a separate and accurate count of summer blend sales, and then

clean it all up at close.

"Yeah, I had forgotten Phil came up with that." Mark smiled as he took off his

apron. Thank God Mark had a sense of humor still. Mark also still wore his black

leather biker jacket, complete with dangling chains. He wore it all the time when he

wasn't at work, even when it didn't make sense to me due to the weather. The jacket

said to me that Mark had a touch of the rebel in him. It was cooler today than it had been, so that explained how busy it was, at least a little bit. I said I would do what I could to get the contest off to a good start. Mark stuffed the deposit in his front jacket pocket. He would not be coming back after going to the bank.

"Great," Mark replied turning to look me in the eyes on his way out. "They will be watching."

That meant sell whole bean. Whole bean sales are great for the bottom line. The more whole bean dollars we made, the more staff we could afford to have on each shift. The floor was under control, so I got to work setting up the display.

I had just finished putting out a few more pre-ground samples of the summer blend and remembering that I liked whole bean sales because it gave me a chance to step out of the trenches for a while. Everything was good to go, and I had just taken a sip of my tripio when a guy walked directly past the drinks line and headed for me at whole bean. He seemed like a big shot and first thought was that he was the new Cosmodemonic regional director. *Crap.*

"Evening." He began casually. "I need a half pound of everything you sell. But ground."

I was relieved. Not the new regional director. But, as it turned out, he was some big shot. But it was with Midas whose world headquarters were here, and he couldn't live without Cosmodemonic coffee. The next day he would head back to his other office and house for the rest of the year, where there were no Cosmodemonics. He planned to distribute some of it to family and friends. After I calculated in my head how long it would take and glanced at the floor, which was busy but under control, I said it would

be my pleasure and began the process,

"Sure, ground for cone-shaped filter or basket shaped?"

***

It felt great to do the recap sheet last tonight. The cash was way less than five

dollars off. No pushing of my knee against the bottom of the table. It was only short two

dollars and some change. No matter how good or bad the day was, I always breathed a

sigh of relief at a balanced recap. And the entry for the whole bean sales was the biggest

I have ever put down in that box. For now, we were hand writing in the summer blend

total, and that seemed fine at four pounds. But that grand total would be noticed. I was

glad I was being watched. It had been a very good day. The bus came pretty quickly

after close. It was Sunday as I headed for my apartment, contentedly slouched on my

seat. And that meant I had a date with Kati in the evening. A good day looms ahead.

***

Back on the bus later that morning, I was too tired to really think of much to

note, to put on paper. I guess the thing that was noteworthy was that I knew what kind

of open I was walking into since I was the one who closed last night. I remembered a

close at #206 when I walked about six blocks up Clark after leaving #206 alone. I

sometimes left with the other closers but not always. It must have been a weekend, so

they wanted to get out as fast as possible. I did too. I had been a lead and key holder for

long enough to have the drill down. It was a grand summer night about this time of

year, so I was walking until I heard the bus noise behind me. I had gotten quite good at listening for the bus approaching from behind and always dashed to the nearest stop in time enough to catch my bus. That night I had the strangest feeling that I had not locked the door. I remembered setting the alarm and seeing the armed light come on. You had thirty seconds before the sensors came on and all you had to do was step on the other side of the door and turn the key. It had become such a routine that I did not even notice doing it. Unless I didn't do it. I tried to reassure myself as I stood on the sidewalk in front of an upscale brick apartment building. I was almost directly across from the Clark Bar, a destination for me and some #206 partners on occasion. Doug never drank with us at #206.

I thought of stepping in for a beer and then after a relaxing cold one, walking back to the #206 corner and checking the door. But I was just too tired. I was too tired to walk back those six blocks. And I was way too tired to miss the next bus no matter what I did. Just at that moment, I heard it. I looked to see its number twenty-two down at the intersection right in front of the store. *Fuck. Now what?* Maybe if I ran fast enough back to the door, the bus would still be sitting at the light, and I could check it and then hop on. I knew it would not work. The light was too short. Nevertheless, I took several quick steps in that direction, staring at the bus over five blocks away in a futile effort to freeze it in place with pure hope. I could forget about the door. Tell myself it was locked and still make my original stop now behind me a half dozen steps. But how could I be sure? Doug might get a call from the scone and muffin company in the middle of the night if they set the alarm off when they did their delivery. He'd be pissed. They'd be pissed. We'd have to pay for the alarm going off. I stood still. The night around me watched. Everyone in the Clark Bar watched. The driver of the bus even watched himself as the bus blew past me. My thoughts went directly to my sore

knees.

I came to the end of the reverie just as the bus pulled up to my stop. I put my

sketchbook in my bag and with store keys in hand, step off the bus, and reach for the

door. Locked. Of course, it was. So were the doors at #206 that night a year ago.

***

I had time for just a quick entry or two in my Sketchbook of the Mind. It was a

good Sunday at #204. Busy, but I was up to it. Since I closed last night, I recharged

myself with the closing energy and let adrenaline take over from there. After the first

sips of my tripio, of course. I took it to the back to set up the drawers and had already

picked out my favorite music to play. We had several options for the store stereo

system, and I liked the jazz with vocals best for Sunday mornings. I liked the classical

for weekday mornings on those rare occasions when I was there on a weekday morning.

As I counted out the drawers, I remembered Denis opening with me on a Saturday or

Sunday around the holidays. It was so busy all the time, and we were all sick of the

Christmas music, so Denis created his own monologue for the open that morning. I put

on the required Christmas music, but he had me keep it as low as possible since the

store was not opened yet. We usually had thirty minutes of prep time. Denis then

proceeded to take on the character and voice of HS, the founder of Cosmodemonic, and

narrated the entire opening routine while pretending HS was watching and often

correcting us. Since he was used to being on stage, Denis could project his voice, and I had no trouble hearing him as he worked on getting the front ready, in character as the founder the of Cosmodemonic.

He began, "Good morning…. Cosmodemonic Partner…. Please commence opening procedures for #204…today's goal, as always, is to create enthusiastically satisfied customers each and every time …. Proceed with the timing of espresso shots…."

And on it went for the entire open… "Now ensure condiment stations are featuring all required milk options: skim, whole and half and half…. Denis, you forgot the skim…. thank you…. Store will open in eleven minutes…"

I wasn't sure if Denis had just seen *2001* and didn't get a chance to ask later as it was busy that day from the moment I opened the door to let in the usual first five or six customers to begin the madness. Of course, the day went well after Denis's one time only performance as HS.

Back to this morning. Patty and Tony got #204 ready, and we were off and running. Mikey G came in at eight. Throughout the day, I remembered Denis's holiday stress antidote monologue from months ago, and it helped get me through the rush, fatigue, and all. I also felt a little guilty that I had enjoyed Denis's parody since the real HS was due to come to Chicago just after the IPO hoopla and I was excited at the possibility of meeting him.

***

Finally made it to the Kingston Kitchen. Kati came to my apartment, and we walked over. She was impressed with my aluminum foil drip control mechanism and even laughed a little at the name I had given it. I got the feeling then that she liked my place and wanted to get to know me by looking around. She started with my bookshelves, or one shelf, and several neatly stacked rows placed on whatever flat area I could find. It was always the first place I looked when I stepped into an apartment or home. If there weren't any books at a certain place, I never returned. That may or may not be true, but it sounded good on paper. But as Kati bent slightly at her waist to look a little more closely at the spines of some of my books, I felt close to her. It wasn't just because she was doing just what I would be doing in her place, but that she was taking an interest in my life, in the things I liked. I wanted to show her *Back Outta the World* and tell her I was finished. I was in fact. But, it hadn't been finished in my mind. It didn't feel finished. Instead, I offered to show her my kitchen and the view of the alley. Didn't matter. It was Sunday afternoon and beautiful out. It was calm and sunny and quiet like the day was waiting for itself to start all over. It matched my mood. I wanted to be the one who started this day and the one who took it where he wanted it to go.

Since I had worked the close and then open and was busy all the time, my hunger for a real dinner had caught up with me. So, I couldn't help but want to get to the Kingston Kitchen as soon as possible. Part of my motivation, besides my stomach, was uncertainty over whether the Kingston Kitchen would be open. It seemed to be open random times, not always matching up with the sign on the door. To me, it was a sign of authenticity and had increased my desire to go. Once there, I inhaled a two-piece jerk chicken dinner with rice, cabbage, and hard bread for under four bucks. Kati ate like a reasonable person. Once I pushed my plate aside, I was a better listener. As I did

that, Kati shook her head at me in a barely noticeably admonition. I remember it

differently. At the time, I thought, "What's the big deal?" But, to my day-later mind, it

was another sign that she cared about me, about how I took care of myself. A day later,

I took in the next part of our conversation differently also.

Gayle and Kati had been talking about moving in together for some time. Maybe

more room. Maybe the same room at a lesser rent. That ended with Gayle announcing

she was headed to Oregon. Over a ginger beer, Kati and I discussed the pros and cons of

roommates, rent, and past moves. It was a familiar story to us both as our age and

income seemed to require these arrangements. She seemed a bit concerned about a

rumor that her building was being sold. I listened silently and was grateful for Karl. I

didn't know his story, but he was a one-man show. I had lucked into the perfect place

for me. I recalled the time early on I told Karl where I worked and his eyes showed

recognition and even relief. He seemed to know I wasn't going anywhere and I knew he

wasn't either. I listened with some difficulty and senseless jealously as Kati told me of

the about the romantic domestic living arrangement with an old flame. She laughed at

the story of how I came to be known as 'The Lover.' I envied her confidence and self-

assuredness. I could not laugh off the old flame of hers as she did mine. And I found

that confidence repeated in her simple appearance: long light brown hair pulled back in

a way it seemed she gave it no thought. But she had to know it simply highlighted her

smooth and square jawline, perfectly placed cheekbones, and dark but at the same time

bright eyes. God damn, she's a beauty. And she is sitting with me having a four-dollar

dinner at the randomly opened Kingston Kitchen.

Later it occurred to me that I should have offered to see if Karl were expecting

any vacancies soon. I only said I'd keep my ears open at #204, which of course she

would also do. At my desk the idea of having Kati in my building was helping to keep

the day mine, mine to create, mine to dream into a temporary reality. After Kati's

approval of it, I didn't feel like having Karl fix my dripping sink faucet. Too late. Part

of the reason I was staying around was to be there when Karl's untrustworthy

maintenance guy shows up to fix it. Karl said he would prefer it if I stayed around in

case there were any questions. Odd, but no biggie. I could always read more of *Parish*

of the Poor. But, I only had today to get things done since Thursday is MIE. As part of

being a unit manager, we all had to be certified by the City of Chicago Health

Department. Candace said the class was quite fun if we got the right instructor. I'll sit

next to Kerry, and we will make the best of it.

Kati and I spent more time trading stories of each other's lives. With a casual,

"soon come," the Kingston Kitchen took us in. No one cleared our plates, even as they

dropped off the ginger beers. No one asked about deserts or left a check. Kati and I

became part of the easy pace of a late Sunday afternoon at the place where the times on

the open/close sign have no meaning. There were a couple other tables with two or three

customers each, but they seemed to be here to stay also. We could hear a radio coming

from the back in and around the sounds of scraping and water splashing into sinks. We

were willing prisoners of the Kingston Kitchen, and in that calm and inevitable drift of a

Sunday afternoon into evening, we united. We drifted together on a current like two

branches that had fallen into the river at different times and spots and come to rest in the

same spot on the bank. They float easily and then pause. They are stuck for the time by a tangle of roots or tree limbs grown out over the shore far enough into the river to halt

what floats on its surface. The two branches wait and float for the time they are meant

to. Then, when the river rises due to rain or a strong enough breeze comes along to free

them from the shoreline tangle, they move on slowly together on the surface. That was

Kati and me yesterday afternoon. We were together on the surface of the water, heading

down the river.

And that river would soon take us together to her family's house in Charleston.

Not river, of course, but Amtrak. We were both set to take that trip and were both

looking forward to it even more than before. I had only been working the extra day a

couple weeks but was missing my time away from Cosmodemonic. I did get the

weekend off with no problem, and Kati only worked weekdays. And to change the

subject again and top off everything, Kati mentioned that she would be applying for

Gayle's old position as lead at Van Buren. She said could use the money, knew the store

dynamic from Gayle, and would have no trouble setting limits with the manager there. I

knew that was true. Even better to my insecure-self was that Kati was then considering

stopping the second job at the Chicago Art Institute. When she told me, I remember

forcing a falsely casual, "Oh yeah?" as a response.

To that, she said, "Lately it has been too much trouble getting there for the pay.

But, mostly you had to concentrate and focus to stay so still, and lately, my mind has

been on other things."

At that, she glanced up to take in my eyes for just an instant. The eye contact

ended almost as soon as it started. But that instant was all it took for me to get the meaning behind it. The Kingston Kitchen finally relented to the passing of time, and our server brought us the check.

We were both at my apartment just last night and even until early this morning until Kati had to get to work. When we got back here, she said she wanted to finish looking at my books. As we did, I pulled a few off the shelves and handed them to her, the ones she remarked about or seemed most interested in. It was then when we were sharing our interest in books that we decided she would stay the night and we would make love again. Not that we even said that or anything close to that at the time. I knew from the way she held the chosen books close to her body, indicating they were precious to her. Kati led me. I took the clues and cues from her. The evening was not hurried. She had taken English Literature classes at Western Illinois and had easily read more books than I had. I didn't have it in me to tell Kati anything about *Back Outta the World*. It seemed out of place. She was elusive when it came to the Beats but had read some of Henry Miller at one point. She didn't finish at Western but had left after two years. Left Charleston. Came back and left again for Chicago. Our stories were similar. I had a well-timed sense of humor that she appreciated and laughed when I joked we had fallen for each other over a cup of the Master Roast and that the Cosmodemonic had brought us together. She briefed me on her family and who would most likely be around when we stopped over in two Fridays. Her mom would talk too much and dad not enough. They had an older, bigger house a little way out of town. I liked the sound of it, placed near woods and fields and trees. I was a city boy, even if Dayton wasn't a big city. I had always thought the farmhouses with the big porches and sheds off to the side were great places to live and especially grow up. On our family drives as a boy, I looked longingly at them as we drove past, mentally creating a room in the house for me, or my favorite spot at the stream that ran out back. Kati advised me not to expect an apple pie cooling on the kitchen windowsill. And, reassuringly, not to expect any trouble when we went up to her old room for the night. Which in turn reminded her to call Sarah and ask her to bring an extra uniform for Kati for tomorrow's open.

***

I needed a new sketchbook for the trip in two weeks.

Noisy neighborhood Monday evening. Evening because I can hear the train stopping fairly often through my opened back door. Jazz archive show is coming from the radio in my bathroom. I did most all I needed to do today. I am quite happy to have finished *Parish of the Poor*. Not too hard at 142 pages. I did not bring up the novel to Kati but did talk about Liberation. That was why I finished it I'm sure. That and *Parish* was easy to carry up to my spot on the roof. I cooked and cleaned and did some laundry. Turkey meatloaf for this week. For the Tuesday close, the Wednesday close, the Friday and Saturday close, and the Sunday open. They were buying lunch on Thursday for the Health class. I'd pick up my cleaned shirts tomorrow. Get paid Friday. I'd call and get tickets in advance for us. Excited for the trip. It was less than two weeks. Excited to see Kati again as soon as I could. As we could. I was restless. I got my vanity sun on the roof but oddly was not tired. It could take it out of me, even though I loved the sun. I mentioned the noisy neighborhood. It's from the night game. That, the radio and the train were filling up my apartment. I was a city boy and liked the noise. It calmed me, let me know I was home. *Not helping now*. It was because Kati was not there. Must be. I crossed most everything off the list, but the edge remains. Going to Liberation tomorrow after I finish the paragraph, then pick up my shirts. Got the day planned. But the edge was there. I was finding reasons not to call her. Or excuses to call her. Just call. I'd make a La Commercial run but was saving for the trip. I would get a bottle to hide in my bag for the train ride. It couldn't be cheap stuff since I'd share with Kati. *Take a bath. To the jazz. That will work. That is the carrot. After I call.*

***

Kati was at the second job last night when I called. Left one of my inconclusive messages. She said she would stay at least a couple more sessions out of loyalty to the artists who she had been working with. But, the bath did work, and maybe my vanity session in the sun did take it out of me after all. I was asleep soon after I finished my paragraph for Parish. My favorite line was "You cannot fight bullets with a handkerchief or a Bible" from Fr. Aristide before he was elected president of Haiti. It captured the essence of the book for me. I can't remember if I told Irene that I wrote. I am sure I did. She didn't remember my phone number the last time I was there, hangover in tow. With the MIE training going well and a relationship unearthing some confidence, I felt like reminding her that I have written a novel. But first, my second cup of the morning's coffee. I went off the varietals and took home some Italian Roast. Hit the spot, just enough body left and the roasty bite I liked.

Felt the urge to glance at some of the old sketchbooks. I'd do that before adding a filled one to the pile on my desk. It is easy enough to create your own fable, your own legend of self. I have been doing that to some degree at MIE. Quite a bit, in truth. The brief recap of my fable is that I took the job at Cosmodemonic to follow my love of coffee, to do what I love and, of course, to "pursue my passion for great coffee and great customer service." I think that was straight from my resume I created for the interview with Doug. There was truth in that. I gave a version of that response to the other MIE's and even to Kerry, my ally in humor. And, without these sketchbooks, it would be set in stone, even to me, and I lived the reality. I would be free to revise and enhance my own fable unhindered by reminders of what my real situation was prior to taking this job. That place was a good place to be. And it worked for the Cosmodemonic, right? I could do the job as well as any of the more management seasoned MIEs. They have written store budgets for places like the Gap. The dark-haired women, Jen, drove a BMW. The fruit of some labor at some other workplace. I had a couple years at a few coffee houses under my belt. I did love the coffee and how I felt like an owner at #204, and before that at #206. No other job had made me feel like that, like a part of something I was helping grow and have a stake in it growing even more. What was good for Cosmodemonic was good for me and vice versa. So, I didn't include the following rediscovered and now recalled a passage in my MIE fable, or even to people I meet.

It goes: "I can't decide if I'm anxious and lonely or just worried more than I should be about not having a job. I had a plan if I got that job at Boston Stoker Roasters. I think everything would have made sense—fallen into place. Six months there, save money living at home. Then out to a place of my choosing. I keep reminding myself to have patience for once. Sure, I'd rather be starting out with Natali in Chicago or my own place in Dayton. But this is the price I pay for going on my mad road trip. As for school. Graduate Degree in English? Possible but I'm not really showing much

inclination, and I don't know why. It'd be cool once I got in…"

Had to go to do my errands. My weekend was coming to an end. I thought it was

best to keep this sketchbook in the middle of the pile, back where I found it.

***

Notes from the Tuesday bus number thirty-six. I was feeling good after handing

in my paragraph to Irene at Liberation. In fact, I felt great. The hangover was no longer

with me. Irene and I had a good talk. The store was slow and appealing. It was different

from Cosmodemonic. Never a line out the door. Never a line at all. It crossed my mind

that I could handle working there. That was before my long stretch at #204 was set to

begin at the end of the bus ride. People looking at a book or two and a stool behind the

counter for whoever was on the job at the time. I could handle "Delivering

enthusiastically satisfied Maoists, each and every time." But that is not what Irene and I

talked about. She was small and intense. She seemed always to be taking the measure of

me when we talked. I had a suspicion she didn't like my vanity tan even if it were

acquired when I was reading *Parish of the Poor*. She didn't ask about the tan. And I

didn't ask if she could help me find a publisher for my book. But that was what might

have just happened. The bus was shaking with every bump and pothole. But Irene had a

friend who knew people and the friend reviewed manuscripts. For a small fee. Pat was

her name. I felt like I came off confident and cool about writing down her number on

the Fall-Winter New Titles Catalogue Irene handed me when she saw I needed something to write on. I did not take that with me. I stuck it on my bulletin board facing

my desk, safe and sound.

***

I hoped Cosmodemonic didn't hear my thoughts earlier about working with the

Maoists. It wasn't a rational thought, but with Cosmodemonic growing as fast as it was,

I had to wonder. Wonder if it was their way of punishing disobedience: Patty is quitting,

and Chuck is cutting his hours to bare bones, just for now he says. That meant he was

finding something else, either sooner or later. Most likely sooner. Patty got a job with a

friend from school or something. Mark didn't feel like elaborating. All he did was hand

me five applications sent over by Katherine and said to find time to look them over. No

warning. I had no idea what Mark's look them over meant. I was afraid to ask Mark if

Kati told him she was going to interview for the Van Buren lead job. I hadn't planned

on reviewing applications tonight. Must be what management is like. But I found the

time. I did a little less cleaning prep than I usually did. I hated not doing what I felt was

my share of the grunt work. But I did find a good candidate. Which to me was someone

with a flexible schedule including weekends. Work history sounded impressive, so I put

it on top of Mark's pile with a post-it note. But I spent a good deal of the bus ride home

second-guessing myself because I was sure I forgot something while I reviewed the

applications. *What if Mark thinks I put Kati up to applying for the Van Buren position?*

What if he gets pissed and doesn't want me at #204 anymore? Anything was possible. I

needed to talk to Kati. I'd call when I got home.

***

I felt better looking at Pat's phone number. A memento of real achievement. I was calmed by it. I realized it was too late to call Kati. It occurred to me that there was no reason why would Mark think I put Kati up to going to Van Buren. If anything, I would want her around when I started working more opens. Okay, definitely, not going to call Kati. I was clean and fed. I was alone, but talking to her would only make it worse. Odd now to recall this image, but when Kati and I walked anywhere, we seemed to literally be in step with each other. First time I noticed this was after the meeting. She was only a couple inches shorter than me, so that helped. And maybe the walking pace came from keeping up with or chasing after siblings in a big family. And she paused before every door we went through together just long enough for me to reach out first to open it for her. Which I always did. That also happened without any words between us. *Good thoughts to close this day.*

***

I felt the desire to and the rightness of sitting down to write, coming back. It had been a while. I wanted to sit and write and drink coffee in my apartment. It was early Wednesday morning. I would call work to talk to Mark about the applications and then ask to talk to Kati or have her call me. That could wait until the rush was over. *It is just starting now. Perfect!* I had three hours or so to write. Then, a call would be the perfect way to take Mark's temperature and the perfect way to look like I wasn't desperate to talk to Kati. Which I was. But I didn't want her to know that, of course. We were in a serious relationship then. Why tell her how I felt?

***

131

It was a beautiful day, my friend. I *finito-ed* the *libro*. I have written a book. Not a book really, but an insult. Walked to the Belmont Rocks to celebrate, I wondered that there was likely no one else of all the thousands I saw waiting for the trains, walking, sitting in cars, etc., wondered if there was anyone else among them who had finished a book today. It had taken not quite three years. I'd spent the whole of my time in Chicago working on it. And I didn't want to say on and off because even when I was sleeping, eating, showering, etc. the book was there, though I may not have been typing it. When I finished, I ate a bagel with some peanut butter and had some OJ. I was hungry and had been drinking only coffee and had become lightheaded. But that is what I did. No cartwheels in the apartment, no champagne. *So, it is done now.* Not like before. Today it ended the way it should have ended. It was an end, but one of a moving on toward another adventure. It was and is as much as anything a book hiding its meaning. I took off into the book much like the trip, with no idea how it would end. My first book was about its own writing. To me, at least. It felt like a manuscript in my hands: thick and heavy. As they say, it hadn't quite sunk in yet. I was done. Completed my first book. I would go to work later, battle the lines, mop at the end of the day, and keep my stock options in place. But first, I'd walk to the lake. It felt right. Literature! Literature! But hey, you can't eat it. Well, time for the walk and then I had things to do. First, one phone call. *Do dat shit!* It felt good to have finished the book. An achievement that stood only for itself. I was in high spirits.

Chapter Four

My new notebook seemed so small and flat. It would bulge and swell through use and abuse. It would be tossed around, crammed into my bag, and written in and on. My new Sketchbook of the Mind. That one was just like its predecessor, which was rare. In looking over the pile of them off to my left, I saw all types. One was small but opened like a book not the flip-over" type, like the new one. But going back several more they were more classic college style notebooks. And yet none the same width. If one had coils, the one before it was held together at the top with adhesive tape.

The Cosmodemonic took more out of me. Work. I was in charge of every shift. But I had been since #206 a while back. It was only two months before Doug made me lead. But trying to think and plan for a future drained me. I couldn't be physically in one place and mentally in another. And, it went without saying that the quick talk with Kati could have gone better. She and Gayle were going to spend most of Sunday taking in Chicago one more time before Gayle left for Oregon. I wasn't invited, although Kati said she was sure it would be fine with Gayle. Just by the tone and delivery in her response, I knew not to push it. I wasn't really invited. Kati and I did have the trip to Charleston in less than two weeks. Maybe I'd see what Natali was doing. Needed to see a friend. Kati and I did quickly talk about getting together some other night. I was too tired for more, even if it was a new Sketchbook of the Mind. A beer and *MASH* episode were what the doctor ordered.

***

Thursday morning before MIE class, I had no time for notes. But I just couldn't

resist the new sketchbook. My entry said, "I have not time for notes." That is all.

***

It turned out Candace was right, and the MIE class was fun. It was the instructor

with the sense of humor. I was certified by the Chicago Board of Health. I had the piece

of paper to prove it. Kerry and I each got a few good jokes in during the day, but our

instructor told great stories and even made the "Temperature Danger Zone" interesting.

Beyond that stuff, he said this was the brightest and most intelligent and engaging class

he had ever taught. I had heard that in some form or fashion from teachers and profs in

my school years. But I felt like our instructor truly meant it about this class. He had to

be telling the truth about us. We were leading the charge of the Master Roast. New

stores were coming. New cities. Cosmodemonic wanted the best managers, not just

bodies. It was both humbling and inflating to hear that affirmed by someone who didn't

really care. He hadn't heard of Cosmodemonic before we turned up on his schedule. He

didn't even drink coffee. We were the best. There was something going on at

Cosmodemonic. The endless lines and countless lattes showed it. And more people

noticed it every day. I was getting a little bit tired of telling people that Cosmodemonic

is not a franchise and has no plans to franchise. It was a coffee company. The standards

were too high to risk franchising. That was why I was there: for the great coffee. Plus

Candace had more good news after class, especially for me. The new regional manager

couldn't make it to our next class. But the Coffee God of Cosmodemonic was coming

town and was going to spend at least an hour with us. Candace said maybe as early as

the next week. No one else seemed too thrilled. But the guy had written books on coffee. I would have the chance to meet him and demonstrate what I knew.   And

after that, HB was coming to Chicago for the IPO announcement. And finally, Candace

also said HS would be in town after the IPO for the open forum on Cosmodemonic and

its future. My future.

***

I still hadn't called Pat about my manuscript. I thought I should be calling *Back

Outta the World* "The Manuscript." Rereading the above paragraph from my

Sketchbook of the Mind helped. I felt strong. I could focus on work if she didn't want to

look over my manuscript. Yeah. No problem. I fell asleep the last night before the beer

and *MASH* were done. I had some left in the fridge. But I had to make them last. I was

still saving for the train trip bottle. I was going to have one, then call Pat.

***

The coffee was good. I had to give it a try. I usually stuck to varietals for my

free pound and stay away from blends. Not sure why. I just liked the single focus of an

earthy Sumatra or winey Kenya. After the big night selling whole bean and the summer

blend, I had forgotten about it. But the floral taste was there with a light mouthfeel. I

would try it over ice later. That was how Cosmodemonic sold it for the hot summer

months. I was pretty sure it couldn't beat my tripios on ice. I was also sure it enhanced

the coffee, and that my mood was good. Pat and I were meeting in two weeks at her

house up north around Evanston! She liked the sound of my book. My manuscript. She

liked that I had a job and could pay for her service. She was also a big fan of

Cosmodemonic and worked near the Merchandise Mart location. We talked more about

135

Cosmodemonic than *Back Outta the World*. Whatever it takes. I would try to remember

to take her some coffee or at least some CosmoBucks coupons when I headed up there.

The place was clean. No more dripping faucet. My radio was on with classical

music, and it sounded good from my bathroom. I was getting out of there in a minute. I

had time that morning. Kati promised to drop into #204 later. She was finally done with

the second job. I'd heard of the manager at Van Buren but hadn't met her. She went

back some and Kati said that Mark knew her. Van Buren was a busy, cramped store.

Kati felt like the promotion and transfer were in the bag. I had no reason to doubt her.

***

A glorious summer storm arrived that night. The winds from the storm at one

a.m. were blowing all through my kitchen. I was there for those winds. They blow at my

screen door so hard. Karl or a maintenance guy at one point patched the screen. The

door itself was older and warped, and sometimes it would unhook itself, and I would

find it open to the back alley inviting the alley itself into my kitchen. Maybe that was

how the two-inch roach got it. It stayed hooked somehow and didn't get blown open.

The rain soaked my kitchen floor, but that's fine since it could use a rinse. The week's

flowers from #204 sat on my kitchen table. Their scent was no longer strong, but the

winds from outside brought their scent alive to my nose. I took them home some

Fridays since we got new ones for the two thousand weekend customers that we

normally got on busy weekends. I took the flowers home on the bus in an empty milk

jug. They were still green, yellow, and purple. It brought a nice lively zing to my mostly

functional kitchen.

It was rainy when I got off earlier but not this hard. I did the big city thing of waiting for my bus under an awning near my stop. Not the green awning of my store. I hated to wait at the end of the night, so I always walked a few blocks if the bus didn't come right away. It really started to rain, and I had my flowers, so I stopped a few blocks north. No one else at the stop. To pass the time, I imagined what I looked like to people driving by. I thought maybe I looked the part of someone from a Jim Thompson novel. Caught in the rain. Holding flowers that his dame had made him take back after the fight they just had. He was glad to have the time to think under the awning. He's watching the rainwater run along the curb in front of him, down the big city drain, taking his life with it. Or not. I'd need a cigarette in my mouth for that, and I didn't smoke.

***

The best part of the night was when Kati stopped by. I didn't really know when to expect her, so starting around six, I caught myself looking up at the door every time it opened. That was not a good idea since we were busy. All types of customers came in. Some were regulars, but most I didn't recognize. All shapes and sizes, one at a time or groups out for the night. They were starting their weekends at #204. Or ending their workweeks. Some were maybe trying to stay up to finish homework or get started on a work project that was due Monday. Or maybe a few were getting coffee for a drive to Des Moines or Dundee, Michigan. Cosmodemonic fit into so many lives in so many ways. But it wasn't fitting into Kati's for a while. She said it would be later because she was talking with Van Buren's manager after that store closed. Kati was wound a lot less tight than I was. Of course, most people were. I guess she meant to interview for the

137

lead position at Van Buren. But she called it a "talk." It was too busy at #204 for me to have a minute for her during the first two or three of hours of my shift anyway. Dennis and I joined forces on the bar and got the lines out. Mark was in good spirits. I needed to ask him when I could start opening more. I was always jazzed about coming in on Fridays after MIE class. Then I always was anxious to get to #204 and start using my new skill set as soon as I could. I wanted to get in and make Cosmodemonic unit #204 better. But I had to close, like that night. I'd like to open since I was not closing Thursdays. I'd have to make myself ask. Then I could have Friday evenings free for Kati. I wouldn't have to see her on the floor like I did then. I knew she'd make it at some point and she finally did around eight. It turned out to be a good time. It was too early to pre-close, and I had Sarah for one more hour. My heart skipped a beat as I saw for sure it was Kati coming in. And she had good news. She was going to Van Buren as the new lead taking Gayle's place. That store wasn't Katherine's so it might take a bit for the transfer to work out. She was going to tell Mark on Monday. I hugged her and held her as congratulation. It was more for me. I rubbed her lower back with my right hand a couple times but caught myself. I was in charge of this shift. It hit me again that things are different for me at #204. It felt different. I was being watched. From Candace's and even Katherine's vibes and the way I was talked to and about, I felt like the promotion to assistant was inevitable. So, I had to be on and set an example while I was at #204. I couldn't just come in, work hard, and leave. I had to do something extra every shift. It was now in my job description to teach and lead and "maintain and enhance self-esteem" of the other partners. Carlos had called me "Mr. Cosmodemonic" way back at #206 since I worked hard and was into it. But even that was different. I didn't get to go to the open forums like the one HS was coming to in about a month. I

didn't make the schedules. My name wasn't on the regional director's big board at the

regional office. I was on the radar now for better or worse. It was far worse at the

moment of the hug because Kati felt great in my arms. Her body told me it didn't want

to separate, but I pulled my hands off her lower back as some customers directly behind

her caught my eye. Some people had been milling around at the retail shelves. I saw

them come in right after Kati. A chance to sell a machine? I had to approach them. Kati

understood. She had to get home before the storms. All and all it was a great shift. Even

if I didn't end up selling any espresso machines.

***

I was up and at it with coffee from my plunger pot. Kati and I did get to at least

form a vague plan to get together on Thursday. It was cool, and the sun was so bright

and clear after last night's storm. So was my head. I owed it to a good night's sleep. I

called first thing and got train tickets to leave Friday evening. I couldn't believe that I'd

have that whole weekend off. With a goal in mind, I could do anything. It was how I

was able to write *Back Outta the World*. I could push through this workweek. I pushed

through three years of writing the book. I couldn't remember if I said I'd meet Pat this

Friday or next. Wrote it down. No. It was next Friday. The confirmation was followed

by quick flashes of doubt. *Should I bother with writing?* Or just make a career for

myself with coffee and Cosmodemonic? After all, it was possible if I applied myself,

like with the book.

I looked up from my sketchbook to the courtyard attached to the building across from me. A guy wearing a beret and dark clothes unlocked his bicycle from the fence. For a few seconds, I imagined I was living in Europe.

I had a lot to do before going in. No chance for anything useful until Sunday after I got home. No Kati and all that went with her being here. Didn't think about her or write anything about her. Just did it. *Take those thoughts somewhere else. Start with Osco.* Needed a few things. A travel size mouthwash and cheapie razors. Then get a good bottle. Maybe some pepper vodka. I'd go to Modi Mahal for some samosas for the train ride. Too far. Then again, maybe not. I'd see.

***

Sunday evening. Knees sore as hell again. Scored a New York Times from the whole bean counter. It was left there. It was mine as of then. Now it is all over my apartment. Read some when I ate at the kitchen table. Saving the Book Review on my bedside table for later. And the rest was scattered near my sofa. Did not feel like seeing people after this weekend. Tony took so long with a customer during a rush that I had to leave the floor or kill him. Not really, but that kind of weekend. So, no people for me. Which was fine. Felt the need to look over *Back Outta the World* for Pat.

***

Something was up with me. I mean I was up and having my plunger pot of summer blend because I needed it. On off day Mondays I loved my plunger but usually didn't need it like this morning. There were times I wrote most of the night and needed the coffee. This was an off day, and I had lots to do yet needed the caffeine to do it.

140

Coffee is a commodity that has a value that fluctuates. Coffee is the second most traded

commodity in the world, next to oil. Something along those lines. One of the things I

learned from MIE class. That morning it was priceless and at the same time free to me.

Combine those factors, and you would drive an economist crazy. Maybe. Didn't do well

in Econ 101 at WSU. The point is I was tired and did not sleep well. Something was up.

Why else would I have started a book like *Back Outta the World?* I picked up fragments

last night and read over them. When I read my own writing, I always wanted to change

it, and I always wanted to keep it as is. No magic revelations or voices told me what to

do. Read the part with Kyle and Jay shooting pool in L'Anse. I liked it, it was me. And I

read and reread the great passage at the beginning of chapter three. We were heading

into Virginia at night: "Ride your lifetime, feel the strength of your living body." I

wondered. Taken out of the book those words felt worth pursuing. And yet… I was

doing it again. The thing that kept me up. *Leave it with Pat or somebody else. Clean*

your place and have some coffee until you are ready. Get out. Get away. Get your bills

paid, calls made, and errands done.

***

Occasionally you do the right thing. Something that is clearly the right thing. It

happened earlier today. It happened when I stepped into #204 at noon just as Kati was

leaving. As she looked up and recognized it was me, I saw the reward for the walk from

Osco, for the walk down Broadway with my bag, for the leaving my apartment and all

those thoughts behind. The reward was the collective gleam in her eyes of relief, joy,

and even, I hope, I sense that she had fallen for me and it was a good choice.

As I left my place, I let my legs, lungs, and body cleanse my self-lacerating thoughts of doubt. As I walked, they were soaked, rinsed, and spun out of me. New thoughts formed as I left Osco. New, better and more productive thoughts came along as I put my pepper vodka in my bag. A small, expensive bottle but good for the trip. I had saved for it. I was thinking of Kati having to tell Mark she was leaving for Van Buren as I left the typewriter store with a new ribbon, bought in case I need to do a lot of work on *Back Outta the World*. And my new thoughts told me that Kati might be having a hard time telling Mark she was leaving. Plus, she had spent yesterday most likely listening to and supporting Gayle. And maybe, just maybe, Kati missed me. Me? It was possible after all.

I knew she did miss me when she quickened her steps and closed the space between us for a long hug. She virtually dragged me out of #204 and without a word, we made a right and headed for the lake to find a spot to sit and talk.

The lake was more like an ocean. The waves were big, rolling, and crashing ashore a few yards from our feet. We didn't bring anything to sit on. Kati's uniform clothes were dirty, and I was in clothes I didn't care too much about. The skyline down to the right confirmed that all was good today. It was alive in the sun. Alive and confirming that by just the fact it that it stood, had been built, that cooperation and working together could produce good, actual results. We both looked it over from our benign distance before we even paid each other much attention. The screaming and shrieking seagulls brought us out of our joint afternoon trance. Neither of us had food for them, and we were soon left alone. Their cries for Fritos or bread crumbs did rouse us enough to slide closer to each other and join hands, leaning slightly against each other at the shoulder.

We talked over the nuts and bolts of each other's lives, and the plans for the time we would share our lives. At least for a day or so. Kati said Mark had known Carmella from Van Buren from way back and she had called him to ask if she could steal Kati from #204. So, there was no surprise when Kati told Mark about the plan. Still, she had wisely waited until after the morning rush when Mark had a minute. Reliable, steady, and good openers were priceless at every Cosmodemonic: five-day, seven-day downtown, Lincoln Park, suburbs. Apparently, Katherine had been screening candidates and applications and had several people farther along the pipeline than I had been told by Mark. Maybe he didn't know himself. Sometimes the world of the Cosmodemonic moved fast, increasingly so nowadays. I was not immune. Two of my calls today, on my off day, involved Cosmodemonic. Candace wanted the MIEs to check in with some measurable achievements from the weekend. Mine was to record and identify a role I or my staff had played in turning a bad, or potentially bad, customer encounter into a resolved or even positive one. And it couldn't just be one when you apologize for forgetting to put whip cream on a mocha and handing the customer a coupon. We were supposed to go over them together Thursday in class but the Coffee God was, in fact, coming to class, and we weren't going to have the time. For better or worse, I didn't have such an incident to record, so I fell back on the one when one of the staff accidentally handed a customer a drink and spills a little on them. They came to me, and I offered to pay their dry-cleaning bill. An oldie but goodie. Then I lucked out with the call to Mikey G, and I was able to switch with him on Friday so that I could open and get out of town around six or so. On that news, Kati looked me

over silently. I noticed the waves had seemed to become less like an ocean. The water

had turned a sun reflected and luscious blue in a fashion that only a large deep body of

water can. We had been there a while, and Kati stood up, offered me both her hands to

help me up, and said it was time for her to get home and out of her work clothes. I

completely understood since I was the same way. I couldn't wait to get out of my work

uniform when that part of my day was done. We headed back toward Lakeshore in a

comfortable silence. I knew she was moved and appreciative that I came to support her.

I felt it as we walked. She was going to splurge and get a cab home, and we headed

toward that goal. Yet, our stride and shared body language had no agenda, no

destination. We had reached the point that we were at times communicating without

words, just intuition and thoughts. I felt it from her as we rejoined hands just before

heading under Lakeshore. About halfway through, I finally comprehended what Kati

was wordlessly getting at. She was a little ahead of me as usual. And it was practical.

Now that I was opening Friday, we could go into #204 together that morning. Made

easy by the fact that we were planning on getting together Thursday night. And sealed

by the fact that it finally dawned on me to ask her to spend the night. Her smile was one

that said, "You figured it out."

On that note, that parting, I got home without really recalling how. I walked, of

course, and got a six-pack of Point at La Commercial. I knew I would be restless after

the long afternoon with Kati at the lake. I was counting down the hours until Thursday

already. The night with Kati, then the opening shift together and the trip and so on. I

needed the break. I had finished *Back Outta the World* but finishing it left me washed out, I think. I don't even recall having much of a lasting sense of achievement and reward. I had been quite busy. But I was liking the Point. It was deeper and fuller than Liene or Old Style. But I was undecided or overwhelmed. Could I be both at the same time? I wanted to read or write but didn't know what or what. I needed to start a new short story or read a biography. *Tropic* was in my roof bag. I wasn't so sure about it that time. Not tonight anyway. Didn't feel like I could spend the money on renting any videos. Saving for the trip. Went from room to room shutting off lights and adjusting the speed on the ceiling fans, sipping Point, and getting hungry. It's just that I felt like blowing things off. No reading, no writing. I was going to try for a chance good movie on the tube that I hadn't seen before. Or a baseball game.

***

I was on the eight heading in for my Tuesday close. My apartment was clean, and I was packed for the trip as far as I could be. I was primed and ready for two great, not good, but great closes. It was my store. I had been made an owner by the upcoming stock options. I had been looking over the books on the stock market that I got out of the library a while before. This was all new to me since it wasn't like my family discussed the New York Stock Exchange over dinner. I read that stock options can be great if the stock in question goes somewhere, like up. I'd do my part. I was on my way to my store. It sounded different in my head. And it even though it looked the same as every other time I've written that mundane line in one of my Sketchbooks of the Mind, it now feels different when I write, my store.

***

It was Wednesday already. Not to repeat myself but I am going to anyway: Vacation starts tomorrow! Not really, but I was not counting Friday as a workday. I had a quick conference with Mark to make sure I didn't have anything extra to do before I left. He complimented me on my close! We had worked together so long I no longer expected it. I was cleared to be off until Tuesday. I met Kati's replacement and the new closer. Monica was Kati's replacement as opener. Dark hair, dark eyes, and a quite serious approach to her position. I was with her for only an hour since she had opened with Mark. I got the sense she was going to be good, so I wanted to present myself as a textbook example of a Cosmodemonic manager. I was being watched and graded on developing new partners. But it was also in my best interest to have everyone at #204 as well trained as possible. After all, I was going to have to work with them. Kati had called when I was training Monica. Denis said she called for me when I was showing Monica how to clean the bar. Denis laughed and said all he had to say to Kati was that I was training a new person. Kati knew how serious I was about training new people but told Denis to make sure I called her back. Before I had the chance, the new closer, Bill, came in for his shift. Mark hadn't told me or just forgot, but Bill had been at a suburban store, Wheaton, I think, for a month already. A gift from the heavens. I did have to show him the specifics of #204 and make sure he didn't bring any bad habits with him. He had been planning to move to the city for some time and seemed quite cheerful and had long blond hair. I didn't love the long hair on guys, but his was kept clean and hidden once he put his hat on and started his shift. And, speaking of coffee heavens and Gods, I was excited to meet Cosmodemonic's resident deity. He came from a small but reputable company in Colorado, Candace said. I wanted to learn as much as I could but really wanted to show that I knew more about actual coffee than anyone else in my MIE

class. Three of my classmates were already full assistant managers at seven-day stores.

As much as Candace pulled her hair out, the pace at Cosmodemonic can be too much

for some. Openings happened often enough. I came along at #206 and got used to the

lines there. Hit #204 and got used to the lines there. So, it was just the drill for me.

Tough to get thrown into it if you weren't used to it. I did feel good enough about Bill

to let him on the floor with Sarah and Denis. Then I took enough time to make a great

but short call to Kati. She was going to try to convert her parents to Cosmodemonic

coffee, but they still had the old percolator. My dad also used one forever. Again, no

wonder Kati and I hit it off so well. It was one more thing we had in common. I

suggested a Columbian or maybe Costa Rican. Nothing too fancy. I offered to use my

mark-out for them. I had a couple half-pounds in my freezer so I could get by. I could

hear the smile on her face, so to speak. The other news was that her upstairs neighbor

did say their building had been bought. Never good. Since I was on a roll, I promised to

ask Karl about any potential openings in my building. After I hung up, I headed for

Denis who was doing the grind for tomorrow. I forgot that I was also going to bring

coffee to my sister in St. Louis. Denis rarely used his free weekly coffee and this week

turned out to be no exception. He let me have his.

***

A couple of cold Points called to me from the fridge. Same restless feeling as

last night but it was being vanquished by physical fatigue. I took advantage of the rare

slow night and a bonus closer and took up the floor mats and sprayed them down in the

corner mop sink. The floor mats saved my knees and those of everyone at #204, but they get so dirty. The process left a waffle-like pattern of dirt and dust on my khaki's

wherever one of the mats laid against my leg as I wrestled it into place. I had no energy

for the last one but did it anyway.

***

It was finally Thursday. I was all ready for the trip to the regional office in my

best Brown Elephant shirt and tie. Hadn't thought too much about where to go tonight.

Maybe nowhere or just a walk. Gotta dance.

***

Kati was due any minute. It just occurred to me that I won't have a lot of time

for the Sketchbook of the Mind until the trip from Charleston to St. Louis and back.

MIE class with the Coffee God wasn't what I hoped. He seemed distracted. But what do

I know? Maybe I was distracted by this upcoming weekend. I could always fall back on

La Bamba with Kati. Next week I'd head to Pat's with the manuscript. Gotta check my

reflection in the mirror. It hadn't changed since I last checked.

***

Under the small red letters that read "Name of Passenger," my ticket said

"Welcome Aboard." That was concrete. That made it a good place to start. That ticket

had my seat aboard my Amtrak from St. Louis to Chicago. And that is where I was. I

had no one next to me. Not sure where to begin the notes of the past weekend. It was

Monday and becoming early evening in the Midwest. I slept from Charleston to St.

Louis on Saturday. The whole way. Looking back, that was not a surprise. I

148

remembered thinking I wouldn't have time to put much down in my Sketchbook of the Mind until now anyway. Here I am, as predicted, on the train home with my thoughts and Sketchbook of the Mind to keep me company.

The train keeps you close to the earth. I liked that about trains. To watch a train passing brings on thought. It provokes thought. To watch a plane overhead brings wonder: How? Where is it going? How far? The train passes, and yet it is almost at eye level and allows you to take it in as it passes. It gives you time to watch. To maybe even make eye contact with a passenger and then to wonder what their story its. Everyone has a story. And it is more interesting than mine. That is what I tell myself when I write. I always felt compelled to wave at any train that passed me when I was a kid. I wanted to befriend it, wish it well. I can't recall waving at an airplane.

My sister and her husband loved the coffee and wanted to buy an espresso machine. I said I could get them my discount if they could wait until the pre-Christmas contests at Cosmodemonic roll around. There. That thought was a good starting place to begin to recall the past weekend.

Kati's mom and dad were split on the coffee we brought for them. Her father promised to try it and offered to put some on right away. In the awkward first few minutes of meeting them, I over explained why percolators ruined the coffee. It sends the same water over the same grounds over and over, thus extracting all the bitter flavor elements. They didn't want to hear so much about the coffee Kati brought as much as the man she brought with her. However, I did manage to backpedal a little and say I'd love a cup. Kati's mom didn't like coffee that much and the silence even less. That helped ease things along. She quickly broke any silence and began talking and asking

questions. Then the dogs had to be let out. One of Kati's sisters came in the door,

getting home from work. Quick introductions to her. The phone rang. To a boy from a

big Midwestern family, it was all familiar. Before I knew it, Kati's dad was back in his

recliner and Kati and I were seated at the kitchen table listening to her mom complain

about him.

Of course, Dennis-the-Juice-Guy came into #204 when Kati and I were standing

a little too close to each other on the bar as a stage. It was Friday morning, post-rush

cleanup, just before I ran to the bank. It was her last hour of the shift before she left to

buy a few Chicago souvenirs for her family members in Charleston. A great thing about

opening at Cosmodemonic was that with an eight-hour shift your workday was over

around three. So, that was perfect for me Friday. I would be back at my place by four or

so and meet Kati there after her shopping trip. I had coffee to give, which had been my

homecoming gift since my first trip back to Ohio a couple months after moving to

Chicago and starting at Cosmodemonic. Even then, I had been taken with how good the

Cosmodemonic coffee was. I pictured myself as a Johnny Appleseed of great coffee,

handing out bags of Cosmodemonic coffee as I was blazing the trail. Kati and I were

simply discussing the last details of our trip as Dennis-the-Juice-Guy came into #204.

Kati and I had stayed in Thursday night. We ordered pizza and rented a movie

called *Withnail and I*. I must see it again. We jammed ourselves into my love seat in the

front room and settled in. After the thrashing, energetic lovemaking, I am no longer in

disbelief when we are engaged as one. My eyes were on her hers, not a street map of

Paris. With that evening under our belts, Kati and I maintained the body proximity and language, which reflected lots of time spent naked together. The next day, Dennis-the-Juice-Guy knew. He smiled at us and shook his head as he walked to the back of #204, a gallon of OJ in each hand. That was also concrete. Well, liquid, actually.

I took a shot straight from the bottle of the pepper vodka. There was a little less than half left of the small, easy to hide bottle. Kati and I toasted the weekend once we boarded, but that was it. I could be quite far away from the dock by the time I hit Union Station. Nobody saw me. If they did, they didn't care or maybe wished they had some of their own.

Out of the window, the Midwest evening just kept passing by. Kati's parents' house passed by several times already. Or ones just like it. Older two story homes with deep front porches. Homes that were not isolated but still separated from their neighbor by a cornfield or two. I liked Kati's house right away. My dad's sister lived on a farm, and we'd visit sometimes when I was younger. Kati's dad wasn't a farmer but some type of lawyer. He bought the place but not the land. Wanted to be just far enough outside of Charleston to feel retired. He liked to walk out back to the stream and woods that marked the end of the cornfields. Kati's room faced the woods and looked out over the cornfields. They moved here her sophomore year. The old man worked in Charleston and all over the state so kept the old house and his practice in Charleston. The mom and kids moved out here but stayed in her same schools. Kati's mom said that arraignment saved their marriage.

After the pepper shot to open the trip, Kati and I talked easily. We covered just about everything. I felt so anxious to share everything with her. As I listened to her, I was ready to share a story about my first car, my broken arm as an eight-year-old, or anything she might be interested in. I felt it from her also. The openness and trust that came, at least in part, from sharing a bed, being naked with someone. She didn't seem nervous at all about bringing me home to meet her parents. She was the oldest of five, two sisters and two brothers. She wanted eventually to get into nursing or healthcare. Kati had been taking care of her younger siblings and her hypochondriac mom for as long as she could remember. As I listened, I thought of Kenny-the-Scavenger. What to do about him when Kati leaves #204? Didn't think Cosmodemonic would be as compassionate as Kati. She had hoped to get a ride back with Emily, the third oldest, and have her take a few boxes of stuff back home. But she wasn't sure who would be around for the weekend and if they were around, how long they would be there. I knew why she wanted to get rid of stuff. Easier than moving it. We jumped off that topic quickly too. I was grateful because I didn't want to tell Kati I had forgotten to call Karl to ask about any impending vacancies.

It struck me that I lived in Chicago. One of the world's great cities and I called it home. Within that city was my apartment. It would be empty when I got back. Empty as it has been every time I have come back. And I knew every inch of my empty place. I always did the dishes before I left. I hated coming home to dirty dishes. Except for a coffee mug, which I don't really consider dirty after one use. It was just going to have the same hot black liquid going right back in it. The heat would sterilize it. At the risk of sounding exceedingly corny, there would be two dirty mugs waiting on me around nine tonight when I step back in. That called for another pepper shot.

As Kati and I drew closer to Charleston on Friday, my life unbuttoned and let

me breathe a little. The approach to and the outskirts of Charleston could have been

Dayton's. I remembered an incident visiting my brother in Dayton. Kati was finding the

ladies' room, and I was taking in lower Illinois through the window. A better view than

the back of the seat in front of me. The memory hit me right then. It was about a year

ago, and for some reason, my brother and I were taking a Dayton bus from somewhere

to somewhere else in the city. The bus pulled up to the two of us waiting at the stop.

Before the door was half-open, I was reaching for the handrail and began to step aboard.

My brother admonished me to stop and "Wait a second!" But I had been so acclimated

to the pace and current of the big city buses and trains that I moved at the pace they

demanded. That current was kept alive in me by the charge and recharging of work at

Cosmodemonic. The lines of customers were never far from my conscious mind. The

only thing worse than the constant moving line of customers deciding on, ordering, and

then waiting for their drinks was a stopped line. Hell was running to the backroom for

change, milk, cups, or any essential item during a rush. Leaving Sarah or Denis or Phil

or whoever on the floor while you ran to the back was just slightly removed from

human sacrifice. But I was beginning to see it. See why it was good for me and see that

human sacrifice can be a necessary thing. Kati sat back down. I had to tell her my

thoughts, my dream, the end result for me of all the lines. In that state of ease brought

on by the sight of soybean fields, I told Kati my newly forming dream. I was going to

stay at Cosmodemonic long enough to cash in some stock options and then move to

Costa Rica, or somewhere where life is cheap, to write. Write novels or short stories of

great significance. I was going to write and live cheaply for as long as I could on my stock sale and either became able to move because I was selling my work or because I

had run out of money and had no choice but to leave and come back home. I felt like

someone had thrown me a life preserver and pulled me out of rapids because she

listened to me. I hadn't come close to telling my family anything like that, even

utilizing the comforting separation of the phone or letter. But I had to tell her, had to tell

Kati. It felt right to tell her my plans for the future. She was becoming part of it.

After our Saturday morning lovemaking by her open window, there was no

doubt. I would close Tuesday and was going to clear it with Karl by phone sometime

before I go in. It is a courtesy for him. Then I would ask Kati to move in with me. There

was one other couple on the first floor already. I saw a change in Kati's eyes as she

talked about her apartment building being sold. It was just as easy for her to get

downtown from her building as it is from mine. We could share expenses and so on.

Beyond the practical reasons, there was Saturday morning, just over a day past. To me,

it was both so far distant yet right before my eyes on the pages of my fast filling

Sketchbook of the Mind. Her bed was flush against her wall. Three tall windows took

up most of the wall and looked out over the yard, the cornfields in back, and then the

stream and tree line where her dad took his morning walks. But on Saturday mornings

Kati's mom and dad went grocery shopping together. They had done it for years and

that morning, visitor notwithstanding, they were at the store. No one else in the house

stayed. Neither Kati nor I were in a big hurry to rush downstairs for the percolator

coffee. We both liked sleeping with the windows open. The sun rose in these windows,

but it was cooler for late summer. Certainly, cooler than the city in the summer. An easy

morning breeze took the curtains back and forth, sometimes strong enough to brush against Kati's bare right leg as she moved slowly up and down on top of me. I reach up

softly with my right hand to run my fingers along the slight indentation formed by the

separation of her leg muscles. The same smooth line of muscle definition I had noticed

at the meeting. Kati's hands framed my head, and she leaned down to kiss me. It was

slow and unhurried. We took each other in, offered appreciation to and for each other in

the way only sex can. A stronger breeze took the nearest curtain and blew it with

enough strength for it rest on Kati's bare, folded knee. If the trees out her window were

watching, they could have seen the curtain stop for a second and not settle back down

on the sill. I reached to brush it off her skin but held it for a moment instead. The

moment we had been working toward. And we reached it together. Out beyond those

watching trees, the stalks of corn settled, moved by the same morning breeze. The trees

beyond the corn rustled too and returned to silence. The stream separating the field from

the trees kept flowing as it always had. From that tree line or the cornfield out beyond

the window, it would have been difficult to see the curtain fall back into place as I let it

go.

The outskirts of the suburbs of Chicago started to appear out the window. Hells

bells. I fought the losing battle to stop the end of the long weekend with one more

swallow of the pepper vodka. I'd save what I had left. I'd have it over ice when I got all

the way home. I'd sit back on the steps overlooking the alley. I told Kati I would call

when I got back. She and her sister would have come back early Sunday. She was

staying at least one day with Kati. My towering, insecure-self hoped her sister liked me.

If not, she had the whole drive back to give Kati her opinion. Plus, she had a car. I didn't. How was I going to help her move into my place anyway? I could ask Natali. She was the only person I knew who had a car.

That line of thinking led to a moment of panic. But I found my keys in my bag that I took on with me. Of course, they were there.

The work schedule was the new usual. Close, close, class, close, close, close, open on Sunday. I had my Pat appointment on Friday before the close. Maybe another shot was in order. *Not now.* My Amtrak was heading into suburban Chicago for real now. Cosmodemonic might have a store in each suburb in a few years. *Is there that much good coffee on the planet?* There were rumblings of another roasting plant on the East Coast. Cosmodemonic didn't play. Still bummed about my meeting with the Coffee God. I had the courage to approach him after class, but he seemed in a hurry to leave and didn't exactly shower praise on his own company. Could be he just didn't have the time for me, the autograph seeker. I was just a poor slob working in a store in Chicago. We didn't invent coffee like the people in the Pacific Northwest seem to think they did. My train was in the city. I also had the IPO and HS visit coming for me look forward to. I had a lot coming my way. Four more weeks of class and who knows? May I'd have a roomie by the time I graduated from MIE class.

Chapter Five

I wrote so much on the train home that I didn't want to write another word, but did anyway. I had my last drink next to me as promised. The train ran late, so it was almost eleven, not nine. I lucked out and caught the train to my place right away. All that was left of the weekend travel was the short walk off the Wrigley platform to my apartment. A little buzzed, I crossed the street with one bag in hand and one shouldered. I glanced sideways at a group of men talking near the station entrance. They were not waiting for a train. Maybe they were waiting for someone to meet them who was arriving on foot. I made eye contact with one of them and nodded casually as I passed close by on my way out of the gate. But, they had no interest in me on that Monday night. I was pleased that they didn't since as I passed them I heard one of them ask the group, "When was the last time you had a gun pointed at your balls?" In a strange way, that question welcomed me back to Chicago.

***

As soothing as last night's welcome back was I had no time to savor it. I was happy to read it in the morning. I was pleased that I wrote it down. But that was what I did. I Thought I would call Natali and ask about the car. I felt like I needed to talk to her anyway. I was sure I came off as a dickhead the last time we saw each other. I didn't have another old friend in town, and I couldn't afford to let her drift away. The food at my sister's was good as always. I was inspired and off to Treasure Island to score some bargains, even if it was already Tuesday. Needed to do laundry, hit the cleaners, call

Karl, and get ready for a long week at Cosmodemonic. I wondered if anything has

changed in the short time I'd been away?

***

I made it back for my Tuesday close at Cosmodemonic #204. As welcomed as I

felt by the group of guys hanging out at the Addison platform last night, the bar at #204

topped that. I had been away enough times to not feel too odd coming back. I

anticipated, created, and sipped my first tripio in days. Then back to business, I

expedited most of the rushes. It was my favorite spot of all at #204. I liked the bar when

I felt up for it. But, I wanted to expedite to get my feet wet for the first lines. I was in

control since it was the position of the first contact with the customers. I pulled the

coffee and pastries and called the drinks to the bar. But, I could pace the line as I chose.

If the bar was behind, I could hesitate in taking the next order. Or, with any luck, the

next order would be drip. Then I would tell the person at the register what the total was

and pull the drip myself. I could tell the customer what the total was, no matter if there

were multiple drip coffees of varying sizes. The register person knew I knew because I

knew every drink price, no matter the size, by heart. With or without scone. From there,

I could see the whole store and jump to the bar to help or to whole bean or run to the

floor to clean or fill a milk thermos. But most important of all, I could keep an eye on

the mighty cash drawer. It could fill up fast and looked too tempting if you didn't keep

it trimmed down every so often. I could easily make the quick dash and drop a pastry

bag full of bills into the floor safe. Then the cash drawer was more like the one at my

coffee house under the tracks where no one seemed to be all that interested. Here, at

Cosmodemonic, it was about the money, the money, and the money.

Bill from Wheaton and Chuck, putting in an appearance, closed with me. As much as I hated parting from Kati and coming back to work, I did feel at home there. As soon as I walked in and heard the music, I knew I was back. I remember at #206 when I first began to feel at home I would glance out past the wall of windows that made up the front of that store. I'd catch a glimpse of the buses packed to the gills heading south toward downtown. The cars at the stop light in front of #206 were lined up deep and their drivers anxious to get to work. And the people, the pedestrians, even the ones not coming into #206 were stepping toward somewhere in the get to work stride. The store music was usually classical. Doug liked it, so he played it. I called it the "Cosmodemonic Work Day Concerto." Whatever classical was playing, that was what I called it. It felt, to me, that everyone outside could hear the same music. It seemed like the Cosmodemonic Concerto was playing for more people every day. And it still does.

So, back at #204, I played my instrument, my expediting, and made it through the close. It would be more of the same tomorrow.

***

I want to call Kati after her rush at #204. But I was stewing a little. I was waiting for Karl to call me back or Natali. Of course, it was only a little past nine. And that means to me that I was almost done with my plunger pot of Sulawesi. I tried an espresso shot of Sulawesi yesterday. It had the body of melted butter. I considered making my tripio with it, but it didn't feel right. So, I stayed with the classic. If I didn't miss working last weekend, I missed my tripio over ice. No Cosmodemonic locations in St. Louis, not to even begin mentioning Charleston. The stewing part came from being a chicken. I couldn't ask Kati point blank to move in. It was not in me to charge straight ahead. I was a counterpuncher, a tactician. If it was not fear of the future, it was lack of faith in myself that prevented direct action on my part. I had a deep-seated lack of faith that things would work out. I could see that in my old Sketchbooks of the Mind going all the way back to when I started them. They have been cheaper than therapy. So, I didn't have it in me to call Kati and ask her to move in based on the belief that fate would fill in the blanks. But, if I called Kati with the news of a car we could use or that Karl had signed off on us living together as validated by the lease, I would have a base of courage to ask officially if she wanted to move in, and when could she move in. She had until the end of the week at #204. Mark's new hires were working out so well that he said Carmella could have Kati a week early. She was needed more at Van Buren.

Kati had been opening for the past nine months or so at #204. As I said before, good openers are quite valuable at Cosmodemonic. I remember the first time I saw her and introduced myself as, "The lead you'll never see." I hoped even then, the first minute of the first time we met, for her to respond along the lines of, "That's too bad." But she stuck to the more formal, "I hear you are the store's resident coffee expert." I liked that well enough as a compliment. But, I truly enjoyed the fact that we maintained serious eye contact the whole time, brief as it was.

The past weekend was so full. I felt like Kati knew she would be moving in. *So why should I have to ask?* Avoid the whole process, that's easier. Like with Natali and me. We didn't break up; we just withered on the vine. It went back to my lack of faith. I guess I was afraid to find out for sure, so I just did and said nothing.

I did have enough faith in *Back Outta the World* to make the appointment with Pat. That would be Friday. Class Thursday. Close tonight. I wasn't sure what Pat could do for me. I didn't expect her to offer to publish *Back Outta the World*, of course, just plot the course for that to happen. Irene didn't have her card, and she was not in the phonebook. *We shall see.*

***

It had been cooler over the weekend in the country. I was lying in my shorts in my bed under the ceiling fan listening to a Spanish language radio station. The last Point was open and, who knows how full or old, sat on my nightstand. The afternoon felt hopelessly lazy. I would close tonight of course but did not ever want to move again. The trip, train, and travel had caught up with me. I sought the cooler, darker bedroom of my apartment. It had purple carpet, and that made it just a little darker and cooler than the rest of the place. Kati was in the bathroom getting undressed from her shift. It was Monday, and I had the whole day off. I was shirtless and listening to her undress, or step out of the shower. That's even better. I could make it as good as I wanted to. Because I had slipped into a daydream.

The phone rang at a bad time. But I arose from my daydream and picked it up.

It was Karl. There was no rule against another person in the apartment. Just no pets. He seemed flattered that I had asked. I tended to over-explain things, but he sounded even better when I introduced the unnecessary detail that Kati also worked at a Cosmodemonic.

161

Couldn't go back to the daydream. However, it occurred to me that I couldn't ask Kati to move in over the phone when she was at work. That was too casual for such a step. I'd call her at her place just before I went in. She should be home then.

With that settled in my mind, I had room for other thoughts. They came in no particular order of importance. I didn't think I had to be poor or be staking everything for the sake of being a writer. I could strike a balance. But what if Cosmodemonic took my life and ran with it for five or ten years? Would I want to go back to writing? I had no plans to marry Kati since I wasn't the marrying type. But as I pondered my future, I saw her there. How could I seriously consider my future as a writer? I had done nothing yet, as far as the outside world knew. Cosmodemonic was a great place to be. But companies come and go. Or, I could work my ass off for them, and it might not make a difference. Someone could take a dislike to me and one day ask me to make sure I bring my store keys in for the meeting we have scheduled.

***

Just got off the phone with Natali. She called at exactly the right time. I needed to stop thinking so much. Things were still good with us. She was a trooper. She had seen me at my worst. I forgot about that. She also sounded genuinely happy that I had met someone and said that I could certainly borrow the car. I had driven it many times and many miles anyway. I couldn't give her the days or dates that I would need it. Natalie had news of her own. Her father had become quite ill and temporarily relocated to his family home up in the Upper Peninsula to recuperate. Natali's brother, Scott, was coming through Chicago to pick her up and go to visit him together as soon as possible.

162

But she, also, was not sure of the dates. Well, it was a start anyway. And it was just the concrete reason I needed to call Kati. Damn, I had met and liked Natali's father. And I lived with Scott for a summer at a house around campus. Natalie and I were together for a while and thoughts of her father and brother combined to create a strong desire to see her. Since I wouldn't see her for real anytime soon, I considered trying for another daydream. I didn't have enough time, though.

***

The Wednesday close was nothing to write home about, so I just put that down in my Sketchbook of the Mind. I did have a good, if not great, talk with Kati before I headed in. Her lease was up at the end of the month, and she was sure the rent would go up a lot. She said again that other apartment buildings in her area have been sold recently and then upgraded. According to Gayle, as lead at Van Buren, Kati would get the position and an increase in pay along with great tip money. So with one job and less hassle, Kati would make as much as she did at #204 and the CAI. But that helped only if her rent stayed as was. Or at least close.

"You could stay with me if when your lease is up." That is what I managed to come up with in the moment. That was all. No wonder there was a moment of silence. Even in that moment of silence, my mind knew it was not enough. I told myself then, right then, to formally invite Kati to move in as part of our progressing relationship. I knew I blew it but was helpless to say anything.

"I need time to think it over," Kati responded. I think that is what she said. All I can recall with any certainty is the silence between us at that moment.

163

It was too late to take it back, to try to fix it. Kati was in bed. Which was also part of my hedging. I didn't want her to be just a daydream. I needed to make it right as soon as I could. It had been so fast, but that didn't make it wrong. It had come to this point so quickly us. For us to fall for each other. To fall in love. *Who cares what anyone thinks?* We were right for each other. There was a reason we were coming together at that moment. *Tell her, not this Sketchbook of the Mind.*

***

I had a thought to drop in on Kati on the way home from MIE class. I didn't because I would have had to transfer. But I would try to call her. Class was good again. Next class would not really be a class, but we were all attending the big IPO announcement with HB. Candace said he really made this market what it is. I didn't remember if I'd seen him come into a store when I'd been in charge. Of course, I'd closed most of those times. I had only two more classes after that, and I'd become a full-fledged assistant manager. Then HS would come to town for the annual open forum. Okay. That was set. Not sure if I could make it as a management cog in the Cosmodemonic machine. It was becoming so real, so corporate. But I felt the same way about writing a novel more often than not. But I did that. Speaking of the novel, I had planned to look over the manuscript some that night. But I was never one to cram for a test or pull an all-nighter. *Why start now? I mean, I wrote it, didn't I?*

I could head to bed and actually sleep in a few minutes with a clear head, conscious, and mind. First, I pitched the stale Point can that had been sitting on my nightstand. My apartment didn't need another two-inch roach. Plus, I had to stay on the cleaning because Kati called me. But that was one small detail. I wished I could say I

had summoned up the courage to call. I could say it. Could even write it down in my

Sketchbook of the Mind. It wouldn't be true, but I could write it anyway. But Kati

called because she is Kati and was always ahead of me. She knew something was

missing from last night's talk.

She said she had to talk to me, but first, she wished me good luck with Pat. It

meant so much to me that she cared enough about what I had spent so much of my time

on.

She simply said, "Jay, Good luck tomorrow."

Her words cracked my defenses and undid my locked up insecurities. Before

they could retake control, I just blurted it out, "Thanks, Kati. That means the world to

me—and, I'm falling in love with you."

I could see a smile on her lips as she added simply in return, "That will help

when we are living together."

***

I think I had only ever taken the El this far north once before. Carlos from #206

and I took it to see a Northwestern football game once on a whim. We walked up and

just bought tickets for a game against Iowa. Can't recall who won. I couldn't think very

straight right then. The train I was on, headed for my manuscript evaluation with Pat,

was dead on the tracks. Of course. Now. Here. Today. I had almost talked myself out of

going a hundred times already. I wasn't sure what I was doing. Now that this was becoming real, I felt stupid for doing it. I could have been back at my apartment doing

tangible things. I could have been going through my closet and getting rid of stuff.

Making room for Kati's clothes. She said she didn't have much. My place wasn't big

but could be utilized better. "Necessity is the mother of invention." An old Russian

wisdom that sounded much better in the Russian I used to know. However, I didn't feel

like a collegiate turning in a late essay. More like a sixth-grader turning in a report on

Mark Twain. A report that the dog ate, but it was so bad the dog threw it back up. A

report I had no choice but to let it dry and bring it with me, even if it was encrusted with

dog vomit. I knew Pat was making me come all this way to show I was serious. She said

she had too many manuscripts that were sent to her and she never again heard from the

person who sent them. I summoned up the courage to start up there, and I didn't think

I'd have it in me anymore. I could get off at the next stop and never come back. I could

call her and tell and her what happened. Or not. No one needed to know. *Back Outta the*

World sucked anyway. I told Kati I was doing this though. She knew of course. We

talked last night. Fuck. Why? I left my place in plenty of time, so I wasn't late yet if the

train started in a minute or two... No announcement. No one else in the car seemed

worried. If today went well, Pat would read and possibly forward the manuscript to a

publishing house in New Orleans. I paid her for her time no matter what. I didn't know

they had publishing houses there. Why not here? I did bring her some CosmoBucks as a

bribe. That couldn't hurt. Oh, Jesus, we moved. We're moving.

But movement was what made *Back Outta the World* what it was. It was the

creation of thought into action written as a road trip. What moved us first was thought,

right? No one else seemed too fazed when we started again. But who else on this whole train had a book to be published? None of them. Or all of them. It didn't matter to them whether *Back Outta the World* was published now or never. And in a way, it didn't matter to me. Okay. I needed to tell Pat that so she didn't find a reason in my desperation to charge more. It wasn't why the book, the manuscript, came to life. In fact, I didn't have a very clear idea why. Maybe I would someday. But that mirrored the book. A thought long ago brought the book to life. But it took about fifteen years for it to happen. Did I make that connection so the readers can? Damn, I had fun writing it. Taking the road trip again. Midwest to Virginia. Cities. The UP. Southwest. Arizona. Mexico. To write it was to take the trip again. They say life is all about the journey anyway so fuck it. The process afterward. Pat. The manuscript. Sod it (sounds better—more literary). Sod it all. It could not have been more random anyway. No one knew what's good. They only knew what they liked. Everyone on this car could have done what I did. Written a book. I know that. And that is exactly what was scaring the shit out of me. It felt good to be underway again no matter what.

My stop. The book didn't matter today anyway. What mattered was the close at #204. And then more closes and the IPO and the promotion. But what really mattered was that Kati was moving in. That was what mattered. Take a breath. No matter what happens now, Pat wouldn't get back to me for a couple weeks. I hoped she liked it.

***

"I'm still waiting for my iced latte."

It was such a long and draining morning. I was too wrapped up in thought to write any notes on the way home from Pat's. And I cut it too close to focus on writing on the way in. Instead, I looked out the bus window as if watching Clark street pass

would make the bus go faster. I did make it to #204 just in time. Boston Dennis was on

the bar, and the usual Friday madness was underway as I stepped into #204. I did feel

relieved to be there. It felt like coming home safely after sticking my neck out and

handing over a copy of *Back Outta the World* to a complete stranger. I hoped it was a

nice enough presentation. She didn't seem fazed. The familiar sights and sounds of the

Friday afternoon rush took me away. The starting of the steam wand. That particular

hissing triggered work mode, and then I was off running. Mark and I had a quick word

in back. We had the big dry erase calendar on the wall for relevant store events. One

date will be marked as the start of a new promotion or the arrival of a new coffee. In a

few weeks, we were getting Ethiopian Harrar back. I loved all the Africans, so I was

looking forward to that. Of course, that month the calendar was full with all the big

shots coming and going. At the bottom, Mark had put an entry for next month for him

only. A lunch with the new regional director. I had forgotten all about him really. I had

yet to see him come through on my shift or around the office at MIE class. Mark said

this new regional director was scheduling a lunch meeting with all the managers. I

wondered if he'd do the same with assistants. I didn't like the sound of it either way.

With that thought in my hand and tripio in my hand, I hit the floor. Boston

Dennis showed up on time and was good with the customers but had never really found

second gear on the bar. I headed there first as I saw he needed help. Denis's play

opened that weekend, so he was off. Mark had asked Monica to stay late, and the

wonderful Sarah was expediting. Kati had left #204 for good. She was winding up her

first week at Van Buren. Wanted to call her. I helped Dennis out by pulling shots, and the first wave was gone quickly. At least this Dennis paid attention to the time of his

espresso shots. Maybe that is why he was so slow. Oh well, I had come to learn that you

can't have it both ways. Dennis was a bartender in Boston and could tell some good

stories. Somehow, between his telling and my listening, we missed a customers' drink.

It was hers.

I can still hear it, "I'm still waiting for my iced latte." That tone expressed such

disgust. So incredulous that her drink had been missed. She had to wait. God fucking

forbid! I did not ask Boston Dennis if the drink was on his list. He used the list. Nor did

I ask Monica or Sarah if they called it out. Already Monica was proving to be mistake-

free at the register. If a person's register was accurate at the count-down at shift change,

then they were calling out drinks and not missing the details. Sarah was a veteran.

"I'm still waiting for my iced latte." I simply asked her turned away face what

size it was. Tall. Skim. Practically spitting the words at the floor. She didn't see the

necessity of facing me. Why it bothered me so much almost nine hours later, I couldn't

say for sure. I just wanted to dump the thing on her head. Instead, I made it, grabbed a

CosmoBuck from the drawer under the La Marzocco, and handed both to her. She took

them without thanks or looking up at me. I was just the lowly dumbass who had missed

her drink.

"I'm still waiting for my iced latte." Why had I written that about ten times?

And barely anything about my hour with Pat? I was too tired to think about it anyway.

There was El Patio, packed to the gills at 1:30 on a Friday night. That was my

landmark. My stop was next.

***

I couldn't sleep last night. So, I came out to the front room and watched *Ride the Wind*. It was about water, cattle, and gunfire. It finally put me to sleep. Did not recognize anyone in it.

I did stay asleep on my small couch for longer than usual. Or, later, really. Last weekend was so long ago. I was back to the Saturday close and Sunday open. But, I did have Monday off. Kati had the weekend off. This schedule wouldn't change too much. At least until I got my own five-day store. Kati and I could work downtown together. Not in the same store but maybe ride in together.

***

I couldn't get into *Tropic* this time. With *Back Outta the World* off to Pat, I needed to find a book to read. I loved the books at my place. I looked at them on the shelves and considered it a good thing to have read almost every one. I loved it when I was into a book enough to pick it up and instantly connect with it. Especially at night when I needed to quiet my mind. When I was in the process of moving up here, I was in the middle of *Literary Outlaw*. It was big enough to form a bridge of connection from my quiet, but stagnant life in Dayton to what became my life in Chicago. I started it there and finished it here. It was something familiar to turn to. By the time I finished it, I felt I was becoming a fixture in my neighborhood and at #206. I loved the book for that more than anything I learned about Burroughs. I saw it on a lower shelf. I had no desire at all to start it today. Even the unread books I bought or been given of recent vintage had no appeal. If I could start a book and quickly get into it, I could form another bridge to the time when Kati moves in. I would see if the Brown Elephant had anything. They had books. I needed a new white shirt for the big meeting.

Kati and I talked a little last night, but it was so hard to focus in the backroom at #204. It was a workplace after all. She had things to do this morning. We talked about getting Greek on Sunday. I liked the tradition of seeing her on Sunday. Still, we couldn't see each other until after my opening shift.

***

Saturday night rolled into Sunday morning. I thought I might ask Mark if I was still supposed to be getting tips. It was just business as usual at Cosmodemonic #204. We measured, brewed, and sold coffee. When I was doing the deposit, I found a pastry bag with my name on it. It had cash inside. It was a good thing. I was officially just in training to be an assistant manager, and that must have meant I was still allowed to get tips. Mark would know. I didn't look a gift horse in the mouth, and gladly put the bills in my wallet. As a result, some of that cash would be going to the good people at Bento's.

It was a rainy summer night in the big, old city. The side door of Bento's was left open to welcome the noise of the rain and train. My first bottle of Old Style was gone in about two seconds, so easy to spend found money. The rest were sipped more deliberately. Bento's was almost empty. I usually liked to sit at a table so I could take notes. Not tonight. I had my choice of bar stools. One table was taken by a group who wouldn't remember they were here. Luckily, they were as far away from me as they could be. The pool table was taken by the only other occupants of Bento's beside the bartender and me. The bartender ignored me unless I caught his attention when I needed

the next beer. Even then, he didn't speak to me. I felt like the odd man out. It felt like I

was drinking my beer among the Blade Runner replicants.

***

A quick shower and I headed back to #204 on Sunday morning. My first thought

was of Kati and our plans for later. I still needed to get my place cleaned out. I did find

a new white shirt at the Brown Elephant. I wasn't so lucky in finding a new book to

read. It would come to me, they always do. I'd have Monday to get organized. Gotta

dance.

***

The Sunday bus rides into #204 were different. It was quiet on the bus, which

only meant you could hear the sounds that it made as we made our way south. It

sounded to me like a whale spouting a shower of water. It must have been related to the

brakes or some other mechanism required to make the bus operate. Quite a few times

that noise had alerted me to its approach. I hated to stand and wait for the bus. I didn't

possess the patience so as I walked toward a destination my back was turned to the bus.

But the whale noise told me of the proximity of any of the three buses I would have

chosen. No need for the whale noise today as I stood for just a minute on the nearly

empty corner, leaning against the sign for number eight. I knew it would be Bill and

Tony for the open. At ten, Sarah would arrive for the meat of the Sunday rush. Mikey G

would close and be in at three. Chuck and Boston Dennis would follow him in, spaced

an hour apart. I'd have Monday off of course. I still checked the schedule board for

Kati's name just out of habit. Not on the schedule of course but I will see her later. I wanted it to be now. I went through my opening motions, not inspired by the prospect of eight hours and about seven hundred customers until Kati. I assigned myself to odd detail tasks as soon as the rush was over. My favorite task of the day was refilling the spools of labels we used for whole bean coffee. The Statue of Liberty and Elephant were down to three or four each on the spool. I put full spools in their place and re-attached the remaining ones by leaving as much paper as I could and sticking them back on. It wasn't so much that I was trying to help my stocks options by saving half a dozen paper stickers. It was the potential loss of time created by running to the back for a sticker during a rush. No use in making things harder on myself. Filling the stickers reminded me that when I started the siren logo sticker was bare-breasted. I miss her.

***

It helped jolt me out of my funk when Kati called me at #204. She was still coming over but a little later than we planned. It would be far and away too late to go to the Greek place we talked about. We could go to La Bamba if there wasn't a game. Or somewhere else. No biggie. She was bringing a few things with her in her overnight bag. Talking to Kati gave me a jolt of adrenaline for the next hour, but it wore off. The rest of the shift reverted to slow motion. Even when I was home and clean, the time moved just as slowly.

***

When my buzzer rang, I ran down the steps in a quarter of a second. Nearly anyway. Kati and I examined each other in the open doorway. It wasn't that that we didn't recognize each other. It was more that we were newly sizing each other up as someone who was now very important in each other's lives and futures. The following hug was simply everything. It washed away the still-waiting-lady, the bus rides, and the whole week. Kati and I had Sunday evening in Chicago together, and that was all right by me.

We did a few quick things around my place to prepare for her move. She had some things for the kitchen that were newer than mine. She had a good sauté pan and a nice set of knives. I had knives of different shapes, but it wasn't much of a set even though I did like to cook. She had good luck getting rid of some old things. Bill from Wheaton needed a bed for his new place in the city. He had been using a sleeping bag. Of course, everyone at #204 knew about us. It was as if everyone echoed Sarah's comment knowing we would make a good couple. And it felt good to plan on sharing the apartment together. Her thoughts and ideas for things never struck me as out of place. We shared the Midwestern practical sensibility. Her dad had that to such a degree he quit his way higher paying position at a law firm and took a less stressful, more stable position as a judge. That was about ten years before. Kati's family wasn't badly off with the big old house and the planned migration to it as proof. But Kati had quit Eastern Illinois and was therefore not going to get any further financial help from her dad. Those were just the rules. She told me that she had always wanted to help people and possibly study nursing or become a midwife. I thought of Kenny. I hadn't seen him in a while. Be that as it may, Kati felt a stable full-time gig at Cosmodemonic would work better within the longer-term plan of getting into night classes when she decided to go back.

At the end of that discussion, and the placing of Kati's overnight bag on the bedroom floor, we headed to La Bamba. No game today. I was happy to keep up the conversation. It was made better by the fact that staff and other customers at La Bamba would see us as a couple talking over our future together. We did just that, with arms across the table to hold hands with the dining room fountain flowing in the background.

***

Kati's black shorts sat on the edge of the bed. She wore them last night. That worked for me. I had a moment of panic as I stirred awake and felt her next to me. It was past seven! The rest of her clothes were on my dresser next to the bed. Then I remembered that she didn't open at #204 anymore. Right, she was not supposed to be at work yet. But the jolt woke me for good. I used the energy to make her some coffee as she woke up slowly. I joked that we had to have a practice morning of cohabitation to help determine if we would function well living together. She didn't have to be in until ten and stayed until close, which was five or five-thirty at most downtown stores. Good hours. Van Buren was small, and the back office was no more than a closet. And true to her prediction, Kati was not having the issues that Gayle had with Carmella, the manager. So, all I could do was finish MIE and see what happens with my own schedule and future. I would likely stay at #204 as a full-fledged assistant through the holidays. After that, I could begin to apply to any five-day stores that come open. Cosmodemonic doesn't seem interested in opening many more five-day stores. Maybe because there were a lot downtown already. I heard that they were opening some kiosks in airports soon. That should spread the word about the Master Roast. I think there are now over one hundred Cosmodemonics.

175

But back to Kati and the practice morning. Since no one would ever see this, I could write the following: "The coffee was hot, but the sex was hotter." Just great. I had no choice, but to get on with my day, just as Kati did earlier.

***

And I did. I walked all over Lakeview to get groceries, haircut (not my Puerto Rican place), to La Commercial for two big cans of Fosters, and to pick up a clean shirt at the laundromat. I listened to bathroom-enhanced jazz to keep my spirits high as I fixed my weekly food: Clam linguini. I couldn't wait for Kati to move in. We would use the kitchen table. I would put the free flowers there, and we could have a real dinner together whenever possible. I felt like my life was working out. Kati, *Back Outta the World*, Cosmodemonic. They were all moving in essentially positive directions. I did admit to checking the answering machine already for something from Pat even if it had only been a couple days. She said two weeks, but I couldn't help myself. What if she loved it and fast-tracked it to her publishing connections in New Orleans? I'd need a lawyer or something. Kati's dad could help. He would be impressed. I assumed they liked me. Her mom seemed to right away. The old man didn't really talk much, but Kati said he was always like that so didn't take it personally.

Dinner preparations and weekly cleaning completed, I opened a Fosters. I liked the Fosters out of my bowling alley glass. The big can warmed up quickly in the warm evening air. I liked the look of the glass as it sat sweating, and surrounded by my papers. It would make a good black and white photo. I kept getting up to pour some from the can in the fridge. On the way back to my desk with a cold glass in my hand, the phone rang. It's Pat! That was my first thought even as I put it out of my head as being ridiculous at best. It was Natali. Almost as good. I filled her in on the status of the manuscript, as I made a point to call it. She said Anita was having a harder time than she thought in getting a space for her play so no news on that. Natali had the dates for her visit to the UP to see her dad. She and her brother were able to make a lot of time in their lives for the visit, so she was leaving for two weekends before the end of the month. She would most likely have to leave the keys at her place with Craig. Those were the last two weekends Kati would be officially moving out of her place. Just the time when Kati would be ending her lease and moving in with me. On that good news, I finished off the glass in one gulp and headed back to the fridge.

It was too late to call Kati and tell her about the car. No. She wasn't at #204 anymore. I would delay gratification and call later. Plus, I knew talking to her would make me miss her. It would make me feel alone. I was used to being alone when I was writing *Back Outta the World*. In fact, I loved my alone time working on *Back Outta the World*. I remembered one all-nighter when I stepped out onto my landing overlooking the alley. The morning was just arriving but more as a mist than glorious sunrise. I heard the train coming to Addison. It seemed to take forever to arrive. When I finally heard it come to a stop, I decided the workday was over. I stepped back inside and had a beer at my kitchen table with the door open, allowing morning to come in and join me.

***

I was up on Tuesday morning and facing the workweek. I'd call Kati when she was in the Van Buren closet counting the drawers down, doing the recap sheet, and all that voodoo. We talked briefly last night. But Kati had to call her mom and needed to get off the phone. Kati was happy to hear about the car but said her mom left a message for her to call right away. She was just going to do that when I called.

As far as the morning went, Mark called. I forgot Mark wanted me in an hour earlier. Glad he called to remind me. He was trying to give Mikey G. some shorter shifts so he could have him work a long shift on Thursday. He said thing were crazy with the IPO Pow Wow on Thursday. HB is no longer coming. It would be Cosmodemonic's coffee buyer instead. The guy who traveled the world buying green coffee for the whole company. That was the job I really wanted. Later, Mark had to go to the regional office to meet with Katherine and her other managers. Two hours early would have been better. I agreed that was fine, as if I had a choice. It was a chance to look good. Who knew who would hear about my sacrifice? Truthfully, I had wanted to head up to my spot on the roof for a few minutes of thinking and tanning, but couldn't now. Two hours out of my day was pretty big. Then again, the manager downtown at what was Cosmodemonic's busiest store had been known to work three or four weeks straight. Or so I heard.

***

It was a long day at #204. The first part was made up of the end of an opening shift. Then it became the closing shift. I sometimes wished I could do the shorter shifts like Monica or Denis or Sarah. I didn't think I ever did. Maybe I did way back on my first month with Doug at #206. I needed full time. I was up here in Chicago with my apartment and bills and only Natali to lean on when she was around. She did what she could. Looking back, she probably let me hang around for longer than she actually wanted because she knew I was on my own. (Or it may have been my dazzling good looks). Not sure if that made me mad or made me miss her. I made it clear I needed full time at #206 and soon Doug had hours available, and the rest is history. Doug appreciated my love for the coffee and soon so did the customers. They came to know that I made good drinks. I came to know their drinks, if not all their names. I could tell what time it was by seeing who was in line. The bar at #206 was elevated too, and so was the first thing the customers saw when they walked in. Back then, when I was just a lowly barista, I could see my favorite regulars as soon as they walked in and then reverse the order of the drink being called. Instead of the customer going to the register, and then the drink being called from there, I called the drink down to the person on the register. Maybe it was "Tall cappuccino," and I'd follow with a nod or smile to the customer who would return the smile. It made them feel like #206 was there for them only. Not an easy thing to do. I caught on quickly and did the same at #204. It gave me a good feeling to see them smile, stand a little taller, or quicken their step a little. And, it never hurt the tip jar much.

I did find a minute to call Kati. She was in back doing the Van Buren closing paperwork. I didn't know why it surprised me when she sounded happy to hear from me. I was sure it was a me thing. They closed at five-thirty, and I knew she would be at the desk, so I timed my call perfectly. She asked me a few questions about the closing procedures. I had been around long enough to be a resource at Cosmodemonic. Back when I started, we took five separate training classes, and almost all were on coffee. During one class, I saw old signage lying around the back of the training location that must have just been taken down. There were signs for things like Panini and spices and

such. Didn't sell I guessed, and they took them away. The coffee sold pretty fast

though. It was in those days that I began to realize that most of the coffee being served

in the USA was not good. I loved my beatnik coffee house in Dayton, but the actual

coffee was no match for Cosmodemonic's. Kati and I didn't have a lot of time to talk

coffee, just a few differences in our respective stores. She said another guy delivered the

juice, not Dennis-the-Juice-Guy. It seemed even Dennis-the-Juice-Guy was expanding

his operation thanks to the growth of Cosmodemonic. Kati said she did miss #204 and

all her regular customers. Mark said that a lot of them had asked about her. When she

was here, more than a few would hang around the bar and bother Kati while she made

other drinks even during the busier times. It never seemed to bother her. I never liked it.

It created a distraction and a chance for an error on another customer's drink. Or, maybe

I just didn't like the attention she got from those customers. They were all men of

course. I reminded her about the car, and she responded that all systems were in place

for the move.

***

I had to get out of there. Not in a bad way. I was just not able to stop myself

from listening for my phone to ring. It was only Wednesday. I met Pat on Friday. That

meant I was only halfway through the first of two weeks waiting. It wasn't very sunny

out so no rooftop retreat. So, I thought I would head to my coffee house under the

tracks. I had been avoiding it because I didn't want to run into 'The Broker.' Come to

think of it, he hadn't been back to #204 since we talked. *Damn.* I'd like to talk to him about the IPO announcement. Not really. He was nuts. And I had my stock market books from the library to study some more. And I could take my MIE homework.

But first, I wanted to find the damn list of books I've read since I moved up here. I kept it in one of my Sketchbooks of the Mind. It would have helped my anxiety to see a list of things I'd done. I started them and finished them. No grey area. That was why I like cleaning. My sink was either cleaner than it was or it wasn't. No grey area. You can't say that about too many things in life, like judging fiction. I found an entry. It was not my book list but might be more relevant. And it was about writing. It was from an older Sketchbook of the Mind and again, I did not note who said it. "The place of the artist: No one owes him anything for writing. He may regret the stupidity or ignorance that keeps his work unknown, but he must accept it as one of the possible conditions under which he must work. No one asked him to write. Let him expect nothing." Wise words. I would add to not expect the phone to ring.

***

I was relieved to be going to work. Comforted by the number twenty-two bus. The drill. Work at Cosmodemonic #204. I punched in, and I punched out. Again, not much grey area. I had to walk a ways before the bus came. That could happen if you were going to work in the middle of the day. If this kept up, I'd never see Kati. She was close to finishing her day. Or would be done in a couple hours. But I didn't think Mark was going anywhere as #204's manager. He never mentioned trying to move up the ladder. But I was doing the schedule then. I admit that I liked seeing my name climb up one notch on the big posted schedule. My name had been on the third line down forever.

It went down from manager, assistant manager, lead clerk, openers (Kati, now Monica), regular closers, and then everyone who bounced around. It went all the way down to Phil who always had one slot at the bottom. Now, though, my name was just one line below Mark's. That made me feel good. It used to be Rebecca's name. Now it was mine, with no asterisks saying in training. There probably should have been, but that was Mark. That bit of non-conformist in him wouldn't go away. I couldn't write a lot on the bus. It was way too cramped. I think it was a replacement for the original bus, which must have broken down. That explained why it was so late. And why it was so crowded. Even if I made the schedule, I couldn't make the schedule fit my life with Kati. That was why I needed to be a manager at a five-day store. So easy. No weekends. I knew they were really busy, but it couldn't be busier than #204 on a Saturday morning. I had my clothes picked out for tomorrow. I even had my khaki pants cleaned for the big day. Pants cost more but were worth it. I was not sure what to expect, but tomorrow would be a different day, to say the least. I read my stock market book at my coffee house under the tracks and now get that as of tomorrow, Cosmodemonic will be a publicly traded company. Traded on the NASDAQ, whatever that stands for. Anyway, I gotta stand up for this old dude. No open seats. I gave him mine. I was done writing in the Sketchbook of the Mind anyway.

***

I had to write. Hadn't since Wednesday. Too buzzed to write much. I hooked up with Mark and Kerry after the IPO Pow Wow and headed to Sterch's. *Great bar. Somewhere. Someone's idea. Had to sort out my options. Stock options that is. Good one. I'd close tomorrow. Good. I could run my pants to the dry cleaners. Spilled apple*

182

cider on them when we all toasted Cosmodemonic going public. It was good to see Doug again. He hadn't changed. Anyway. Not done celebrating. More beer in the fridge and these are free. Gotta sort out my options. Look into my options. See what my options are. Jocularity. Jocularity. Father Mulcahy from MASH. Good one.

Chapter Six

I woke up with a dry mouth but didn't feel bad otherwise. Some of the past evening was coming back to me. First, I hoped I didn't call Kati last night. I would have woken her up. If I did, I invited her to spend the night tonight. Friday night. Made sense at the time. I assumed she was coming over Sunday. When I got Natali's car, I could start bringing Kati's things over for real. Until then, she was bringing over what she could on Sundays. The dry mouth reminded me that I wanted to get back to the Red Lion. It wasn't close. I had been taken there for my send-off from #206 by Carlos and a few of the partners there. I had wanted to get back. I felt rich after last night. Kati and I could take a cab. We could have a good dinner of bangers and mash. No beers until we got there though.

The message light on my phone was not on. The coffee water for my plunger pot was. I remembered most of the day, but the end was fuzzy. I knew for sure that I had a blast with Kerry and Mark. Kerry seemed likely to get his own store soon. We traded Kenny stories. It seemed Kenny had migrated down to Sue's store on Halsted. He had to because Kati left. He'd have to go a long way to find her again. But, he just might. Damn, it felt great to be at that table with those two. I looked over everyone else in the bar. Not just the women. But everyone. As I did, I imagined that Mark, Kerry, and I had just found a buried treasure. We had that secret on everyone else at Sterch's. We had found the treasure, made a map of course, and reburied it somewhere safe so no one could come back for it. Or, better yet, they would come looking, but only the three of us knew where the treasure was. They would walk right over it, not even noticing the displaced sand under their feet. We were just waiting to go back to get it. And to repeat:

only we three knew where it was. It was ours. Not everyone was eligible for the options on Cosmodemonic stock. You had to be full time for the prior year. That was me, Kerry, Mark. And Sarah. And Doug. And some more in Chicago. Candace. Sue from Kerry's store. It wasn't that many. I wasn't sure if the pints were giving me the buzz or it was dawning on me just what I lucked into and had buried. Just by staying employed, my treasure, that is my stocks, grew. And what if Cosmodemonic doubled in size in a year or two?

I needed to take a walk, get the blood flowing to help clear my head. I'd drop off my cider stained khakis and head out from there. The Belmont Rocks were a possibility as always.

***

It was too nice not to end up on the rock slopes between Belmont and Fullerton. I dropped my laundry off. I did remember to stuff a bathroom towel into my bag along with my sketchbook and a bottle of water. I'm feeling much better thanks to the walk here. It is sunny and not as humid by the lake. The last time I had been here, it was with Kati. That was happening more and more. My places were becoming hers. Well, ours.

***

On the walk, I passed a bus stopped for no apparent reason at a green light. It must have just died at that light. Or it would have been moving with the changing light. The guy in the car behind the bus kept blowing his horn. Over and over. It was doing no good at all. I was sure the bus driver wanted to move. And so did all the passengers on that bus. The horn kept blowing. Uselessly, needlessly, pointlessly, stupidly.

***

I still needed to clarify what becoming a public company meant for the future. I had to understand more fully what vesting meant. I didn't recall my dad ever discussing his stock portfolio. I was sure there were people at work to ask. Or there would be soon. Those who were eligible would be getting more info in the mail.

The view of the lake and its waves generated thought. Waves of thought. Corny. But, maybe the guy behind the bus needed to come here. It had been just a week since I dropped off my manuscript. Already though, it is fading from my reality. *Back Outta the World* is something I wrote, taken from a yellow legal pad full of notes and reminders: matchbooks, receipts, a Greyhound schedule. I found those tangible reminders in that beat-up legal pad and knew that I had been at The Shanty in Tucson, drinking beers at nine in the morning. The writing of the book seemed like vapor, like the lake effect. Yes, I felt that I wrote it. But I couldn't see it. It was with someone named Pat who freelanced in publishing, whatever that entailed. I could see the revisions and working copies. But I couldn't see the writing. I couldn't see it happening even when I was writing.

With all that was happening and going to happen at Cosmodemonic, I needed to make a decision about work based on, in part, that writing that I couldn't see. It needed to be clear for me. But I hadn't been writing so how could it be clear? I sat just putting down thoughts, hoping to come up with something useful in some way. It still felt good to do it. The work path was so much clearer. Maybe I could do both. I knew for sure

that going to visit Kati was the right thing that day we ended up here. Something told

me it was right. I guess everyone has those visionary experiences from time to time. I

do. I could use one about now.

***

I was wet. Dripping wet from the waist down. I had my bathroom towel

wrapped around my waist. The lake told me to. I walked into it until I was waist deep. I

stood in the waves, looking outward, and pretending that Costa Rica was the shoreline

behind me. It would be years from then. I relished my life, having just written another

best-selling novel. And looking back on this day.

***

No one took a second look at me while I was walking back to my apartment

wearing a wet towel around my waist. I was close to being dry when I got back to my

place. I needed to make a key for Kati. I should have done that today. Maybe she could

come over tomorrow and spend the weekend in my empty apartment while I was at

work. Wouldn't be too much fun for her. I would still call her tonight. But, I was feeling

a bit tired. Damn. It seemed like I should have been thrilled to go in and start increasing

the value of my stock options. But, I just didn't want to. I couldn't remember if I had

called in sick since I started at Cosmodemonic. I couldn't bring myself to call in. At

least the big shots watch was over. I was sure they had all left town by then. It would be

just another day.

***

Well, I was wrong. I didn't take my *Sketchbook of the Mind* on the bus in. I must have been tired if I left it behind. Thank God for my tripio when I got in. And for Sarah and Denis and Bill. We kicked ass. But, I was wrong about the big shots being gone. Partly. Because Katherine dropped in just before the after-work, pre-weekend crowds started coming in. At least no big, big shots were with her. And at least I was filling the condiment stations and had a bar towel over my shoulder and was looking the part of a committed Manager in Education. We talked for a second on the floor. She was nice enough but was always keeping something back. Like they all did. A smile almost crossed my face as we talked. I was facing the bar, and I could see out of the corner of my eye that Denis was looking for the timers we use to time the shots. They should always be on top of the La Marzocco where we can see and set them easily. They did get used in the mornings and sometimes at shift change. I only used them from time to time since I felt like I knew a twenty second shot when I saw one. After a few seconds of fumbling around, Denis managed to find a timer and put it in its required spot. After that, I ran a tape with the counts for Katherine and we just more or less talked in back. I knew I scored by being out on the floor when she walked in. I had heard that even established managers were known to lounge in the backroom, or closet, as in Van Buren's case. She seemed to want to make sure I'd be at the open forum the next week. No reason not to be since I was not even scheduled at #204 that day. It used to be my day off, I mentioned. I'm pretty sure that Katherine let that comment go by intentionally without acknowledgment.

***

It was one week since I dropped off the manuscript and I felt better. A hard day's work had a way of purifying the mind and body. But making the knees feel sore. I felt a delayed jolt of enthusiasm come back to me from the IPO meeting. As such, my store, #204, looked better than usual at close. That was not up for discussion. That would not keep me up tonight. In fact, I'm calling it quits in a second. No book yet but I can read some of the *Time's* book reviews. I might be able to pick up Natali's car this weekend. I was glad I got ahold of Kati for lots of reasons. She would be able to come over Sunday after I opened. Just what I needed to hear. I did say I could pick her up if I got the car in time. We would have to communicate via #204 now since she is discontinuing her phone.

***

I was quite enjoying my second cup of Sumatra when the phone rang. It was Natali. She and her brother were leaving for the UP today. As in this morning. That was one time that I didn't recall Natali and our time together too fondly. I was hoping to see her and to see Scott again somehow during this car lending. I had further hoped that she could find a minute to drop the car off over here. Not to be. Her free spirit and beauty attracted me, but the free spirit in her sometimes didn't plan very well. Not sure if you can be free-spirited and detail oriented. Kati does both, though. So, as appreciative as I was for the use of the car it did not surprise me when the last thing she told me was that the car really needed gas. And there was one more thing. The apartment key was in the mailbox.

So here I go. It was early enough to make my way over there, find a gas station (and if I remembered how), gas up the car, and make my way back in time for the Saturday close. It would be busy of course. I was trying more and more to see every customer as someone helping my portfolio. Still, it didn't make it much easier to get excited to close on yet another Saturday.

***

I was a bit apprehensive as I stepped off the bus at the White Hen Pantry. It was the landmark I had used before, and it hadn't moved. Why should it have? It had changed for me though. It felt different now that Natali had officially ended the romantic part of our relationship. "The Lover" was no more. The White Hen had changed for me. It meant something new. It wasn't that White Hen; it was this White Hen. Funny, but this truly sounds like someone who has written a book called "*Back Outta the World.*" Her street was residential but sedate compared to mine. The life-sized cut out of Jack Nicholson was still in the window in her half of the double she shared with Craig. The landlady who gave me the nickname lived in the other half but was nowhere to be seen.

I had to get into her place to get the keys to her car. That was why Natali more or less insisted I come over today. She didn't want the key to be left in the mailbox overnight. Craig was also gone for the weekend. I would have given the key to the landlady, who still knew me, and gone from there. Kati would have done that I am sure. I found the car keys in the drawer where she always kept them. With the car, I felt I had the time to get back easily. The freedom of a vehicle. Maybe it made sense to try to start saving for one. If I had a financial future, I could buy a car. But for now, I took the time

to head upstairs to Natali's room. I slept here for my first few nights in this city. This

city that I became more and more a part of. In fact, I was a unique part of this city, and I

found treasure there, thanks to Cosmodemonic. Craig's room was across the hall, and

that door was closed. Natali's door was open. The first thing I did was step over to the

window, push the curtains aside, and look out over the neighborhood. It was a Chicago

neighborhood, and it too had changed since the last time I looked out this window. It

was like I was stepping into my High School on the first day of my junior year. The

buildings looked the same, but I saw them differently. There is always movement. No

day was like the one before. It couldn't be. Natali and I moved apart, and Kati and I

moved closer together. Cosmodemonic was moving fast. I wondered, standing in

Natali's bedroom, how the manuscript would have moved or changed when I looked at

it next.

My window memory time lingered longer than I thought. And so did the drive

back to my place. I parked several buildings away from my place. It struck me that I

was not sure where I would park at #204 since I'd never had to think about it before. I

decided to leave the car on my street and take the twenty-two for today. I could find a

parking spot close to #204 a lot easier at 6:30 on Sunday morning.

***

My day started hectically and maintained that pace for hours. It was busy but not

so busy for me to feel as out of it I was feeling. I was not all there mentally, but not sure

why for most of the rush. Even my tripio didn't help all that much. So when I had the accident at the condiment station, it wasn't all that surprising and could have been worse. I tore open the paper wrapping that held about 500 logo napkins, and they busted open all over the floor. I decided before I did anything, on beers and TV when I got home. It had been that kind of day. But the napkin explosion woke me up at last. The shift got better as the evening wore on, as the pre-close was efficient. And saving the best for last, there was no last-minute group coming in off the street just before we locked the doors.

Once I made it home, the beers in the fridge and mindless TV called to me. But I wanted to write down the job offer (or whatever it was) before I collapsed and forgot. I thought she was a customer who needed help at first. Sarah came into the back as I was dropping a pastry bag of money into the safe and said someone was asking for me. I saw her standing by an empty table. She smiled and held out her hand as I approached. I knew someone buying an espresso machine or grinder wouldn't want to shake my hand. And so, I knew she had something to talk about with me. I might have been able to get a better idea of what she wanted, but I had one ear on the floor. We were just beginning the pre-close and were not out of the woods yet. The growth of Cosmodemonic had attracted attention. There must have been more good coffee beans on the planet than I thought. The reason she was here was that she represented a coffee company just getting started on the Atlantic Coast. Was I interested? Cosmodemonic had bought a good-sized competitor in Boston not long ago, so I knew there was competition out there. My ego was happy to be talking to her. But I was an owner here at my store. This was my store. Here in my city. And it struck me that Kati would figure in all these decisions now. That was it. The source of my distraction most of the night. Only I hadn't realized it. A big change was coming in my life. So, I turned the competitor down. Looking back, I don't think she sought me out personally. I have a feeling she was canvassing the nearby, if not all, Cosmodemonics to see who was interested. I did put her business card in my bag, however. I would ask at the MIE meeting one of these Thursdays if anyone else was approached. Maybe a beer and TV for maybe the last time in my place alone. It was still a long day.

***

Sunday morning and I was driving. Driving a vehicle to work. Then I was going to Kati's right after that. It was becoming real, and I could hardly wait. It seemed like forever since we'd been together. Last night was tough in a way because there were Kati things in and out of boxes all over the apartment. I wasn't able to enjoy the beers and mindless TV as much as I had hoped. I wanted her to be there with me.

I did not need to make coffee. I had a cup of day old Italian Roast at room temp. It was slightly sweeter that way. This was the week HS was coming on Thursday, so there was not a MIE meeting so I couldn't ask the group about the job offer. But I might be able to talk with Kerry if I sat by him at the open forum. My first open forum also. I was becoming a regular at the management only events. I must have been climbing the Cosmodemonic ladder.

***

Fuck Cosmodemonic! Fuck the Open Forum! All of it. Kati is not here. I am alone again. I had to work a double. Chuck did not show up to close. No one else could come in. Not sure if Kati was pissed. She said she understood that I had no choice. But,

193

she had to stay alone in her empty place. That was my only concern. The car was

useless. Alone on a Sunday night after literally working all day. The beers in the fridge

were a must. I was still too pissed to do much more. Plus, my knees were sore and

aching.

***

Okay. The anger was gone. That thing of energy in my stomach that grew and

grew as I figured it out. I figured out that Chuck was not five minutes late, not fifteen

minutes late, not forty-five minutes late. He was not coming in for his closing shift. I

was doing the schedule on Tuesdays. But I was doing it in my head. Who gets his

hours? Who can work when? I was doing it in my head that morning instead of all the

other things I could be doing. I thought I had even promised to take Kati to work this

morning. From here, of course. She is likely on the train now. Once again, it seemed

like forever since I had seen her. The anger thing was returning when I thought about

not seeing her. The anger was not all gone. I had never been so happy to lock the doors

as last night. The Christmas week shifts came close. We had two coffee shipments that

week. One was only Holiday Blend. Coffee makes a great all-purpose gift. Like booze.

My beers did taste good last night. The two and a half I had before collapsing in my

bed. It made me feel better if I made it to my room to sleep. *I should think of it as our*

room now. Kati was so smart and level-headed. I was too pissed to think clearly. After

all the calls to all the staff who didn't answer or couldn't work and all the calls to Kati

with increasingly bad news, she had a partial solution.

So, I was off to her place to pick up the boxes and things she was going to bring

over last night. That works. A solution. I was too, make that way too, all or nothing. A

good thing Mark didn't pick up last night. I was blaming him. Everyone knew Chuck

was leaving—not his fault. Mark could have just forgotten to tell me to leave Chuck off

the schedule. Maybe Chuck told me last week, and I forgot. I did have a lot on my

mind. No way. I would have asked for something in writing. No matter. I was not in the

mood to be reasonable. But today is today, not yesterday. I did still have the car and

needed to use it. Better do it then. I could pick up Kati at least. I could still make the

day work. Better call Mark. I knew he got my message and note. But I better call before

I headed out, even if it was my day off.

***

It was nearly noon on Tuesday. Felt odd to have skipped a day and a half of

writing. It did happen now that I had a six-day Cosmodemonic schedule. I wrote a lot of

Sketchbooks of the Mind when I was hammering out the novel, or the manuscript, *Back

Outta the World*. It was a good way to warm up. The rest of Monday, I was too busy.

Just got back from Van Buren. Kati and I did run some errands, and I helped pack more

of her stuff. The car was back to being useful. We made love on a hand me down quilt

that had seen better days. Her bedroom was almost empty, and our noises made it feel

like her whole building could hear us even as we tried not to be loud.

I closed Tuesday and Wednesday. Candace left a message saying that Thursday

was going to be half MIE class and half open forum. Kati and I decided it was now or

never with the car, so she would move in Friday. Or most likely Saturday morning. We should be able to get the rest of her stuff in two trips in the morning, and she could

make herself at home all day. When I'd get here Sunday, we would be roommates or

lovers, or you name it. There were so many benefits. Life would be enjoyable,

shareable, meaningful, and just plain full. I might have to get used to missing a day or

two in the *Sketchbook of the Mind*, but it would be worth it. I could pay compliments to

Kati in person. There was a time when I didn't have a journal at all. Let alone a

Sketchbook of the Mind. And on Friday, Pat was due to call with a verdict on my

manuscript. Verdict. Sounded so bloody final.

***

I rode in for the Tuesday close. I didn't find that driving in saved any time.

There was never any place to park. And I am a creature of habit. At least I used the time

on the twenty-two destructively. I mentally created scenario after scenario of worst-case

fallout from the Chuck episode. I hadn't been to #204 since the Sunday I stayed all day.

In that time, the close was reborn in my head and sucked. And it pissed off Mark when

he came in to open. Customers complained all morning about the condiment stations

being dirty. And the morning shift ran out of coffee because we didn't prep enough drip

on Sunday night. There was not enough change for the cash drawer because I forgot to

divide it out of the Monday drawers so Mark could buy some at the bank. And no one

did mark-outs for the whole bean. There were three drawers of stale, old whole bean

left. We had a week to sell an opened five-pound bag. Monica had to run to the back to

retrieve a new bag one for a customer in the middle of the rush. The line slowed down.

Customers complained again. And because Monica was in the back, no one stayed on

the drip. Sarah was too busy looking for the second set of tongs. They were washed but left on the drying rack in back. She had dropped hers on the floor in front of the customers and couldn't pick them up in front of everyone. No drip for a few minutes meant unhappy customers. More of them. Boston Dennis would have to make them Americanos on the bar for them. If that was okay? It was fine with some but, not with everyone. Plus, his slow ass wouldn't be able to get the drinks out fast enough. It didn't help that he was looking for the flat lids. Some customers insisted on flat lids on their drinks. There were no holes in those lids, so no spills during the commute. It made sense. We had a small stack of flat lids placed at the bar next to the regular ones. I noticed the empty spot Sunday night as I carried a drawer to the back to count it. I told myself I'd replace them when I came back out to get the second drawer. Never did. Boston Dennis was looking for a backup sleeve which wasn't there because it was not a high-volume item and we didn't have room to store an entire sleeve at the bar. The line grew longer. (That happened to me once. I simply used two regular lids and reversed them so that the slots were on opposite sides, eliminating spill possibilities. The customer appreciated the maneuver and smiled as they left.) Mark saw Boston Dennis on the bar looking for something and not pouring shots or steaming milk or handing out drinks. He was just looking for something as the line grew. Money stayed on the wrong side of the counter when customers couldn't pay. It was my fault. All of it. I knew it.

Except that Mark was glad to see me and apologized to me as soon as I stepped in the back. Chuck hadn't quit. He had a family emergency and had to get home to Colorado. So, it was no one's fault. And Mark told me to keep him on schedule when I did it later. Before leaving for the day, Mark added that even if HS was most likely not in town until Thursday everyone was on edge, so I should do my usual great job at

close. Which I did.

***

One thing that had to stay the same when Kati moves in was the location of the

coffee, plunger pot, and mugs. A lot had already been changed in my apartment, but I

made my way to the kitchen and coffee error-free in the morning. If I could start each

day of living with her having easy access to caffeine, we would get along famously. I'd

close later. Needed to make her a key. I'd meant to. I must have walked past five lock

shops every day but couldn't picture where any were when I needed to.

***

Got Kati's key made. It sometimes pleasantly surprised me that I lived in this

neighborhood. I found the lock place. Next to that a nails place. And next to it, an

empanadas place. And above them apartments. Living spaces. I always felt that a

diverse combination of spaces under the same roof declared that you were in a big, old,

important city. Not the tall buildings, giant parks, or even the history. This combination

of needs met in one building said big city to me. In Dayton, we had a couple such

buildings downtown. Here, just in walking distance, there were too many to count.

I did a deep cleaning. Not that I expect HS to stop by my place. Nonetheless, I

improvised a mop using a small push broom I found in Karl's laundry room. I

proceeded to wrap some bar towels I brought home from #204 around the brush part.

Then I used the bathroom tub as a bucket. So equipped, I mopped my kitchen and

bathroom floors. Then I cleaned the tub, of course. Kati called, and we had another good talk. She was like me. I got the sense anyway, that when she was at work, she didn't like to get too off base. We made plans and filled each other in on the move details. Not much touchy-feely talk. Especially since she was in charge of the shift. Fine by me, I supposed. I wouldn't have minded some. Then again, I could have taken the initiative for a change. Kati was getting used to the five-shot mochas ordered by the guys in smocks who work the floor at the stock exchange.

Hoped for a quiet night at #204, I wanted to clean the vestibule. And even clean the ledge that ran along the window facing Diversey. The counter for customers sat above and ran along it. Thus, crumbs from scones and muffins plunged over the counter to rest on the ledge. Very hard to get to in order to clean. But, it was just the kind of spot the big shots noticed.

***

Up to the alarm. Thursday and the open forum. Not my first thought though. I could drive in. Kerry drove and knew where to park. Drive in and pick up Kati afterward at Van Buren. No use asking why this didn't occur to me sooner. *Call Kerry.* I remembered Candace mentioned something about where we could park at the end of last class. If Kerry doesn't answer, I can most likely recall what she said after cup of Sumatra.

***

Tired, but had lots to recall before some of it faded away. Kati had to get back to her place to hand over the key and let somebody in to do something so she could be officially out of the lease. It was the representative from the building owners or someone like that, and he had to do it tonight. A lot easier for me to just talk to Karl.

But this person had to check the walls for scrapes or some other evidence the lease

hadn't been violated in some way. So, she was back at her place and not spending the

night. But she did have her key. Bill from #204 was getting the rest of his stuff Friday

after Kati got home. She was not sure when exactly Bill would be over, so she was

planning to spend the night on her sleeping bag and read by candlelight. The candlelight

joke made me smile. I had the car and picked her up after the open forum. I made it to

her store in plenty of time. It was different from my two Cosmodemonics. It was not

much more than a kiosk in a hallway in a bigger building. Looking at it, I could not

believe they could generate the customer count Kati told me they did. But it was 5:30 in

the afternoon and not seven in the morning. And it was a Cosmodemonic. That meant it

was going to be busy. There was re-circulated, spent air wafting through the corridor.

There were a few food places open, but most everything else was shut or was shutting

down for the day. There was no call for most of these places to be open after the

workday commute had ended. I waited for her out in the corridor. I didn't want to hurry

her close. Occasionally, if it were cold enough and I was closing at #204, I'll let a friend

of Phil's or Sarah's stand inside and wait for them to get finished. But, I didn't even like

when I had an out of town visitor come in and wait for me to leave after a rare day shift.

I felt hurried and anxious and that in turn made me feel as if I forgot to do something

before I left for the day. So, once Kati saw that I was there and we hugged and kissed

quickly in the corridor I excused myself and waited. I wanted to show her my new

award. But we had agreed over the phone to have a quick beer before we went our

separate ways for the next couple days, so I waited.

MIE class was disjointed. Candace was not there. So, we had a fill in. Some guy I had never heard of. He was a new district manager for stores that didn't exist yet. At least some did and some of them didn't. I think his name was Kyle. Speaking for myself, I didn't like it. It threw me off. Our MIE class had become close. Candace had been our instructor but yet had felt like one of the class also. Why this new guy?

At the open forum, I saw a lot of faces I didn't know. But plenty that I did. Of course, it was a lot of the same people from last week, management, that is. The big exception was HS of course. I had never seen him in person but liked his vibe even from across the room. When he got up to speak, he sounded different from Denis' impersonation from last Christmas season. I did smile to myself, recalling that, as I applauded HS taking the podium.

Like everyone else in the audience, I sat in silence and listened intently. It was mostly all great news. Cosmodemonic was just getting started and not taking any prisoners. HS didn't put it in those terms, but that's how I remember it. And I very clearly remember HS saying, "They are going to write books about Cosmodemonic, people." That stuck in my head: write & books. The reasons are obvious. The reason I don't remember much of the rest is that a few minutes after the speech was over, HS called some partners to the stage for recognition. I was one of them. He called my name about halfway through the presentation (he mispronounced the last name, and I politely corrected him), handed me a Cosmo Bravo award and shook my hand. It was for "Superlative Service" demonstrated to the Midas guy who bought a half pound of everything. I took my place in the small line of other award winners forming next to HS. I couldn't look out to the crowd in the chairs in front of me. I glanced down instead to read a line on my Cosmo Bravo award: "Recognizing Initiative, Resourcefulness, and Action in Service, Sales, and Savings." It was indeed recognition, and it was in front of everyone. It was signed by HB and even HS himself.

Recounting it with Kati at the Duke of Perth later, I was still on a high from it. I was just doing my job, I told her. And, I don't remember if I thought that there was an option other than taking the time to make the guy happy. Mail Order? Come back tomorrow, and I will have it ready? I guess. But, I just did it. Is that all it takes? Easier than writing novels.

I wanted to stay at the Duke and celebrate. But Kati was still in her work clothes. I wanted for us to dash back to the apartment and have celebration sex. Again, Kati had to get back for the last-minute inspection tonight. At least, I did make the effort to ask her about her day. Damn though, I really wanted to talk a lot about me. I wanted more time to celebrate me. So, here I am writing about me instead.

***

The neighborhood seemed so quiet. Opera music was filling the air of late summer. I wondered which window it was coming from. Which apartment? It was Italian. That I knew.

I could do my part. For me to be successful, or on the way at least, and living in this city would be great. Opera out of the window on a Friday morning. Walking out of my gate and turning left or right, I was never sure what I would encounter. Wrigley one direction, Boys town the other. I wanted to continue writing. But with Kati moving in, I was willing and able to postpone it for a while. I could restart in January, but it is a clichéd month to renew. And the New Year seemed far away, as I sat with my *Sketchbook of the Mind*. I was pretending to be busy so that when Pat called, I could pretend that I was in the middle of writing something new and inspired. When I answered the phone, I would act like I was hard at work on my second novel, which would be way better than *Back Outta the World*. The irritation will be heard in my voice. Pat would hear that I had already moved on to bigger and better things and barely had time to listen to her thoughts on *Back Outta the World*.

Was it too far ahead to try to imagine where I would be three or four years later? How many more actual novels might I have written? More Cosmodemonic options would show up every year. I should have been getting a statement soon of exactly how many options I had been granted. And, last but not least, Kati and I would still be together. I knew it. Not sure how, but I did. Just like I knew it when we parted ways after the L'escorgot night. Imagine if I was freer financially. If I was farther along writing and have a real grasp of possibilities involving stock dividends, portfolios, and shares. At that point, Kati and I could get to the real Paris, or anywhere in the world we wanted to go.

It wasn't bad to have this quandary. I mean, I liked my job. Is that wrong? It didn't exclude being creative, did it? Aren't writers supposed to be poor? But at Cosmodemonic, I might have found my mini-generation of peers who I respect and like and we've all come along at a time when we could really make a difference. My Beat Generation of coffee, if you will. I'd always hoped to find a situation like it. I had been hoping over the years to find a band in writing (WSU friends, non-theatre), but it never materialized. The forces weren't there to put it into place. It wasn't anyone's fault, but I was sure it didn't happen for the lack of possible talent and ideas.

Instead of sitting and writing in my *Sketchbook of the Mind* and waiting for Pat to call, I'd leave. If I left and did my errands before I headed in for the close, I would come back to the message light on. That had to work.

But why care what she says? Because as I sat and listened to the opera music filling the space between my building and the one across the way, I could see it all. *Back Outta the World* was selling. It found an audience. Plus, it was garnering critical acclaim. Why mess with that? In my apartment, that was the reality of it all. Not all over the apartment but in my head, which was in the apartment. Why care at all? I had it all in my head, and I really liked what I saw there. I liked what I put there.

Mark must have told everyone that I had received an award. Dennis and Sarah told me congratulations when I arrived at #204. Mark greeted with a smile and shook my hand to emphasize how genuinely happy he was to see me. Then we did have a good work-related discussion in the back. He said that Chuck was back to stay and wanted to return to his normal twenty hours a week. And Mikey G is officially a full-time lead. He could open or close any and all shifts. Katherine was already asking if Mikey G has any interest in becoming a manager at some point. Cosmodemonic was always on the lookout. I didn't say that I thought I was better than Mikey G was at the lead clerk position. I was grateful that he was as good as he was because his success meant good things for me. It meant that once I graduated on Thursday, I would go back to a five-day schedule, provided I opened or closed, of course. Cosmodemonic was not wasting all my training on a mid-shift. They had higher expectations of me. I understood. I was a key holder forever and had closely observed Rebecca when she was here. I saw that Mark was a bit rough around the edges recently but attributed that to trips to Boru's. The stress and strain of being a manager at Cosmodemonic would not get to me. I had a plan. I would be getting a five-day store as soon as I could. With that, I immediately planned on scheduling myself off next Sunday. I wanted a whole weekend day off with Kati. Mark never seemed to mind working Sundays since his wife also worked most weekends at her salon.

I had tonight to live it up, but there was no reason to celebrate. I had a couple beers and watched some reruns. Wow, how in the world was I going to do without this? Tomorrow at this time, Kati would be here. Hard to believe. It happened fast. But, like I said, that doesn't make it wrong.

I should have known. I checked the message light as soon as I got home from #204. There was no message from Pat.

***

It had been too busy at work and at home to write much at all. The starting of the second novel for Pat remained only in my head. I looked over my desk a few times during the weekend. I asked Kati if we should move it somewhere else. Kati thought that the desk should stay where it was. More importantly, she said it was nothing to worry about if Pat didn't call exactly on the day she said. Things happen. I knew that. But hearing someone else say it to me turned my Saturday mood from apprehensive to appreciative of the fact that Kati was here on this Saturday afternoon. Kati was here to stay. Yet that made it harder to leave for the close, even taking the car, which made the physical commute easier. I had become better at finding parking spaces. The return would be that much sweeter. Coming home from the crowds at #204, shaking off the constant currents of the big city and stepping into my place to be greeted and hugged by a warm, beautiful human being was better than I thought it would be. I was restored by the presence of someone who could relate to my workday, recognize my coffee scented body, and engage equally with my stories of the day. I was revitalized by a woman whose eyes told me she was truly glad to hold me for a minute or two, or as long as I needed. I still needed a shower, but that was about all that felt the same about that first night coming back to my apartment, our apartment.

***

Sunday crawled by at work. It was slow at times. I was able to clean and dust the retail shelves. That needed to be done more often than anyone did it. I volunteered myself just to get off the floor away from the customers. It had been a long haul since MIE started and I was tired of being "on" and "creating enthusiastically satisfied customers." I wanted to plan the week ahead in my mind. The apartment was already redone. It didn't change all that much. We moved the bed to create more space in the bedroom. I did have a lot of wasted space there. Other than that, we were done. I suggested we order pizza, stay in, and get used to the place tonight. And have as much sex as possible. The last part stayed in my mind only, but Kati agreed to the rest. I finally did make it home.

I was through the shift. I parallel parked the car with almost no room in front or

back of the bumpers. I had to admire my skill when I stepped out. As I did, a passerby

walking his dog commented to me that he loved our coffee. I drove home and so hadn't

changed out of my Cosmodemonic gear. It was a little thing, but it happened a good

deal. People forged a loyalty and connection with Cosmodemonic that brought them

back time and time again. I smiled and said thanks, but stepped quickly on my way. I

didn't want to talk to him about Cosmodemonic. I was done for the day, the week, and

had a Monday off awaiting me. Plus, I wanted pizza, wanted to stay in, wanted to adjust

to the newly remade place, and have lots of sex. Thank God, Kati and I thought a lot

alike.

***

I nearly fell out of my desk chair when the phone rang. I had been giving way

too much thought to my Cosmo Bravo award. The recognition felt great. It meant a

good deal in and of itself, but it stood in contrast to the silence from Pat. She could have

a least called over the last two weeks to update me. The actual physical sheet of paper

was still in my bag. With Kati moving in, I hadn't had time to put it anywhere else. But,

I decided to frame it. Earlier, I stepped into a frame shop located in one of those multi-

use building I liked so much. It wasn't the kind of shop I needed. Everything was too

expensive, and the frames were for pieces of art, not awards. I felt like I was out of

place and self-conscious about my appearance. I had no money to frame art. I looked

around long enough to make it appear that I was actually shopping and not wasting my

time. My other reason for leaving was that I wanted to be home when Kati got back

from her day at VanBuren. I wanted to greet her as she had greeted me Saturday night.

207

She had the place in shape and even had a candle burning to enhance the serenity and calming feel of our new place. I had offered to pick her up, but she knew I had things to do and said that she didn't mind her new commute that much anyway. So, she was taking the train to the Addison stop with all the cars of current and future Cosmodemonic customers who were ensuring my financial future. That worked for me.

After the frame shop and store and cleaners, I got home way before I needed to. I had it in my head to be there at 5:30. Kati closes at 5:30 but will get home closer to 6:30, depending on how the commute shakes out. That only occurred to me when I stepped in the door, put my keys in the chipped bowl by the door, and looked at the message light on the phone. Nothing. The workday was over for most people. And it was for Kati, who was just leaving work. I had scored a nice flower vase at a resale shop. I had decided to upgrade from the milk jug for obvious, aesthetic reasons. It was quickly rinsed set upside down to dry at the kitchen window. It occurred to me I had time to kill. Feeling a bit greedy with that time, I sat down to take advantage of it and felt a pang of near guilt opening the *Sketchbook of the Mind*. That was when the phone rang.

I regained my upright posture and reached it in three, rather than the usual four, steps. It was not Pat, but Natali. I was oddly relieved. It may have been that I was terrified of what Pat would say. "Not worthy of forwarding to my New Orleans publishing connection. Please pick up manuscript when convenient. Thanks, and continue writing, even though you suck."

There was a little more to Natalie's voice this time than just relief. Natali was now a confidant. No couple karma remaining to fog things up. She sounded good, and the news was also good on her father's condition. On that, she didn't elaborate. Only to say that for the time being he was having a friend stay with him. She and Scott would be back tomorrow, and this time, they would pick up the car. Scott had wanted to see some of Chicago before he left for Cleveland. Perfect. I wasn't sure when I was going to able to drop her car off anyway. Natali said they would swing by #204 and get the keys and that Scott wanted to see me for old time's sake and try some of this Cosmodemonic coffee he'd heard Natali talk about.

I hung up. Anita's play popped into my head for the first time in a while. It occurred to me in the next instant that Natali wouldn't have heard anything in the UP anyway. The third thought that appeared in my head was the similarity between Anita's play and my book. Each was looking for a home. A vehicle to allow the world to take part in our efforts. Good. I was not alone. I remember Anita's dark curly hair and eyes that poured intensity. She was the most noticeable on stage of any of Natali's friends from school. It would be a shame if she couldn't find a place for her play. Ned the affected warbler performed regularly at Lower Links. There was a lesson there for me. It might have sunk in except an overdue wave of disappointment hit me at not hearing from Pat. Kati was due home. She would get rid of that for me just by stepping in through the door. We would have tonight together. I had scored at Treasure Island and was going to grill some chicken thighs for dinner. Didn't think Karl would be thrilled at me using my hibachi on the wooden steps out back, but he has never said anything.

***

I graduated from MIE. A great peer group, baby. It was a boost to the ego to be a member. A good feeling came from us as a group. It struck me, possibly for the first time that everyone else in the class (except maybe Kerry) had chosen to come to Cosmodemonic. Me? It just happened. I did feel a sense of pride in that I had helped create that destination for them.

Still nothing from Pat. The week was flying by. If I didn't hear anything, I would call her on Monday.

***

Sunday morning and a day off.

I was listening to Kati's Cocteau Twins tape from the bathroom. She is in the shower with the door closed, but I can still hear it. Back from Osco with celebratory breakfast supplies. I already brewed and placed Sumatra in the thermos. It was a great rainy morning for coffee drinking. I woke up with cramps in my calf, which happened from time to time. Kati and I had a long session of sex this morning, after one like it last night. Plus, I was on my feet all week, and that surely helped to bring them on. I bought juice, bagels and cream cheese, grapes, sausage links, and a few butter croissants. I felt great coming off a painless shift at my Cosmodemonic yesterday. I would go in all next week and do all I can for the cause. I had a glorious Monday off to start. It had been the drill for a while. I still stuck to my routine. I did not expect to have two days off in a row on a regular basis. Kati and I were already a team. But not because we both slaved for Cosmodemonic. No. She and I insisted on clean bathrooms and kitchens but stop there. Neither of us were clean freaks about all rooms and places. She worked hard at

Van Buren and hated to be late. Swallowed coffee without cream or sugar. She favored the Sumatra over the Africans. Not a deal breaker, however as I remain loyal to the Africans. I loved the rain on a summer morning, as she did. Kati compliments me apropos of nothing. Just out of the blue. I fake a dismissive smile but know that I am great, special, intelligent, handsome, slim, and on and on. Why deny it?

"We earned dirty sheets." As the saying goes. I would take them down to the still new laundry room later. Or Monday. Not used to being home Sunday. On second thought, I bet the laundry room is busy. Kati brought a set anyway. Her being here has also uncovered or recovered or discovered a confidence in me. Just by her being with me, I feel more impressive at #204. Sarah and Dennis and Monica and everyone else knew it was my shift Saturday. They always did, but now when they were talking with me they stood just a little bit farther back from me, a more respectful distance, I thought. I knew that I could write for a living. Kati knew I could do better than steam milk for the masses. *I'm a writer.* I was not trying to *be* a writer. I had opened up to her more about *Back Outta the World* and how it came to be. How organic I felt the process was. There were people out there being writers who would remain clueless, even as their efforts are published and praised. The same goes for street cleaners, major leagues umpires, musicians, generals. The majority don't know what the hell they're doing. Why or why not. They are trying to be instead of just being. I am a writer. Not trying to be one. I finally believe that now.

Perfect timing. The tape ended. We were in synch. The lattice of coincidence could not be denied. I compiled the late, rainy Sunday breakfast. I never felt better.

***

Thursday, Mark had the day off. He requested it. Mikey G was closing, and Kati was not home yet. I got off at four and had a good day if not for the not so perfect timing of the surprise visit. It was perfect, however, to get back to the *Sketchbook of the Mind* and see the last entry from several days ago. It fit again because it made me feel better. I needed to feel better after the already mentioned surprise visit.

The surprise visit refers to the new regional manager coming into #204 about three hours into the morning rush. He was, in fact, carrying a small tape recorder. He spied me at once in my white shirt and tie in my usual expediting spot. When I saw him step into #204, I was transported back to the somewhat foggy Thursday of the IPO. He and I had shaken hands and traded names after a quick intro with Kerry via Candace. That moment was easily forgotten because of the event itself, the spilled cider, and the debauchery at Sterch's. I smiled and nodded but didn't feel I could step out of position for another handshake. The end-of-rush regulars were in line, so I thought it best to stay put and get this last line out. That is also why I hadn't yet cleaned the spilled mocha on the outside door. It was about knee high on the glass. I had noticed it a while before and saw no urgency in cleaning it up. Of course, just after the regional manager (Stan) made eye contact with me, he turned back to look at the door, and the spill launched earlier from a customer's to-go cup. The customer didn't seem to care, didn't get any on him, and so took off down the street. Again, no emergency on my part. Yet, it was obviously tape recorder worthy. Because regional manager Stan did a half turn to get another look at the offending spill, held the recorder to his mouth, and quickly dispatched something into it. But, he had to know that I had my reasons. That is why he gets paid, to know things without being told. I was in the trenches. Always have been. I knew where the

landmines were.

Once, at #206 during the morning rush, I almost stepped on a landmine but

defused it. I recall I was expediting and as such could step over to the La Marzocco and

fill up the espresso hopper for Tracy, who just a little behind on the bar. And damn if

the hopper didn't crack right at the base. Right where the hopper connects to the

grinder. I must have reached for the lid with too much force or something. A few beans

spilled, but I was able to shut off the bean flow with the sliding latch designed for just

such purpose (it was really there to shut off the bean flow so the grinder itself could be

emptied and cleaned). I remember muttering sarcastically to myself "I'm glad that

happened" and getting a giggle from Tracy. I think the humor was brought on by

confidence. I had been lead at Doug's store for a while and had led many a charge

across no man's land. In any case, the humor relaxed me. I cupped the bottom of the

hopper with my hand. I placed the hopped on the counter, quickly removing my hand to

spill as few beans as possible. I then grabbed a tall paper cup, inverted it, and then fit it

in the hole where the hopper went. It fit perfectly! A cast of sorts. I then put the hopper

gently over the tall cup and slowly opened the valve. It worked. I left the hopper mostly

empty but kept an eye on it. All this happened in about a minute. Tracy caught up. Next

day, Doug ordered a new hopper. In the meantime, I cleaned both hoppers before I left

for the shift and switched the way, way slower decaf in place of the regular. Just one

example of prioritizing and surviving in the trenches I could tell regional manager Stan.

Of course, we did not discuss that incident during his visit. He and I talked briefly. He asked me to run a tape from the register. I did, while he introduced himself to everyone

else. And quickly left. The spill was not discussed. I had Denis clean it.

***

All that time and effort devoted to Cosmodemonic. None on Pat and the

manuscript. I did leave a message on Monday. But it was Friday and three weeks past

drop off day. I thought of running to Liberation to see if Irene could tell me anything.

Not likely. And, she would likely try to get me to review another book, and I didn't

have the time.

***

It was good to see Natalie and also Scott earlier in the week. It looked like I

would have to get used to playing catch up sometimes in *Sketchbooks of the Mind*.

Living with someone could throw off your routine. Not a big deal. I gave Natalie and

Scott each a free half pound mark-out. Natalie's as payment for the use of her car and

Scott's as payment for long ago beers I took from his side of the fridge. I bought him a

grande to jump-start the drive back to Cleveland. If I thought Cosmodemonic would be

opening in Cleveland soon, I would have given him some Cosmo Bucks also. I thought

Washington DC and San Diego would be the next beachheads for the Master Roast.

Then, dare I say it, New York City.

***

Kati called to talk before she left Van Buren. She sounded a bit tired. I forget

how busy her Cosmodemonic was. She was also getting used to a new position, store,

214

and apartment. No wonder she sounded so run down. I was going through something similar of course. I thought she sounded better when we talked about the upcoming weekend.

I kept waiting for the other shoe to drop, so to speak. I went ahead and scheduled myself off on Sunday again. No protest from Mark or Mikey G. I closed Friday and Saturday. Still yet to officially celebrate the promotion with Kati. She and I were both making more than we had been and splitting expenses. A cab to Greek town, I thought, on Sunday. Maybe that carrot would give me the incentive to call Pat tomorrow morning. I'd send some postcards to the family and announce the promotion. Wasn't feeling ready to say anything about the book, yet.

We had a quiet night in. I made a decent weeknight dinner of Treasure Island jarred pesto and grilled a few bockwursts on the hibachi on the back steps. We split a bottle of Econo vintage white wine. Kati and I then settled in on the love seat and fell asleep somehow. Not a lot of room but we did it. Possibly overcome by all the changes we were going through. Also, gratitude induced fatigue may have set it. We were grateful to have each other. Our bodies found now familiar places, and they fit themselves together without trying.

***

It didn't make sense, but I wanted to send a postcard after I hung up with Pat. I had a good morning cup of coffee with Kati, and her energy was back. We had Sunday to look forward to, and that propelled me through the Friday and Saturday closes. We walked to the platform together and said goodbye under the rush of passing train above us. I wanted to get back and call as soon as possible before my confidence or

hopefulness brought on by proximity to someone who loves me no matter what wore

off. And that worked. I called Pat as soon as I got back to the apartment. She had been

meaning to get back to me. It was just that the manuscript was a little difficult to get a

handle on. It didn't possess a clearly defined beginning, middle, and end. All novels,

books, stories, fiction have a beginning, middle, and end. Pat explained that it took

longer to read than she expected. She explained to me the main character (me) lacked

direction, a clear motivation and was the least interesting of the three main protagonists.

She explained that if readers are to sympathize with and thus care about a character then

said character must have clear motivations. She explained to me that no, no, no, and

clarified that no, no, and no. I nodded to the receiver, as she simplified no, no, no.

However, there were no additional charges to me due to the extended time spent

reviewing the manuscript. But back to the manuscript. No, no, no. She said the

manuscript did possess the seeds of something unique. I managed to ask how I would

get my manuscript returned. She reminded me that the cost of returning it was included

in her fees, and that if I knew anything about writing a novel, I would have remembered

that.

I'm not sure that Pat actually said the last line. However, I do think I heard her

think that. I just wanted to send a postcard. I had to close later. I had no grand thesis to

defend my writing. No proclamations about how I was ahead of my time. About how all

great novels and novelists got rejected first then resurrected by the passing of time.

None of that. Besides that little bit. It would come. I did find an old postcard. It was a

Jim Thompson book cover, *Recoil,* I didn't remember where I bought it or why I hadn't sent it yet. Hadn't read the book, just liked the card. I'd send it to my old wannabe

writing friend back in Dayton. A good friend once. We corresponded from time to time.

I'd tell him about my promotion at Cosmodemonic. And that I finished my novel.

***

I did not call Kati. I had to let everything settle in. I did manage to have a great

day at work. I had to. It was my company now. I was going to help it grow, and in turn,

it was going to help me out. Yes, indeed. There was no subjectivity to the twenty

second shot. Well, there was a little. The acceptable range was eighteen to twenty-three

seconds. Earlier, the shots for my tripio were closer to twenty-three, but I dumped them

over my ice. I ran hot water from the La Marzocco over the shot glasses. I wanted them

to be clean. The line and retail floor were busy, but under control, so I headed to the

back to talk with Mark. He had waved to me to come to the back when he saw me come

in. Fuck, he's going to write me up over the spilled mocha recorded for all time by

regional manager Stan. That would fit with my current day, I thought, as I walked

slowly to the back. I picked up a lid from the floor behind the counter. I did not pitch it

at the nearby trashcan. I held onto it in order to throw it away in front of Mark. It would

allow him to witness my still present devotion to the Master Roast, even if I had

allowed a mocha to tarnish the front door of one of its outposts. Of course, it wasn't

about the spilled, recorded mocha. Mark had wanted to make sure I remembered to

come in early on Tuesday since he was leaving early to have his lunch with regional

manager Stan that day. It was on the monthly store-planning calendar, but he hadn't put

it down in the request book. I had, in fact, forgotten about it but would gladly come in

early on Tuesday. Not a big deal. He asked how Kati was doing and wanted me to tell her that a lot of the regulars missed her. And that a week from Sunday would be the

store meeting. Katherine said she'd like to sit in, her schedule permitting. Mark didn't

say this particular bit of news with much excitement. But, he perked up as he slipped his

customary leather jacket on and headed out. Kati had sounded tired yesterday. Today,

Mark looked tired. Thanking the Creator for my tripio, I headed for the floor, tossing

the lid in the trash before I did.

***

Kati was racked out from the day, the week. I showered off the Friday close and

soon would ease in next to her. She was just as beautiful asleep as she was awake. To

begin the next day correctly, I wanted to head to Nookie's and have an unhealthy, salty

breakfast of bacon and eggs. I might take my own thermos of coffee though. I'd done

that before. They thought I was just being cheap, but their coffee just was not good.

During the fortifying meal, I would discuss the rejection with Kati. Them bacon and

them eggs. Kati was asleep. It made no difference. She was here. Here in our apartment

in our bed. The talk with Pat earlier was slowly coming back. I lived alone here for over

two years. Tonight I couldn't imagine having had to come home and be alone.

***

I wanted to delay gratification. I wanted to prolong the anticipation of climbing

into bed next to Kati. And I did need to wind down a little. So, I would certainly have

the beer in the fridge as a reward. Just one left. Perfect. A Liene from last weekend.

Damn, did it taste great out of the bottle. I faced the future in great shape. All else being

equal. I had a career now. A career which in twenty years, if I'm still around, would be the type which people would wonder upon me telling them about it, "Why didn't you get in me on this?" I had a soulmate who believed in me. Or would until after our breakfast conversation. Ha-ha. I also believed in and respected her. She respected me also. Made a little bit of sense to use the word *respect* here, I think. A soulmate I respected. That may or not make sense, but that's what I wrote my *Sketchbook of the Mind*. I mean that she was meant for me. And I was for her. Not just for now, for the coming years. But it was not because of anything to do with Cosmodemonic employing us both. As Hooper told Brody in *Jaws*, "There's something else out there."

***

One more thing to get out of my system. One more thought to finish the beer to. My place next to Kati's warm, almost naked body awaits. It was the third part of the equation. That was, of course, my "mountain of futility, my slimy and always fecundating slag heap of wretchedness." That referred not only to *Back Outta the World*. But all of it. And even that reference needed work. But it referred to the writing I did before the road trip, the journals I kept that are still in my mom's basement, these *Sketchbooks of the Mind* and even what's to come. All written in earnest! Bogies, boils, chancre sores, pus dripped onto paper. But written in purity, in earnest effort to better who I am—and thus the world. Futile? Yes! Wait... No! In those lines was validation. I knew it was there. It was all in earnest. Change that to honest. It was an honest effort, above all. And all of it was as honest as it was hopeless! And I would take that deal. Carry on, Jay. Carry on! Good night.

***

219

Sunday morning! I had two days off in a row. I thought it would be the last time. When Mark and I were talking earlier about me coming in early on Tuesday, I felt that he was going to say something about managers typically not getting two days off in a row. But he stopped because he was asking me a favor in coming at noon Tuesday and then to close. But that is why I was planning on applying to any five-day store that came open. He and I both knew two days off in a row were not kosher. Especially if one of the days was Monday. All the new voicemails and announcements came in on Monday. I hoped to keep my Sundays. Or Saturdays. I could go in on Monday with Kati, arm and arm to fight in the trenches for Cosmodemonic. To win the war one latte at a time. Mark, for his part, didn't tell me up front that it wasn't allowed. He seemed to hold himself back from enforcing all the rules. He always kept his rebellious streak alive via the leather jacket and hearty appetite for pints. He looked over the schedule book as it sat on our desk in back and just stared at it lost in thought for a second. I clearly pictured him as he sat there a couple days later. He was weighing something else in his mind beyond whether to have me redo the schedule that week. I just breathed a sigh of relief when he said nothing. I would make sure he didn't have to give the schedule a second thought when I posted the next one.

Nothing was simple anymore at Cosmodemonic. Every day the stakes seemed to get higher. New stores were opening in the burbs. Our coffee was being served on an airline. The company is growing every day, literally. That lifts the water level. Not in the plunger pot, I mean. We got more and more store voicemails. And not just on Mondays. There were always some we had to listen to. Doug would have me listen even as a lowly lead at #206. Those days seemed like a million years ago. I was making great progress on the book and working for a small coffee company with stores in three cities. Now, my book was dead in the water, and it was getting harder and harder to recognize that small coffee company. New policies and procedures arrived on the voicemail constantly. Mark used to tell me what the voicemails said. Now, since there were so many, he just asked me to listen to them as soon as I could. And he left the brown envelope that followed the voicemails with the detailed explanation of said voicemails, in my mail slot above the desk. He knew I'd see them. He used to make time to sit and go over them with Rebecca. Maybe he trusted me more. Maybe he was just treating me as an equal. Maybe he just didn't care all that much anymore.

***

Kati had the ability to sleep in. A talent I lost in college, oddly enough. I never pulled an all-nighter, never slept until noon. I did pull a few all-nighters when I was working on *Back Outta the World*. Then again, the fuel to do so, as in the coffee, was so much better.

When she got up, we were both ready. The plan was to go to Osco together and food shop for the week. Just like her parents did. I fondly recalled the morning Kati and I shared during our Saturday in Charleston. Later, after more arranging and changing of the apartment, we might possibly be off to the lake and then the Red Lion. Kati and I talked a little about the rejection. Another reason it was good to be living together was that I could talk things over and get things out. She didn't seem overly concerned. Kati hadn't read the book but had faith in me. I could feel it. I knew she had faith in me the person. Faith in me that I could handle the future, whatever it brings. That future might include more novels and rejections, a career at Cosmodemonic, and all the ups and downs of a relationship together. Since that faith in me came first, I took it by extension she had faith in the book, even if she hadn't read it. Not that she's had a chance. She really did seem to like the "seeds of something unique" critique. Which I over analyzed to the point that it meant nothing to me. Neither good nor bad. Just unique. What could I do with that? Be that as it may, I was off the celebratory mood that flaming cheese brings and felt more like the common fare of bangers and mash and pints.

***

We were home from the trip to the lake. Kati was on the phone with her mother, filling her mother in on the big move in together. Kati's is actually doing more listening than talking. Her mom could really talk, I learned quickly. The fridge was full. A newly filled refrigerator filled the soul as well as future stomachs. It was assurance of survival, at least in this day and age. Kati and I shared stories of store day at our respective childhood homes earlier on our walk. We each had a sibling who would sneak items of their own choice into the cart if they were forced to go on the store excursion. And we shared the sibling who would hide a favorite item after said excursion was over, sneaking into the kitchen cabinets after the dust had settled and made their move. We discovered as we continued our increasingly animated and reassuring conversation that we had one more sibling in common. And they possessed the most soul-crushing talent of all. This sibling returned the empty, or nearly so, box of goodies to the shelf upon annihilating its contents. This was cruel beyond measure since it gave hope that since the box was still on the shelf, there were some prized Cheez-Its remaining inside, only to find upon opening that the box had been returned empty! Who could be so premeditated yet so falsely thoughtful toward others? At least in my house, there would

be two or three Cheez-Its left in the bottom of the box. But the culprit in Kati's' home

left absolutely nothing. We debated which was worse for a bit longer as we slowly

made our way to our favorite spot on the shore.

That was where it came out. My bile, my anger, my defense of *Back Outta the*

World. On the phone with Pat, I was diffident and courteous. I was pretending to be a

seasoned and professional writer. One who had been rejected before and could take it

because he understood the process. In fact, I had no idea what it took to get a

manuscript published. But it was important to me to impress upon Pat that I did, even as

I was being told that wasn't close to happening.

The lake had its own pace, always a little different than the day before. It was

cool and sunny at the shore that afternoon. Seagulls and dogs were everywhere. That

was where I dreamed of being a writer, a successful writer. I would be a household

name, rich, and living in Costa Rica.

I thought Kati and I were just talking about food. We were trying to decide

where to go for our day off reward. I no longer wanted to go anywhere in public and

suggested Comastro's, which was on the way home. Kati was good with it. That

decided I let out my cost, my time, my effort, my three years' work on *Back Outta the*

World. I had occupied that space at my desk for so many hours and now Kati, not Pat,

had to listen to what it meant to me.

"It's your own life. Not anyone's view or opinion of what your life should be. It

is up to you to live it. Then, for me, to write about it. My life will not be the result of someone else's expectations. My life is not a puzzle piece, left off to the side of the

puzzle with the other middle pieces, just because it is harder to find a place for it than

the edge pieces. That is me, the middle piece. That is a good description of my writing

in fact. The puzzle is not complete without my piece! Sure, it is harder to see its place.

Yet that difficulty validates its place on the rest on the cardboard next to the partly

completed puzzle."

Kati nodded a few times as I went on. Such a beauty in profile. So simple in her

beauty. No adornments needed. I recognized underneath that face, the expression she

wore when listening to her mother go on and on.

"Then just put my puzzle piece aside until you are ready for it. I leave the

obvious vague, as Van Gogh did. And I do it for a reason. I want people to think! Does

any story or novel really need a beginning, middle, and end? It isn't up to me to choose.

I write what I see, what I know. I can't worry about when my piece of the puzzle will fit

on the board. They can't finish without me, can they? I can't waste my time on how I

should write! I leave that to the ones who are being taught how to write. The editors and

namedroppers and reference makers and trail followers. Pat and others can purr and rub

the legs of those that came before them. I don't, I won't. It is my life, as I said before.

How can I even write for someone else? If my story doesn't comply, then that *is* my

story. Doesn't she get it? What it the point if I am not me? How to use my life, my point

of view best? Honest effort. All I want is for people to think. To use their heads. Is this

about me and my thoughts when they read my book? Yes, but only because it has to be.

But it is really about us all. If you try to see that hard enough. Try to think, at least. You

can wipe your eyes clean if you only try! I believe that, so does Jay. Through me, see.

See your own life and think about it, really consider where you have put yourself with those thoughts. Like, Jay. You know, the least interesting character in the book. You know, me."

I apologized to Kati after we left Comastro's. The delivery driver cooked for us. Kati smiled and said that is what we do for each other. Sometimes we just listen. And, she said she has had lots of practice listening to her mother over all the years, which I already knew.

***

I felt better after that lakeside diatribe. And much better after we had eaten, tossed out the takeaway trash and had a large glass of wine. Kati showed me some of her postcards with photos of Paris in the '20s and '30s. She loved the era and its look. We talked about maybe going to Paris one day. We tried not to talk about Cosmodemonic. That was so easy to fall into when we both worked there. Kati liked to put small colorful cloths or thin scarves over the two lamps in the bedroom to diffuse the light. It was a simple way to fashion a secretive feel to the bedroom. It was her way of recreating the photos she likes so much. Her lighted candles helped the ambiance, too. It helped keep my mind off the rejection, the book, and all that went with it. When we settled into bed in the half-light, we talked and eased slowly closer to each other, taking our time before making love.

***

I walked Kati to the Addison Station. I would close the next Monday, I was sure. I couldn't schedule myself off two days in a row, even if it wasn't premeditated.

Thursdays and Sundays as days off would be good for a while. As long as I had one full

weekend day to spend with Kati, that would be fine. I had mixed feelings as Kati

disappeared through the turnstile. It was a becoming a ritual already to see her off on

Monday morning. It was an event we could look back on to mark our early days living

together. It was close to nine, late for a start to the day for a Cosmodemonic open. Then,

I had to remind myself it wasn't an open, but a close. She would get home early then,

for a close. It didn't matter, she was gone. It struck me that I was walking back to the

apartment to find it empty. The walk back retraced my old routine, my former steps

when I was alone and writing so much of the time. It was a short stroll, and I would

travel back in time. I knew that as soon as I stepped back into the apartment, it would be

our apartment and this odd feeling would pass. It would be the present. Two empty

coffee mugs on the counter could tell that story all by themselves. But, I wanted to keep

walking, to prolong this time travel. I wanted to know, feel, and appreciate the

difference. And I had an excuse. I had wanted to buy an *Investor's Business Daily*.

There was going to be a short article about Cosmodemonic in today's edition. I had lost

that intention for a moment as I watched the crowd fill in behind Kati. She was off to do

her bit for Cosmodemonic. I was off to buy the *IBD* and read about the result of her, and

my, hard work.

 I made my purchase and went on with my own day. I sent a few postcards. I was

slowly telling everyone I'd moved in with Kati. I had too many brothers and sisters all

over the country to call or write to all in the same day. I spaced out the news in an effort

to keep the news fresh each time I told or wrote it. Kati only had to tell her mother and

let the news sprint forth from there. I did the usual Monday cleaning and laundry.

Didn't have to plan so far ahead on work food which helped. Kati didn't seem so food dependent as me and promised me any leftovers from her dinners without me. Thursday, we would dine together, and that would be our nice meal, perhaps with a glass of vino, as we did last night.

I did some sit-ups and jumped rope until I felt invigorated enough to call it quits. I had given up on more regular exercise to work on *Back Outta the World* seriously. I depended on my walks to keep the blood flowing and mind clear. That worked, but I wanted to tone my body more in proportion to time spent naked with Kati. I was out of the shower and cleansed as the midafternoon faded. I spent some time staring at the original notes and notebook that spawned *Back Outta the World*. Then, I remembered my Investor's Business Daily. I had about thirty minutes before walking to meet Kati. Plenty of time to pull a kitchen chair out to the back steps, have a cold beer, and read the article. I could pretend I was Thurston Howell.

***

Tuesday night and Kati was asleep. I missed Mark earlier at #204. He must have left just before I got in. I'm sure he didn't want to run any risk of running late to for his lunch meeting with regional manager Stan. And he knew I would be in and on time because I always was. The odd part was getting in at noon for close. But, it felt easy to go in because I didn't have to leave Kati and the options her company brings. Saturday would suck when I leave her to go in close.

***

I was left uneasy, with a bad taste in my mouth. And it wasn't from a thirty second, over-extracted shot. Mark and I were going to have a quick meeting on Thursday at Boru's to go over Sunday's store meeting agenda. Normally, we'd talk just before the meeting for a minute, even when I a lowly lead. That never made Rebecca happy because technically I wasn't supposed to have access to some of the stuff to be covered. But, Mark always liked me and paid just enough attention to the formalities to keep everyone above him happy. So, he gave me the highlights and let Rebecca stew about it. With Katherine due to stop in for our pending meeting, Mark and I decided to put on a unified front. As much as I was looking forward to renewing the Boru's tradition with Mark, he didn't seem too enthusiastic. We didn't have a lot of time to talk as Tony was running late again and the store was trashed, especially for a weeknight Wednesday shift. All Mark said was he'd meet me after my shift Thursday and that he needed help with Phil.

***

I had to note the time and day more often now. My own *Sketchbooks of the Mind*, reflecting my own life were becoming scattered. It was Wednesday night, and Kati was asleep. I told her she worked too hard. Of course, I did the same thing and often wondered why I didn't listen to my own advice. As I adjusted to missing days in my *Sketchbooks of the Mind*, I felt the need to put in a day to orient my thoughts. I didn't keep a journal to compile the story of my life, as such. I found that I was really tracking my mind. Hence, *Sketchbook of the Mind*. Although I'd been journaling for years, I just named these notebooks a few months or so before. The physical chronology of my life is not what I want to catch. The progress of my mind—Progress?—was what found most interesting. But the where and when were also important. With everything

else going on, I was finding it took more time to figure that out based on my last entry.

***

I was on the Clark bus heading in for the Thursday open. Kati was up with me

and thankfully had coffee ready. The bus was crowded with commuters. I would give

up my seat soon. I had a shorter trip than most. Kati said goodbye standing at the door

wearing a white V-neck T-shirt. I said it looked familiar and she replied that she had

found it in the corner of the closet when she was moving in. Still in the package. As we

hugged goodbye for the day, I ran my hands underneath it to feel her body. Warm and

smooth skin. I stopped at her hips and rested my hands there on the slight curve. Over

her shoulder, I saw the futon. We kissed for a second more, but a door opened on the

floor above us. Thoughts of being late for work ended. So I ended up on the twenty-

two, heading in to work. A mother and baby got on. *Now that's a full workin' day, lad.*

Couldn't resist a Monty Python reference. No one else seemed interested in giving up

their seat. I would. It was the thing to do.

***

Mark said that Cosmodemonic stock options statements were due at the end of

the week. Kati should be eligible soon. I still had to get up to speed on the stock market

and all it means. There was a lot to learn.

***

229

Kati was off to work, and I had my errands done. I felt great after morning sex. We had the time. Our only time really. I felt empty, yet full of hope. I was doing the laundry, the V-neck T-shirt included and waiting for the mail to arrive. I wanted to see if I could figure out what the options would mean in money terms. I think I still had those library books. Might have taken them back. Mark didn't seem too anxious about his. He planned to pay off some credit cards right away. I was going to save mine for the shack in Costa Rica on the water. Complete with cot, desk, and one lamp. We had some quick pints at Boru's. More methodical than celebratory this time. Boru's wasn't much to look at, but most, if not all, bars were better in the midafternoon. I opened so got there before four. Mark arrived just after me, and we found a clean table by the wall. A few other people, all at the bar, were there with us. No jukebox or TVs on. A bar poised for the evening held promise. The end of the previous night's ugliness was mopped, wiped, and swept away. The first beers were always the best tasting and most meaningful. Even from the plastic pitcher and flimsy cups at Boru's. They didn't have to be grand. That would be put in by the drinkers. I finished my first in short order and ran to call Kati. I said I was going to be at Boru's but wanted to make sure she could meet me after her shift. She said she'd rather stop by our place and change. Then she would meet me at La Bamba. Sounded good. I would be hungry. Boru's was not a place to dine.

Mark hit the highlights of his lunch with regional manager Stan. A re-districting was coming. Regional manager Stan hired a new district manager besides what's his name. He was not sure if Katherine was staying with #204 or not. Candace might bail. Seemed they wanted a new training module for the expansion to come. Less coffee training, more money counting. I thought quickly of my autograph-seeking with the

Coffee God. More stores here. More stores in other cities. Lots of opportunities. Mark

had to find a way to get rid of Phil. New recap sheets and voicemail codes for Monday.

New ordering forms. No more deposits done in pastry bags. On and on. I sipped my

second plastic pint and listened. Nothing really surprised me all that much. Most of it

sounded good. I was into Cosmodemonic for the all I could get. At least until I could

get to Costa Rica. And, I mentally added to my shack as I listened to Mark. I added

electricity and a coffee maker. Mark said that I would "be fine." I liked the sound of

that of course, even if I wasn't entirely sure what it meant. Best of all for me was that a

five-day store was soon to come open. I thought Van Buren. But before I could even

ask, Mark told me it was Illinois Center. I didn't care to ask why it was coming open. I

was going to apply and have my five-day schedule. The next sip at my plastic pint was

deeper and fuller and tasted even better. The first beers, plural, always taste better. And

so, I asked just before leaving to meet Kati, "Do I just leave Phil off the schedule?"

A good, buzzed stroll up Clark followed my meeting with Mark. I had to

announce some of the new procedures at the meeting Sunday. No biggie. A chance to

demonstrate my leadership skills in front of Katherine. But, that meant going in for an

hour or so on Sunday. My Sunday with Kati. Damn. I was not going to get paid for it. I

was now on salary. There went my buzz. Wasted the best Boru's has to offer. I had to

close Monday. So, I'd figure out what to do when I talked to Kati. Maybe L'escorgot

again on a Sunday after the meeting?

***

It hadn't come yet. I hoped it would arrive as I was writing in my *Sketchbook of the Mind*. The noise of the mail arriving would interrupt me at a critical part of note writing. Then, I would have to refocus and keep writing or run downstairs for the mail, trusting I would remember where I was. That is how it usually worked. When the writing was going well, I got interrupted. And when I was stuck, no suitable distractions arose to give me an excuse to step away. No need to worry since there had been no noises from down on the landing. I had to head into #204 just as Kati was ending her week. The Illinois Center would be mine. I could ditch the weekend-close drill. I closed all three weekend nights when I started at #206 for about a year straight. I didn't complain. No wonder Doug loved me.

***

At least Kati loved me. All joking aside. She said she would wait up for me. That would get me into, though, and over my shift. It would be Bill, Chuck, and Boston Dennis tonight. We could handle it. It would be worth it to get back here later. Last night was okay. I was worn out from the open following a close and then the long walk to La Bamba after several pints. Kati was at La Bamba, and there was no game. We sat by the fountain, which was our spot. Going out twice a week worked for me. Kati talked about Cosmodemonic. I was done with it for the day but listened. It was what we did. Her manager at Van Buren freaked when a brewer went down. They had the big, old, canister drip brewers. The pots looked like metal butter churns with handles. It was a bad day. Kati said she wanted to call Gayle and see how she was doing. Maybe she was right about Carmela. I said it was a good idea to stay in touch with friends. Of course, it was something I never did. I barely kept my family in the loop. I told Kati that Mark

232

said hello again. I didn't tell her how Mark seemed to be acting less and less interested in #204.

***

I didn't want to be burdened with money's inevitable outcome: acquiring things, accumulating accumulation.

***

Friday afternoon, the options statement didn't come. My rejected manuscript did. I had hopes that it would not be sent back. I fantasized that *Back Outta the World* kept coming back into Pat's world. Her head, I mean. In that, it got to her a little more each day, and she had to read parts again. Then she read the whole thing again. All the time not letting me know. That she now saw what I was saying. That it was unique because it was from me. We are all unique, but the seeds of my writings took time to take hold. That my manuscript was on the way to New Orleans for review. That she would only let me know when I needed to know anything. And that would only be after her connections had approved the next step in getting *Back Outta the World* published. That was the imaginary outcome I had sown in my mind. I liked it. It filled my head on the bus and at work. But the reality came Friday after I left for work. Kati put in on my desk. I saw it there lit by Kati's candles when I got home Friday. I stuck it under my desk on top of a pile of some old magazines. It belonged there for a while. Kati said she thought of calling me when it arrived. But she knew how busy Fridays could be and thought better of it. Excellent judgment on her part.

233

Besides excellent judgment, Kati had excellent financial sense. We split the bills, paid the bills, and bought the food together. The #204 store meeting was a couple hours off. Kati was talking to Gayle in Portland, and I was looking over the "Revised Unit Procedure" handout Mark was having me discuss at the meeting. Not much about coffee. But no need to change a winning formula. That was my ace. I was the coffee resource at #204, just as I was at #206 before that. Cosmodemonic is a coffee company. Anyone could enforce, handle, and apply these new procedures. After the meeting, I was going to ask Katherine for an interview for the manager position at Illinois Center. I had no desire to go to the meeting later. It was easier when I was already physically at #204 and had no choice. It was easier when Kati was not there. Even the otherwise wonderful reality of her living with me, sleeping with me, sharing expenses wisely with me, had a downside. She had to be here in order for me to have to leave her on a Sunday afternoon. She worked in the morning on Monday. I didn't. I worked in the evening. She didn't. We made the money work. We could afford to go out on this glorious town a couple times a week—at least out to cheaper, nearby places in our neighborhood of this town. But, we didn't see a lot of each other. Not enough anyway. So, it made me want a five-day store more than ever. My seven-day store experience would make a five-day store seem easy. My coffee knowledge would enhance the Illinois Center. I'd never been to that location but was sure I would know the most about the coffee when I got there. So, it was decided. Kati and I would go to the Thai place she likes before the meeting, part ways, and spend the evening relaxing back home. Monday I would prepare for my interview, wherever and whenever it would be.

***

I felt good this morning, even if it was a Monday. Almost great, in fact. I got a lot of sleep. I had an appetite, and I'd put a few things of mine back in place in the apartment. Kati had moved or changed a few things in the apartment we hadn't discussed beforehand. I had a calendar on the back of the bathroom door. It was an odd place to hang a calendar, but I would always look at it when I was drying off my body or face after a shower. It was a habit I used to get my week planned. I must have had one up there since I first moved here and started working at #206. I needed it to keep the days straight since I worked so many weekends and would have a Tuesday and Thursday off one week and Monday and Wednesday the next. I was conquering Chicago alone in those days, adjusting to life in the big city. I wasn't sure when she took it down. It may have even been a week ago. I wanted it back up. I'd check for it among the empty cardboard boxes that I was planning to take to the alley later. On that note, it was sunny but almost cool in Chicago. Kati was safely off to work. I had some things to do. It occurred to me that I was still getting to the *Sketchbook of the Mind* on a regular basis.

I ran out to buy some postcards. Kati was a good example as she communicated with her family, mother that is, on a regular basis. I would send these cards to family. I needed to do this more. Kati called Gayle yesterday to see how she was doing in Portland. Of course, they talked about Van Buren. Kati and I tried but could not avoid some talk about Cosmodemonic on our Sunday night time on the couch. Gayle said people on the west coast thought Cosmodemonic was putting the local coffee houses out of business. It might or might not have been true, but the official Cosmodemonic gospel was that when they open stores the interest in coffee spikes and generates more business for local coffee places. Gayle also said that Carmella did lose it from time to time but don't take it personally. I had the Illinois Center interview with the district manager, Kyle, on Thursday. I didn't lose it when things went bad. He'd see that if he didn't know that already. Cosmodemonic liked to do important things on Thursdays. Unless it was my imagination. Not likely. Cosmodemonic was not the type of company that did anything randomly. That was how we became the largest coffee company in the country now. Customers asked me things like "When are you putting one in my neighborhood?" or "How do I buy a franchise?" more and more. I smiled and gave them a card with the main company number on it. I wished I could tell them more. Now there are more official sources of information on the goings on at Cosmodemonic than Dennis-the-Juice-Guy.

I felt I was bound to get Illinois Center. My MIE class had three or four who were already managers. And we were peers. If the people from my class were making manager, then it followed that I would also. And that was just one of many reasons I had this position in the bag. However, Mark did say at Boru's that #204 was not going to be a training store for the time being. That might keep me there. Mikey G is a strong lead but didn't seem to want to move up. Then again, Allyson from #206 could take my place, and #204 could run with two leads until I was replaced. All kinds of options. Kerry could easily take my place. I know Cosmodemonic likes to move newer managers around. I could spend all day trying to sort it out. Come to think of it, where was Dennis-the-Juice-Guy when you needed him?

***

"To prove yourself to the world through writing is impossible unless you spend time with each and every one of your readers." I found this sheet of paper folded in the back of a *Sketchbook of the Mind*. Not sure of its origin. It was not attributed to anyone, but I knew it was me. Sometimes I did that. Find whatever sheet, piece, or scrap of paper is at hand and put down what is in my head. Nothing to define the paper itself. But it was folded neatly in the back and smashed flat. Hence, it stayed put until it slid out as I put the *Sketchbook of the Mind* in my bag. "One person at a time. It is impossible."

Not sure what to make of it. It must have been written on the way home from dropping off the manuscript at Pat's, or sometime soon after. Maybe it's from copy paper I took from the regional office on a break. I would have been feeling that way around them.

***

My favorite Brown Elephant tie awaited. One good thing about Monday close was that it could be actually slow. I could clean the retail shelves or wipe out the oily coffee drawers. And that would keep me away from the customers. I could do a rough draft of the schedule. Mark said he would talk to Phil over the phone. No need to put his name on the one slot this week. The jokes about the Master Roast wouldn't seem so funny anymore.

***

I just made the twenty-two. I guess I didn't hear the mail come. I checked the slot on the way out. I had music on when I was cleaning. My Cosmodemonic Initial

Public Offering Options statement is here. I didn't want to take it on the bus. Ran it

back upstairs and tossed it on my desk. I had to hurry to the stop. It reminded me of the

days when I was deep into working on *Back Outta the World*.

***

Back at my desk Tuesday, and once again, Kati was off to Van Buren. We made

love last night, and I didn't think we changed positions afterward. She woke up to the

alarm from her side of the bed. Her right leg over both of mine. Where they met a film

of sweat had formed. It was no longer as cool as yesterday was. The sheet was at our

waists and Kati on her side, her head on my shoulder.

A double bed would be a must for the shack in Costa Rica. And a ceiling fan. I

might even upgrade to a bungalow or cabana. The ceiling fan in the bedroom here

worked wonders. There was no AC in the apartment, and by that time of year, the

Midwest humidity and heat dragged on. I was letting my mercenary side take over. Why

not? I dug up Kati's calculator this morning. Mine had gone dead a while before. Once

in a while, I'd use #204's if I needed to figure out when or how much to pay on a bill.

The calculator was in the only unpacked cardboard box remaining. It was under the bed

but worked when I hit the button. I opened my options statement yesterday and quickly

looked it over. Today, I was examining it more closely. I had options on 268 shares of

stock set now at a value of $8,408.50. So in three years, I'll get at least that. If I

understood options, it meant I could do what I wanted with them, more or less. So, as of

today, I was planning to buy forty more shares of Cosmodemonic at $17 now valued at

$1,255.00. So, even as I dreamed of being a writer, the practical side in me said to keep

238

the job for three more years. I'd be vested in even more shares and options by then. I think that I could keep my stake going even at twenty hours. We got health insurance at twenty. Kati was more interested in that crap than I was. She asked me about it the other day, in fact. For today, my only concern was prolonging my relationship with Cosmodemonic. As long as I didn't use Dennis's Death Ray on the I'm-still-waiting-for-my-iced-latte-lady, I would be fine. Think of it. If I stayed long enough to get all that stock, I could keep writing and not kill myself. I could make it happen, Pat or not. It was almost too good to believe. All I had to do was slave for the Master Roast (sorry, Phil). I had shown great ability to do that already. For two and a half years. Nobody, but nobody in Dayton knew Cosmodemonic when I told them I was taking a job with them. No need to put pressure on myself. How could I fail? I could write without worry. Until we have our shack or cabana in Costa Rica, I would just have to learn to manage my portfolio. We had been assigned a broker. One in San Francisco. Good. I assumed they would know what to do. To think of more and more stock bringing more and more money was madness. But, I couldn't help it. I just had a quick daydream. Kati and I were at our cabana in Costa Rica. We were poolside taking in the afternoon sun. Her legs darker brown than they are now and just mouthwatering. I had on a Hawaiian shirt and sunglasses, cocktail in hand. We had nothing to do until dinner later. The dinner would be with my publisher or publicist. Daydreams don't get too specific. But, to keep thinking of more and more options to cash in was madness. *Remember your entry about accumulation!* Yes, settle down. I'd plan carefully to have just enough and know just when to quit Cosmodemonic in order to fulfill my calling as a writer. *That's better.*

Chapter Seven

Thursday before my interview for the manager position at Illinois Center. It would be at two at the same office where I had my MIE classes. I thought about going to a museum after the interview. I still wanted to see the Van Goghs and Hoppers and Picassos again. I remembered the first time I took the El from my apartment to the art museum and saw Blue Boy. It was a milestone day for a boy from Dayton. That day, if all went well, it would be a great way to kill time until Kati got off. Maybe we would have a beer and talk about our days before we headed back. In the world of Cosmodemonic, an assistant at a seven-day store usually moved up to a manager at a five-day store. If my MIE classmates were any indication, I'd have a great shot. They were my peers and had a great track record at getting their own stores. My own Brew Generation. That didn't work. I was only a little bothered by not knowing new district manager Kyle. I hope he at least drinks coffee. It was odd to me that he interviewed me and I felt like he was the new guy and outsider.

The interview took longer than I thought it should, or would. I didn't know if that was good or bad. In any case, I'd close Friday and Saturday and Monday, and we'd have Sunday off together in between. I felt good about the interview, even if it drained me. I was nervous, and in that state, it was hard to recall details and specifics. I had to skip the museum but met Kati just in time for her usual train back. Kati was getting cleaned up, and I forced myself to remember more of the interview, but because I was forcing it, the well was dry.

***

Friday morning I was back from mailing postcards to family. I didn't say I had

an interview upcoming. I didn't want to jinx myself. I was just trying to stay in touch. I

somewhat replaced working on *Back Outta the World* with writing postcards. Hey, it's

writing.

I walked for a while around the neighborhood after I mailed the postcards. I was

almost back home and mentally planning my workday when I passed the Jardin. It

smelled of frying meat: greasy, chunky, floury, wet. I saw a beer sitting on a table

inside. The bottle was sweating in the midday heat. It looked better than any beer I

could recall seeing in my life. Because I couldn't have it.

***

The close was a good one Friday and better Saturday. In spite of how busy it

was both nights. Or sometimes because of it. There was no time to lean. If you were

busy, then you tended to do things without even noticing. I thought Sarah should look

into MIE, or at least being a lead. She was at #204 forty hours. Why not? It was

working for me. I knew that some stores had two leads. I knew Mark would hate to

have me go. But, if I could at least get Sarah interested in being a key holder that might

help him a bit.

Cosmodemonic was in my head too much. I used to write my novel, write in my

sketchbooks, and barely mention it. As I looked back in my Sketchbook of the Mind, I

found an entry on every page—at least. That day was going to be different! Kati and I

were breaking free from the Master Roast and heading to some friends of hers that she

made when she first moved here. It was a couple throwing a backyard party for no

241

reason. Sounded great. It wasn't too far from Natali's. I wondered how she was. Her

dad? Needed to make time to check in.

Kati and I needed the getaway. She seemed tired a lot, and I was in a rut

creatively. We had been at each other for the first time in our relationship. I put my

calendar back up, and that didn't go well. I should have explained why, but couldn't

really. I needed to clean the kitchen while she did our room. It was too small to let it get

dirty, and we agreed that it was better to come back from a party to a clean place. I

would bring Kati's friends some coffee as a party favor. Easy choice and free. Of

course, if I brought it, that would lead to a conversation about where Kati and I worked.

And then we would end up talking about work anyway. At least by then, I didn't have

to explain what Cosmodemonic is. More and more people already knew.

***

The party was great; we drank beer in the sun all day. I didn't feel as bad as I

should. Kati felt worse this morning. It was still worth it though. For a second, I thought

she was serious when said she was calling a doctor. Our hangover that morning was

something else we shared. I walked her to the station. She seemed better by the time we

got to the platform. I was sure she felt way worse than me because she had a workday

ahead. I didn't, and I was glad we got everything done yesterday. I didn't have a lot to

do so I thought I might go back to bed. I'd still have time later to get to Treasure Island

for the Monday bargains.

***

A call from Kati woke me up. She asked if I was sleeping. I had set the alarm

clock but had about ten minutes to go when she called. Kati said she made a doctors'

appointment for Friday morning. I was still too cloudy to get all the details before she

had to get off the phone to run to get the five-shot mocha line out the door. She didn't

sound hungover, or even tired. Good to hear Kati's voice though and the guilt of her

being at work got me out of bed. I took comfort that I wasn't alone. I needed that when

I wasn't feeling quite so good about myself. Plus, what helped my frame of mind the

most was that Kati said she would have gone back to bed if she were in my place, too.

***

Monday night was another slower night of cleaning. I did the condiment stands

again. I was able to shut one down early. I took it apart and tossed everything into the

sanitizer. I had the coffee order to do, and so I did that while the milk thermoses and

condiment shakers were going through. There was one box of four five-pound bags still

not put away from Thursday. That never would have happened if Mark were still paying

attention. However, I put the coffee on the shelf in its proper place. Every five-pound

bag has a roasted-on date, and the newest was put behind or to the left or even under the

older. It all depended on the space available. I rotated the espresso even though there

was never any danger of it going bad. Not even close. I did the same with Christmas

Blend. Maybe the Decaf Espresso or a Swiss water processed decaf varietal would be in

danger of expiring. If a whole bag was in danger of going bad, we simply used it to

grind for coffee of the day. I hated it when there were three or four different coffees for

the morning rush. That situation would be precipitated by the above-mentioned scenario

of multiple coffees due to expire. It wasn't that big a deal to some partners, even at

#204. They didn't bother changing the sign indicating the regular varietal of the day. I always changed it. I always wanted the right coffee with the right sign. Most customers didn't care all that much if the sign was Costa Rica Tarazu and we were serving Panama Boquette. But it bothered me enough to quickly grab the correct sign and replace it, even if it was in the middle of the rush. After all, we were a coffee company. One thing I didn't mind is when there was maybe just a half pound of Sanani, Harrar, or Sulawesi set to expire. That was not enough to grind, brew, and change the sign for. It was just enough, however, to fit in the drawer of my freezer at the apartment. Be that at it may, I was glad the box the coffee was shipped in was around. Empty, it served as a good cover the for the cleaned and closed condiment stand. I cleaned the other after close, as usual.

I noted the above in my Sketchbook of the Mind since, as expected, Kati was asleep. Sunday beers in the sun and then going into work caught up to her.

***

Store #204 actually received a voicemail from HS in the Monday messages. He didn't ever leave voicemails on the storewide system. But there was some concern about the stock value going down. He essentially said not to worry, although I didn't quite understand why. I tended to get anxious whenever people talked about Cosmodemonic stock because I still didn't know enough about it all. When I was anxious, my memory was not as sharp. Also, regional manager Stan left a message informing us that we did, in fact, have three district managers now. Katherine, Kyle, and Ted, who ran the country's busiest store right here in Chicago for as long as I'd been with Cosmodemonic. Since he was an old-timer like me, I hope he ended up being

my district manager at Illinois Center. I wondered if there was a lunch with regional

manager Stan in my future.

***

Thursday morning meant that I had today and Sunday off. All I asked for is a

postcard in the mail. A reply to one of mine. I had seven brothers and sisters and my old

writing colleague who could possibly have sent a response. I usually called my mom

since all of her children had moved out, and she lived alone. She had for a while. I still

thought about writing and needed to start something. I couldn't look over *Back Outta*

the World just yet. It sat under my desk at shin level. Mornings like these at my

apartment, I still got echoes from writing the novel. I wrote so much on days like this.

Plus, the writing would help to keep my mind off the Illinois Center. From the sound of

things, it might take a while for the Cosmodemonic wheels to turn. New district

managers, new districts, new stores—the Cosmodemonic Empire rolled on.

***

I couldn't resist a walk to the lake. It was hot, and the lake was too close to say

no. I could get some vanity sun, and that would keep my mind off things. I didn't start a

new piece of fiction, so it wasn't like I was running away from anything. I noticed a

house I had never noticed before. It was old. It must have looked out over the lake

before the city and highways came this far. This was the suburbs eighty years ago. But

the house had survived. I loved the porch. It wrapped around all the front of the house

and about half of one side. Best of all, there was a ceiling fan above the chairs in front. I

245

imagined a spring day with clear skies and clean air. A breeze. I was sitting on that

porch, healthy. With money. That was what that house, porch, and outside ceiling fan

said in their day. I thought that chair was for me. And that time more for me. I belonged

under that fan, feeling the slight breeze on my exposed arms.

***

Got back to the place and heard the phone ringing. The entry hallway echoed

since it was mostly just painted wooden steps. I heard the phone halfway up the first

flight and knew it was Kati. She wanted to stay in tonight, not go out. Good to hear her

voice. I didn't even think for a second it was district manager Kyle. Maybe a half

second. In that case, I would make a decent pasta. Got a small block of real Parmesan at

Treasure Island on Monday. Needed to run over to La Commercial and get a semi-good

white wine. It is all they have. The semi-affordable. Then maybe a movie. Kati said she

still felt a little off but wasn't going to the doctor for it anymore. I had forgotten she

talked about it.

***

I always knew how many beers were in the fridge and how much coffee was on

hand. I honestly couldn't remember the last time I had to buy coffee though. There were

four beers left over from the weekend. I knew that on Monday, Tuesday, and

Wednesday. But I didn't drink them. Tonight, I knew it was time for one. I picked up

Kati at the station. The person you are looking for stands out in a crowd. I think their

own special movements catch the eye before the eye recognizes the face. I knew it was

Kati before she emerged from the crowd of commuters coming out of the gate at

246

Addison. Of course, I noticed the dumb ass guy who watched her from behind as she approached me. She almost jumped into my arms and squeezed me tighter than usual. I wanted to flip the dumb ass off but held on to her instead. Over and over again I saw how well we fit together. For that embrace and all others, I barely bent my knees to meet her at the perfect level to take in her upper back, just below where the arms meet the shoulders. And that angle allowed me to straighten my knees for just the slightest lift. That lift expressed how happy I was to see her. Not an affected twirly Hollywood lift, but just enough for her to feel it. And for me to do it naturally, without effort, like it was meant to be.

The beer tasted great. Liene in the red and white bottle. Kati was cleaned up. I had dinner under control. Kati said she had to call her mother in Charleston. And it had to be before they had their dinner. At first, I was a little irritated. I knew how long her mother can stay on the phone and that a lot of those calls turned out to be not very urgent after all. But then I remembered the four cold beers in the fridge. I would simply relax with one while Kati called home.

***

Friday morning and I had two more closes for Cosmodemonic until I'd have Sunday off. I told myself that I wouldn't hear anything before Monday about my interview. Monday was when things were announced so I was not going to think about it if I could help it. Kati was gone again. I was not missing out on writing as much as I anticipated. Then again, I wasn't seeing Kati as much as I anticipated. We had a good walk after dinner. She wanted some ice cream, so we went out in search. Not that I hated the idea. We didn't talk much at all. Kati and I both seemed to be sizing up the nicer apartment buildings we passed. I think we might need a transition place to live before Costa Rica. Our place was great but small. She pointed out a park I had never noticed. It, too, was quite small.

I had a feeling that Kati wanted to tell me something. Maybe she wanted to tell me that she didn't like the place after all. And that, if I got promoted, she hoped we could look over one of these nicer places and consider moving. I usually took my walks in the day. My walking at night was done to get somewhere. But last night was relaxing and soothing. Kati was likely talked out after the almost hour-long conversation on the phone earlier with her mom. Kati became restless and spent some of the time on the landing. At one point, she even stepped in and motioned for me to open the wine and pour her a glass. She was in full listening mode, and later I thought more than anything she just wanted to walk in silence for a while.

Laundry day could no longer be confined to Mondays. There was always some to do for the weekend. I thought I might finally look over Pat's notes on *Back Outta the World* between loads. I was ready. I thought I was feeling the desire and could make the time to go back to writing seriously. Kati and I had settled quickly into our life together, and it had its own rhythm. With that came the confidence that the writing would follow.

Chapter Eight

"Natali never got pregnant," I said when she told me the result.

Kati and I had talked about adopting someday a long time in the future. We discussed adopting, among other options, because she had a double uterus and couldn't get pregnant. But it was a conversation that included many other details of our future together also. Now it was too much to think about. I had to close later. Kati bought a pregnancy test and used it the previous Friday. She knew. She bought the test to confirm. Kati told me over coffee Saturday morning. The remark about Natali may have been the worst thing I've ever said. That was the least of my worries.

***

I had my Sketchbook of the Mind with me. We were at the appointment Kati made to confirm the positive test. I was having trouble getting things organized in my head. She was told by their family doctor, an old friend of her dad's, a long time ago that a double uterus precludes a pregnancy. I remembered the talk when Kati stepped out on the landing to talk to her mom before dinner. It was during that conversation that her mom confirmed Kati's memory of his diagnosis. The old quack was wrong, but he was already retired.

I had no idea what to do. I didn't know if I'd even held a baby before.

The magazines in the waiting room didn't help. We needed so much stuff. We'd have to get a bigger place so we can outfit a room. Boy or girl? We couldn't start buying things until we knew. We'd need to get ready. I had no idea we'd have to buy all

this stuff to get ready to have a baby.

When and what should I tell the family? Kati's mom knew. She had to because

Kati had to ask if that doctor was still around. He was no use now. Kati found this

doctor from a partner at Van Buren who had a toddler. I had just thought Kati was tired,

but she told me that she had suspected for a couple weeks. Plus, she had done some

reading beyond what she was told years ago in Charleston. A didelphys uterus could

mean premature births and early miscarriages were more likely. It was hard to be sure

because it could appear to be just like a heavy period. I knew all this now, but I couldn't

tell anybody in my family anything. If I told them about Kati and me, I sure as hell

didn't say we were planning on starting a fucking family. Maybe I wouldn't have to tell

anyone anything. It was not a done deal. The double uterus was not ideal for carrying a

baby to term. Maybe I could just wait and hope it didn't, that it fixes itself.

Kati was filling out forms next to me. She had more time to deal with this. She

seemed strong here and now in the carpeted, lamped, and end-tabled waiting room. But,

I felt like everyone in the office knew we didn't plan this.

***

We would be going back there a lot. To the OBGYN so they could check on

Kati. She was pregnant for sure. And apparently in the left uterus. But the Charleston

Quack was right in that having a full-term delivery isn't likely at all. It must have

happened during the Charleston weekend from the timing of things. And by early

spring, there would be a baby. A baby, here in the apartment. Maybe. Possibly. If all went well. Kati was a mix of joy, beauty, and worry. I knew I was supposed to be a

writer, but words escaped me. Helpless came to mind. Terrified. Mad. Angry. Why me?

***

I was picking up where I left off a week or so ago. I didn't know what to do,

where to go. Maybe that was why I had had the longtime habit of keeping a Sketchbook

of the Mind. I couldn't tell anyone I was close to about the pregnancy. We didn't send

postcards out to everyone saying that Kati and Jay had moved in together and so expect

a baby in nine months. I couldn't tell anyone because there was a distinct possibility the

baby wouldn't carry to term. I read some of what Kati had given me. But these types of

discussions were long gone in my house by the time I was growing up. People in my

family, cousins, neighbors, and friends, stopped having kids by that time. If I told

everyone and something happened, then... I didn't know. I wasn't sure how my family

would feel. No one had met Kati. We should have visited. If only she'd gone to St.

Louis with me. Then everything would have been okay. If only we hadn't gone to

Charleston. If only her mom and dad didn't go shopping on that Saturday morning. If

only her old-fuck doctor in Charleston knew what he was talking about.

I did have my Sketchbooks of the Mind to tell. No one would see or read what I

wrote in them. A lot like my fiction. I needed a new one soon anyway as I was filling

this one up fast. I'd go for a different style. Just wanted a change in format.

But now I'd have to think about things before I did them. Not a lifestyle I had

ever been good at. A thought to call Natali popped into my head. Maybe. My mind kept

racing ahead like a dog, your favorite dog as a kid who's busted off his leash. It was free and running straight into a busy rush-hour intersection. The dog had never been off

the leash before and had no idea what moving cars were. Those were my thoughts now.

Kati had already been told she would have to take it easy. The longer the pregnancy

went, the less they would let her do anything. That meant no working. Money. Money.

Money. All that stuff in those magazines. We had nothing like that. I had no idea what

to do about it. Kati was fine physically. Always took care of herself for the most part.

She was truly excited about having a baby. She had relationships before and obviously

never had a baby. Why now? Why me? I never even thought of starting a family. Never.

I had a plan. Keep writing. Keep working. Cash in the Cosmodemonic options. Then it

would be off to my shack on the beach in Costa Rica. I was getting hungry for the first

time in a while. My appetite was gone for the most part. Anxiety was gladly taking its

place. Kati would be a great mom. And we were a great couple. Sarah said so months

ago. Such a simple time then. *God damn it!* It was simple then. Work. Sleep. Sex.

Coffee. It seemed like a long time ago. Maybe the Brown Elephant has a Nursery

section. I doubt it. Not much call for one. I did talk to Kati. She had faith in me. As a

father. Me? I once told Kati a story about how I liked taking care of my childhood dog's

paw after he stepped on a shard of glass. That was way back, and my mom told me she

thought I'd be a good veterinarian when I grew up because I liked taking care of things.

I took care of a stoop kitty once in a while. Kati liked the dog story and remembered it.

And stoop kitty. But neither was in this context. The context of a baby, raising a child.

It didn't apply here and now. How could it? It was just an animal. I had no idea what to

do with a baby. I sometimes hoped that it wouldn't happen. Go to term. I couldn't

handle it if that happened. I just couldn't. No one else needed to know about this, but it crossed my mind. The pregnancy would just turn out to be something that was not meant to be. Then Kati and I could go back to the simple times. Work. Sleep. Sex. Coffee. Maybe I would even go back to writing.

And just to show how bad things could be, I didn't get Illinois Center. District manager Ted wanted to talk to me Thursday. I wasn't sure why. Wasn't sure about much those days.

***

It was good to go to Cosmodemonic store #204. The twenty-two bus had always been there. It was relaxing. I took refuge in the routine of the coming Friday closing shift. I was close to finishing three full years at Cosmodemonic. I took comfort in the sound of the filter baskets thudding as the grounds were emptied. And I took comfort in the sound of the milk steaming. The grinder whirring. I knew how long it would grind when triggered. It was loud, but I had the duration of its noise set in my head so that if it was grinding and I was talking to a partner or customer, I would look over to it with a finger up. I then turn around and face them just before its noise ended. On cue, I'd pull my hand down and resume the conversation. The pace and demands of the day-to-day existence of #204 took me away. It made me happy to sell a pound of whole bean Sumatra or Kenya. I could roll the top back and fold over the metal twist tie part to tie it shut. Whole bean sealed evenly. The French Roast would almost fill the bag completely. It had almost no moisture left in it after being roasted the longest of all the coffees. Thus, the pound filled the bag to the very top, making it more difficult to wrap the tie over it. Sometimes, I took a second sticker to seal the bag. Then I could affix the proper sticker evenly and centered on the front of the bag. Again, so much easier to

achieve with whole bean than ground. Then I'd take the tightly sealed, evenly stickered

pound of coffee and hand it across the counter to the customer. But always handed over

with the label facing toward them, thus completing the presentation. Those things

provided reassurance. I did them before. I still did them now, even with a baby on the

way. And, I would still be doing them when—if—the baby arrives.

And then, the future ran into the busy intersection, and tires screeched, and

horns honked, and I looked for somewhere to go. But it was too late. I'd never been out

of my yard and had no idea where to run. I stood frozen in the path of a car that didn't

see me. What if the baby didn't go to term? How would it hurt Kati? When? The longer

it went, the worse it would be for everyone. I wished it would happen soon. We could

move on.

"I heard you and Kati are having a baby," Dennis-the-Juice-Guy said as soon as

I walked through the vestibule of #204. At least that is what I thought I heard. I had not

seen him in a while. It was late in the day for him to be making his rounds. But, he had

to make a second run to some of the Cosmodemonics before the weekend. One in the

morning and a second run later to get some stores through until Monday. Dennis-the-

Juice-Guy had always been great. We never ran out of his juice. As great as he was, he

couldn't read my mind. He had heard that Kati and I moved in together. Not that Kati

was pregnant. It felt to me that everyone knew. How could they not know? It was such a

massive event that the world must know. Except for Dennis-the-Juice-Guy. We talked

shop. He asked if I knew that Candace had given her notice. I had. I think. I wanted to

tell him why my mind had been elsewhere. I wanted to tell Dennis-the-Juice-Guy everything then and there. On the floor of #204, in front of the whole bean counter, I wanted to spill my guts to him. I didn't even know if he had kids. He would offer words of wisdom that would help me get through. I would be strong then. Strong enough to get Kati through whatever happened. In reality, I did not have it in me. I would have to use someone else's strength and wisdom. Why not Dennis-the-Juice-Guy? He had to have the answers. The answers had to be somewhere.

Instead, Dennis-the-Juice-Guy took off for his next Cosmodemonic, and I punched in. I caught up with Mark on the day's priorities and ran yet another shift. I wrote all of this in my sketchbook on the bus to and from work. Back at our small and quiet place, I looked in on Kati. She was asleep. I expected her to look different. I expected her to look pregnant. She didn't.

***

I wanted to talk with her. But everything was different. If Kati was asleep, then she needed to stay asleep. At least she was done with Cosmodemonic for the week. The anxiety and fear came and went. Kati was in our bed at almost one a.m. on a Friday night in our room. She looked like she had been a part of my life for a long, long time. I took comfort in that. And a little bit of belief stirred in me. Maybe I could do my part. She always slept with her feet uncovered no matter how hot or cold. I knew that. I knew her likes and dislikes. Most of them anyway. This was real responsibility. A life was in our hands. I wasn't worried about her. She was the oldest in her family and, to some degree, helped raise her younger brothers and sisters. She had a thriving babysitting business by the age of ten. I had not changed a diaper in my life. Never, not one. Why should I have? There was no reason to. We would have a baby by the time baseball

starts again. Impossible. When would I ever get to do what I wanted to do? Like, sit in

front of a baseball game? But all kinds of people have babies. Everyone has done it.

How hard could it be? But they all had room for a crib. And a bed in a separate room.

And they had a bed with matching Star Wars sheets and pillows. And shelves for toys

and books. The magazines in the waiting room wouldn't leave my head. Each one had

something else I had no idea we needed. Next time, I wouldn't look at them. I needed a

beer and TV. I'd never fall asleep at this rate. Writing things down used to help. Now it

just brought up more questions than my mind could handle. I'm quitting the Sketchbook

of the Mind for now. It's been good, but it seemed selfish now. Maybe selfish isn't the

right word. For now, I hoped an old *Columbo* was on. *McCloud* would do, too.

***

He took me to lunch. It was a great company, Cosmodemonic that is. I knew I

swore off writing in my Sketchbooks of the Mind. I did stay away for almost a week.

The week that Kati and I had a disagreement. Our first real one. Disagreement was what

I called it a week later when I was not so mad at her. We fought and even yelled some.

Kati didn't get it that I couldn't come and go as I please as a manager at

Cosmodemonic. I told her that my schedule might not be as changeable as hers, in spite

of the fact that I could make it up. She said I used to do what I wanted. I told her that

was only because Mark let me get away with it and those days were over. He said, she

said. It didn't matter now. We needed to figure out her appointments at the OBGYN.

She wanted me there for all of them. It was just not possible. But, I did not pick up my

Sketchbook of the Mind to write about that.

I had to record my lunch with district manager Ted. I met him at the regional office. It felt good to be back there. It carried good memories of the MIE classes. There was not a lot going on, so district manager Ted and I walked to a Vienna Dogs, and he bought. Earlier, I told Mark that district manager Ted had wanted to see me, and Mark said it was most likely because Cosmodemonic was rolling out a new review process. But he wasn't sure because he hadn't bothered to read all of the memos he had been sent about it. But, once he found them, he would put them in my mailbox at #204. That didn't happen but fair enough. I didn't need the memos anyway. The meeting was not formal or official. District manager Ted took the time to give me a pep talk about how to get promoted at Cosmodemonic. He is not even my district manager. Katherine kept #204. On his own time, district manager Ted gave me some insights and advice. My wish for wisdom was answered. His main point of emphasis was for me to get to know the store I was interviewing for inside and out before the interview! Spend time there as a customer, just observing. Maybe even work a shift there, unpaid of course, since I was now on salary. Then, from there bring a plan to improve store in question to the interview. And be ready to discuss it. The interview really had nothing to do with what I wanted from the store. It was all about what the store needed, and what you could provide for the store. I must have come off as arrogant in the actual Illinois Center interview. Well, I was as humble as hell now. I was sure my humility came off as real to district manager Ted. I was humbled tremendously now. But not from not getting Illinois Center. There is nothing as humbling as staring fatherhood in the face.

The most amazing thing about the Vienna Dogs lunch was that district manager Ted wanted to help. He wanted to but didn't have to. He made the time to help me out. I knew him a little. It was impossible not to. I was going on three years at the

Cosmodemonic. And district manager Ted was almost a legend already when I started.

It was all about feeling empowered at Cosmodemonic. At least for me, it was. The free

coffee was great, but I felt like an owner with my options, and I was nowhere near

being a big shot. HS made everyone owner of their own Cosmodemonic. And it showed

as it grew. District manager Ted cared enough about his company to help someone else

so he could benefit the company in turn. In return for that, Cosmodemonic benefits

district manager Ted. Yes, we sold great coffee, but it was only the vehicle for that kind

of empowerment and ownership that I had. I felt ready to go in and kick ass, just like I

did after MIE class. Ready to go in tomorrow and grow my stock options.

Kati was due at the platform, and I was going to meet her like I always did.

***

When Kati got back, we got in the shower together. We had a long talk

afterward. Kati lit some candles, and I put a blanket over the window in the bedroom.

We made dusk out of an afternoon. Nothing might happen to her. All of a sudden, the

pregnancy could be over like a bad, bloody period. And that would be it. Anything

could happen. I was early for my birth. I almost didn't make it since I was only about

three pounds. Kati came easily to a mother younger than mine. I was still afraid to tell

my family. I was glad I sent those postcards so at least they know Kati and I shacked up

a while ago. I was afraid of what might happen to Kati and the baby-to-be if that is the

right word. I couldn't tell them that we were expecting a baby. We didn't know. We just

didn't know. I was also afraid of what they would think and say. This was an accident.

This was not planned. We didn't mean for it to happen. None of it sounded good. I should have stayed in touch more often. This news would come out of nowhere. They didn't even know the novel got rejected. Or even submitted. Maybe submitted, but it didn't matter either way. Kati told me during our post-shower talk in the dim bedroom not to say anything yet. We should wait a month and see what things were like. After that, anything that happened to Kati and the baby would be more serious. A miscarriage then would put her in the hospital for sure. I wouldn't say anything for a while. That would be long enough to wait. We'd just have to wait and see. It sounded so easy.

Kati was going home the next weekend. I thought it would do some good for both of us. The OBGYN said she could still travel. And we did have sex in the shower. She said, "It felt huge," so matter-of-factly. Maybe the last time for that, but so far Kati and I were in agreement to not ask about sex at the OBGYN. During the wet and upright lovemaking, I was able to hold off for a while. That, and trying to keep safe footing on the slick tub, left me with shaky knees. The after-sex conversation in the bedroom left us in a better frame of mind. She wanted me along on the visit to Charleston, but I couldn't swing it. Kati said it was fine. I truly did want to make the OBGYN appointments with Kati. If only she could make them for my days off on Thursday, then I could go. But, it was better for her Van Buren Schedule to go on Friday. She would have to tell Carmella at Van Buren soon. I didn't feel like telling anyone at Cosmodemonic. What would they think? Should I act like it was the plan all along? Maybe I could try that with the family when the time came. Of course, they'd say I had never even mentioned starting a family before. They would be right.

***

The week was going by fast. It almost felt like a normal week. Fall was just around the corner, and Cosmodemonic customers were already asking about Christmas Blend. Couldn't they wait?

Kati and I decided to hold off on names, regardless of gender. We would wait to see what happened. It was another thing we had to wait on. A name would make it tougher on Kati if something happened.

***

I did end up somehow working Thursday instead of Friday. Mikey G was a saint since I just asked him last minute to switch. Sarah and Denis would also be closing on Friday. It was a close I would have looked forward to since Denis, the actor and comedian would have made me laugh, and Sarah would just have been her beautiful, efficient self. There were some truly fun shifts at #204, I must admit. The whole crew used humor as the antidote to the thousand-customer mornings. Mark used to be funny, too.

Kati was performing her ablutions and packing her kit bag in the bathroom. She was going from the OBGYN appointment directly to the train. She used a personal day. If she kept this up, the forethought, the planning, we would be fine. She saw the dominos falling in advance. The OBGYN was downtown so why backtrack? She was less nervous today. So was I. I only looked at the magazines last time because I thought it was the thing to do. I put down my Sketchbook of the Mind and glanced casually at the magazines, pretending to pick and choose. When, in fact, there wasn't anything in them I could afford. I thought I was more ready for this appointment. I was always ready to leave before she was. But not ready in that way. A few minutes before, Kati

said I looked great. I got more dressed up than usual on purpose. I figured that I could at

least look like I had some money. People like nurses and doctors treated you better

when you looked prosperous financially. I'm not sure why but they just did. With that

in mind, I had a great idea. I'd leave the Sketchbook of the Mind behind and take the

Barron's with the latest article about the Cosmodemonic. I'd stroll into the office with it

casually under my arm and read it in the waiting room, nodding significantly as I did.

***

It was a mistake not bringing my Sketchbook of the Mind. I could have written a

lot on the train ride back. It took forever. But it was not a mistake hitting La

Commercial for some Lienes in cans. They were quite cold. Cans are always colder.

Mistake. The same word applied to forgetting to bring something and to creating a

pregnancy, to making a baby. It was a mistake.

But, how could it have been a mistake when the sex was, and still is, so great

with Kati? I didn't know about Kati's other lovers, but I must have fit her better, just

right, in order to get her pregnant. I must be bigger. How else to explain it? Sound

plausible to me because it also explained why I hated condoms. Not like other guys hate

them but because they were always so tight, especially at the bottom. I used the biggest

size with Natali and before. But a lot of those times, I was too inebriated to discern

much. Yet, I blamed myself somehow for not fitting into them. Or, at least I didn't see

that being too big for them as a possible attribute. My lack of self-worth told me it was

my fault somehow. Natali once jokingly compared me to a beer bottle. She and I compromised, and she tried other methods to avoid using condoms. But, damn, with

Kati it felt like I was going in twice sometimes. The double uterus was somehow in the

way. But in a good way. I felt it on the way further in. Sex without a condom and, at

times, double penetration? How could that be a mistake? It must have been the time at

her parent's house. I know I felt something twice then. With her on top by the window.

It felt so good. It had to be then. It had to be due to my width that she got pregnant.

Right? If it were just a misdiagnosis by Dr. Quackenbush, then she would have been

pregnant before. Her other lovers must have used condoms. Can't afford not to, in this

day and age. Kati kept her fertile times in a small notebook so she'd know. I didn't want

to know, so I didn't' ask. It had been that we just fit together. I didn't think she wanted

a baby now. She wanted to get back to school. And maybe later, when it would be a

good time when it was good for us, we'd think about kids. Still, it could be a mistake

either way. She said she'd call immediately this weekend if she saw any blood. Part of

me really hoped she did.

***

I thought I better get a different Sketchbook of the Mind Saturday. I'd hide this

one away, at the bottom of the pile. Kati called me "an inveterate note taker." She knew

I did this. And I didn't hide them. Still, since I needed a new one anyway, I'd put this

one out of sight.

***

I thought a bit ago that I would become more responsible and not have so many

beers. I didn't say when I would start. That Liene was just too good. I was free until

Sunday besides the Saturday close of course. I thought it would be Wheaton Bill, Tony, and Chuck. Good crew but not as fun as it could be. I'm drinking the beer and listening to Steve Earle quite loud. Those Leinenkugels were going fast. Just enjoying beer and music at home. Steve Earle could have been from my neighborhood in Dayton. He could have lived next door and worked on his Mustang all weekend in his driveway. By Sunday evening, empty beer cans stood guard around the still unfinished Mustang like sentries.

***

I stayed in by the phone last night to make sure I didn't miss a call from Kati. Plus it kept me close to the beers, except when I ran back to La Commercial for six more. When Kati called, she sounded relieved and happy to hear my voice. But at the same time, she sounded so far away and like she wanted to be back here with me. It was like that now for us both, I think. We no longer could feel one emotion at a time.

Was I always looking for a way out of responsibility? Habitual? I went to La Commercial with the fear. Walked to and from with the fear. A line I remembered from the movie *Withnail and I* was something about making enemies of our future. I did that, more than ever. At the same time, I knew it was not worth it. I needed to live the life of dad-hood. Where was I really headed before? Becoming a writer? That was a one-in-a-million dream. Would it be worth it? I was a writer regardless, so who needed the stamp of approval of a published book? I can be a writer without being published.

***

263

Overall, I enjoyed my night of freedom. Again, people do it. Everyone figured out a way to have a family and still go to baseball games, and go bowling, go to concerts, see friends, make more kids, take a pearl diving class, whatever. People do it, have done it. I am here. Everyone on the trains or buses or apartment building next door was there because their parents raised them, were able to do it.

I had to make a decision: Make coffee or go back to bed?

The winner was bed. Saturday closes took a lot of energy. Three beers were still left. They would be there when I got back.

Kati and I talked. I might get out of here and head to my old coffee house under the tracks. I needed to think. She had good news, besides no bleeding. There was a crib and changing table still in her basement along with some other things. It took me a second to sound happy. I had to piece together what the changing table was for. And it didn't sound like her parents hated me. I talked to her mom for a few minutes. She had been reading and rereading all she could on the double uterus. There could be healthy, full-term pregnancies with it. However, there wasn't much of a database. She did say a genetic component may be a factor, but only sometimes. It sounded like she didn't want me to blame her.

Off the phone, I did blame someone. Not bad enough that Kati was pregnant. We were helpless to do anything but wait. Kati was bringing home some books they had from when she first found out. Kati wanted me to read at least some of them. Infertility is quite often associated with her abnormality. No such luck with the two of us. Blame.

It was not going to help me by blaming anyone. Blame wouldn't stop the pregnancy.

Blaming someone wouldn't enable me to picture myself as a dad. I still couldn't see it.

Chapter Nine

I couldn't face any place based on selling coffee, so I took a walk to kill time. I still took my Sketchbook of the Mind. When I got back, I reread the last paragraph. It wasn't entirely true. I could see myself being the loving father. The veterinarian father, who loved little things. I could see myself tossing a baseball in the street with my son or daughter. Not my street now. But a neighborhood street that had more room, more trees, and fewer cars. I saw myself helping with homework at the kitchen table after a workday. I'd still be in my work pants, but have taken off my work shirt and have on my white V-neck T-shirt. I could do things like that.

I stopped off for bubbly water at La Commercial. The daughter was there, looking older and better than when I first started my beer runs almost three years ago. I sat for a while on a little wall in front of a different apartment building and thought. I had a great life and a great future regardless of the current stasis horrors. A favorite term of Burroughs. The stasis horrors. I had them now. I shared that with Burroughs. Proud to say. But not because I was marooned in a jerkwater town deep in the Andes. I shared that with a famous writer. A good description of the current pregnancy. The confidence begins to fade away, to weaken its hold. The leash on the ground, tied to a fence. It became useless. The knot wasn't tied well enough where it met the collar. The intersection was Diversey, Clark, and Broadway. My dog mind was standing there, and there were not only cars going by but also buses and cabs. They kept honking but just missing me. Just then, at least. The baseball-tossing dad didn't get it done. That was not enough. It couldn't be enough in this country today. The good ol' USA demands more. Way more than I could handle. Way more than I'd ever be able to give.

266

My fears happily found their confirmation on the way back home from the rest

of my walk. I passed a house fire. I had walked quite a way, lost in thought. Time went

fast like that when I was concentrating on *Back Outta the World*. It seemed like I had

only walked for ten minutes. I passed through the watching crowd in front and across

the street from the fire. I didn't stand there with them but circled around and past the

burning house to the alley behind it. A much better view. I watched a kitty cat being

saved from a second story window ledge above the backyard. The kitty was black and

white, and even from my distance, I thought I saw soot on its fur. I don't like fires,

public calamities—what's the use of watching? It could one day be me. But it wasn't

today. I was glad it wasn't me. And I was sure everyone in the crowd felt the same

unless they knew the people in the house. I didn't. I was smart enough to be alone, still

sipping my bubbly water and sitting. Not standing among everyone else. I had the best

seat for this calamity, and I was glad for it. It wasn't me this time. It took my mind off

miscarriage and premature birth. And money and insurance and responsibility and being

a provider. All that stuff that I had no stomach for. For just those passing minutes, those

realities all went up in someone else's flames. And, I felt better for it.

***

I was smart enough to bring my Sketchbook of the Mind and a *Reader* with me

to pass the time while I waited for the train. I had hoped Kati would just get a cab and

get back. I had to silently backpedal on that hope as we talked on the phone. I said I

would gladly come downtown and meet her. That was three hours ago, and she was

calling to tell me that the train was leaving on time. Its arrival time here passed about

thirty minutes before. If it weren't Sunday, I would have walked over to Kerry's store.

He just got Two North Riverside. I was a little pissed at Cosmodemonic. I didn't even know it had opened. I called his old store last week to borrow a case of hot cups, and he told me the news. It is a five-day and rocked out. The mornings consisted of super intense rushes. Every morning it was just waves of people pouring off the commuter trains like zombie sardines. Instead of brains, they wanted lattes, mochas, and grandes. For three hours, there was no room to stand or move, according to Kerry. He'd take over in two weeks. I didn't know who the manager there was before. Kerry was good but not as good as I was. He did say he didn't have much choice in the matter and that made me feel better. But I wished I hadn't been given a choice and had already been sent to a five-day store. I still had Sundays off. And I felt like I was the manager at #204 anyway. Everyone there could tell Mark had checked out.

I saw in the *Reader* that Ricki Lee Jones was coming to town. Kati loved her, and the concert was not going to be too far from our place. She was playing a small place by the tracks off Belmont. I'd get tickets. My first thought was to surprise Kati. Once I'd had time to think, I decided to check with her first. She'd be excited either way. I still had to get used to this planning ahead business.

All those people coming and going. They all began their life somewhere, and we're here now. A soothing thought.

I just walked to the bathroom to get rid of my morning Sumatra. There was an empty Cosmodemonic cup sitting on the shelf where you could toss your bag while you relieved yourself. Must have been bought at Two North. Or maybe it was carried down here from Bannockburn or Wheaton. I remember early on when I saw a Cosmodemonic cup in the trash at a bus stop or crushed along the curb, I would think that is a good sign

that my company is growing. It was beginning to spread outward. The trashed cups,

appearing in odd places around the city told me that. I took comfort in that because that

was my employer, my logo, and I may even have steamed the milk that once filled that

cup. I didn't think that anymore. There were too many stores around and too many

empty cups on the ground. Almost no chance there once was a drink made by me in it.

I knew if I moved, the train would come. I was glad I came down here. I was

excited to see Kati. It seemed like a lot longer than two days since we had been

together.

***

I got back to the Sketchbook of the Mind on Monday. Hard to describe how it

felt to see Kati coming toward me yesterday. I tried to see if I could tell she was in fact

pregnant. She had on jeans and a sweater and looked great as usual. I took the heavy

bag with the books in it from her right away. She felt the same as we hugged. She didn't

feel pregnant to me. I decided to splurge on a cab. Over the weekend, I had only spent

money on the Lienes. She had been on trains enough.

I felt her confidence in me physically transfer over to me. Like she cast a good

magic spell, if only temporary. We talked and planned in the cab. We had only six

months until the baby. The longer, the better. I agreed to start to read the books. She got

some newer ones than the ones her mom had kept. I had no clue how many books there

were on pregnancy, planning, and expecting a child. Odd thought: I never did come

269

across the list of books I've read since I moved to Chicago. But I knew I sure as hell

didn't plan on having to add *What to Expect When You're Expecting* to that list.

***

I didn't know how long it was going to be until I got back to the Sketchbooks of

the Mind. I might just ramble on about kitchens until I fill the latest one. It was Tuesday

after the close. Kati and I agreed to a three-week moratorium on worry. That was when

we would go to the next appointment. I had one page to fill. I thought about just ranting

about how pissed I was at Mark. But, I wasn't really. He was suddenly taking the next

week off, starting tomorrow. Katherine approved it. I guess she had faith in me. This

was not all that new to me. After all, I was used to being in charge, but that time I felt

more was expected of me. Mark was fried. I didn't hate him for bailing for a week.

***

Kati was fine, and she wanted me to start referring to her in the plural. Her

appointment was on a Thursday. The trip to the doctor downtown could be a pain. I

wouldn't write or even make journal entries if I was watching a baby when Kati is gone

or at work. There is no way.

***

I was energetic and on edge but in a good way. I wasn't sure where it was

coming from. Possibly, it was just the energy of changing surrounding and situations.

After several weeks, It felt good to be back to writing. Not a novel or a short story or

even a letter. Sure, it was just my new Sketchbook of the Mind. But it felt good to be back. I'd keep writing, though at times I'd hate the uselessness of it. I'd been through it

for years. It was the fourth or fifth "room" for this pursuit. I didn't want to set up any

artificial barriers to my writing. I could write at any time of the day or night. Just write,

baby or not. Or not. I didn't want to go to the doctor. I wanted to write instead. *See why*

I can't have a baby in my life? How would I write when it is wailing in the other room?

How could anyone do anything? That sounded selfish or blind, but I needed to try to get

all I wanted. I wanted my place in Costa Rica. I wanted to wake up to the crashing of

ocean waves outside my kitchen window. I wanted to sit with my first cup of coffee

looking out onto it. That was what I wanted. It could happen. More and more articles

and publicity about Cosmodemonic showed up every day. I was fully in the middle of it

all. Foolish dreams? I knew myself better than that. I was awesome and seeing that I

could achieve it made it more painful at times. It could be done. I'd always known I was

meant for something. I'd carried that confidence with me all over and around Dayton

and in buses and in bars. It brought me here, come to think of it. But, at times, I'd

forgotten it is even here.

***

I placed the first order for Cosmodemonic Christmas Blend. I couldn't

remember when we started selling it last year. I liked it, only so much though. We

would make it the coffee-of-the-day every weekend until Christmas.

I heard Kati turn the shower off. I was ready. We still shared the on-time gene.

Kati was never late for anything, and neither was I. It didn't seem to matter at the doctor. We would be on time and still wait an hour. I hoped Rikki Lee Jones tickets arrive later that day.

***

It turns out that I didn't need to haul the Sketchbook of the Mind with me on the train and back. Kati and I talked the whole way. The baby was due on April eleventh. Kati wasn't so sure. Not about the date, but about the doctor. Her dad was a professional, and so she was not as intimidated as I was. I nodded my head and mumbled an affirmative. I was certain they knew it was an accident. They all did.

At first, I took small comfort that the woman behind the glass window loved Cosmodemonic. "I love their skim lattes," was her exact response when she found out we both worked there. I went on about how I love my tripios, but I didn't think she was listening. She said she didn't like the lines at the one down the street. She glanced up from checking my information to make eye contact. For a second it seemed like she expected me to fix that for her. I wasn't sure which Cosmodemonic we were closest to. We were somewhat close to Van Buren, that much I knew. I also knew that customers had taken to trying to call their orders in, especially in the mornings. I had heard that Mark flipped out when Monica took an order over the phone and promised to have it ready. It was before Mark's much-needed vacation. The lines were bad enough to sort out. Mark's meltdown was just before #204 received its policy update on phone orders. There was so much stuff coming out of Cosmodemonic HQ that it would have been easy enough to forget some, if not, all of it. Even Cosmodemonic couldn't keep everyone happy. Yet, sometimes it seemed within reach. Especially when the holidays hit. A vision of #204 packed to the gills came into my head as I waited for the woman

behind the glass to finish her task. I heard Christmas music playing under the steaming,

grinding, and ringing of the cash register. I'm not ready for it. The woman handed me

back my card, and I replied that there are more stores on the way. I slowly turned

around and walked over to sit next to Kati. The whole exchange was just a few seconds

long, but it had made me tired.

***

They wanted to see Kati in two weeks. Not to worry. Everything was fine, but

since the condition is uncommon, they wanted to see her again soon. I had no idea what

to make of it. It made me feel better in one way that the OBGYN and staff didn't know

much about a pregnancy in a double uterus. That excused my complete ignorance. In

another way, it magnified how little prepared I felt. I didn't remember many, if any,

pregnancies from my childhood, adolescence, and so-called adulthood. Nothing to

recall that would make me feel sure that it would work out. Or even sure, that it

wouldn't work out. If we knew either way, then we could plan on what was going to

happen. The easiest would have been a miscarriage very soon. The longer it went, the

harder it would be on Kati. They were doing what they could at the OBGYN, which

wasn't much as far as I could tell. They did mention cutting work time for Kati and

even bed rest. That sounded impossible. Going to part-time was an option because

Cosmodemonic would let Kati keep her benefits. Bed rest sounded like she'd need a

full-time nurse to move in with us. None of the options sounded appealing at all. Even a

full-term birth meant having a baby, caring for it, being a real dad. None of which I ever

saw myself doing. That was why I wished it would fix itself in the next couple weeks.

The Rikki Lee Jones tickets came for a week from Sunday giving us something to look forward to.

***

Friday night and I grabbed a bottle of vino cheapo at La Commercial. Kati still allowed herself to have one glass. But she was asleep. She was so tired after the workday and from the emotional toll the appointment always took. We got the news yesterday her work hours needed to be cut. That put us back to square one financially. Kati already thought she would go to twenty hours but just had to talk to Carmella on Monday.

My first glass of wine was gone. History, L'istoire, or whatever it is in French. I wanted to wash work off my mind, but I had to review applications and hire a couple people pronto. At #204, we had been lucky to keep a standard crew for a while. We still had a reputation as being a little offbeat, but I liked it. Mark seemed better. He cut his hair short and lightened it. His wife did it, actually. She was a stylist. Mikey G, Sarah, Denis, Chuck, and Tony were all heading into at least their second Christmas. I had to do all the hiring process this time. I made the initial appointments, did the interviews, and even offered the jobs to the right candidates. And, I had to get it done in the next two weeks or sooner. It was not a good time for me to be doing this. It meant more time at Cosmodemonic as the holidays approached, on top of what was going to happen anyway. And no more money for that time. That was the on-salary deal. If Kati went down to twenty hours and I couldn't get overtime or tips anymore then where would we find the money?

274

***

Kati missed Gayle more than ever. She needed to talk to a woman who was not her mother. I could only do so much. I took the more mellow thirty-six bus heading in for the Saturday close. I had not even thought about trying to apply to a five-day store. Just another thing I didn't have time for. It felt worse than usual to leave Kati. But she was going to call Gayle, and that would help her get through the night. We'd have tomorrow together at least.

Kati was playful and excited about the baby. A good night sleep did her wonders. She told me stories of her childhood. She had a small stutter when she was little. She was a bit of a tomboy but still remembered the names of her favorite dolls. She told me about the Goth phase she went through as a teenager. I knew she had always read a lot. She was looking on the bright side of everything and was planning on reading a lot if she had to go on bedrest. As I listened, I wanted to speak up. I had a sudden urge to tell Kati about my secret hope that the baby wouldn't come. I was standing in the kitchen making my lunch. But I was stopped by my age-old fear of speaking up, opening up. And by seeing that the prospect of a baby was making Kati happy and lifting her spirits. I read that moods change as a pregnancy progresses. But I grew up telling myself that speaking your mind can lead to bad things. Hence the resorting to journals. But, what would be so bad if things were back normal in a month or so? I almost started by saying "We do have to keep the other possibility in mind" as a way of breaking the ice, of slowly making my way toward verbalizing my hope for miscarriage. But the last obstacle to that I could not overcome was Kati's belief in me. It always came up at these times. She said she could see me changing diapers. And that was based on Kati watching me pack my lunch as we talked. I always had good hand-eye coordination. I smiled a little and responded that in little league I was a good-field, no-hit second baseman. And that I could see myself playing ball with and especially reading to the baby when it got older. I said that instead of saying it wouldn't be so bad if the baby didn't come after all

***

Taking the lead from Kati as usual, I found myself looking forward to the very near future and the zoo at #204. The bright side of the zoo was that it would be too busy to think about anything but getting through the close. I managed to get two interviews scheduled. The week was going by fast. No changes with Kati.

***

"You are more capable than you know, than you even begin to realize." I put that randomly down in a Sketchbook of the Mind. I don't know why or when.

***

I called Dayton and talked to my mom. It was great to simply hear her voice. And nearly impossible not to tell her. She raised a big family, and it wasn't easy for her. She did it and so can I. Again, I almost spoke up but instead said it was too busy to come for either holiday weekend. I could have done it if I really tried. Another problem for a manager of a seven-day store was that I had to say no to requests for time off, including my own. She understood. I felt like I was off the hook for a while. But it was getting harder not to tell my family.

***

On the bus home Wednesday. I decided to call Natali and tell her. I felt like that would release some steam. I would call and ask first about Anita's play and then tell her about Kati and the baby.

***

Kati couldn't work up the nerve on Monday to tell Carmella about the twenty hours. At least not yet. What if something happened? All that energy wasted for nothing. So she decided to wait until it becomes necessary then bring in something on letterhead from the OBGYN. I almost chickened out but called Natali. She sounded truly happy to hear from me. Her dad was doing better. A friend had moved in to take care of him. I had a fantasy for a second that Kati and I could move up there and have this friend take care of her. No Cosmodemonics in the UP. Never will be. Detroit would be the closet. Anita's play had a location. Natali said it was amazing that I called because she had just found out that it was all set for Saturday and Sunday. I had to tell her that I worked Saturday and that Kati and I were going to see Rikki Lee Jones. I said to tell Anita and Craig I said hello, and I sent my regrets. After all that, I hung up without telling Natali anything about the pregnancy.

***

Sunday I made a plunger of Italian Roast. I loved the Christmas Blend but not at the apartment. Kati and I had to spend some time looking for an outfit that fits her for the Rikki Lee Jones show tonight.

277

***

That damn diva canceled the show. She claimed it was too close to the El tracks, too noisy. Kati was crying in our room. Again. Still. More later. Shouldn't we decide if it is too loud?

***

Kati sat in the cab next to me. She seemed normal. I had said we could just get some beers somewhere. We'd get our money back. At that point, I just wanted to blow off steam. I had actually wanted to see Jimmie Dale Gilmore at Schuba's instead but knew Kati's preference. I was good with Bento's or somewhere close for some Old Styles to wash the bad taste away. I hadn't given up on that as we passed halfway on the short cab ride back home. Then Kati just started crying. I was just glad we didn't have one of the talkative cabbie types. My words missed the point as I look back now. I just kept saying it was all right. That we would get our money back. That we could still make something of the night. For the last minute of the cab ride, she leaned against me. I could feel her body make the effort to stop the tears. I had told her all day that she looked great in her new outfit. She did. I said so. But she said she didn't care. I stayed quiet after that. She stopped crying while I paid. I pitched the Bento's or any Cub's bar in a storm idea again. Kati just wanted to get home. We could still fix tonight. That was all that occurred to me. I wanted to drink, to unwind, to forget about babies, double uterus, pregnancy, and full term. All of that crap. All of it. This had had the feeling of a great night out in Chicago. It could have been my last one for a while. If ever.

I looked up and down the street as we got out of the cab, searching for inspiration. A spot Kati might just agree to go and drink with me. Blow off steam with me. Forget with me. All gay bars. And they all seemed to be packed on Sunday nights. A little farther up Halsted were a couple places. No dice. Too far now. We could still fix tonight. Kati stopped actively crying, but her eyes were shiny from tears. If the light from the Manhole Bar were brighter, maybe I would have seen that she wasn't crying about tonight. Maybe I would have seen in her eyes that she was afraid too. Maybe I would have seen that she understood what I didn't. She understood that there would be other books and coffee companies and concerts. But there would never be anyone like our baby. If it gets here. Never. No other person ever born before or since would be like this baby. The same for all people who have come to be. I couldn't see it then and as we left the corner and headed home. We walked slowly toward the apartment. It got darker and quieter, and I had missed my chance.

Once upstairs and home I gave up on a bar but not on saving the night. We talked for a little while. Kati said to just let her be. She was really all right. But tired. Just leave her alone. I said that was fine. And I would be out in the living room watching a movie after I called Rikki Lee Jones some names in my Sketchbook of the Mind. Kati smiled just a bit. I felt relieved to see her smile in the shadowed room. I asked if she wanted anything at La Commercial. She said no and shut off the light.

***

I walked Kati to the station as usual. She was running out of believable excuses for time off at work. She was also beginning to show. At least she felt she was. Kati was sure that Carmella had guessed anyway. If true, she had most likely talked with Mark.

I'd keep an ear open for hints that Mark might know. There would be coffee and all

kinds of Christmas mugs, thermoses, and crap to order. I knew Kati was going to tell

Carmella today, even if she didn't say so on the walk to the station. The Friday

appointment would be here before we knew it. Two weeks already. Seemed impossible.

I asked if she was all right but only once. I could tell she was back in form. Kati didn't

bring up me saving the night with my beers and movie. I think she knew we were going

to need each other quite a bit in the next six months or so. And we would each have

times when we were not at our best. She seemed to understand that we were in this

together. And there likely would be a good deal of worse along with the better.

***

I just put down the Back Outta the World manuscript. I did not pick it up with

any intention of reading, editing, or revising a comma. I held it and wondered about the

author. He had the courage, if that is the right word, to take a VW van across the

country. He had moved out of his apartment in Columbus, Ohio, and didn't have any

home but that van for a couple months. That journey ended up being the manuscript.

Where was the faith the author had to do that? Why was it not in him now for the

journey to being a parent? Not only a parent but the father. Because they were two

completely different things? HS started a coffee company. A lot of people along the

way thought he couldn't do it. Now, look at it. Onward, the Master Roast! I can see

myself doing that too. I still had the card from the woman who was recruiting

Cosmodemonic managers. Call her. Get started. The official word from Cosmodemonic

was that they actually helped other coffee companies when they opened in a city. It created a buzz and interest in all coffee businesses in the area. Seemed plausible, and

feasible. All I had to do was help set up a few stores in Raleigh, North Carolina, or

Norfolk, Virginia, and wait.

I had to go in an hour early for one more interview. Had to run to pick up my

clean shirts. Didn't mind going in early. I really needed a tripio. Maybe the guy who

wrote *Back Outta the World* was still around. If he was, he better show up soon.

***

Kati and I had a good Thursday dinner of spinach rotini with mushroom sauce.

We shared a good Frenchy wine with it. I had most of it of course as Kati had one glass,

which seemed to be okay. It was turning chilly out at nights. Kati and I decided to stay

in to dine, which was cheaper and easier. We were also eating to fortify against the

cold. Eating to survive the cold. Eating to live to see the next day. Heavy, I know, but

with the appointment tomorrow, it seemed a significant dinner. For entertainment, we

had a BBC series on tape called *Lovejoy*. It was easy to watch, just challenging enough.

Neither of us had been prepared enough, or really wanted to ask about sex at the

OBGYN appointments. Assuming it was fine, we kept it up. We still felt right for each

other. She found the *Lovejoys* at the library. Also, a cheaper option and I liked them

right away. I felt restored by the food, the wine, the lovemaking. Kati was reading one

of her pregnancy books. Okay. Gotta clean the kitchen up. Scrape, scrape, scrape…

***

Early Sunday afternoon Kati was off to Osco for a few things she needed. I just

remembered the promise made over the summer to buy an espresso machine for my sister in St. Louis. I was working up the nerve to call her and let her know I have picked

out the best machine for them. It was a durable one that was not complicated. But it did

make a true shot of espresso. It had the necessary force to propel the water through, and

not around, the ground coffee. That was what differentiated the machines we had on

sale. We had all types of espresso machines on the shelves, along with plunger pots,

mugs, chocolates, thermoses, and on and on. But, I digress. I had to ask her for her

credit card information so I could buy it tomorrow when I go in to close. Still, I digress.

I decided to tell my sister about Kati, the pregnancy, the condition, and now the

fact that the OBGYN said Kati must cut her workload to twenty hours. Kati and I had a

day to digest, dissect, and discuss it. It was all the standing we do at Cosmodemonic

that concerned the OBGYN. What concerned us is that it seemed too much of an

overreaction. But, I did as I was told. Kati was less awed by those people than I was.

Hence, she intended to continue to take walks, go to the store on foot and do most other

day-to-day stuff. The idea of walks was appealing to me. They didn't cost anything. The

news has put us back to square one financially. And we had Christmas coming up. The

easy gift choice was coffee for everyone, which Kati and I decided and announced at

the same time to a shared and stress releasing laugh. After the call, I would call my

mom in Dayton. But that would be all. I'd let the news circulate throughout the rest of

the family. It would be way too tiring to repeat the entire story a dozen times. Kati was

starting twenty hours the next day. She told Carmella last week, as I guessed, and was

basically keeping her closing responsibilities intact for now. I would tell Mark

tomorrow. It is all the must-do things in my life. Now my life was mostly just things I

must do.

***

"Kati and you going to get married?" Mark jokingly asked when I arrived in the crowded backroom at #204. All kinds of boxes and bags for coffee gift packs were piled everywhere. The seasonal red aprons had arrived. We had to wear them all month. I had forgotten about that. We had to assemble Christmas Blend gift boxes for quick and easy gifts. Hell, yea. It was tiresome and monotonous work, but I breathed a sigh of relief as the memory of last year reappeared in my head. I would assemble them behind the whole bean counter, just as I did last year. I could keep an eye on things from there, get something done, but only deal with retail or whole bean customers. Just what my tired mind needed. Repetition. Work that was rewarded by a simple, tangible result. That result was a half-pound each of Regular and Decaf Christmas Blend boxed, labeled, and stacked on the counter or shelf. Ground for drip or left whole bean. That would be repeated most of the shift. It was necessary because these boxes would be bought almost as quickly as I could assemble them. Two or three at a time seemed to be the usual purchase. My closing shift became something to look forward to in that instant I stepped into the backroom at #204. I had all this racing through my mind as I looked up to see Mark smiling at me.

Scoop, weigh, seal, box, shelve. It was wonderfully repetitive. I thought I could do this forever. Not that I was going to have much choice in the near future. There were a few declarative statements included in my conversation with Mark in addition to his question about our future plans. The first was that my regular Sundays off were a thing of the past until after Christmas. Not a shock. Second, one of the new hires is going to start tomorrow, and yours truly would be training them. Again, no surprise. The third item was so obvious that Mark saved it for last and simply said, "Whole bean."

I just nodded because I understood. Cosmodemonic #204 had to hit a higher per transaction amount than last year. Of course. Why not? If we didn't do better than last year why even exist? After all, it made so much sense. Bigger, faster, stronger. Just like Steve Austin. I wished he was coming tomorrow. Judging by the crowd and sales a week before Thanksgiving, we would be in good shape. But then by next year, this year would not have been good enough. Why? There was no way my current mind should pursue this line of thinking. I had a tough time with it when back when things were easy. I was happy to scoop, weigh, seal, box, and shelve. I'd let district manager Kyle figure out why it made sense to exert all this human energy and life force just to flush it away next year. Let me mindlessly scoop. I had to reserve my mental space for me and Kati. I tried to recollect if we had even really discussed marriage. We were too concerned with the immediate reality of a miscarriage, bleeding, double uterus, bed rest, and the like. The fact that we hadn't made a memorable discussion about it made me wish I were with Kati now. We thought so much alike that we must have both known now was not the time for superficial things like marriage. That would come later. It made me think that she and I were in it for the long haul. That we were meant to be together. But that, in turn, made me feel bad for still hoping things would take care of themselves.

As these competing thoughts battled for space in my head, I finished off one box of Christmas Blend, which held forty pounds of coffee. Under it, another forty pound box waited, unopened." Perfect," I said to myself.

***

How could I smile and pretend it is great to be expecting a baby when I hope it didn't happen? I saw this line from this Sketchbook of the Mind from weeks ago. It was even more relevant now. My knees ached from the long day and the longer than usual wait for the twenty-two bus. If Kati saw that entry, would she maybe understand? Not a good feeling to end the day.

***

How could it work out? How would it? Every day was so confusing. I loved being by myself. On a random Thursday between the holidays, I was taking notes in relative silence. I dreamed of the same time of day, a calm afternoon in my shack in Costa Rica. Away from this big city. Did I waste years of my life chasing a lifestyle that just was never really there? Close enough to mentally touch on occasions, maybe. Real to me, but invisible to anyone else. Did I expect it to work? How did I expect to live life without a skill? A trade? A profession? Did I expect to write? Or did I not chose? Too late now. I had a child on the way. Did scrapping by always seems okay? Yes, looking back in dishonesty. I pretend I was choosing it. But, I was not really choosing anything. It was a happy existence and meant for me. Looking back in honesty, maybe. No direction. No real realizations in High School. It was only a place to spend four years as a teenager. More drifting in college. I chose what was beyond me in both. High School playing tennis, a rich man's sport. In college, languages and travel to see the world. But only applying once to teach overseas. Not getting that position. I guess the real question was why? Did I think I was special and that everything would work out just for me?

285

I did not date either of the above entries. They could have been written years apart but were not. At Cosmodemonic, I'm back to the old Saturday close, Sunday morning shift. At least I didn't open. Saturday morning Kati and I were off for a walk. We might make it as far as the lake. Kati said the walking and movement made her feel better. I worried about it of course, but Kati insisted the OBGYN is overdoing it on the restrictions. I agreed it would be nice if she were still full time. We talked about names and all the things we had to have for this baby. It shouldn't have been this complicated. Kati looked the part now. A baby coming into our life seemed even more real.

***

I had the last drops of my second tripio counting down the drawers. I was energized by the fact that at least a small, small fraction of this money would find its way back to me via my options. I had caught my second, third, and fourth winds. I was wide-awake on the bus. I should have gone home and started a new novel, possibly the length of War and Peace. It was war on the floor those days. I walked into a packed #204 at three to start my shift. Customers were covering every inch of the floor. I remembered that I had scheduled everyone at #204 to work that day. Mark, Sarah, Monica, Denis, and others were there, and more were yet to come to help me close. Mikey G was on the bar, and for some reason, he was alone. I did not punch in or put down my bag and stepped up to join him. He had just moment between rushes, oddly enough. I simply said, "I'll be in back counting money so don't bother me."

He turned at me and smiled. Amid the hand-to-hand combat all around, I found humor. Mikey G had been in the trenches with me and saw in my joke that it all would be fine. That even though it was going to be, as projected, the busiest day of the year, it

was going to be fine. We would all go our respective ways after I locked the doors that

night. That was going to come to an end. It was only coffee, after all.

***

Truth is stranger than fiction. I couldn't make this up. You had to be there. They

all apply. And no one would believe me, so I only told my Sketchbook of the Mind after

a busy Sunday catching up errands with Kati when I was alone at my writing desk. My

writing. That reminded me that no one would ever read this anyway. Kati, possibly, but

why would she? She had stacks of books on baby preparation and classic fiction to keep

her company. She had no interest in my Sketchbooks of the Mind. I hadn't seen my

desk looking disturbed or different in any way when I came home than when I've left it

hours, or even days. It was so quiet. Kati was asleep in the room that we started to

rearrange. We snipped at each other quite a bit while doing it. I was wiped out after the

close then open during the holidays and only wanted to have some beer and watch

football. I was not in the mood. More than that though, I wanted to tell her what had

happened to me that morning. I couldn't bring myself to, so it came out in grunts and

smart-ass remarks that only I found funny. So, I have the time and solitude to recall this

morning in my Sketchbook of the Mind now.

I took the thirty-six in for the morning shift but did not have to open. The shifts

on Sundays took some time to get a head of steam so that I got to #204 just in time for

the first lines to form. Then it was busy for the entire shift. The thirty-six bus was so

mellow and nearly empty that I almost fell asleep. Maybe I did doze off for a moment or two. My third or fourth wind from the Saturday close didn't subside until sometime

after three last night. I was both way too tired and wired from my adrenals and tripios

kicking in to help me finish the crazy day. Once I made it back home, I didn't want to

watch a *Lovejoy* without Kati next to me. Wasn't much on normal TV and I just

couldn't read. I tried the two beers from the fridge to relax, but they only confused my

system even more. So, maybe I did fall asleep and dream about it. The thought crossed

my mind throughout the long, busy day. But, no, it happened when I stepped off the

thirty-six early this morning. I turned facing it. No doubt it happened. I dragged myself

off the bus and stood facing it as I waited to cross the street and head for #204. But the

bus was blocking my view toward the lake, down Diversey. It must have been waiting

for a late passenger I didn't see coming, or was ahead of schedule and had to sit for a

minute or two. After another moment, it pulled away and allowed me to look east

toward the lake. My view down Diversey toward the lake was now clear. I had a clear

view of the sun rising over the lake. It was a sun rising only for me, pouring toward me

out of the sky. Clear and bright and powerful. Not blinding. It was shining as clear as

I'd ever seen it. And it was silent on that corner that morning like everything had come

to a momentary halt, maybe for a half a second, maybe for five minutes. I don't recall

exactly what happened, how long it took. I just stood at attention and knew. I felt it. I

knew that that sunrise meant something. I knew that it was telling me that I was going

to have a son. Me.

Chapter Ten

Kati talked to her mom almost daily. Her parents were coming up between the holidays for some Chicago-style Christmas shopping and, of course, to see Kati. Everyone in my family knew by then. I had been able to space out the congratulatory phone calls and didn't have to deal with any in-person visits real soon. My birthday was in January. I'd been promised a visit or two around then. I had been on the phone with Kati's mom several times. I found being put on the phone by her command to Kati both intrusive and refreshing at the same time. Since she had few, if any, boundaries, I could open up to her. It was easier to talk to her than even to my own family. By January when I'd get my visits, I hoped for a reason to put their collective minds at ease. We were a family of worriers. I wanted to be able to put their minds at ease with something a little more substantial than, "a sunrise told me everything would be okay."

***

Another OBGYN visit was the same as the ones before. They were still in a wait and see mode. No changes. I wanted to tell Kati about my sunrise vision. The worst part was that we had to cut out the sex. They acted surprised we hadn't been told already. By then, we had cooled it a great deal anyway. Kati and I agreed that we might be asking for trouble. I had been able to make a little time to read some of Kati's pregnancy books. She thought it would a better use of my time than writing in my Sketchbooks of the Mind or watching football or basketball on *el tubo*. I said, "Two out of three isn't bad." I was feeling better about handling it all. However, Kati and I agreed not to buy anything baby related for each other for Christmas. No need to jinx anything. The

horrible, high-stress time of year we call Christmas was almost over. About time.

I had never started a Sketchbook of the Mind on New Year's Day. No reason to,

I supposed.

***

A good snow was going outside, and I was feeling much better. Drinking estate

java because I liked the full-bodied coffees in the winter. I was getting ready for a day

of slaving. Kati was going shopping with her mom and dad. They were taking us to the

Pump Room the following day. I guess they didn't hate me for knocking up their

daughter. According to Kati, They had wanted grandkids for a while. They hadn't liked

her partner in her first, real adult relationship. The one I was jealous of when we first

met. Anyway, he couldn't, or wouldn't, hold down a job. At #204, my hires did well. I

was in management in an increasingly well-regarded company with limitless hair-

pulling-out opportunities. What else could in-laws want? Not that we were getting

married. With a couple days left in this year, slaving at the Cosmodemonic was not such

a bad place. Happy New Year, early.

***

I set my alarm those days for 3:55 a.m. That was the new time I got up to take

two trains to Oak Park to open *my* store. Store #308. I was the acting manager. It was

like walking on the moon when I left to catch the El to downtown to switch to the

commuter train—the Metra. It had been three weeks or so since I got the call from district manager Kyle. It was so cold. It was like the moon. Cold, empty, dark. It was so

early. So early that there were only two cars on the train. Two.

On the train, I read the sketchbook entry from before New Year's. The entry

about the Cosmodemonic not being such a bad place to be. It had been a while since I

even had a chance to think about anything but work, Kati, and the pregnancy. I reread

that entry many times over and about the only use I had for it now was to burn it in

order to warm up.

I had managed only two days off so far this year. It sounded dramatic, but it was

technically true. Oak Park Cosmodemonic store number #308 was a seven-day store. A

slower one. My marching orders were to guide it to its future as a profitable location.

How? It was sedate out there. The suburbs. An older suburb. Frank Lloyd Wright's old

stomping grounds. Not that helped me create more transactions per hour. He wasn't

coming in any time soon. A better location, a better physical location would have done

that. What did I know? That was why I had wanted a store near Wrigley or a five-day

store. When district manager Kyle called, the first thing he said was congratulations.

Then I heard promotion, acting manager, and Oak Park. My first thought was, where

was the car I needed? Must have? I couldn't do it without one. Didn't they know?

Didn't Cosmodemonic preach to set others up to succeed? Didn't I hear over and over

at MIE class that firing someone was the fault of the manager? Weren't we mandated to

treat other partners as we expect them to treat our customers? By customers I mean,

meal tickets. I was just one domino. Carmella went to Sue's old store on Halsted.

Somebody I never heard of got Kati's five-day store. I could only stand that because I

could see the logic of not having us work together. Especially now. Sue went to #204, and Doug went to Sue's store. Bowtie got my venerable #206. And by the way, Mark just quit.

***

The only bright side to my banishment to the gulag of #308 was that the Chicago to Geneva Metra was a great place to write and read. After three, actually going on four weeks, I used it as my escape. The seats were bigger, cleaner, and the cars themselves were quieter. A lot more opportunities to score an old *Barron's* or *Investor's Business Daily* to see how my stock was doing. Those papers were all over these trains. A quick glance usually revealed that Cosmodemonic stock had moved upwards in value. Hardly any *Readers* to be found though.

I opened for the most part, with a few closes thrown in to get a feel for all of #308. I had been trying to hire a few partners with help from district manager Kyle. Cosmodemonic #308 wasn't a mess, but it never had performed up to expectations either. District manager Kyle tells me that my experience, solid leadership skills, and demonstrated ability to drive whole bean sales are the reasons for my exile or promotion. All three were true, although I would say that I was a natural, instead of solid, leader. But it was true that I kicked ass since the MIE class ended. I just didn't get why I couldn't have just replaced Mark when the dust settled. I would have been close to home and would have been more engaged in my job there. Because I would have been near Kati all the time and I would be near when the baby was due on April eleventh.

When I opened, I had to switch from the El to the Metra downtown. I had to walk a few blocks to get to the Metra station. It took just a few minutes to make my way across Jackson Plaza when it was deserted. The rest of downtown was standing empty waiting for the arrival of its business day occupants. No one out yet. Just me. Me and the Picasso Horse statue. I crossed under its watchful eyes every time I did the open commute. It stared at me as I walked quickly past with my backpack shouldered for the long day ahead. It was a statue, yet its eyes followed me. Only when I was not looking up at it though. As soon as I looked up, the Picasso Horse looked away reverting to the form it kept to fool everyone else. I know the Picasso Horse was awake in this quiet, cold predawn. It was awake only for this secret time of day. I knew it. And it knew I knew.

***

The birthday visits came and went. The first round was from my from my older brother who brought my mom. Their meeting with Kati was awkward at first, but that was quickly overcome by my older brother's quick wit and perfect comic sense of timing and delivery. The next visit just a couple weeks later was from my sister who lived in Texas. She was in Chicago on a business trip. Just about everyone had reason to come to Chicago at least once. The visits consumed my only two days off during that three-week period. I was tired and distracted. I thought everyone liked Kati. It was good to see everyone. Then they had to leave.

One more birthday event, I got a birthday card signed by HB himself. It was the second or third one he had sent to me.

293

***

Kati went to two appointments on her own. There just wasn't any way I could go with Cosmodemonic #308 and the commute consuming so much time and energy. Kati wasn't happy about it and seemed to blame me. It sucked, but the exile was not my idea. I just put my head down and went to work. That was what I did. It would serve us better in the long run if I obeyed the terms of my exile. She said the best long-term solution was for us to be together on all facets of the pregnancy and beyond. I told her I couldn't be in two places at once and that I would get a raise when the Cosmodemonic made me manager for real. We'd bicker and make up, argue, and make up. It all put us back to square one money wise. We had to stop things now that Kati was part-time. The big one was that we didn't go out as much. Plus, I couldn't get to Treasure Island for bargain Mondays. On top of all that, Kati was beginning to buy things for the baby. She had to. Of course, the calls to her mom and all my long distance phone calls were mounting up. My commute made the city seem big, cold, and like it didn't give two fucks about us.

***

Cosmodemonic store #308 was not the home away from home that #204 was. It seemed like just another Cosmodemonic. It was on street, and there were stores and people around it. That much was comparable. It just felt different to me. I knew in part it was because #308 was all mine. I had to look at it differently because I was responsible for every bean in the place. But something was missing. I knew #204 existed when I was at #206. I had been in there. I had heard of Van Buren and of Sue and Kerry's store. It was like #308 just fell from the sky.

***

At least my #308 crew was good. Michael K, Hippie Dave, Gail (not Gayle), the voluptuous April, and Connie the new key holder. Plus, in the Kati and Monica role as a five-day opener is Cynthia who lived so close she could walk in when she didn't feel like driving. I can't name the rest now but they all showed up. That was quality number one for me in these partners. According to district manager Kyle, #308 would be due an assistant manager spot when the sales justified. Hence, my challenge according to district manager Kyle was to keep building whole bean sales and increase transaction averages. My challenge was magnified by the fact that I felt disconnected and powerless by being so far away. I was too far away to cover a shift last minute at #308. I wanted to tell district manager Kyle this fact prohibited me from taking ownership of #308. When I was there, all I wanted to do was get back closer to Kati. I was too far away to quickly get home to help in an emergency. But, what could I do anyway?

Out my Metra window was one of the landmarks from my new commute. The Mars candy plant. Halloween. Kids and candy. I had some good memories of my Halloweens growing up. My brother and a couple friends heading out in the old neighborhood just getting free candy. Such vibrant times. All full of life and energy. Just aware enough of a life of some kind ahead of us all. I saw myself more as the dad who would take his kid out on Halloween.

295

The condition has not fixed itself. Maybe it was meant to be. I was meant to be a Halloween dad. Maybe that was what my sunrise was trying to tell me. We'd see.

*** *

Those days I got home to the hissing of our Franklin stove. It always made the hissing sound when it came on. I never appreciated that that sound meant heat and warmth until after coming home at the end of a fourteen-hour day. Kati was hot most times now. Another change her body was undergoing. She didn't have any interest in listening to me wax poetic about the hissing Franklin stove.

Kati was planning to rearrange our room to make space for a changing table. Her mom would be bringing it soon. She and one of Kati's younger sisters would bring it on a visit. I had no idea what a changing table was until recently. Against my better judgment, I looked at some in one of the waiting room magazines. It was a good thing we were getting an old, but free, one. Our place was small, but how big could a changing table be? Where would it go anyway? Kati would know. I had enough on my mind.

I was back on the Metra train riding and thinking. Underneath all the events ahead of me was the understanding that it had happened and was taking place in Chicago. Chicago had been a near-mythical land for me for years. In college, my writer wannabe friends would sometimes concoct a beer buzz inspired plan to run to Chicago for a weekend, or even just lunch. It had been just over three years of my life spent here. All of it gainfully employed by Cosmodemonic. Every day I went in something big could happen: a stock split, a new market, a headline in Barron's about some agreement we've made to buy a competitor. In fact, we were soon going to have cafes going up

inside mega-sized bookstores. And I was one of the quickly shrinking percentage of

people who got the first stock grant. There wouldn't be a second one. No second chance

to spill apple cider on my khakis as a toast to the event. I had taken to telling customers,

"You will never see a Cosmodemonic at a rest stop along the highway or in a strip

mall." I couldn't be sure of anything anymore. People I started with three years ago

became scarce. The Coffee God was long gone. So were Candace and Mark. Lost track

of Doug. Kati might be next. I knew the OBGYN wanted her to quit working altogether.

Kati didn't want to. I didn't want her to. I was getting used to her walking and looking

differently. The second trimester was well underway. More than. I could see evidence

of the baby. It became so real. I thought I was even more scared. Shitless, in fact.

Beginning to brace myself, if that was the correct term. Never doubted my writing so

much before. I did, but in a way that agreed that I was the source of the fear and doubt. I

created it in my head. The baby visible in Kati was not in my head. But I did have a part

in creating it. No question that I did. Come to think of it, I helped create the

Cosmodemonic experience for thousands of customers over the previous three years.

No question about that, either. I was getting near Oak Park all of a sudden. That

happened fast. Time flies when you are lost in thought. Not sure if I even waved to the

Picasso Horse on my way past.

***

Whenever we had things break down in the city stores, we called Darrel. Out

here in the suburbs, we had a list of companies we had to use. One company did the ice machine; one did the La Mazarco, which was only a three group, by the way. And there was no sign of Dennis-the-Juice-Guy way out here.

One thing I liked was that we had a basement and thus more space to get away on a break. Down there were lots of shelves and even a bathroom that was all our own. There were a table and chairs for us. We were never supposed to take our breaks on the floor at #204 or #206, but when it was cold, or there was simply no room in back, I let the staff do it. Plus there was a full-length mirror to check ourselves for the customers. I still packed my lunch. I could check to see if there was anything stuck in my teeth after eating. Or, as time allowed, I could check my reflection just to feel good about myself. I could also get away with having more lids, cups, and things in stock since there actually was space to store them. That would especially come in useful if we ever got busy enough to need them. When I did the deposits, drawers, and recap sheets, I could escape down to the basement. I needed the separation to concentrate since the register drawers could be noticeably off here once in a while, going back to the previous regime. District manager Kyle presented that as just another challenge for me to work on. Of course, what goes up must come down, so hauling all the coffee downstairs on delivery day was a pain. Then again, #308 was not as busy as any other Cosmodemonic I had worked at before, so there was not as much to deal with. The customers were fine and liked me well enough. We were not as busy as the Wheaton store, father out west. Then again, we were not on a busy corner like they were. District manager Kyle was lining up events to cater in the area in order to get us out to the customer. It sounded like a good plan to me. If I had to work with any of them, it would give me a chance to explore this part of the city.

The schedule had fewer names and fewer hours to fill, especially compared the

weekend shifts at #204. Thank God. It wouldn't have been so bad if I could walk to

#308 like Cynthia, or even just catch one bus to get home. I called Kati at least twice a

day. She called yesterday to tell me Raymond Burr just died. She knew I loved the old

Perry Masons. But that was just an excuse to talk to me. She needed it. She needed to

be reminded that I was available, even by phone, for her if she needed me.

Kati also wanted to know how I was doing, how I was holding up. She could tell

that the whole #308 exile was taking too much out of me. She needed me to be present

when I got home to her. And maybe Kati could tell something by the way I described

April. By trying not to describe her physically. By not saying that the stupid green

aprons that we wore had no business covering up her body. Even when the apron was

on, the fact that it was there only called attention to what it was unable to fully hold

back. At times on the long train rides, I daydreamed of April's physical attributes as the

carrot to get me to #308. I took any motivation to get me there, especially when I didn't

want to leave Kati, the apartment, the neighborhood, and my life before the exile.

This Metra trip was long enough to get some sleep on the way back. Metra-The

way to really sleep. I did. And I would. But before I did, I had to say the trains could

use a separate car for a Cosmodemonic. The first-ever mobile Cosmodemonic. Maybe

I'd suggest it to district manager Kyle. I realized that what Kerry said about his store in

the train station was true. These people lived, breathed, shot, and shit their

Cosmodemonic coffee. Since I was on the train at all hours, I smiled when I saw a cup

in someone's non-briefcase or -umbrella hand. If they were headed to the city, I guessed

the cup came from Wheaton or Bannockburn. If they were headed to the suburbs, my first guess was Kerry's store and failing that, any loop store, even Kati's. Maybe made

by Kati. Hmm, she was never too far from my thoughts. I remembered that she gave me

Heart of Darkness to take on my endless train rides.

***

I was home from opening #308 on Saturday. I got up at 5:12, which meant that I

slept in. Oh, joy. Actually, I didn't feel too tired. I sat down and finished a few quick

postcards to family, short on detail, but everything was going fine. There was no dad for

me to send one to. No reason to for years now. He might have come in handy about

now. He did his part to bring eight kids into this world. But he was gone most of the

time by the time I was old enough to notice him not being around.

I was listening to Kati's Matthew Sweet tape. Kati moved my radio from the

bathroom. Oh well. We watched, or we started a Wim Wenders movie last night. I was

out in seconds. Kati must have lasted a little longer. I got about five hours of sleep. But

I was energized by being home alone. The echoes of my writing days were still there. I

could hear them at the times when I was alone at my desk. Kati was out with her mom

and younger sister buying clothes for Kati and the baby. We didn't know the sex and or

gender. I knew it would be a boy. The sunrise told me. I hadn't said anything though.

We were going out later for dinner. I was feeling self-conscious that I had not paid for

much for the baby. And I would not be able to contribute to dinner later. Kati's family

didn't say anything about it.

***

I tended to worry about things I couldn't control. I could control my diet,
though. And the beer is tasted great. Not a coffee stout I assure you. An amber ale. I
loved my coffee and beer but would not mix the two. If I didn't get a release once in a
while, I was afraid I would end up as about as imaginative as a drying puddle. I felt
better with Kati's family in town. Why did I move here? Why did Kati? We had no one
around.

Maybe I would use the Metra time next week to look over *Back Outta the
World*. It sat at my knee under my writing table. The physical place didn't mean much.
It did not change. But *Back Outta the World* changed in my head constantly. Always
had. Those days, it was less there than anytime I can remember. It was a dream I
dismissed. Hence the thought of physically moving it again. I fully intended to bring it
back to life.

***

For me, it was a Monday morning. The night was not over for most everybody
else. I saw one pathetic soul on our street walking their dog and carrying a plastic bag. I
would never have a dog. I couldn't do this much longer. I stood freezing for about five
minutes before I boarded the warm two-car train to downtown. I couldn't keep this up.
Exile. A day in the life of Jay, a Cosmodemonic manager. I think I would apply to
occupy the stool behind the counter at Liberation Distributors. I was sure the Maoists
didn't get up this early. Instead of *Back Outta the World*, I would work on my
confessions. I apologize for the Master Roast jokes. I was wrong.

Kati was feeling the baby, and she thought she might be having contractions. Or not. We had over three months until the baby was due. I read some more of the books. I thought I knew what was going on, but most of it went out the window due to her condition. She got into the OBGYN tomorrow instead of Thursday. She would have to tell them about the contractions if that is what they were. That meant Kati would soon be forced to quit Cosmodemonic. One paycheck, here we come. I did ironically have Thursday off that week. We had a better handle on the staff now at #308. I wanted Kati to wait so I could go with her. She said she knew her body and that something felt wrong. I suggested she read things into her head from all the books she had read. She only glared at me and said I should just switch my days. It wasn't that easy. It seemed like we had this fight before. We were at each other more. The city was ugly and unfriendly in winter with no snow to decorate it, especially headed west out of town. It passed by my window. Chicago, this train, and Cosmodemonic roll on oblivious.

It had been way too cold for Kati and me to share in reveries, walks, or time by the lake. To relax and escape we watched *Lovejoys* together at night when I didn't close. Or sometimes we'd start a movie I'd never finish.

It was too much work to read. And it was too much effort to try to write anything new. I still liked to write in my Sketchbook of the Mind at least. But, I need to review the old budget from #308. District manager Kyle was hosting a seminar on store budgets at the regional office. I should have been getting ready for that. I didn't want to do that either. My Metra was taking me back to my city. Then to my El and up toward the apartment and Kati. The appointment was not dramatic. But Kati was no longer allowed to be on her feet for an extended time. The pains might or might not have been related to work hours on her feet. The OBGYN saw no reason to take any chances. Kati had to call Van Buren and take a leave of absence, immediately. One more thing that was not easy for her to do since she still liked working at Cosmodemonic.

***

Wednesday on the way home, I dreamed I am back in my shack in Costa Rica. I felt like being alone there. No Kati. No one else. I was sitting in one of those old aluminum lounge chairs with the plastic straps. The kind my parents had on our front porch. Some of the straps are frayed in the places they always frayed. The ocean rolled in my ears. I had a beer in my hand and was on my small back porch taking in the ocean and sky in front of me. A lizard or two skittered around on the wooden slats of my porch floor. I was confirming that I always knew this would be my destination. I was sitting on the frayed chair and happy with my life choices. The latest novel would be finished soon. I was at the point where it had no choice but to finish itself. I knew this was my future. It was just a matter of time and million more double tall skim lattes.

***

No two days were ever remotely alike. Wednesday was the night Kati and I didn't sleep. Something seemed wrong with Kati and the baby. It seemed wrong enough for us to head to the hospital.

As I tried to write about last week and all that happened, I started with the Bulls game on the TV. It was on in the hospital room where Kati and I ended up. There was so no sound on. There was no one else in the room. Kati was on the bed surrounded by tubes and monitors. I sat on a stool next to her, and the TV was on the wall above her.

303

The Bulls were playing the Suns, and even with the sound down, just halfway into the first quarter, I could tell it was a great game.

We had been there since the morning. By game time, Kati was fine. The baby was fine. They couldn't and didn't find anything wrong. We were waiting to be processed and sent home. So, we were left alone in that hospital room. It was quiet now. There was nothing for anyone to do. We had made it this morning to a different part of the hospital in the cab. Kati had already had the number of the taxi company stuck on the fridge. After that night of no sleep, decisions to go, decisions not to go, I called around nine a.m. I kept my wits about me. Maybe all the experience from handling the holiday rushes at #204 helped keep me calm. We made it to the hospital with the bag Kati had already packed and waiting for the birth. She had not wasted her time when she had not been working. We finally made it, got checked in, and met the nurses and the doctor on duty. The doctor was a tall guy who was confident enough to use some humor to help Kati relax. Mostly though, we waited in one place and moved somewhere else. Waited there and moved somewhere else again. To everyone else at the hospital, it was just a day on the job. I suppose that is how they have to treat it.

As inconclusive as it turned out to be, I looked back on it a week later as good practice. Kati had abdominal pains for the next day or two. By Saturday, they were all but gone. Most importantly, Kati knew she was all right. She could feel the baby and knew it was all right. I worked Sunday because I took that next day off. Kati's mom and dad came up Friday night late. They only got in the way this time.

We got discharged before halftime of the Bulls game, and I joked to Kati that we would be home in time to see the end. I remember that she tried not to smile. She did though. She looked just great again. Tired and a little pale but great to me. Great mostly because she knew she had somehow helped her baby when she was called on. The staff and such at the hospital didn't seem to do much. So, I smiled too as I held her bag while we walked slowly to a waiting cab. It wasn't at my dumb joke. I was smiling for myself. I was happy for the man who would no longer recognize himself alone, in a shack in Costa Rica. Happy for the man who spent that whole ordeal wanting the baby to be okay, realizing that the man who would be a father in a few months had finally shown up.

Chapter Eleven

I found myself walking near #204 yesterday. Running odd errands for things I used to pick up on my walks to or from work when I had the time to walk. I would not usually do this on days when it was midwinter. I must have needed the walk for the exercise mostly. I passed the old Love Transient Hotel and saw a group of people through the window huddled around coffee cups. I got the impression the coffee was Cosmodemonic. A guy walked toward me from the same hotel lobby from that group. That small scene brought on a pang to write. I still needed to keep it up. "Work toward a dream, and it will happen," I told myself as I started walking once more.

***

Life around our apartment was feeling better. Kati and I had been at each other less. She was cleaning and moving and rearranging smaller things when she felt like she could get away with it. She called it, "building a nest and it is quite common."

Our place was going to be even smaller. It wasn't like we could afford to add a lot to it or had the time to move. My family offered to help with money. So had Cosmodemonic. Not directly, of course. I had been considering exercising some of my options.

Got a call from my wannabe writer colleague in Ohio. He was boozing before he called, but it was good to hear a voice from back in those days. He had just wanted to talk. It was a Sunday afternoon. I had the day off. It had been too many workdays in a row since the hospital stay. I was going to start a countdown until full term for the baby and keep it in my Sketchbook of the Mind. Didn't have the time. But, I had some beers while we talked, and that helped along with the nostalgic phone call. My friend

remembered we planned to start a writer's colony in New Mexico where it was always

warm. I hadn't thought of that in ages. The hissing of our Franklin stove seemed to

taunt me as we talked. I loved the idea of someplace warm.

I was hoping for the baby more than ever before. I was sure nothing would go

wrong. I remembered my sunrise. Did it happen as I remembered it? It did, the account

is in the pages of my Sketchbook of the Mind. Maybe that sunrise helped me stay calm

during the hospital ordeal because I knew we would be fine.

***

More proof that the Picasso Horse lives. It is Monday on the Metra after leaving

the El and crossing the couple blocks to the commuter station. The city streets are even

more barren and moon like on Monday predawn. On the way past it, I saw steam

coming from where the Picasso Horse's mouth and nostrils would be. Steam, but it was

breath.

Not much to tell about life at Cosmodemonic #308. There had been a slight

improvement in whole bean, just from communicating to newer customers that we

actually sold it. The closing drawer was short $20 a couple nights before. I had to leave

district manager Kyle a voicemail when it was short more than $5. I could replace it

with money from the tips and repay it like I used to. But, I didn't get tips anymore. And

I was broke as a joke now. One more reason to miss #204 and #206 was that I had some

spending money due to those cash tips. And I had some kind of ceiling to my hours.

Now, I don't. Plus my commute took forever. Whose idea was this? But at least, the staff was holding steady and showed up for their shifts.

***

I got a letter from my sister in Texas. She and her husband had been parents for several years. She was excited and helpful about planning for the upcoming baby. My sister and her husband slept on an air mattress and weren't rolling in money then. They lived in a house with rooms, however. A room for each of their kids. Kati bought (with money left from her last paycheck) a lambie, as she called it. It looked like a rug of white lamb hair and was about the size of a doormat. But soft. It was for us to put the baby on when needed. That would be the baby's first room, more or less.

One more thing. I felt like I have to be home. Close to Kati and our baby-to-be. That feeling was stronger than ever. I wasn't sure why. There wasn't a lot I could do.

Kati alternated between hopeful expectation and fear of the worst. I did too but didn't say anything to anyone. Just put most of it in my sketchbook. She couldn't wait until full term arrives so she could do more outside. She had already repacked the hospital bag and had me put the changing table together. It was way bigger than I pictured it. It took up half of the remaining floor space in our room. Kati was thinking of life after the baby. She considered becoming a midwife. I could see that. I could see her becoming a midwife after all the reading and studying she had already done. She read so much on pregnancy and the whole process that she had a great head start. I guessed that meant she had no desire to return to Cosmodemonic.

The long Metra ride lent itself to daydreams. Especially the return trip. It was not a long walk from #308 to the station. I was going in the opposite direction of the masses heading home. If all went well, I could leave #308 when Connie showed up to close during the week. Homeward bound around 3:30. Sometimes I had my tripio with me. I swear it was not quite the same out there. Made on our three-group La Marzocco. A newer one of course. The machine just needed to be seasoned more to give the shots depth. Just a theory of mine.

In my daydream, I was living in a lakeside home like the one Natali's dad had in the UP. Or better yet, having it for the most of the year, except when it was cold. I was too sick of being cold to include winter as an option in the reoccurring daydream of mine. Ideally, I was going up there to live and have space to write. That required the financial freedom of a man with lots of time. I would have cashed in my options to write full time and would have sold some works. Kati could be a midwife with no specific workplace or boss to speak of. We could have the baby with us until school age. Then, who knows. That was my daydream moved from Costa Rica to accommodate some reality. The house would be big enough for visitors, like our families. Over an evening bottle of wine, I would entertain them with my writerly wisdom and humor. If all this could get me there. If this commute, the 3:55 alarms, the hours, the time away. If this would get me there, then bring it on, my friend! Think of all the problems like the aforementioned commute, missing till money, transition amounts, budgets, and partner reviews as obstacles or mile markers on the road to the dream house. *Work to achieve it!* I was already on the right road, just needed to pass those mile markers as I come to them. I was getting closer.

***

The hospital bills came rolling in. I sent in an order to exercise fifty options of Cosmodemonic stock. Would I regret it? Who knows? I could be hit by a bus before I get the check.

***

I had to run to Treasure Island early. I used to have a routine. Now, I did things when work allowed me to. I did things that Kati wasn't supposed to do. Those days were coming to an end. The baby seemed to be growing and would soon be defined as "full term." Every day the pregnancy went on the chances got better and better for a healthy, normal birth. Kati did not want to schedule a C-section. I agreed, not because I knew anything at all, but because she seemed sure about it. My sunrise vision made no distinction, but I had a feeling from it that the boy would be delivered by Kati. Not that it mattered anymore. Just as long as he made it.

***

When I was looking for a bargain at Treasure Island, I noticed an older guy sitting in the Treasure Island Café eating, thinking, and looking sad. The next thing I glanced at was a magazine cover that read "Chicago's 50 Richest." The guy at the Treasure Island Café wasn't one of them. It was too easy to measure something like richest. Money was too easy to use. Money was just a default. It was too easy a path to follow. The title should have been "Fifty People Being Told What to Do." It was a boring story. Fifty boring stories. I would have rather heard the story of the Treasure Island man. Or I could write it.

***

It suddenly occurred to me on the train trip that I could exercise some Cosmodemonic stock and buy a crappy car. Insane? No, but I should have thought of it sooner.

And, that I needed a Brown Elephant trip. There was no longer any time to walk up there. It had been almost three months of exile but felt like a century. My white shirts were not as white because I hadn't been able to take them to the cleaners. Karl's laundry room didn't quite get it done. Would I have time to get to my space on the roof when it warmed up?

I needed to get off the train and stop those negative thoughts. I took care of Kati when she needed it. It was practice for later, for the baby. I could do it. But the commute wore me out. I should change my thoughts after I change trains. There would be different ones after the transfer.

Made the transfer to the El. I found a good seat on a Thursday night. A benefit of being the anti-commuter. The drawer was short ten dollars. I closed with April and Hippie Dave, who had a long ponytail but wasn't really a hippie. I had to send him home at eight. We closed at nine out in the burbs. One good thing about #308 was that it was a more serene weeknight vibe. Store #308 did not produce the revenue to warrant three closers, so I usually asked for a volunteer to leave early. Thankfully, Hippie Dave needed to go to band practice. That meant it was just me and April, a good closer in addition to being easy on the eyes. In fact, the more we worked together, the more appealing she became. It seemed that she was looking better than when I first saw her several months before. Her new short haircut highlighted her big, light brown eyes. Those were the eyes that met mine down in the basement after close earlier. Well, the reflection of those eyes.

April had told me she was meeting Gail (not Gayle) at Punky's, a few Metra stops west, for Thirsty Thursdays. She was changing in the bathroom as I counted the short drawer over and over. I was dreading placing the call to district manager Kyle. It was only ten dollars, and I was preoccupied with the idea of reaching into the safe and taking the ten from tips. It would have been so easy. The actual tips payout was a week away. My options check would most likely be in by then, and I could easily repay it then. I liked the way the broker asked me about the sale. Kati and I joked about it because I sold it at street value. Made it sound like a shady mob style deal. I didn't ask how long it would take to arrive, the tax implications, or any of that. I just hung up and felt like it might have been stupid to do what I just did. I didn't remember if it was the fortieth or fiftieth time I had debated that in my head when I heard April's voice ask, "What's wrong?"

I looked up and to the wall to my right, where the mirror was hanging. It was strategically placed just before the stairs so we could check ourselves before facing the loyal customers. I had been so involved in my mental war that I hadn't heard her leave the bathroom, changed and ready for the night out.

April's back was to me. I was sitting at my desk, right knee pressing the bottom of the desk and staring at the unbalanced till. Her eyes were looking at me via an angled reflection in the mirror. Her light brown eyes were wide from asking the question. She held a lipstick tube in her right hand after just applying. She held the case next to and slightly away from her wonderful face as if to show me just how great she could look when made up. And more to say, "How do I look?" than "What's wrong?" I knew from her reflected eyes that is what she meant. I said nothing for a moment. April did not attempt to break eye contact. She wanted an answer. I couldn't give it. I broke off the reflected stare with effort. Looking down on the way back to the till, I took in her black sweater and wonderfully fitting jeans and replied with no enthusiasm at all, "Nothing. Just tired."

There was a pounding on the front door. We both knew it was Gail (not Gayle) coming to pick up April for the night at Punky's. April quickly put the lipstick case away, grabbed her purse and bag, and headed toward the steps. Just before she took the first step, she hesitated and aligned her enveloped, and thus highlighted body, and said, "Have fun."

Whatever scent she was wearing finally awoke my conscious mind, edging out the ten dollars. It lingered for a few moments as I heard the door open. I knew I had to get up there to lock it again. April didn't have a key. I suddenly felt like I had to get home to Kati and all she meant to me. I tossed the till together and called district manager Kyle and left the voicemail. There were more important things in this world than ten bucks.

***

I lucked into a weekday off at last. I rose early to drink coffee, lengthen the day, and hang out with Kati. She is asleep under our quilt. I heard the beeping of the garbage

313

truck from the alley. The noise carried right up the back steps into our apartment. So annoying. I hoped it didn't wake her up. When she felt up to it, we were venturing to Osco for supplies, including rubber pants. Up until a few days ago, I had no idea what they were and was too embarrassed to ask. I figured it out just yesterday after Kati said she had called and set up a diaper cleaning service. Her mom gave her the money for it.

The coffee tasted fine this morning. I didn't recall which varietal it was. I guessed Central American by its light body. I got so sick of unfurling the bags to get to the coffee I put it all in a glass jar for easy access a week or so ago. No big deal, but it saved a little time every morning. Every second mattered when I got up at 3:55 for the commute to #308.

I still had to clean the bathroom. Someone was playing Jackson Browne from another apartment. We had only three more weeks, or hopefully more, until the baby could be born safely.

Damn if district manager Kyle didn't call a few minutes before. I had to meet him in the regional office before I closed next Thursday so we could figure out the missing money. The last thing I wanted to do was to spend it thinking about Cosmodemonic. Couldn't they leave me in peace?

Got a letter from my older brother in Cincinnati and a postcard from one of my sisters. Both wished me well. My brother had been looking to open his own Volvo repair shop. He was bummed because the spot he wanted had been taken. Long story, but it was one of the dominos that fell from the new upscale shopping center planned in that area. He needed space for lots of cars to stay parked while he worked on one or two of the others. Never thought of that. Wish Cosmodemonic had been that careful when

planning #308. It is in a bad location, parking or not.

Getting ready for a family wasn't easy. Or cheap. I worried long term. Kati had

read so much. She said that she would like a natural, home birth. But she knew that

wouldn't happen this time. The baby was in the right uterus. That seems to be the good

one. Since she wanted to be a midwife, she'd like to experience a natural birth. We

talked on the slow walk to Osco. She would like to have more than one. I agreed. One

was not a family as I had lived it. Kati and I both came from big families, and it made

sense to want the same thing. I said, "Let's just get through this one first." Of course,

Kati agreed. But, thinking ahead, as she always did, Kati wanted to breastfeed and stay

at home. She wanted to give the baby a hands-on style of care and upbringing. All the

new data, according to Kati's books, suggested that it was best for the baby to have at

least one parent engaged and around for years, not just weeks or months. She filled me

in as we walked all over the Osco. We had a cart full by the time we left: onesies, diaper

pins, disposable diapers for early days, lotions for mom and baby, and on and on and

on. I had to charge it all. Kati had no income at the moment. We had to get a cab home

because we had too much to carry, which in turn cost us more. Mo money, mo money.

At least breast milk was free.

***

Tomorrow I'd be back to work at #308. The day off went too fast. With all that

that was coming, at home and at Cosmodemonic, I still thought of writing. I wanted to

start something. It would be good for me. The morning at home triggered the feeling of those days writing *Back Outta the World*. It was not easy to sit down and write a lot of

times when I had better things I could be doing. Was I already that nostalgic for it?

***

Kati and I had formal dinner at the kitchen table that night consisting of bread,

broccoli, and Polish sausage. I washed mine down with a couple Lienes. Best I'd felt all

day. I left the close to Connie and Michael K. She knew what she was doing. District

manager Kyle suggested I review the closing and deposit procedures with her tonight.

Didn't he know I didn't have a car? There was no chance of me staying the entire shift

to do that. Store #308 had two drawers, so I reviewed them on the second drawer, the

bean drawer that we never used. It was the best I could do. I was a phone call away.

And there was no way was I going back, even if I could. My place was here with Kati.

She and I put together a mobile thing to hang over the crib. The crib was big too. No

room in our room. I asked Kati why we needed one if we were doing the breastfeeding,

family bed thing. She said it was for naps or when we needed a place to put the baby

while she made dinner or what have you. Again, I had no idea. Kati also told me that

her mom talked to my mom yesterday.

***

Monday Metra Madness. I used to read Si Burick in the Dayton Daily News as a

kid. He wrote about the Reds, Bengals, and the Dayton Flyers. He'd name his columns

thing like that: Monday Musings or Friday Fodder. He may have inspired me to want to

write. I wondered if the baby would grow up to like sports. The Metra Madness referred

to the Picasso Horse. It still watched me with unblinking intensity as I passed in front of

316

it. It would normally be bad writing to refer to a sculpture as unblinking. But, this sculpture continued to be an exception.

We were rapidly going broke.

I never did start *Heart of Darkness* but started *Cadence* by James Crumley instead. I did that though. I usually waited until a book called to me. Even if I got some books for Christmas, I'd wait for months and sometimes longer. Or, I'd start it right away. Depended on if I heard the call. This was his first book. I realized that I was a writer when I read it. A writer and soon to be a father. But, would that last? Maybe realized wasn't right. Maybe I remembered that I am a writer. That would not change. *Back Outta the World* expressed ideas that I didn't fully understand yet. But, that didn't stop me. "By writing one becomes a writer" meant that writing was there in me. Crumley started slow. It seemed obvious to me in *Cadence*. It was equally obvious that it was the one and only Crumley. That's the way it's gotta, or gonna be. For better or worse, my friend.

***

On my commute, I was on the El daydreaming of the back porch of my shack in Costa Rica again. Just me and the lizards. It was because I was headed to #308 and didn't want to think about it until I was there. District manager Kyle did manage to send an MIE to help. It sounded good, getting forty free labor hours. That was how district manager Kyle saw it. But he was new to Cosmodemonic. He came from Pier One or somewhere. I thanked him, smiling over the phone, but knew that the MIE would end up needing a lot of attention from me. I didn't have it in me then.

317

I forgot to tell Kati I was meeting district manager Kyle. The OBGYN appointment was that same day. This missing money thing had me preoccupied. Cosmodemonic wanted me at #308 even more, to track it down. I thought I had just been hoping it would go away.

Kati didn't want to hear about short tills or Cosmodemonic. I remembered that I told her I would go for sure that time. This OBGYN appointment would be too important. We had the same fight. She said needed me more than Cosmodemonic did. It rolled on, gaining steam as it went. There were enough people out there to help it now, too. More and more people knew about it and wanted to work for Cosmodemonic. Where were all these people when I started? I tried to explain it to Kati. I said the new MIE guy had no real experience, that Connie was good but couldn't work overtime and that the sooner the problem was solved, the easier life at #308 would be. Kati brought up the obvious fact that I didn't get paid for all that overtime after they made me a manager. I couldn't be in two places at once. It felt like thoughts kept leaving my head, brewed in, poured out, brewed in, and continually poured out until it was dry. Nothing left to brew into my mind. My mind was empty and hollow like our brewing canisters left overnight. There were ground thoughts in the basket waiting to be started tomorrow morning. But now it sits empty. That was my mind, empty and waiting to be filled again. I just wanted to sleep until I got downtown.

I found last week's Barron's, checked the stock, and then put it over my face. I had to try to doze.

***

The walks with Kati used to be getaways. Now they are not. Does anything, anything, stay the same when a baby is on the way? Because now when we walk, it is no longer fun. We tried to take a short walk on Saturday. It was late winter, and everything was grey, and even the crust of snow remaining had turned black on the curbs. All the bits of hibernating trash had been revealed by the thaw. A little warm air brought too many people out on a late Saturday morning. And with that came too much noise. Kati was not as nimble as she was when we first met. We couldn't even go a block, and she had to stop and step aside or have someone step aside for her. We tried to hold hands for a while, but that was a no go. There were also the obstacles that didn't move such as telephone poles, parking meters, and the bicycles chained to them. We did make it to the one and only park in the neighborhood. I had thought of it as a quaint and pleasant spot but never once before in all the times I passed it, did I really look it over. Today, it looked cramped. It was a playground, but there was no room to run. Just run for the sake of it, to play chase, or even toss a baseball back and forth. Plus, it was like a cage, surrounded by bars. I remembered the occasional break at #206 when I went to the Lincoln Park Zoo. It always depressed me to see the animals in those cages. On top of that, I had to show the closing procedure at #308 to new MIE guy later. I didn't want to be embarrassed by having the tills short in front of the new guy. I was lost in thought and began to cross the street to the command of the walk sign. I made it just about halfway across when I heard my name. It was Kati calling to ask me to slow down.

***

I thought the close or open at #204 or 206 were bad. There was an old Day's Inn on across the street from #204. Some nights after closing #204, I would step out of

#204, lock the door knowing my key would be the next one to fit the lock in about six hours. I would turn to head home and see the neon Days Inn sign and ache to cross the street and check myself in for the night. I did not discover such a daydream option on the commute to #308 for this weekend. It was Sunday evening, and I did somehow make it through. Store #308 didn't stay open as late or open as early on the weekends as my old Cosmodemonics but that time was eaten by the commute. The two days ran together. District manager Kyle suggested it because it gave me the opportunity, his word, to schedule and then work with everyone on #308's staff. I spent both shifts trying not to be conspicuous as I watched the registers open and close. Mostly, I felt useless spying on everyone. But the new MIE guy was fine. He had only just started his training and had no background in coffee. They didn't need it much anymore. But, I was glad he was around to take some of the responsibility of #308 off me at some point. Of course, he had a car.

***

Kati and I were ready. It was exactly two weeks until full term as determined by the OBGYN. I felt like we'd reached a truce about the appointment. I couldn't be there. I didn't even try to change it. The meeting with district manager Kyle would be Thursday, and I had a case of fear. I splurged on a Winter Lager on sale. Kati also had one before her phone call to her mom. There was a school of thought that in the advanced state, an occasional beer was good for you. I'd buy that. Made me feel less selfish. I wished the missing money thing was done. I hoped I could figure it out before the baby. I couldn't have that hanging over my head at a time like that.

I had next Tuesday off. It was my only day off that week. And it wouldn't do me much good unless the baby showed up. I couldn't do this when the baby comes. I would need more time with Kati and the baby. Did they expect me to work all the time to chase some money? Didn't Cosmodemonic have better things to do? I would clear it up with district manager Kyle.

On my second lager and thoughts of my meeting with district manager Kyle were coming along easily. I would simply tell him what was important in this world. During the ultrasound they did at the hospital, I saw the baby. For the first time. I would simply tell district manager Kyle that I had to be there when the baby was born and therefore could not work, commute, sleep, work, commute, and sleep. I wasn't sure how exactly. But, I could tell district manager Kyle that I had had a vision on the corner of Diversey, Clark, and Broadway that spoke to me. It told me what to expect, what to prepare for, and that I was not getting out of it. Those were the facts of my life, and the understanding would come later. No promises other than that. So, I would tell district manager Kyle that I knew what was important in life and that it was not the recap sheet at #308! Yes! He would get it. I wasn't sure if he had kids. I couldn't keep up with all the new people at Cosmodemonic, especially without access to Dennis-the-Juice-Guy.

***

Tuesday the two of us were holding steady. It was impossible for Kati to sleep soundly most nights. She usually could get to sleep around four or so. Apparently, we could expect a similar schedule from the baby when he arrives. I still know it is a boy. I hadn't told Kati about my sunrise vision experience. But it happened. I know it did. It was for me. As for today, sun was out for a change. And it was almost warming up. I thought I would head up on the roof to my spot. I'd keep my clothes on of course. It was quiet and calm here. Kati had finally fallen asleep. My coffee was made. I was paying the bills. *Have faith. If you ever think you are not good enough, think of the sunrise.* Why did its power go away? I knew it happened but the strength from that moment evaporated so quickly. It did come back. But was sure as hell not here as I tried to pay the bills sitting ay my old writing desk with *Back Outta the World* collecting dust at my knees.

Paying the bills. That reality overcame the long gone two-lager buzz I had when I had my pretend meeting with district manager Kyle. In reality, he was all business. I was not impressive at all. I said nothing but a small "Thanks" when he wished me luck on the birth. District manager Kyle was more interested in the progress of the MIE guy than anything else. I wondered if district manager Kyle knew I didn't really care anymore about Cosmodemonic #308.

***

I went out to put the bills in the box, along with a few postcards. Then I hit Treasure Island for a few provisions. Not as good as my Mondays used to be. I returned a video. I came back to find Kati was reading and doing fine, at least now that I was back. She said she got nervous a little while after I left. She felt like something was going to happen when I was out. But, it passed. Nonetheless, she was glad I was back. The walk in the sun had convinced me it would be a good time to hit my spot on the roof. But, as I stood next to our bed, Kati motioned for me to come closer. I sat next to her and put my hand on her baby belly as she had taken to calling it.

"Do you remember that note I left you?" Kati asked me out of the blue. I took my hand off her body and took her left hand in my right. I did it as a sign of affection but also to buy me some time. I didn't remember, exactly.

"The one I stuck in your bag the night you got no sleep?" Kati looked softly up at me.

"Yea, I do. It took me a minute. A lot on my mind." I said buying more time.

"Join the club" She smiled back at me.

In her smile, I remembered. It was the morning of the sunrise vision. I read that note Kati had written for me. I stuck it in the pile of my Sketchbooks of the Mind some time ago. I began to remember as I sat on the edge of the bed, feeling her warm body meet mine at our hips.

"You said to me that you hoped the situation would take care of itself." Kati looked from me for a second and continued, "Or you would leave me."

"That was before," I tried to speak up, to explain. Kati didn't want either. She calmly went on.

"Just now, I was trying to imagine what it would be like if you were gone—for good." Kati continued holding up her free hand to stop me from interrupting. "Because I knew the baby would make it. Even if all the books I read said it was almost impossible. And I knew if you left—"

"It would be some kind of sick lie, and we'd both be miserable." I quoted her

words back to her. It was the part Kati was waiting for me to remember. Our held-hands

squeezed a little tighter. Kati silently acknowledged that I got the quote right. That it

was the part she was getting at from the note. My deepened clasp of her hand

acknowledged that Kati did, somehow, know me better than I knew myself.

***

I made it up to my spot with no surprise to see that my chair was still there. And

the bottles from last summer were still in the same spot. They were not mine, of course.

I always brought mine back down. I'd never been up there in a sweatshirt and jeans. It

went on below me. The city. I only had my Sketchbook of the Mind and no book. Too

distracted to read those days. I'd been watching the trash truck making its rounds below,

beeping as it backed up. I remembered I'd found an old copy of *Big Table* in the alley.

It was when I had just moved up here. It was in good condition with writing by some of

the Beats. It was a good sign, I thought at the time. The guys in the truck went about

their business. If I'd thought I could make it in time, I'd climb down to the apartment

and retrieve the manuscript. I could then toss it down to them. I assumed they didn't

know I was watching.

They were doing their jobs. Not much chance they had stock in Cosmodemonic.

I was lucky. I needed to tell my family to buy some Cosmodemonic stock. I'd meant to.

I should have felt so lucky to go to work and just by showing up, ensure a future.

Things were just getting started at Cosmodemonic. It would be nationwide one day. But

I couldn't do it. I just didn't care. All the Cosmodemonic was to me now was the

324

missing money from the drawers. Did that ever happen to Mark or Doug? Around $150 missing. Not much to the Cosmodemonic in the grand scheme. I'm not Colombo. Someone must have been stealing. But they must have known the safe combination. I did an extra deposit when I was on. I went up there to get those thoughts out of my head. *Stop*. I needed to go back downstairs and tell Kati all this. I would, but she was reading.

The sun is coming in and out; it was an early spring sun, in and out from behind the clouds. Every day was so different from the one before or the one to come. The early spring sun was helping to warm me a little. But it had yet to help my mind, my confidence. In fact, I couldn't do this either. I couldn't handle fatherhood and Cosmodemonic at the same time. Sitting on my chair of past summers and beers and vanity tans and *Tropic*, I was lost to myself. I wanted the oblivious Jay to return. I wanted the Lead Clerk Jay back. The Cosmodemonic lead with just enough responsibility. I wanted the wannabe writer Jay back in this chair. He had a plan. A plan for a shack in Costa Rica. I wanted that Jay to wake up again next to Kati and later take her black shorts to the washer four stories below and that would be it.

The armrests on the beat-up old chair are still cold to the touch. Just like always, the city went on about its business. I could still hear the trash truck, but getting farther away. The beer bottles. They were strewn exactly how they were months and months ago. They have not moved, changed, progressed in any way. They could be me. Should be me. The changing of the days, the energy of the moving world hadn't touched them. But I got caught up in it. I should have stayed up here. Not meant to be. I thought I heard Kati.

"Jay! Jay! You better get down here!"

Epilogue

It has been a while since I've done this. At Midway at gate twenty-eight, waiting for a flight to St. Louis I needed to get some water. Planes and airports and traveling made me thirsty. I had to buy a cheapie, imitation Sketchbook of the Mind. More like a tablet a server would use at a restaurant. It was all they had. It would do. I didn't have a lot of time.

Kati took the boys on a stroll before our connecting flight to St. Louis. I think the last time I was there was before Bill was born, almost three years ago. Kati stayed in Charleston. And just like that time, my sister was helping pay for the flights. So were Kati's parents. They were driving over from Charleston to meet us for the weekend.

I just had to take a few notes. I passed a Cosmodemonic next to the magazine kiosk. Not like I hadn't seen one since we left Chicago but this one struck a chord in me. The tall blonde guy working the register reminded me of Phil from #204. It wasn't, of course. Cosmodemonic was in big cities everywhere now. And in airports. And grocery stores. You name it. It showed no signs of stopping. Onward, Master Roast! I almost got a tripio at this one but was too thirsty. Plus, I knew it wouldn't be the same. The store wasn't busy. They never were, at least to me and Kati. Not like the weekends at #204 or #206.

The tripios at my current store came close though but were still not quite the same. The heart and soul were not there. I ran the Cosmodemonic Café inside Mega Books in Cincinnati. It is on the same location that my brother wanted his Volvo shop to go. It all worked out though. He got me word that the Mega Books was planning to open and it would have a Cosmodemonic Café. And he ended up with a better location for his shop after all.

I saw them way down the corridor. It looked like they were looking at the vending machines. Kati never let Bill have junk if we weren't traveling. It gave me more time for this Sketchbook of the Mind.

Bill was born a few weeks early after all that double uterus pregnancy stress. A healthy and beautiful baby boy. Kati knew it was not a false alarm when she yelled to me from two stories below me. The next morning at 6:14 am, Bill was born. But, I still haven't told Kati or anyone about my sunrise vision. I imagined there was no need anymore. I saw him on the warming table, pink and a picture of health. Kati was strong as ever. I was there for it all. Turned out she was right about me. She always knew I had it in me. We saw it through together. I wasn't in the waiting room handing out cigars. After we were discharged, I remember waiting for a cab. Kati was in a wheelchair because they required it, holding Bill. I had the bags and watched the world go by. It had kept going, oblivious. I shook my head a couple times to make sure I was seeing what I was seeing. No, it was true. The world and all of its people kept going about their lives, even if Kati and Jay had just had their first child.

I didn't get a feel for the city out at the airport, but I missed Chicago and especially the neighborhood. I was happy, I guess, that we moved, now that we have two, but no one will ever be able to tell me there is a better neighborhood in a better city anywhere.

With help from my older brother, Kati and I found a half a duplex close to work. I walked to my Mega Café when Kati needed the car. The walks were functional, practical but couldn't compare to a walk on Halsted or Clark after close on a Saturday night.

The best walks we took now were with the boys in a double stroller. Kati and I took turns pushing the boys along the quiet, older neighborhood streets of Cincinnati. We lived in an upstairs apartment, and that worked. But, I looked with envy on the lamp-lit living rooms of the homes we passed. Kati would take a walk with the stroller when I was at work and knew a few different paths. One we took I called the Chicken Run walk. That was the name of the old restaurant we passed on our evening walks when she hadn't done one earlier. The fried chicken coming from it smelled so good. So good because it was good. But also because I always wanted to go in and have it. Then and there. But, it was not in the budget. We had to try to save to buy our own house. A house to raise the family. I couldn't help it, it filled my mind. Only because it would have so easy—if…

Maybe that is why I didn't keep a Sketchbook of the Mind anymore. I would fill it with ifs. If only I had stayed at Cosmodemonic. If only I could have found the missing money. Instead, district manager Kyle let me step down, resign from being a manager at #308. Looking back, he seemed relieved. I think he knew my heart wasn't in it. He let me step down, and my Cosmodemonic career slowly ended at the Dearborn and Division store #236. I worked with Candace's brother who coincidently had also stepped down from just being a lead at Armitage. So, it was as close as district manager

Kyle could get me to Kati and the baby under the circumstances. The end result was that it gave me more time to plan the move and try to find a job.

When I took a break at Mega Books, I sometimes headed to the newspapers and periodicals. I still looked at a *Barron's* or *Investor's Business Daily* and checked on Cosmodemonic stock. The last time I did, it had just split. If I had held on to it, I could pick and choose any house around here to make a down payment on. With a yard as big as the one little park we had in our Lakeview neighborhood. If. If. If. See, I knew it.

Of course, the Cosmodemonic stock paid for Bill's birth. And for Jack's too. Twenty months after Bill, Jack was born. Kati couldn't keep her hands off of me (ha-ha). The OBGYNs and hospitals down there were no more capable than Chicago's. Kati ended up having Jack as a C-section. That took care of the rest of the IPO money. In and around all of that, Kati and I had a legal marriage officiated by a Justice of the Peace. My older brother came over to watch Bill. One day we plan on renewing our vows and having a party. For now, no time, no money.

No matter. *Here they come.* Jack, the pre-existing condition, as he was labeled and therefore not covered by insurance, was in the baby backpack. He was almost too big and insisted on being put in facing out. He wanted to see the world. Kati didn't work yet but hadn't given up on being a midwife one day. For now, she spent so much time with them that it was hard to do anything else. But she knew them so well, and I had begun to see the benefits of her staying with them. For one, she could breastfeed them which was free. And they were smart as hell, and never sick. Kati read to them a lot, which helped. One benefit of working for Mega Books was access to cheap books.

Once, I came home with two big shopping bags of children's books for them. There

must have been forty in total, and I paid less than a dollar for each one. I loved to read

to them too. But I spent time with them doing everything else. A lot of time. It felt like

time well spent, though. It felt like the best investment I'd ever make. And it was

getting more valuable every day, like my stock used to.

I hate to admit it, but on slow nights at Mega Books, I did wander the aisles and

imagine I see the spine of *Back Outta the World* on one of the shelves. In real life, it

was safely stored in my old room at my mom's house in Dayton. It was there, slowing

becoming a classic work of fiction.

Okay. Here they come now. Break over. Bill was running ahead of Kati and Jack

with a vending bag of chips in each hand and a big smile on his face. He was a mix of

us, so I'm told. Jack was looking on from the Snugli. Kati too, had her beautiful,

inviting smile back. The one with a bit of mischief in it. It is the one she had on when

she asked how boot camp was, a million years ago.

"I hope you haven't started that again," Kati asked me, seeing the pad and pen in

my hands, as I stood up to greet them.

"Oh, I am just killing some time," I leaned over to kiss her on the cheek and

touch Jack's shoulder. At the next instant, I looked down at Bill and asked, "What have

you got there?"

"Chips from a machine!" He chirped back, eyes wide with achievement.

"He wants to show you how the machine works," Kati responded knowing how and what Bill is thinking without being told. A benefit of spending so much time with him and Jack.

"Yeah, dad, come on. Mom's right. I want to show you."

"We do have about fifteen more minutes," Kati confirmed. "Plus, I need to sit for a minute in peace. Here take Jack with you. Mr. inquisitive wants to see everything also."

"Here, take my water and notes." I agreed, trading for Jack and the Snugli.

"Daaad!" Bill said to me, starting back down the corridor.

"Just a second. Got him. Don't read it."

"Okay, I won't. Just like all the other ones I didn't read."

The way Kati said it, I knew she had read them all when she was on bed rest. It never really occurred to me. At that moment, it didn't matter. I didn't mind. That meant she knew everything. Had read all my old Sketchbooks of the Mind. And she still loved me for all my mistakes and faults and fears. She always knew we were in this together. We had to be. She was and still is ahead of me.

"*Back Outta the World?*"

"Of course."

"Tell me what you thought on the flight."

"If we have the time. I think, for now, it is right where it needs to me. You better go. He wants to show you." Kati nodded in the directions of the vending machines. "Have you got some change on you?"

"Uhh, yea…I didn't buy any coffee…Okay, guys lets go…See you in a few. Love you"

"Love you too. Have fun."

"Dad…let's go…Daaad…"

THE END

Made in the USA
Columbia, SC
31 May 2021